THE DIVA HAUNTS
THE HOUSE

THE DIVA HAUNTS THE HOUSE

Krista Davis

CHIVERS

British Library Cataloguing in Publication Data available

This Large Print edition published by AudioGO Ltd, Bath, 2012.
Published by arrangement with The Berkley Publishing Group, a division of Penguin Group (USA) Inc.

U.K. Hardcover   ISBN   978 1 4713 0420 0
U.K. Softcover   ISBN   978 1 4713 0421 7

Copyright © Cristina Ryplansky
A Domestic Diva Mystery

Printed and bound in Great Britain by
MPG Books Group Limited

For
Janet Bolin and
Daryl Wood Gerber (Avery Aames)
with love and appreciation

ACKNOWLEDGMENTS

I am so grateful to all the wonderful people who gave of their time, expertise, and imagination during the writing of this book. Special thanks to Rhonda Dossett, who shared her childhood memory of wrapping socks around her neck to prevent vampire bites! Also to Julie Hyzy, who so kindly filled me in about the details of a séance she attended. Naturally, any errors in the séance in this book are my own. I am also grateful to Beth Solheim for her expertise on coffins and caskets.

I was overwhelmed by the generosity of Mary B. Smith-Morrison for sharing her famous Sweet Potato Pie recipe, and I thank her daughter, Patsy Smith Morgan, for coaxing it out of her. This is the real thing, and has already become a favorite at my house. Many thanks, too, to Meg London for the fabulous microwave risotto recipe, which I turned into Bat Cave Risotto by adding black beans for a creepy touch. And what would I do without my wonderful friend Amy Wheeler, who patiently mixed ingredients until she achieved the delicious Immortal Kiss.

As always, I'm grateful to my mother and Susan Smith Erba for their suggestions and enthusiasm. My friends Meg London, Kaye George, Marilyn Levinson, Laura Alden, Janet Bolin, and Avery Aames are always there to help me get over humps and think outside the box. Janet and Avery also keep me on track with their insightful critiques. I can't forget my dear friend Betsy Strickland, who is my best first reader and biggest promoter. Her support surpasses anything I could possibly deserve.

Many thanks to my delightful new agent, Jessica Faust, for staying on top of everything. And very special thanks to my editor, Sandra Harding, who is always such a delight, not to mention patient and fun! Thanks also to the very talented Teresa Fasolino, who has once again painted a cover that is a perfect window into Sophie's world.

I must thank the charming Robin Bierlein, who told me about the Dracula orchid when I was on tour in North Carolina. Last, but not least, I thank Brach's and Dianna

Dailey of Kroger for providing a case of candy corn off-season — for free!

AUTHOR'S NOTE

Old Town Alexandria is rumored to have plenty of ghosts, as one might expect of a historic location. However, Viktor Luca is totally a figment of my imagination. If any vampires have resided in or passed through Old Town Alexandria, I have no knowledge of it.

BUBBLE & TROUBLE
A COFFIN & CAULDRON FOR
OTHERWORLDLY TRAVELERS

ADULT VOLUNTEERS

Bernie
Humphrey
~~Frank Hart~~
~~Lulee Jenkins~~
Nina Reid Norwood
June Winston (Mars's mom)
Wanda Smith (Natasha's mom)

OWNER OF BUILDING

Ray Barnett

STUDENT VOLUNTEERS

Jen Bauer
Vegas Lafferty
Jesse Unterberger
Blake Bennett

PARENTS/GUARDIANS

Me
Mars Winston & Natasha
Dana Unterberger
~~Patrick Starski &~~ Maggie Bennett & Dash
  Bennett

ONE

Dear Sophie,
My neighborhood goes all out for Halloween. I'm planning to use pumpkins, but I'd love for my house to stand out. What can I do to my front door that no one else will have?
— Not Spooky Enough in Spook City,
Colorado

Dear Not Spooky,
Cut bare branches, or small dead trees, and spray paint them black. Wrap them with strands of orange lights, then arrange them in an arch around your door. They'll be creepy during the day, and when those lights glow in the dark, you'll have a super spooky entrance.
— Sophie

I balanced on the ladder, aimed my gun, and squeezed the trigger. A gossamer string

15

of wax shot out, creating a creepy cobweb. I cackled with glee. Pointing the gun at the gauzy black curtain covering the front window of the haunted house, I let fine threads fly. In seconds, it looked like no one had cleaned the place in years.

A shout upstairs interrupted my fun. It had to be my neighbor, Frank Hart.

I stepped off the ladder. "Frank?" A thud upstairs worried me. Had he fallen? I dashed to the foyer in time to see Frank slam against the built-in bookcase at the top of the stairs and stumble down.

"Frank, are you okay? What happened?"

He brushed past me as though I wasn't there, fumbled with the door handle, yanked the front door open, and staggered out to the sidewalk. His chest heaved as he gasped for air and stared up at the windows on the second floor of the haunted house. The skin on his face had turned ashen.

"Frank?" I hurried down the few steps to the brick sidewalk.

He blinked at me and his Adam's apple bobbed. "There's some . . . one, some . . . thing up there, Sophie."

A tall runner in his thirties, Frank owned a wine and cheese shop in Old Town. He'd generously and most enthusiastically donated time to the creation of a community

16

haunted house. I'd never thought of him as skittish. In fact, when another volunteer, Lulee Jenkins, bolted out of the haunted house a week ago, declaring she would never step foot inside the building again, Frank had chuckled about it.

Maybe humor would be the best approach now. Like the kids who pitched in to help with the haunted house and loved to play pranks on each other, I sang, "Psych!" With a big grin, I added, "Isn't it great the house is so scary that we're spooking ourselves?"

Frank didn't laugh. Not even the hint of a smile crossed his face.

A cool October wind kicked up and shuttled dry leaves past our ankles. Frank finally shifted his gaze from the windows. He grabbed my wrist with icy fingers. "Do *not* go back in there, Sophie."

"Now, Frank." I tried to keep my tone light. "Exactly what happened?"

His eyes were wild with fear. "Heed my warning. Close it down, Sophie." His voice rose. "Close it down!"

His words and behavior alarmed me. I couldn't disappoint everyone by closing the community haunted house. I made my living as an event planner but in my spare time had taken on the creation of the haunted house as a volunteer community project, and I intended to deliver. This was my first year in charge of the haunted house, and I was determined to see it succeed. The community haunted house idea had nearly died the year before, thanks to an uninspired effort of hay bales and plastic ghosts in a school auditorium. We'd lucked into a historic building in a great location this year. The Ye Olde Candle Shoppe building was a little creepy, but that made it perfect for a haunted house. Besides, Frank really hadn't told me what frightened him.

He took off at a jog, nearly colliding with Bernie, who'd gone for midmorning coffee and pastries. "What was that about?"

"Another defector. Frank says there's something upstairs."

In his charming British accent, Bernie said, "Never would have expected it of a solid fellow like Frank." He shifted the coffees and bag of pastries to his left hand with the ease of a restaurateur and high-fived me with his right hand. "If Frank is scared — we must have nailed it." He shot me a wickedly amused look and ran a hand through his perpetually mussed hair, which, along with the slight kink in his nose from an old break, gave him a grown-up Dennis-the-Menace appearance. Bernie, who was inclined to wear Birkenstock sandals, except in snow, had surprised us all by becoming an outstanding restaurant manager for a British absentee owner. My ex-husband's best friend and the best man at our wedding, Bernie had flitted between jobs and towns around the world before settling in Old Town. I was a bit surprised that he'd hung around as long as he had. Maybe even vagabonds eventually found someplace to call home.

Ray Barnett stuck his head out of his store next door. Inappropriately named Le Parisien Antiques, the hazy, smoke-filled shop was closer to an indoor junkyard. "Bernie! Found what we were looking for. Could you give me a hand?"

Bernie held up the bag. "How about a pastry first?"

Ray bustled out of the shop, wiping his hands on baggy trousers. "Don't mind if I do. Can I have a peek at the house?"

Hefty Ray led a beer-swilling, chain-smoking, bacon-gorging life that left him looking haggard. Dark semicircles hung under slightly bulging eyes. He could have made a living doing voice-overs. I didn't think he was capable of a whisper with that deep, gravelly voice. He'd lived over top of the shop since his wife passed away. I shuddered to imagine what the upstairs apartment might look like.

We ushered him inside, thanking him yet again for his generosity in lending us the empty building for the haunted house. His last tenant, the Ye Olde Candle Shoppe, hadn't fared well and had closed down after less than a year.

"I'm hopin' some of the folks who go through will get ideas and want to lease it. It's a right good location for a business. Gets lots of foot traffic, seein' how close it is to King Street."

Bernie handed out coffee and chocolate croissants in the small foyer where visitors would enter. We faced a stairway and a narrow hallway. To the left visitors would see the lights leading to the witch's lair, where they would eventually exit, having come full circle.

"One of the kids, who have named themselves the Ghastly Guides, will emerge from the hallway to lead a small group on a tour, beginning with the stairs," said Bernie. "They'll wind through the upstairs rooms, down the back stairs into the kitchen, out into the small backyard — which we're transforming into a mock graveyard — back through the kitchen, and end in the witch's lair in the front of the house."

Ray and I followed him up ancient stairs

that creaked with our every step. Our presence triggered an automated ghost that flashed over our heads.

Upstairs, I realized that Frank had knocked over the black pumpkin we'd placed in the recessed bookcase to the right. Sometime in the checkered history of the building, a skilled craftsman had built an arched top with glass doors over a cabinet. I opened a door and set the pumpkin straight before joining Ray and Bernie. All the rooms upstairs had been decorated as bedrooms for different ghoulish creatures. The first one we took Ray into was my personal favorite, the vampire's bedroom.

"When y'all asked if you could paint this room shiny gray, I thought you were off your rockers. Shoot, I'm no vampire, but I'd move into this room." Ray covetously eyed a black and red smoking jacket Frank had hung on a valet.

I loved the way dim lights reflected off the walls. Heavy red velveteen curtains shrouded the window to protect the vampire from any hint of daylight. My niece had found an oversized painting destined for the trash and transformed it into a portrait of a lovely woman, complete with two holes dripping blood on her swanlike neck.

An old console had been repurposed into

a bar. Frank had donated empty Vampire brand wine bottles and displayed them with elegant glasses. The opposite end of the bar featured burgundy martini glasses and a rack of test tubes, which the kids had labeled with blood types. A heavy walnut coat tree featured a cape with the opening tacked back to reveal a sumptuous blood red satin interior. A resident of Old Town had donated the clothes valet, along with the smoking jacket and black velvet slippers. My favorite part, though, was the dresser, where a gleaming manicure kit was displayed along with dental files.

The next room belonged to a werewolf. He had left bloody bones and body parts lying around, but slept in a fancy dog bed. A room belonging to hairy spiders who had cocooned their next meals against the walls creeped me out. But I thought the most ghastly bedroom belonged to the axe murderer, who had mounted a collection of axes on the wall. His trunk was rigged to open and display fake decapitated heads.

To raise the scary factor, we had scheduled at least one person to pose in each bedroom motionlessly and move when visitors were least likely to expect it. Frank had been our vampire bedroom attendant and now that he had bailed, I would have to find a substitute vampire.

Lucky me — I would be the witch in the lair, located at the end of the looped tour. As the designated witch, I could keep an eye on the front door as well as any rowdy visitors.

The doorbell rang and I went to answer it, leaving Bernie to show Ray the rest of the bedrooms. I took the back stairs down to the kitchen and passed through the witch's lair, which featured a large display window that overlooked the street.

The screech of metal on metal drew me to the window. A Hummer was parallel parking in front of the building, but the driver didn't seem to care about hitting the cars around her. She backed up and tried again, a cigarette hanging loosely between her lips. Finally, even though the rear of the car stood out in the street, she cut the engine and stared straight at me, mere feet from the show window, all without touching the cigarette.

I continued to the front door and opened it. Black branches arched over my head.

"Is this the haunted house?" Although he wasn't smoking, the man standing in front of me reeked of cigarette smoke. He wore his hair short, slicked back in a way that made him seem slimy to me, but I was willing to bet other women chased him. Slender, he dressed impeccably in Old Town style — khakis and an expensive designer shirt with a fancy logo sewn just below the shoulder. High cheekbones and full lips surely drew attention to him, but I was wary of the sultry eyes that flashed with dark energy.

"Yes. Did you want to volunteer?" I hoped not, but I did my best to appear welcoming.

He assessed me, making no effort to hide his critical gaze. I'd dressed in work clothes, comfortable jeans I could throw in the wash when they were dusty from toiling in the vacant building and a simple oversized mock turtleneck in a peachy color. I'd pulled my hair back into a ponytail and for fun, I wore dangling earrings in the shape of ghosts. Somehow, under his scrutiny, I felt as though I should have dressed more formally. I held out my hand, ready to introduce myself.

Instead of placing his hand in mine, he plunked something hard into my palm. Without thinking, I pulled my hand back and whatever it was fell to the brick sidewalk, landing beside a giant pumpkin.

He picked up the item, an annoyed expression on his face. "We found these in Blake's room, hidden under his socks." He opened

24

his hand to reveal teeth — teeth with prominent vampire fangs jutting from them.

I shrugged, clearly irritating him even more. The only Blake I knew of had volunteered to help but had never shown up. Before I could say that, the man launched into a tirade.

"We don't want him exposed to this sort of thing. Maggie doesn't do vampires, and I will not stand for this kind of behavior." He spoke with authority, his tone tinged with hostility.

He'd obviously mistaken me for someone else. Maybe he was talking about a different Blake, not the kid who was supposed to help but hadn't shown up. "I'm sorry . . ."

"Look, Blake will be here this afternoon, but we will not have him playing out any ridiculous vampire fantasies. And another thing, I have tried, but I cannot reason with Natasha, so I have to come right out and say this as plainly as possible to you so there's no mistake between us — keep that little tramp away from Blake! We're certain that she's the one fueling his interest in vampires."

Just who did he think he was? I felt terrible for the girl he'd called a tramp.

I glanced at the woman in the car for a clue. There wasn't much space between the house and the car, just an old red brick sidewalk. Although she remained in the Hummer, I could see her well. Her hair appeared to be naturally dark in contrast to my bottle blond, and she was painfully thin, while I needed to shed a few pounds.

He studied me, holding the teeth in a palm that was extended toward me, as though he expected me to address them.

"I'm very sorry, but I really don't know what you're talking about. Blake has not been here, there are no tramps, and I know nothing about the teeth in your hand." I started to close the door, but he stepped forward and pressed a hand against it. His eyes narrowed. "You're not the domestic diva in charge of the haunted house?"

I couldn't help grinning at the title of "domestic diva." I still wasn't used to it. I supposed I was one, but not in the flashy, in-your-face way that Natasha was. We'd grown up in the same small town, always competing with each other. She'd made a huge career of being a domestic diva and even landed her own local TV show about all things domestic. Somehow, along the way, she'd managed to end up with my husband, living in a house a few doors down from mine. In fact . . . I took another look at the woman in the car whose cigarette hung between her lips. With her thin figure and dark hair, she resembled Natasha.

"I'm Sophie Winston. I am in charge here, but that doesn't change the fact that I don't know what you're talking about." I didn't extend my hand this time, lest he put the vampire orthodontia in it again. "And you would be?"

"Patrick Starski. I don't want our Blake getting cozy with that homeless girl, Vegas. Blake will be along shortly, and I expect you to watch them like a hawk and keep them apart. There's to be no involvement with vampires for Blake, either. His mother, Maggie," he said, gesturing toward the car, "will not have it. Understood?"

I understood all too well. My first instinct was to defend Vegas. She wasn't homeless. The poor kid was living with Natasha and my ex-husband because her mother had absconded while her father was on military duty overseas. If anything, she needed our support and understanding. Patrick's attitude made me bristle, not to mention the fact that we had plenty of work to do on the haunted house before it opened tomorrow, and I didn't plan to babysit anyone. Plus he was fighting a hopeless battle trying to keep his kid away from vampires. They were everywhere — books, movies, TV, bill-

27

boards. It took some forbearance on my part, but I smiled and said, "We would love to have you help us. That way you could watch him yourself."

He saw right through my diplomatic response, and his coal eyes seemed to spark with anger. "I don't need your snippiness. When I found out Vegas was involved in this project, I tried to get the school to pull Blake out, but that didn't work." His jaw twitched. "We all know everyone has a soft spot for people who remind them of their first love. I will not have him spending the rest of his life chasing cheap girls like Vegas."

"They're twelve-year-olds," I blurted. "And I am not babysitting. They're here to work, but if you want to be a helicopter dad and hover over your baby, you're welcome to stay and help us."

He pointed a long forefinger at me. "You have crossed the wrong man. People don't mess with Patrick Starski."

Two

Dear Natasha,
A coffin would be just the right touch for my Halloween display. I'm a decent crafter, but cutting plywood and building are beyond my skills. Isn't there an easier way?
   — Afraid of Power Saws in Grave Creek,
                              West Virginia

Dear Afraid of Power Saws,
Did you know that a coffin has a narrowed toe area, while a casket is rectangular? Either way, you can build one out of a large sturdy cardboard box, Styrofoam, or foam board. Cut the pieces, assemble with a glue gun, and paint. You can even use a sharp comb to create "wood" striations before painting if you like.
                              — Natasha

Patrick spun and ambled back to the Hummer, his chin in the air.

I closed the door and returned to the front room, where I pulled the gauzy black curtain aside a hair to see better. Maggie cupped her hands around her mouth, trying to light another cigarette. When Patrick climbed into the car, she listened to him before launching into an outburst. His face contorted with such anger that I was frightened for her. She looked up at the windows on the second floor of the haunted house and swallowed so hard I could see the muscles in her neck tighten. Her gaze drifted down to the window where I stood, and I thought I saw fear. She put the car in reverse and hit the gas, nearly causing an accident when she pulled out without bothering to look for oncoming traffic.

Now that I had met the dreadful parents, I was almost afraid to meet Blake. I was still thinking about them when I retrieved two four-foot-tall electric candelabra from the kitchen and positioned one on each side of the entrance to the witch's lair.

I plugged in the candelabra and stood back. Three orange faux flames flickered on each as though the wind was blowing into the house. The spiderwebs and bats that adorned them added to their appropriateness for the room.

Bernie and Ray emerged from their tour to admire the candelabra. Bernie hooked a thumb over his shoulder. "We're going to get the crowning glory for our favorite witch. Leave the door open, okay?"

We had found a heavy black cat doorstop upstairs. I propped it in front of the door and returned to the front room to place a selection of potions on the counter where a cash register had probably stood for the candle shop. The kids had had fun printing labels in freaky letters and pasting them on colorful old bottles. I had eye of newt, dragon blood, bat's toes, dried rat tail, peppered spider spit, and frog tongues. Those kids had let their imaginations go wild. I couldn't believe they were lucky enough to get school credit for working on a haunted house.

Their voices filled the foyer, cluing me in that it was already lunchtime and the Ghastly Guides had arrived to work. I wandered over to the door and watched the two boys and two girls in the foyer. I didn't recognize one of the boys and guessed he might be Blake. No one noticed me. Preteen hormones practically danced through the air.

Vegas and my niece, Jen, wore their hair long and loose, and the gleaming chestnut

31

color was almost identical. But Jen was petite, like her mother, and still had a baby-ish face, while Vegas was growing into angular features. They wore miniskirts with tights, so similar that I was certain their outfits must have been a major topic of a telephone discussion the night before. Their mock turtlenecks resembled mine, only tighter. Who knew I was on the forefront of teen fashion?

Deep in a typical twelve-going-on-thirteen conversation, they all spoke at once. They shrugged off their backpacks in the hallway. Jesse, a boy with lank light brown hair that fell into his eyes, dug into his backpack and withdrew a wrinkled sheet of paper. High cheekbones and a slightly pudgy face combined to give him a cute rascally look.

Jen reached for the paper. "It looks like you slept with it." It may have been a derogatory statement, but the lilt in her voice left no mistake that Jesse was special to her.

He tossed his head to the side to sling the hair out of his eyes, and said simply, "Hey, Sophie."

Vegas, a pretty girl who had already shot past her classmates in height, chimed in, "Sophie, this is Blake. He's late joining the Ghastly Guides because he's on the tennis team and couldn't come until practice was over. Doesn't he have a sexy haircut? A lot of our friends volunteered to be spooky characters in the house, but you wouldn't believe how picky they are about the costumes they might have to wear!" She held her hands up in a prissy manner like she was mimicking someone. "Oh! I couldn't possibly be a mummy or a zombie, it might mess my hair!"

They all giggled, and Blake said, "You crack me up when you do Heather."

I wasn't sure about Blake's haircut being sexy. His short nutmeg hair looked like an ordinary barbershop cut to me, but then I didn't know much about boys' fashion. I did notice, though, that Jesse wore baggy pants with a loose untucked shirt that matched his unkempt hairstyle, while Blake's preppy shirt bore the Lacoste logo and was neatly tucked into khakis.

"When we met at camp last summer, Blake's hair was long enough for a little ponytail," said Jen.

"I thought that was a girls' camp."

The girls giggled and Jen said, "It was, but the boys' camp was just across the lake and we had boats."

Vegas flicked her long tresses over her

shoulder. "Come on, Blake. I'll give you the tour."

I watched the kids race up the stairs. The girls met last Christmas when Vegas and her father came to visit their cousin Natasha. While Vegas was spending Christmas with her dad, her mother disappeared. When her father returned to military duty, Vegas continued to live with Natasha and my ex-husband, Mars. She seemed to have adjusted to her new life, though I suspected she often put on a brave face.

Jen lived in another neighborhood with her parents and went to a different school than Vegas, but the two sly girls had managed to wangle time off from school for participating in the haunted house. Whatever happened to being a candy striper and helping those in need, I wondered. Halloween fell on Saturday this year, perfect for parties. Jen and Vegas would be staying with me for the next couple of nights and the weekend — one long slumber party — while we worked on the house and opened it to the public. Jen's thirteenth birthday happened to fall on October 31, which caused a great deal of consternation for my brother and his wife when the opportunity arose for a trip to Rome. After endless discussions, they decided to take the trip, because I promised to have a little Halloween birthday party for Jen, a few of her friends, and the volunteers at the haunted house after it closed.

For part of their school credit, the kids were supposed to come up with a spooky story to tell about the haunted house. I hoped that the wrinkled sheet of paper that passed from Jesse to Jen meant they'd finally made some progress.

Ray's gravelly voice bellowed, "Out of the way, Sugar Pants!"

I winced at being called *Sugar Pants*, but I knew Ray didn't mean anything by it. He was a character and too old to change his ways.

I scooted aside to make room for Bernie and Ray and the enormous black cauldron they carried down the sidewalk between them. Their faces beet red, they huffed and groaned as they inched it up the front steps and inside the witch's lair. Fortunately, the historic house had a huge fireplace, big enough for me to stand up in, that really was used for cooking at one time, though hopefully not by witches. The cauldron fit perfectly, as though it had been used there before.

"Is that cast iron?" I asked.

"Yes indeed, and it's far superior to any

modern plastic version," grunted Bernie. "We'll set dry ice in the bottom so that a fog will wisp out of it."

Footsteps, giggles, and occasional screams grew closer, and I looked up to see Jesse casing the room with Jen right behind him.

"Witches just aren't scary anymore. Well, maybe for little kids because they don't know any better." He flicked his hair out of his eyes with a head toss again.

If I were his mother, he'd be taken for an immediate haircut. But, from the adoring way Jen gazed at him, I gathered the constant snapping of the head didn't disturb her.

"Jesse's right, Aunt Sophie."

Gee, how did I know she'd agree with him?

"How about ghosts?" I asked.

Jesse snorted, and Jen flashed me an I-could-just-die-right-now-of-embarrassment look. "Ghosts are juvenile," she explained with a disdainful shake of her head.

As much as I'd have liked to ignore their opinions, they were very much our target crowd. "So what's scary? Something Harry Potter-ish? A Hogwarts-like school?"

"No!" they protested in unison.

"Shape shifters." Jesse held up his hands like claws and hunched over like an animal.

36

"Vampires and werewolves." Jen bared her teeth.

"I suppose I know what sort of costumes you two will be wearing," I said. "Is there a way to be a shape shifter, Jesse?"

He leaned back and with the smugness of an overly confident man forty years his senior, he said, "I'll think of something."

Vegas and Blake finally joined us. *Was that lipstick on his collar?* I sidled closer while Vegas bemoaned the lack of a scary story to accompany the tour. *Not only was lipstick smeared on Blake's shirt, but I thought I saw the beginnings of a hickey. Oh no. No wonder his parents were worried. They had no right to talk about Vegas as though she were a tart, but I understood their concern a little bit better and anticipated another angry visit from them.*

Ray wiped his forehead with the back of his hand. "Well, I'll be. Take a look at that." He tilted his head toward the window, and his laugh bellowed through the house.

The kids gathered at the window for a nanosecond before racing out to the sidewalk with the adults behind them. The boxy, elongated shape of a shiny black hearse maneuvered into an empty spot in front of the haunted house. Gleaming chrome ran along the length of the bottom and circled the windows. I guessed it to be 1960-ish vintage because of the prominent fins on the back.

Humphrey stepped out, his huge smile showing he was pleased with himself. His pale skin and almost white hair gave him a ghostly appearance, not the best look for a mortician.

I'd grown quite fond of Humphrey, but in a strictly platonic way, and I made sure he remembered that. When we were Jen's age, he had an obsessive crush on me, to which I was embarrassingly oblivious. Humphrey meant well, though, and had proven to be a good friend, even if he hadn't progressed past high school when it came to romance and chasing women. All he wanted was someone to return his affection. Surely that wasn't asking too much. As a mortician, he had a slightly different view of the macabre, so I hoped his contribution to the haunted house might spur an idea for the elusive scary story the kids needed.

The kids zoomed around the car. "Where did you get this?" asked Jesse.

Humphrey puffed his chest proudly when he said, "A friend of mine collects funeral memorabilia."

"Eww." Vegas sounded like a spoiled Valley girl. "That is sooo gross."

Jesse peered inside. "Hey! There's a coffin

in here."

Everyone laughed except Humphrey, who patted the car. "She's in perfect condition. And the crowning glory . . ." He placed a life-sized skeleton in the front seat and wrapped the fingers around the steering wheel as though it were driving.

"Is the casket for the vampire's bedroom?" asked Bernie.

I thought Humphrey might melt and sink into the pavement on the spot. He glared at Bernie, mashed his lips together, and tugged at his collar as though he was uncomfortable and hoped to change the subject. Bernie looked to me quizzically.

"Is there somebody in it?" asked Vegas.

Simultaneously, Jesse and Blake breathed, "Cool!"

Surely it didn't contain a corpse! Humphrey would never be that unprofessional. Or would he? Were dead people so matter-of-fact and everyday to him that he would carry one around?

Ray clapped Humphrey on the back. "Who've ya got in there, buddy?"

Humphrey's wan body shook from the force of Ray's hand, and he had to take a step forward to regain his balance. Looking like a kid caught in big trouble, he dragged to the back of the hearse and opened the rear door.

Ray followed him, but his expression changed from amusement to horror. "What the dickens? That's my wife's casket!"

THREE

Dear Sophie,
My sister-in-law always manages to top my Halloween decorations. She comes up with one-of-a-kind items that can't be beat. This year, I'm determined to outdo her. Where can I find unusual decorations?
— Boring Mom in Deadman Crossing, California

Dear Boring Mom,
Haunt junk stores, secondhand shops, and stores featuring donated items. Don't worry about anything being perfect — a slight cant, age, or major crack will only make it look more authentic and spooky. Think creatively. Use old balusters as candleholders. Find uses for chipped crystal, weather-beaten books, and oddball objects. Don't be afraid to

use spray paint liberally.

— Sophie

Humphrey turned beet red. "Well, it's not like she's in there!" He expertly released legs with wheels, pulled out the casket, and shut the hearse.

"It looks real." Blake was duly impressed, as well he should be. Brass accents gleamed against highly polished wood the color of coffee beans.

"It *is* real." The maroon shade of Ray's face made me worry about his blood pressure. His wife had died years ago. I must be missing something.

Bernie flicked Humphrey a thumbs-up. "It's fantastic! Can't you imagine a sophisticated vampire residing in there?"

"I can imagine *my wife* in there. Y'all use it for the haunted house, but then I want it back. I paid for it! Shoot. I've got a customer. I'm not through with you yet, Humphrey!"

Humphrey relaxed and released a huge breath when Ray scuttled back to his store. "It's been taking up space at the mortuary, and it's true he paid for it, but what's he going to do with it? Wait until you see the interior." He lifted the lid to reveal a garish red lining.

I ran my hand across it. "Is that velvet?"

Bernie laughed out loud. "It's worthy of a Victorian bordello."

Humphrey closed the lid and rolled the casket toward the front door. "We special-ordered it for Ray when his wife died. He paid extra for that lining and expedited delivery. But when his wife's sister saw it, she was so traumatized at the thought of her sister spending eternity in that 'gaudy nightmare' that she returned later in the day with a shotgun tucked inside her coat, and blasted a hole as big as a fist in the side, rendering it useless."

The kids couldn't resist. They trotted around to the other side and, sure enough, Jesse inserted a hand in the coffin. He arched his back and screamed, as though something inside had grabbed his hand and wouldn't release it.

"We couldn't bury her in it, and even though it's state-of-the-art, we couldn't use it as a model with that hole and the taste-less interior, so it's been taking up space at the mortuary. They were delighted it could be used here at the haunted house."

Bernie helped Humphrey bump it up two stairs and into the house.

Humphrey collapsed the legs of the roll-ing gizmo, and Bernie grabbed the far end, pulling it up the stairs toward the vampire bedroom. Humphrey pushed from below with no effect, except that his normally pale face flushed tomato red. He bellowed like a bear when he heaved the end of the coffin up one step.

"Come on, old man, you can do it." Bernie peered over the top at me.

"Can't we enlist some of the young bucks?" asked Humphrey.

"We're not allowed to send them home broken," I reminded him.

"What's the problem? You move these things all the time," Bernie said.

Humphrey thunked the end of the casket on the next step up, turned around, sat down on the step below it, and wiped perspiration off his face with a handkerchief. "Sorry to disappoint you, but I'm not some kind of superhero. We wheel them around. I've never carried a casket up stairs!"

"Are you taking a break? Sophie, prod him a bit, will you?"

I couldn't help teasing them. "Are you sure Ray's wife isn't in there?"

Jesse emerged from the front room and puffed out his slender chest. "I could give you a hand." He sat next to Humphrey on the step and said, "On the count of three, we heave with our backs."

44

"Wait!" called Blake. We could hear the pounding of his footsteps as he ran up the rear stairs and across the second floor. He reappeared beside Bernie and grabbed onto the coffin.

"We could help, too, if the stairs weren't so narrow." Jen pouted.

"Why don't you hustle up the back staircase to the second floor and make sure the path is clear from the top of the front stairs to the vampire bedroom?" I suggested.

With the boys' help, the casket was nearing the top of the stairs, and I returned to the witch's lair. I had strung tiny purple lights around the corners and the ceiling and shot cobwebs over them. I still needed to add a witchy broom or two, but the room had come together nicely, except for the bright brass chandelier hanging from the ceiling. Large and authentic for Old Town's historic style, it would have been coveted by many homeowners, but was surely a humiliation for a witch.

Bernie spoke behind me. "The casket made it to its destination. I think we did a decent job of hiding the hole. It's on the side that people won't see. Humphrey adjusted the lining so the hole isn't visible when the lid is opened. Okay if the kids help Humphrey and me finish the graveyard in the back?"

"Perfect. I need to run some errands anyway. I'll bring back Chinese takeout for lunch."

My first stop was Ray's shop, Le Parisien Antiques. Like the haunted house next door, it featured a large picture window to showcase the interior. Cigarette smoke hung heavily inside, giving it a gloomy, hazy appearance. Two plastic side tables, probably worth less than ten dollars when new, occupied a place of honor in the window. Stacks of old books surrounded them, as well as a genie lamp, a pair of ratty slippers, and an old tire. Ray Barnett sure knew how to dress a window.

Gulping a breath of fresh air, I pushed the door open and a flat clink, barely audible, announced my arrival. Ray heard it, though, and shuffled toward me through the cluttered mess.

"Howdy, little Miss Sophie."

"I'm sorry about the casket. That must have been a shock."

"Tell the truth, I forgot all about the thing until I saw it again. I like to fell over. But I'm a tough old geezer. What can I do you for?"

"I'm looking for old, chipped, okay —

cheap — chandelier crystals for the haunted house."

"I have some beauties in the back corner." He motioned for me to follow him. "I plan to be first in line when you open up for business. I love me a good haunted house." He grinned, displaying large yellow teeth. "It better draw some potential tenants. It's been empty since Patrick Starski defaulted on his rent."

"Patrick Starski just paid me a visit. He owned the candle shop?" No wonder he didn't want to come in and help with the haunted house. He was probably still upset about losing his business.

"He's not much of a businessman."

I knew nothing about him. "That Hummer Maggie drives couldn't have been inexpensive."

"She's got money. I imagine the Hummer came from the car dealership — she's part owner. That Patrick is a parasite, though. There you go." He pointed at a dirty corner. "See anything you like?"

Ray didn't believe in high-wattage lightbulbs. Maybe that was just as well given the clutter. Still, I could make out an amazing array of dust-encrusted crystal chains and prisms of every imaginable size and shape. "Oh, that's the door. I must have another customer." He patted my shoulder. "Since it's for the haunted house, you take whatever you need for, say, five bucks."

He shuffled off toward the front of the shop. Funny, I hadn't heard the dull clink of the bell on the door. I spent a few minutes pawing through the crystals. I really didn't need many, and since he was being generous, I felt even more compelled to snag broken ones. A spritz or two of black spray paint would add just the gloomy touch I sought.

Ray's voice bellowed through the cavernous store. "How dare you come onto my property and threaten me? Git! Git on out, you sorry fancy-pants Yankee."

I didn't hear the response, but an ear-shattering rumble of items falling to the hardwood floor suggested someone had bumped into a stack of goods. I hurried to the front to see if anyone needed help, and arrived just in time to see Patrick Starski pointing a finger at Ray, much as he had at me. He backed through the front door and fell flat on his face on the sidewalk outside. He rose quickly and glared into Ray's store.

Ray nodded once with apparent satisfaction. "Yellow-bellied sap sucker." He pulled out the drawer of his old-fashioned cash register and even in the dim light, the metal casing of a gun shone as he stashed it away. "Hey there, little lady. You find what you need?"

"Is everything okay?"

He snorted. "Some of these young fancy-britches fellows don't know how to conduct business. I'd be plumb ashamed to come around asking for extensions and favors." He accepted the five-dollar bill I held out to him. "You see? That's how you do business. Fair and square."

"Patrick likes to point his finger and threaten," I observed, in the hope of learning more about him.

Ray waved a fleshy hand through the air carelessly. "I've dealt with his kind before."

"All hot air?"

"Not unless you think a striking rattler is full of hot air. You steer clear of him, hear? I've already spread the word about him. No one in Old Town is going to rent him a place to do business. Don't need folks like him around these parts."

Even though I barely knew Patrick and wasn't really worried about his idle threats, I found myself on the lookout for him when I left Le Parisien Antiques. I picked up an assortment of Chinese takeout, bought a can of black spray paint, and headed back to work. The house was still when I entered.

I carried the food through the hallway to the kitchen and set it on a 1950s-style laminated dinette table. Through the windows, I could see Bernie, Humphrey, and the kids working in the backyard. I was about to call them to come in when I heard something.

A whimper.

I listened intently.

I heard it again — like a dog's whine. I scanned the yard for any sign of an animal.

A creak behind me made the hair on my arms rise. I swung around and Natasha rushed at me, her hands raised, witchlike. My own sweet Daisy, the hound mix Mars and I shared, bounded toward me, her tail spinning in a circle with joy. I sank into a chair and hugged her while Natasha laughed.

"I love Halloween!" Natasha dropped Daisy's leash and promptly wiped dog fur off her gorgeous, fluffy robin's egg blue sweater and skinny pants that made her look even more slender. "I thought I'd drop Daisy off. I have so much to do before tonight's big Halloween party."

"I'm sure it will be marvelous." When my pulse returned to normal, I set the kitchen table with paper plates and napkins that featured a creepy house with ghosts hanging out the windows. Natasha reached out and clutched my shoulder with such tension that I could feel her superlong, perfectly manicured nails digging in.

"I need your help. I'm desperate, Sophie."

I'd grown up with Natasha and was used to her drama-queen behavior. I turned away, stifling a yawn. "I'm up to my eyeballs with the haunted house."

"Pleeease, Sophie. My mother arrived unexpectedly! She just assumed she was invited to the party."

"That's nice."

"Noooo," she whispered. "Not at all. You know my mother. I can't have her at my party tonight. I've invited everyone who is anyone. It has to be perfect. I have a lot riding on this." She picked at an errant dog hair on her trousers. "Frankly, I'm still miffed that they didn't ask me to chair the haunted house. I have to prove that I can out-haunt you."

"That's why you're throwing the party?" Natasha and I had a history of competition, but we were adults now, way beyond the nonsense of high school. "You could have volunteered to assist with the haunted house, you know."

She shifted uneasily. "You would have gotten all the credit."

As far as I was concerned, it wasn't about credit. It was about fun for the kids.

"So you see how vital it is that *my* party be *the* party of the year. I need it to be the party against which all other parties are measured. The most incredible Halloween party ever thrown in Old Town." She raised her gaze to meet mine. "You know my mother. I can't have her showing up in some strange outfit, talking about spirits. Please, please ask her to help with the haunted house so she'll be busy?"

I found Natasha's mother, Wanda Smith, fascinating, but then, she wasn't *my* mother. Prone to dressing like a teenager, Wanda was the antithesis of her conservative daughter, who considered her public image in everything she did. Wanda was likely to turn up at Natasha's party as a sexy witch or a call girl. She was also inclined to spout superstitious sayings and read palms or tarot cards. The more I thought about her, the more I thought she would be perfect to spook kids at the haunted house. We could place a chair in the foyer for her, and she could entertain waiting groups by telling fortunes.

"I would love to have your mother help us. As long as she doesn't dress in something too revealing, she would be fantastic. Can't you just see her being mystical with the kids who come through?"

Natasha's perfect eyebrows shifted together in a frown. "I hadn't thought about it that way. This is the ideal time to introduce her to important people. No matter what she says or wears, it will all be embraced in the spirit of Halloween. They won't know she's always like that."

I pretended to be disappointed, so she wouldn't change her mind. "Oh, but she would be so great at the haunted house! Maybe she could help out tomorrow instead? I'm sure she'd rather be at your party tonight." Truth be known, I was very happy that Natasha *had* changed her mind and wouldn't hurt her mother's feelings by trying to get rid of her.

She eyed each container of Chinese food as I opened it. "Would you care to join us?" I asked.

"I'm so starved I would even eat takeout, but I don't dare eat anything today. My costume is skintight. Oh, but it smells good. I'm turning Daisy-the-fur-factory over to you, okay? I don't have time for her right now."

"Why do you insist on talking about her that way when she saved your life last Christmas?" Like me, my ex-husband Mars

53

was crazy about Daisy so we shared custody. If only Natasha would be kinder to her.

"Nonsense. That was nothing but a fluke, dumb luck at best. Must run, darling, so much to do!"

I rubbed Daisy's ears. "It was very generous of you to chase the person who attacked Natasha. Especially given the way she treats you. *I* know it wasn't accidental."

Her tail wagged so hard that her hind end wriggled, and she panted a doggy smile at me.

After lunch, we decorated like fiends for hours. By seven o'clock, we had accomplished more than I expected, and it was time to feed the troops again. I had anticipated being dog tired and had prepared pizzas in advance — the cheese, pepperoni, and slices of peppers arranged in jack-o'-lantern-style grimacing faces. All I had to do was pop them into the oven.

Humphrey and Bernie headed to work. I felt guilty that they'd spent their free time laboring, but Bernie assured me that he enjoyed working at the restaurant during the evening hours, and Humphrey reminded me that morticians have to be available around the clock.

The kids went home with me. Blake had

already called his father and asked him to pick him and Jesse up at my place. I dreaded another encounter with Patrick. We walked the few blocks to my house, the boys constantly trying to spook the girls.

We approached my block, and Jen held out her arm to stop us from walking. "Do you have company?"

I didn't. Yet candles flickered in my kitchen windows, the little orange lights around my front door glowed, and the three pumpkins that scowled at the base of the door had come alive in the dark.

The kids clustered behind me, whispering.

"We'll protect you, Sophie," said Jesse.

"Maybe Nina wanted to surprise us?" But honestly, I doubted Nina Reid Norwood, my neighbor across the street and my best friend, would have gone to the trouble of turning on the holiday lights. My pulse raced as we crossed the street and walked toward my front door.

FOUR

Dear Natasha,
My out-of-town cousin is coming for a pre-Halloween dinner with her five small children. I don't have children, toys, or games. How do I keep her brood occupied while I'm cooking dinner?
— Nervous Wreck in Sleepy Hollow, NY

Dear Nervous,
Keep those little hands busy! Set up a children's table with a plain white cotton tablecloth. Tell the little ones you need them to decorate it for Halloween, and pass out nontoxic crayons. Swap it for a plastic tablecloth when they eat. After they've left, place a piece of waxed paper over and under each image, and apply heat with your iron. Present their original work to Mom and Dad as a gift. It will make a delightful keepsake.
— Natasha

As I grasped the door handle and pushed, my throat got tight. The front door opened with a creak, and the skeleton that hung from my foyer chandelier rattled, every bit as creepy as I'd imagined it would be. I let Daisy lead the way, but she didn't appear to be perturbed.

"Hello?" I called.

I tiptoed inside, aware of the rich scent of wood burning in the fireplace. With Jen on my heels, I peeked into my kitchen. An elderly woman wearing cat ears and a costume of ocelot-spotted fur snoozed in one of the comfy chairs by a crackling fire, her feet up on an ottoman with Mochie, my Ocicat, nestled on her lap.

"June?" I said it gently, hoping I wouldn't scare my former mother-in-law.

"Faye? Is that you?" she murmured.

Oy. Faye was June's deceased sister, and the previous owner of my house. Maybe June had been dreaming about her. "June! It's Sophie."

She woke fully, flopped her feet off the ottoman, and set Mochie on it before rising to give me a big hug. "I hope you don't mind, dear. You said I could drop by anytime."

I had said exactly that and had given her a key, too. "I wasn't expecting you."

57

"That's why I turned on the lights around the front door. A burglar wouldn't do that." She twirled around to show off her costume. "Do you know who I am?"

She'd used makeup to skillfully draw an *M* on her forehead, along with cat whiskers and exotic eyes. "Mochie?"

"For Halloween I have his jumping ability. I can leap to the tops of cabinets and sneak into rooms on silent cat feet. I'm agile and limber again." She peered past me. "This couldn't be Jen?"

Jen had met June years ago when I was married to June's son, Mars, which led to the inevitable my-how-you've-grown comments. If the light in the room had been stronger, I felt sure I would have seen Jen act embarrassed. Vegas clearly knew June, since she was living with Mars. I introduced the boys, but within minutes, the kids were engaged in their own conversation, excluding June and me.

Although I was tempted to turn on more lights, the crackling fire and the candles offered a spooky ambiance that I enjoyed. I preheated the ovens and pulled spiderweb guacamole out of the refrigerator for munching on as an hors d'oeuvre.

I shook tortilla chips into a basket lined with a black Halloween napkin and noticed

58

that June was listening to the kids.

"I have a scary story for you," she offered. "A true story."

Even in the dim light, I could see their lack of enthusiasm. As though the spirits knew what she had in mind, the wind howled outside. June settled into her chair by the fire, which caused shadows to dance across her feline face. She didn't wait for the kids to indicate an interest.

"My sister, Faye, threw loads of fabulous parties here." She pointed to the portrait hanging on the stone wall of the fireplace. "That's Faye." Candlelight flickered below the picture, casting an unearthly glow.

Mars and I had inherited the house from Faye. When we divorced, I bought him out, so I was now sole owner. But it seemed right to honor Faye's memory by keeping her portrait above the fireplace. Slightly risqué and incredibly romantic, the painting depicted her holding a pine-colored drape around herself with one shoulder bared.

In years past, June had insisted she could hear Faye's ghost in my kitchen. I wasn't so sure about that, but my house qualified as a historic landmark and was over one hundred years old. If ghosts lived anywhere, it would be in the historic houses of Old Town.

June continued. "It was the sixties and

everyone was open to new things. Much more than today. We liked to say, 'Anything goes.' " She flashed a glance my way. "I was never as adventurous as my sister, but I loved to come to her parties."

Jen and Vegas settled cross-legged on the floor, with Mochie and Daisy between them, enjoying the attention. The boys clustered by the food, munching.

I put a pot of cider on the stove to warm, with a cinnamon stick for a hint of zing.

"One of Faye's regular guests was the very dashing Viktor Luca. He absolutely enchanted all the women. He spoke several languages, could discourse on any subject with astounding knowledge, and, oh my, was he handsome! Wavy dark hair brushed his shoulders. His skin was gossamer, as though he had never seen the sun, and his blue eyes bored into your soul."

"Like a vampire," breathed Vegas.

"You're so smart, Vegas. He talked with an accent and spoke intimately of Paris, but we were fairly certain he wasn't French. Viktor was on the guest lists of all the chic hostesses in Old Town. He was the life of every party. The only one who wasn't completely taken with him was my husband, the judge. Viktor seemed to have an abundant source of money but he never worked, and he lived over at the Widow Nagle's boardinghouse."

I chuckled. "Abundant money but he took a room at a boardinghouse?"

"She called it a pension, like they do in Europe, to class it up. But my husband said the same thing. He never trusted Viktor — unlike the ladies in this town who enabled Viktor to live the high life. Plenty of widows asked him to travel with them as a companion. He went on cruises and tours around the world."

Viktor sounded like a gigolo to me. I poured hot cider into black mugs dotted with images of candy corn so bright they seemed to glow.

"One night, Faye's party broke up quite late, and Viktor offered to walk one of the guests, Peggy Zane, home. My husband and I stayed here with Faye, and we were all awakened in the morning when Peggy's husband called to ask where she was. He'd been at a business meeting and had skipped the party. She never came home that night!"

I handed mugs to everyone while June told her tale quietly but with dramatic emphasis. She'd definitely gotten the kids' attention. The boys were so mesmerized that they'd stopped eating.

"We went straight to the boardinghouse, and when the Widow Nagle unlocked Viktor's room — he was gone. It was as though he had never been there. His clothes and all his possessions had simply disappeared. The bed was stripped, the mattress bare, the dresser and closets empty. There was no sign that the room had ever been rented. Even the trash can was clean."

Jen and Vegas sat up straight. "What happened to Peggy?" asked Jen.

"They found her down by the Potomac River, completely hungover with no recollection of what had happened the night before. But she had two puncture wounds on the side of her neck . . . and she died three days later."

The girls squealed in fright and exchanged wide-eyed looks.

I'd always enjoyed June's company but had no idea she was so talented at spinning tales.

"But that's not the end of the story. You see, my husband prided himself on his ability to assess a man's character. He was always suspicious of Viktor, and his sudden disappearance bothered my husband, so he did a little investigation of his own. The peculiar thing was that except for a few pictures of him, and an address in Paris that he'd given the Widow Nagle, we couldn't find anything to prove Viktor had ever been here. No bank accounts, no post office box or mail, nothing that a regular person would have. Well, when my husband suggested we take a vacation to Paris, I wasn't about to say no. He packed all sorts of papers to prove he was a judge and off we went. He thought Viktor was probably a scam artist, so we started at the police station. The young man there dismissed us as silly Americans and denied having any knowledge of Viktor. So we went in search of the address."

I leaned toward June. "Let me guess — it didn't exist."

"Oh, but it did. It was the address of a cemetery."

Vegas and Jen screamed and clutched each other. Mochie leaped to the safety of the window seat.

"We couldn't believe it. It was such a spooky day, with a bitter wind and dark clouds roiling in the sky. We strolled in, and I was certain we'd come to the end of the road. Viktor probably never lived in Paris. And then we saw it — a mausoleum with Viktor's name on it." June sat back, apparently pleased by our stunned silence. "He had died one hundred years before."

The girls issued screams worthy of a horror movie. Although I'd been skeptical, a

63

chill shuddered through me.

"And he was here? Physically in this house?" asked Vegas.

"Many times."

"Aw, come on. That didn't really happen," said Jesse.

"Oh, my dear, but it did. Exactly as I told you."

Every one of us looked around as if we expected to see Viktor emerge from the shadows.

We all jumped when the knocker on the front door sounded.

"That'll be my dad. C'mon, Jesse." Blake rose from the table. "See you in the morning at the haunted house. Thanks, Mrs. Winston."

Jesse followed him to the foyer, still eating tortilla chips. I assumed his hand gesture meant "ditto for me." I opened the door, hoping Patrick would be in a better mood. The man who stood on my stoop said, "I'm here to pick up Blake and Jesse?"

The boys walked by him and out into the night.

"Smells great! Thanks for taking care of them. I'm sure they would thank you, too, if they had any of the manners we try to drill into them." He shouted the last part over his shoulder, as though he hoped they would hear. Smiling, he wiped his forehead in an embarrassed gesture, nudging waves of short toffee-colored hair into an unruly peak. He wore a Redskins jacket over a button-down shirt and jeans.

"Blake was very courteous." Who was this guy? I didn't see any vampire partials in his hands, so I extended mine and said, "Sophie Winston."

"Dash Bennett, Blake's dad."

I wondered if I should ask for identification. Blake was old enough to know his own dad, though. Surely he wouldn't have waltzed out if this man were a stranger.

Using two fingers, he gave me an informal salute. "I'll drop him off at the haunted house in the morning." He turned and hustled down the walk, leaving me to wonder — *If that was Blake's dad, then who were Patrick and Maggie?*

When I returned to the kitchen, I asked, "Does Blake have a stepdad?"

"Nope," said Vegas.

A well of horror rose inside me. "Then who are Patrick and Maggie Starski?"

Vegas tossed her long hair back. "Maggie is his mom but I think her last name is still Bennett, and Patrick is Blake's albatross. He's Maggie's boyfriend. Blake *hates* him."

I could understand why. I enlisted the

girls' help in setting the table with shiny black plates. Before I left in the morning, I had thrown an orange tablecloth over the kitchen table. Anticipating the need for access to the pizzas, I skipped a centerpiece. Vegas added black napkins, and I pulled the hot pizzas from the ovens. As I ran a pizza cutter through them, I couldn't help noticing that June had acquired admiring new friends. I didn't often see preteens mesmerized by adults, much less anyone June's age, but they peppered her with questions and hung on her every word. A considerable feat given that they usually weren't interested in anything that wasn't connected to a screen of some type.

At my urging, and undoubtedly, the fabulous scents of oregano and baked pizza dough, everyone except June moved to the table and took seats.

"June, will you help us with the haunted house?" Jen asked the question, but Vegas folded her hands in a pleading gesture.

"I would love nothing more. I'd also like to stay for dinner, but I'm told I must make an appearance at the grand party across the way," said June. "Better get it over with."

I saw her to the door. "Sophie, dear," she said, "do you still have those boxes up on the third floor? The ones that belonged to Faye?"

I was a little bit ashamed to admit that I'd neither gone through them nor cleaned them out.

June was ecstatic to hear that. "Marvelous. It will be like a treasure hunt through the past."

She walked out into the night. I could hear voices and car doors around Natasha's house and hoped June would enjoy herself.

When I returned to the table, Viktor continued to dominate the conversation.

Without warning, Jen screeched, "It's perfect! Our resident vampire at the haunted house has a name — Viktor. That makes it so much more real, doesn't it? It's a boardinghouse, run by the witch. What would a witch call a bed-and-breakfast?"

"A Dead and Breakfast," suggested Vegas with a giggle.

"A Coffin and Cauldron?" Jen laughed.

After dinner, the girls watched a DVD of old Vincent Price movies while assembling little packets of candy corn for the haunted house visitors. I washed the dishes and cleaned up, planning to join them.

Mochie, his tummy full of sliced ham from the deli, sat by the window, no doubt interested in the sounds emanating from the party. He perked his ears and peered out the window on alert.

If Daisy hadn't run to the front door and scratched at it, I never would have heard the knock. Someone rapped on the door down low, and not very hard, but with a rat-a-tat urgency.

I didn't see anyone through the peephole, but Daisy's enthusiasm gave me the courage to open the door. I hoped it wasn't some sort of ugly Halloween trick. Holding onto Daisy's collar so she wouldn't barge out, I swung the door open just enough to see a little boy dressed as a devil.

"Gabriel Hart! What are you doing out by yourself?" I reached for his hand, peering outside for his father, Frank, or his mother, Anna. Surely the little three-year-old hadn't walked over from his house by himself at this hour of the night.

He willingly took my hand but refused to enter the house. He tugged at me, saying, "There's a bad man outside."

FIVE

Dear Natasha,
I'm throwing an adult Halloween party. I've looked at invitations, but they're all cheesy or babyish. I think the invitations should set the tone for the party. What can I do to make them chilling?
— Frankenstein's Wife in Scary,
West Virginia

Dear Frankenstein's Wife,
Bathe your card stock in a tea bath. Let dry — it's okay if it wrinkles a little. Run through your printer with a chilling scene involving a noose or a dagger, and your spooky invitation details. Then carefully char the edges with a match.
— Natasha

"Honey, it's Halloween. Lots of people have scary decorations. Let's go inside, and I'll call your mommy."

"No! It's the *bad* man." He held his ground but appeared to be on the verge of tears.

I hoped nothing had happened to Frank. After all, there had to be some reason Gabriel had turned up by himself. "Okay. Come in for one second while I get a leash for Daisy."

That must have sounded reasonable to him, because he ventured inside and bravely waited for me to pull on a vest and snap a leash on Daisy's collar. Vegas peered around the corner and gushed about the cute little devil. Jen promptly joined her, and the two girls made a huge fuss over Gabriel. A good thing, because the commotion probably caused him to forget about the bad man he'd seen.

"I'm taking him home," I said. "Be right back."

"Wait!" The girls cried in unison. Jen opened the closet and they grabbed fall pullovers that were the latest craze. Made of soft, warm fleece, the black tops snapped at the neck. When opened, they revealed a bright color inside. Jen's was her favorite color — purple — and Vegas's top showed bright orange. The pullovers reversed to the loud colors.

When I opened the door, each of them

took one of Gabriel's hands, and he seemed quite content to be propelled along the sidewalk by his new friends. We neared Natasha and Mars's home at the end of the block, and the three of them stopped dead.

Lights glowed in every window of the house, and Natasha had rigged panels of some type so that it appeared that skeletons hung from nooses in two of the front windows. No wonder Gabriel had been afraid.

She'd taken great pains with the entrance to the house. A long, curving staircase arched upward from the sidewalk to her front door. The railings wore heavy garlands of shiny black magnolia leaves that must have taken Natasha forever to spray paint. Tiny lights intertwined with them for an elegant but slightly dark effect. Vultures perched on each side of the stair rail, and pumpkins glimmered on the landing at the door. Matte black pots hung from the main floor windows by chains, and real flames flickered in them. The deep notes of haunting organ music floated to us.

"Wow!" I wasn't sure which girl said it. They appeared transfixed.

A rolling fog offered glimpses of the nook created by the curving stairs. Tall dried cornstalks formed a backdrop for hay bales that extended to the service gate, which led

71

to the backyard. A flame in a post light oscillated as though it burned kerosene. More pumpkins with horrifying faces sat on the hay bales and the sidewalk.

"Over there." Gabriel pointed a chubby finger at the hay bales.

We crossed the street for a closer look, Daisy leading the way. "Did you help carve the pumpkins, Vegas?" I asked.

She sounded hurt when she replied, "No. Natasha's crew did it for her TV show, and they said they had to be perfect, not amateurish."

Ouch! Nothing like losing sight of the fun part of Halloween.

A pirate lolled on one of the hay bales, the fog drifting across him. He wore a patch over one eye and a dark scarf wrapped around his head. His ruffly white shirt with a deep V-neck and puffy sleeves had been crammed with something to make him appear real. He wore black trousers, stuffed into huge knee-high boots that were turned down at the tops.

The grim reaper hovered over him in a ragged black robe with a hood hiding his face.

A vampire posed on the other side, in a floor-length black cape with the collar turned up. A mask, complete with bloody fangs, made him even more frightening.

Natasha hadn't considered children at all when planning her decorations. The ebbing mist sent shivers down my back, even though I knew it was all pretend.

Gabriel shook loose from the grip the girls had on him, grabbed my hand, and tugged me toward the pirate. He jerked on my arm and pointed at the pirate with a wail.

"Oh, honey," I said, "these are all make-believe. They're like . . ." I sought an analogy in a children's fable. ". . . like the witch in 'Hansel and Gretel.' There's no such thing as a witch. Look, it's all stuffing."

I reached out and pressed on the bared chest of the pirate, marveling at Natasha's ability to make it seem so real. But my fingers didn't press into packed shredded newspaper like I expected.

Six

Dear Sophie,
I would love to put glowing eyes on some of my Halloween decorations. Unfortunately, power cords would have to crisscross the front walk and kids might trip over them. I'm afraid to use anything with a live flame. What to do?
— Chicken in Black Cat, Arkansas

Dear Chicken,
Battery-operated tea lights are perfect for Halloween. You can even turn them on and off. Make a small hole where you would like an eye. Glue a tea light to the back side of the decoration where you need an eye, being sure the "flame" portion goes through the hole. Repeat for the other eye. No open flames and no cords!
— Sophie

I pressed again, my mouth suddenly dry. Soft flesh yielded ever so slightly to my touch. I shrieked, scooped Gabriel up, and backed away a step, shaking. The pirate didn't move. Daisy strained at her leash, sniffing the legs of the vampire.

Stressed, and unable to pull because I was holding Gabriel, I growled, "Daisy, come!"

She ignored me and stuck her head deeper under the vampire cape. One of the vampire's legs twitched, as though to discourage Daisy. My gaze climbed to his mask. Like an eerie painting, his eyes shifted. For one long second, my eyes met his in horror. Then he bolted away, a black cat crossing his path as he disappeared into the night.

Gabriel and I screamed, but we were no match for the demonic howls coming from Vegas and Jen. The shock knocked the breath out of me. Vegas and Jen clustered close to me, but Daisy pulled at the leash, eager to run after the vampire.

Vegas shrieked and pointed at something behind me. I pivoted, new fear welling up inside me.

"What about him? Is he real?" Vegas indicated the grim reaper.

Holding Gabriel as tightly as I could, I struggled to speak calmly over his crying. "No. Definitely not." *It was a total lie. I had no idea.* "Do either of you have your cell phones with you?"

They shook their heads.

Could Gabriel cry any louder? Poor baby. I suspected he could feel my tension. I couldn't make my heart pound less or slow it down. "Everything's okay," I cooed. "Vegas, Jen, run up to Natasha's and call 911."

Clutching each other, they stumbled toward the base of Natasha and Mars's stairs. A couple dressed as Superman and Wonder Woman approached and headed up the stairs behind them.

"Call 911!" I shouted.

They laughed and the woman said, "What a great gag. Natasha always has the best ideas. Who would have thought about adding a mom and a kid to that scene? Makes it seem so real."

Gabriel wailed in my ear, and I patted him on the back. Vegas and Jen made their way up the stairs and into the house.

I breathed just a hair easier, knowing they would summon an ambulance. But they came rushing out the door and down to the sidewalk seconds later. They couldn't have made a call that fast. "What happened?"

"A vampire threw us out. No kids allowed," said Jen.

"Do you think it could have been the same vampire who ran away?" asked Vegas.

For pity's sake. "Vegas! You live there! Here, hold Daisy's leash." Carrying Gabriel, I climbed the stairs, out of breath by the time I reached the top. The door wasn't locked, and from the sound of the crowd, I didn't think there was any point in knocking. I opened the door to a horror house that looked like a college reunion for vampires. I'd never seen so many caped creatures in one place. Werewolves, witches, mafiosi, skeletons, and at least one Tootsie Roll mingled among them.

I would have to wind through the packed house to reach a phone.

Gabriel screamed anew at a particularly scary vampire who bared his teeth at us. The kid was going to be scarred for life.

"This is a private party." The vampire swept his arms wide, opening his cape to reveal a red satin lining. "We're not trick-or-treating. Remove this ear-shattering child immediately."

"Could you call 911? There's a . . ."

He closed the door in my face so fast that I didn't think he heard me. For a second, I contemplated asserting myself, but Gabriel's frightened screams made me reconsider and a new chorus of horrified howls

77

came from below. It had to be the girls. I staggered down the stairs as fast as I could.

Vegas, Daisy, and Jen had migrated to the pirate. "Touch him," said Vegas. "I dare you."

"Aunt Sophie, I think the pirate is real." Jen chewed on her upper lip.

I set Gabriel on the sidewalk. "I want you two to take Gabriel home. It's across the street, third house down on the next block. Then go straight home."

"With a vampire on the loose?" shrieked Vegas.

She caught me by surprise. He wasn't a real vampire, of course, but what if the man in the vampire costume was vicious? What if he lurked somewhere on the next block, waiting for hapless children in the middle of the night?

"Okay, let's go there together. Hurry."

I lifted Gabriel so we wouldn't be slowed by his toddling legs, but I wasn't used to carrying a baby around, much less one as hearty as Gabriel, and by the time we crossed the street, my breath came heavy and hard. Mindful of the pirate who appeared to need medical assistance, I didn't dare stop.

Unfortunately, the street lay quiet. Lots of orange Halloween lights glowed on the houses, but no police cruisers were parked on the street. I was relieved to unload Gabriel again when we reached his house. The old Williamsburg-style lights on either side of the front door glimmered, illuminating a child-friendly Halloween wreath of Casper-like ghosts on the door, but I didn't see lights on inside. I banged a knocker in the shape of a squirrel.

No one answered the door, elevating my concern over Gabriel's parents. The girls clustered close behind me, each one holding one of Gabriel's hands. They whispered about keeping an eye out for the vampire who had vanished into the night. I knocked on the door again, this time with more fervor.

Something squeaked inside and after what seemed an eternity, the door swung open a crack. A safety chain hung about the level of my nose.

"Yes?" I couldn't see much of the speaker, but the outdoor lights revealed tousled blond hair. A sitter? I wondered if she knew she'd lost Gabriel.

"I'm looking for Gabriel's parents."

"They're out." She started to shut the door, but I applied a little pressure with the palm of my hand.

"Not so fast." Did she know she'd lost her

charge? "Where is Gabriel?"

Her eyes narrowed to wary slits. "None of your business!"

"When did you check on him last?"

She studied me. "Is this some kind of mean Halloween trick on the babysitter?"

"He turned up at my house earlier" — I put a little bit of motherly guilt into my voice — "all by himself, and I wanted to be sure he made it home safely."

"A three-year-old out all by himself? I don't think so." She slammed the door, and I heard her turn the bolt.

"Was that Heather Corbin? She didn't even notice Gabriel!" Vegas's voice reflected the shock I felt. "You can't give him back to her."

"You know her?" I asked.

"Ugh." Vegas made no secret of her feelings. "Miss Snoot Face thinks she's better than anyone else in the entire universe. She's in my class at school, and she's always flirting with Blake."

"I agree with Vegas. What if Gabriel escapes again but doesn't come to your house next time?"

They were right. I couldn't leave him with an irresponsible sitter. Why was all this taking so long when the pirate needed help, too? *One thing at a time, Sophie.* If I took

Gabriel with me, his parents would be shocked when they came home and found his bed empty. But the risk of leaving him with the inattentive sitter was just too great.

I'd have to deal with informing Gabriel's parents later. I swung him up again, and our little parade hustled home as fast as we could go.

As we crossed the street, Vegas screeched as though she were being tortured. "There he is!" She pointed toward the alley. "It's the vampire, coming for us. Hurry, Sophie!"

Gabriel's loud cries began again, even with me murmuring comforting words to him. I couldn't run with Gabriel in my arms. As it was, my lungs burned by the time we reached my house.

I flung open the door, set Gabriel down, left him to the girls, and dashed to the telephone. I called 911 and blurted the information about the pirate in front of Natasha's house.

"Is he breathing?" asked the dispatcher.

My heart still pounded and her question caught me off guard. I was going to feel really stupid if that pirate turned out to be a prop. "I didn't check."

Gabriel toddled into the kitchen, crying, but with less intensity. I opened the refrigerator and pulled out a white-iced cupcake for him. It worked like magic. The second he held it, he appeared to forget all about the monsters he'd seen. He tasted the frosting like it was an ice cream cone, getting it on the tip of his nose. Daisy assisted by licking his nose, but the sweet girl didn't lunge for the cupcake, which must have been tempting. She sat in front of Gabriel and waited for crumbs to hit the floor.

Assured that an ambulance was on the way, I hung up but still trembled. "Jen," I called. "I have to go back." Where had they disappeared to so fast?

Jen and Vegas reappeared in the kitchen. They'd taken off their outerwear, but both of them wore knit collars of some kind.

"Will you two be okay watching Gabriel? Just don't open the door for anyone. Understand? Here's the number for Gabriel's dad. See if you can reach him. He'll be worried sick."

They nodded, and I took off, leaving Daisy with the girls. I shut the front door behind me and jogged back to Natasha and Mars's house. How long would the ambulance take? I didn't see any sign of it yet. Had the dispatcher written me off as a kook because I didn't know if the pirate was breathing, and I'd blathered something about a vampire? What if she thought my call was a prank?

Nothing had changed at Natasha's. The eerie music and party sounds continued. The fog still rolled through her decorations. I took a deep breath and walked closer to the pirate, who didn't appear to have moved.

The grim reaper still stood over him, leading me to believe that he was a prop. Still, after the vampire had turned out to be a live person, I wasn't taking any chances. I reached toward his black shroud tentatively, wishing I'd brought Daisy. Like a darting snake, I poked him with a finger, and hit what I'd expected to feel on the pirate — some kind of crunchy stuffing.

Bracing myself, I reached for the pirate's wrist, but a tightly fastened sleeve with a fancy ruffle as long as his hand prevented me from feeling a pulse. The hand was cold . . . bone cold. It was real, though. Even Natasha wouldn't have been able to make a fake hand that felt so authentic.

A wave of mist flowed around us when I reached for his neck in search of a pulse. I bent closer and yanked my hand back in horror.

SEVEN

Dear Sophie,
I'm having a small Halloween dinner party for friends. I have the menu and decorations worked out, but I can't think of anything original to do with the bar.
— Spirit Hostess in Wine Hill, Illinois

Dear Spirit Hostess,
Decant your libations into plain glass bottles and dress them up with scary labels you make on your own computer. Red wine might be *Blood of a Three-Toed Man,* vodka could be *Zombie Acid,* and olives can be labeled *Eye of Zombie.*
— Sophie

The fog rolled on, and clear as the back of my own hand, I could see the pirate's neck. Two blood red round spots about an inch and a half apart dripped rivulets of red. The howl of a siren finally drew close, and I decided it would be best if I didn't touch the pirate. The professionals would be there momentarily.

I dashed to the edge of the brick sidewalk, waving my arms over my head as soon as the ambulance came into view. It pulled to a halt in front of Natasha and Mars's house, and two emergency medical technicians jumped out, while a third took his time. One of them took in the elaborate scene and muttered, "And I thought I went all out by carving a pumpkin."

I led them to the pirate, and they wasted no time starting CPR. Unfortunately, since I didn't know the guy, I couldn't answer most of their questions. Once again, I dashed up the stairs and barged into the party. The vampire who guarded the door raised his arms so that his cape fluttered out, and he looked menacing. "Didn't I make myself clear? What don't you understand about *private party?*"

I pushed past him, even though I could hear him shouting at me, and kept going until I found Mars, my ex-husband, in the dining room refilling his glass with red wine. A black cloth topped with a lace spiderweb covered the sideboard. Natasha had followed our lead in labeling various bottles with poisonous-sounding names. She certainly hadn't skimped on Vampire wine. Among the sinister bottles stood several labeled *Absinthe.*

"Sophie, sweetie! I thought you were home taking care of the girls. I'm glad you came, though you might have dressed for the occasion."

"Pin-striped suit, narrow tie, and cheesy mustache. Who are you supposed to be?"

He lifted my hand, kissed it, and pretended to nibble at my arm. "Gomez Addams, my lovely."

Under other circumstances, I might have thought his clowning cute. "One of your guests is injured, and the rescue squad needs someone to identify him."

He set down the wineglass. "Lead the way!"

It was with a modicum of satisfaction that I paraded Mars by the doorkeeper vampire. I couldn't help shooting him a patronizing smile. We ran down the stairs, and as soon as Mars saw the pirate, he said, "Good grief, that's Patrick Starski! What happened?"

Patrick? I took a closer look. Between the eye patch and the pirate wrap on his head, I hadn't recognized him.

"What's wrong with him?" asked Mars.

The EMTs kept up CPR, but a look flashed between them that worried me. "He have any next of kin?"

At that exact moment, the obnoxious vampire and a handful of guests stepped out the door and peered down at us. Maggie was among them, her hands already cupped around a cigarette to light it. She took a deep drag, placed a hand on the railing, and casually stared down at us.

"Maggie!" Mars shouted. "Patrick's had some kind of accident."

It took a few seconds to sink in. Maggie shuffled to the top step, leaned over, and unsnapped something on the bottom of her dress. She made her way down, slowly, one painful step at a time, as though she had difficulty walking, but she still carried the cigarette. When she reached the bottom, I realized she wore a Morticia Addams dress, skintight, all the way down to her ankles. I guessed she'd unfastened something that allowed her to walk more easily, but she still couldn't do much more than shuffle over to Patrick.

"Patrick!" Her cigarette fell on a bale of hay when she screamed.

The spark ignited a loose bit of hay on the top, and it blazed like a dry Christmas tree. Simultaneously, two police cars arrived, and a crowd of partygoers rushed down the stairs, adding to the confusion.

I grabbed the Grim Reaper's cape and threw it over the hay bale, dousing the fire. As I recalled, hay bales were packed so tightly that they didn't burn easily. Nevertheless, my heart thundered from the brief flare-up of loose material.

With the fire under control, I paused to catch my breath and saw Wolf, the homicide detective whom I dated. His presence told me everything I needed to know — Patrick was dead.

Wolf took charge of the scene, finding a few seconds to kiss me intensely on the lips before calmly moving everyone away from Patrick and the EMTs. Our relationship wasn't a secret anymore, but I was stunned by his public display of affection, however brief. Mars scowled at me, and I couldn't help noticing that Detective Kenner, who'd been chasing me in spite of my relationship with Wolf, was watching. There was nothing wrong with Wolf's kissing me, yet I couldn't help wondering if it had been for the benefit of Mars or Kenner.

We clustered at the edge of the sidewalk. Partygoers lined the stairs to Natasha and Mars's front door, their assorted gruesome costumes bestowing a surreal atmosphere. The fog machine continued to blast a pea-soup cloud over Patrick, contributing to the eeriness.

I hadn't known him really, and our one encounter had been decidedly unpleasant, but the shock of his death stunned me. I looked on with the others, watching the horror unfold.

Maggie stood near Patrick, clinging to Mars. Her hands clenched his jacket so tightly that her knuckles shone white in the semidarkness.

One of the EMTs called Wolf. "I think you should see this."

I knew what they were showing him — it had to be the two blood red spots I'd seen on his neck. Wolf, characteristically calm, took it in stride. His voice low, I heard him ask, "What is that?"

The EMT didn't have Wolf's tact. "Vampire bite?"

Maggie bent forward to have a look, and screamed as if a vampire were biting *her*. If it hadn't been for Mars wrapping his arms around her waist, she would have fallen. She stopped screaming as quickly as she had started and muttered, "Three days. He'll be dead in three days."

Unless I missed my guess, he didn't have three minutes left.

She turned around and scanned the crowd. I followed her line of sight — a weird collection of people dressed as vampires, interspersed with traditional witches, skeletons, mummies, and scary TV characters. Her head fell back, and she collapsed, nearly taking Mars down with her.

Wolf lunged toward them and helped Mars lower Maggie to the ground. An EMT came to her assistance, and I wondered if they would have to cut the tight dress off of her to restore her circulation. Not on the sidewalk, I hoped.

She came around quickly, struggled to sit, but she couldn't stand up by herself because of the tightness of the dress. Over the EMT's objections, Wolf and Mars helped her to her feet. She took a couple of tiny Morticia Addams shuffle-style steps, bent over, and ripped the seam of her dress, right up to midthigh. "Blake. I have to warn my son, Blake."

Warn him? Of what?

The woman beside me shuffled closer to make room for the growing crowd and jingled when she moved. In spite of the gypsy costume, I easily recognized Natasha's mother, Wanda. She wore a turban with her hair tucked underneath it; a gauzy loose blouse unbuttoned too low, showing off too much cleavage; and a long skirt. She gave me a quick hug and said, "I sense danger for that woman."

Even when I was a little girl, Wanda had claimed powers of prognostication. It didn't take much, though, to guess danger lurked, since something sinister had happened to Patrick.

Wanda closed her eyes and held out wrinkled hands covered with enormous gemstone rings. "She's afraid. Very afraid. I'm getting the name Lucas."

Okay, that *was* a little creepy, given June's tale about Viktor Luca.

I heard Mars offer to help Maggie up the stairs. Strain showed in her expression as she gazed around at the other guests. *Looking for a friendly face?*

"Which hospital will they take Patrick to?" she asked.

I froze. I'd guessed he was dead, since Wolf had been called. Either I was wrong, or Maggie didn't understand yet.

Wolf ran a hand over the top of his head. "I'm sorry . . ."

Oh, not in front of everyone! I stepped forward. "Would you like to come across the way to my house for a little privacy?"

Mars immediately said, "Great idea." He took Maggie gently by the arm to lead the way, but she recoiled at the sight of me, as if I were a threat. She pulled a pendant on a chain out from under her costume, spun around, and stood with her back to me for a few seconds. Looks passed between Mars, Wolf, and me. *What on earth was she doing?*

She turned toward me with a weak smile and dropped the pendant under her dress again. "Thank you."

The crowd opened for Wolf as he led the way for Mars and Maggie. I was in the middle of the street, bringing up the rear, when I heard someone shout, "That's her!"

EIGHT

Dear Natasha,
Everyone in my neighborhood has long stairs leading up to the front door. I'm so tired of a lantern or a pumpkin on each step that I could scream. I would love to do something new and different. Any suggestions?
— No More Pumpkins in Gourd Neck,
Arkansas

Dear No More Pumpkins,
Buy glow-in-the-dark paint and paint scary sayings on the riser of each step: "You're getting closer to doom." "Run!" "Prepare for the worst." "It's not too late to turn back." Paint freehand and let some of the paint drip down. You'll have a very original entrance!
— Natasha

I looked over my shoulder and saw Gabriel's

babysitter pointing at me. "She's the one who kidnapped him."

An African American woman, only slightly taller than me, with a flawless complexion, accompanied her. The trousers of her police uniform cinched her waist too tightly, creating ample rolls above and below. Her shirt strained to contain a generous bosom. "Hold up there a minute, ma'am. I need to have a word with you."

I waited for her to catch up to me. "Gabriel is fine. And I did *not* kidnap him or anyone else."

She looked around. "Where is he?"

"He's at my house with my niece. Come on. You can see for yourself."

By the time we reached my foyer, Mars and Wolf had escorted Maggie to the living room, and Jen and Vegas were eavesdropping.

"What's going on? Is that Blake's mom?" asked Jen.

"Heather! What are you doing here?" Vegas blurted.

I ignored their questions. "Did you manage to reach Gabriel's parents?"

"We only get voice mail," said Jen.

Vegas and Jen were still wearing something wooly wrapped around their necks. "Please tell me you're not coming down with colds.

Do you have sore throats?"

A pink flush flooded Jen's cheeks. "It's a precaution." She held a kneesock out to me. "We have one for you, too."

Aware of the horrible moment that must be transpiring in my living room, I wanted to get them out of the foyer. "Everyone into the kitchen. You're sure no one is sick?"

They promised everyone was fine. The girls had turned on spooky lights and lit candles in the kitchen.

"Where's Gabriel?" I asked.

Jen and Vegas shrugged and raised their palms as though they had no idea.

Panic surged through me.

In a loud, teasing voice, Jen said, "Where could Gabriel be? I haven't seen him. Have you, Vegas?"

"You see? They're hiding him!" said Heather.

The officer frowned at us, her forehead furrowed.

As though on cue, little Gabriel, still wearing his devil horn hat, gleefully ran into the kitchen from the family room. He looked far too angelic to be a devil. He giggled and charged past us into the foyer.

"Is that the missing child?" the officer asked Heather.

"Yes! What a relief. Thank you, Officer."

She took a couple of steps in the direction of the foyer but didn't realize that Gabriel was making a circle. He toddled toward us from the family room again, obviously delighted with himself.

Heather held out her arms to him and he stopped cold. His happy expression morphed to one of displeasure, as though someone were trying to feed him bitter medicine. "I don't like you."

The officer's eyebrows shot up. "We'll let him play for just a little longer." She bent toward him. "Hi. I'm Officer Wong." She lifted his necklace and sniffed it. "Garlic? You afraid of vampires?" She directed her question to Jen and Vegas.

Heather snorted. "I *have* to send a school-wide text about this!"

Vegas jutted her hip with attitude. "You think you're so smart. Well, if you'd seen what we saw tonight, you'd be wearing garlic, too. But that's okay. You run back on down the street by yourself without any vampire protection and hope he doesn't drink *your* blood."

Heather tried to snicker, but her doubtful expression suggested her bravado had been shaken.

The officer appeared confused. "You three take the baby and protect him from vam-

96

pires." She pointed straight at me. "I'd like a word with you."

Jen took Gabriel's hand and led him to the family room. Vegas and Heather followed her.

"Hot cider?" I asked.

"Sure." Officer Wong stood at the island, watching me. "How come you have the baby?"

"He showed up at my front door all by himself. You can ask Jen and Vegas. When we took him home, Heather didn't even know she'd lost him. I didn't dare leave him alone with her again."

"Uh-huh." Disbelief drenched her tone. "A three-year-old just happened to escape his sitter, walk to your house, and knock on the door."

She clearly wasn't buying my story. "I don't know how he managed to get away from her. He was scared when he got here. There's a very creepy Halloween display between our houses, and I think it spooked him."

The corner of her mouth twitched, and she studied me while I poured the cider. "Cupcake?" I asked, placing a plate of them on the counter. "Those are devil's food, double chocolate." The dark cupcake was topped with a chocolate ganache. I had drizzled white powdered-sugar icing over top in circles and used a toothpick to drag it into spiderweb designs.

She lifted one, pulled back the wrapper, and bit into it. "Umm, these are good."

"Wong?" Wolf's voice came from the doorway.

Officer Wong gasped as if she'd just had a eureka moment. She licked ganache off her forefinger and waggled it at me. "I know who you are. They warned me about you!"

What does that mean? I wanted to ask, but Wolf shot toward the cupcakes.

"Buttering up the cops?" he teased.

I poured him a cup of cider. "How's Maggie?"

"Taking it hard. For some reason, she thought he was unconscious and would die in three days."

Wong squinted at him. "Why do I feel like I've missed something?"

Wolf brought her up to speed. "Is that why the girls are protecting the baby with garlic?" she asked.

I relaxed a bit. Wong was obviously sharp. It had been such a weird and confusing night that it was getting to be a little bit hard to explain everything. "The vampire was standing in front of Natasha's house, posing like he was part of the display. Then

Daisy stuck her head under his cape and he took off at a run."

"You saw the murderer?" asked Wolf.

I nodded. "So did Vegas and Jen, and, alas, Gabriel. I don't know that he was the murderer, but he was wearing a vampire cape and a mask, and he took off running."

Wolf scowled. "Did you recognize him? Hair, shoes, voice?"

"I thought he was a prop, a mannequin. If I'd known he was a killer, I'd have paid more attention." I thought back. "He didn't say anything. The collar of his cape stood up, hiding his jaw, and he wore a horrible mask." I shook my head at him. "I'm sorry. Everything happened so fast."

Jen stomped into the kitchen. "I am so mad!"

"What's wrong? Is it Heather?" I asked.

Jen waved her hand in a familiar gesture she must have picked up from her father. "She's obnoxious, but that's not why I'm upset. I love mysteries. I devoured *Nancy Drew,* and I didn't notice one clue about the identity of the vampire."

Wolf bit back a smile.

"Vegas and I talked about it, and we can't even remember how tall he was. How pathetic is that? I have to start being more observant."

"You'll tell me if you recall anything?" asked Wolf.

She threw her hands in the air. "We're useless!"

Raised voices came from the family room. "That stupid Heather. Man, but she's mean." Jen rushed back to the family room.

"Mars is going to drive Maggie home, and I have to get back," said Wolf. "I want you to be very careful."

"We'll be fine," I assured him.

He frowned at me. "Soph! Until we catch this guy, you and the girls need to be on alert. He may come after you if he thinks you can identify him."

"Don't be silly. We didn't see anything. You heard Jen."

Wolf leaned toward me and in all earnestness, said, "But he doesn't know that."

Wong and I watched as Mars and Wolf accompanied Maggie out the front door. Instead of the broken, weepy woman I expected to see, Maggie stood erect, her alert eyes taking in everything.

The door had barely shut when Wong said, "Did she look like someone who just lost her man?"

"I don't think I'd have been so together."

"Me, either. Unless she was happy to get rid of him."

A whiney voice arose behind Wong and me. "Well? Can I take Gabriel home now? His parents will be arriving anytime, and I wouldn't want them to find an empty house." Heather had the good fortune to be a very pretty blonde with a pert nose and great hair. Unfortunately, she acted like she had figured that out and was used to getting what she wanted.

Officer Wong sipped cider and didn't appear to be in any hurry. "What time did you put Gabriel to bed?"

Heather's eyes widened in surprise. "I wasn't watching the clock. He's a baby. He goes to bed early."

"And then I guess you watched TV?"

Heather recovered and if her sly look and sassy tone were any indication, she thought she was onto Wong and her line of questioning. "No. I read a book."

"I like to read. What book was it?"

Heather couldn't stop a sly smile from creeping onto her lips. "My biology book."

"I like biology, too. So how come it took you so long to answer the door when Mrs. Winston came by?"

How could Wong possibly know that?

Heather had to think for a minute. "I was in the bathroom."

"I see. How do you think she got inside

101

the house to snatch Gabriel?"

I almost began to feel sorry for Heather when she paused, unsure of herself. "I heard something in the backyard, and I went outside to check on it. I guess I left the door unlocked, and she was lurking outside, waiting for the opportunity."

"So, you weren't reading your biology book. You weren't even in the house."

"You're not allowed to question me without my parents present. I know my rights! My daddy is very influential in this town. He will not be happy to hear about the way you've treated me. I'll . . . I'll get you fired!"

Wong appeared nonplussed. "Perhaps you're not aware of the penalty for false charges." She brushed by Heather into the family room.

Heather turned toward me. "You wouldn't dare!"

"I don't think I have anything to do with it." I said it with smug satisfaction, and immediately wished I hadn't, even if she was a spoiled stinker.

Wong returned, carrying a sleepy Gabriel. Addressing me, she said, "I'd better get this little guy home in case his parents return."

I nodded and opened the front door for her. "Wait. How did you know she didn't answer the door right away?"

Wong grinned and whispered, "There were Heathers when I was in school, too. And they were always outside necking with some boy."

Vegas darted up from behind and draped a second garlic necklace over Gabriel.

Heather pinched her nose shut with her fingers. "*Ugh.* You are so weird. No wonder your mother ran off and left you. I'd abandon a kid like you, too."

It was mean. Low-down, dirty, and aimed to hurt Vegas where she was most vulnerable.

To her credit, Vegas didn't cry. When Heather was out of earshot, she said, "I hope she gets in big trouble for ignoring Gabriel."

I had a feeling that wish had already come true. Between Gabriel's parents and the very astute Officer Wong, Heather had some explaining to do — no matter how important her parents might be.

"In fact, I hope the vampire does bite her!" Vegas crossed her arms over her chest and pouted.

I had just begun to close the door when I heard a blast. Holding the door open just a crack, I peered out. Doors opened up and down the street. Daisy and Mochie ran to my side in alarm. The acrid smell of burning filled the air. I hoped it wasn't some kind of gas leak. I'd seen TV news reports of entire blocks being demolished by a gas leak. Maybe we would be safer outdoors?

"What was that?" Jen gazed up the stairs.

"I don't know. Put on your jackets." I buckled harnesses on Mochie and Daisy. I wasn't about to leave them behind. Although Mochie knew how to walk on a leash, he gladly rode on my shoulder, which I preferred at the moment in case we had to run.

The girls beat me out to the sidewalk.

"It's at my house!" Vegas ran across the street with Jen on her heels.

"Girls, wait!" There was no stopping them.

Fortunately, all the police cars had slowed traffic to a standstill. A golden glow spread in the air in back of Natasha and Mars's home. Harder to see was a plume of inky black, darker than the night sky, that rose in terrifying billows.

The crowd in front of Natasha's house had retreated into the street. Maggie stood by herself, staring at the house in shock.

I hurried to her. "Where are Mars and Wolf?" Hopefully they hadn't gone into the house.

She pointed to the street that ran along the side of the house. I jogged in that direction, trying not to jostle Mochie too much. Sirens filled the air. I moved to the opposite sidewalk to clear the way for fire trucks. From my vantage point, I could see that Natasha's kitchen was on fire. Amid the flames, part of the wall appeared to have been blown out. Firemen and police ushered us out of the way, blocking me from returning the way I had come.

Bernie watched from a spot a little farther along the street. He wore a cat on each shoulder.

"What happened?" I asked.

"I have no idea."

Bernie lived in an apartment over Natasha and Mars's detached garage. "Must have been loud at your place. Have you seen Vegas or Jen? They got away from me."

"Haven't seen anyone. I was in my apartment when I heard the explosion. I could hear glass from the windows shatter as it hit the street, so I grabbed the kittens and ran outside — just to be on the safe side."

The flames began to subside, but the clouds of dark smoke continued. I searched faces for Vegas, Jen, Mars, Wolf, and yes, Natasha. With the firefighters blocking the side street, I would have to walk along the alley and cut through Nina's yard to go around to the other side of the house.

Talking fast, I filled Bernie in on Patrick's death.

"Do you think the explosion is related to that? Someone set the kitchen on fire to hide evidence or distract everyone so he could escape?" he asked.

That idea hadn't even crossed my mind. "It is awfully coincidental."

I breathed a sigh of relief when I saw Wolf standing among the firefighters. He made his way over to us. "What a night. Are you two all right?"

"I'm worried about Mars and Natasha. It's a lucky break that so many people had gone outside to see what was going on with Patrick. I hope no one was hurt." Daisy strained at the leash to be petted by Wolf.

He rubbed the scruff of her neck. "They're fine. I saw them on the other side of the house with Vegas and Jen. The firefighters say it should be under control shortly. It's in the renovated section of the house, so it's not a tinderbox like some of these old buildings."

As though his words were magic, the flames tapered off significantly.

"Crikey, look at that." Bernie adjusted an increasingly restless cat and motioned toward a jagged hole gaping in the second story of the house. "Reminds me of those pictures from war-torn countries where a bomb hit a house."

"Except for one big difference." Wolf studied the damage. "This bomb went off inside the house. It blew the wall and the glass in the windows outward."

"So Bernie might be right? The killer could have set it up as a distraction." I set Mochie on the ground to let him sniff around a bit.

"If that was the case," said Wolf, "he didn't plan well. Seems like he would have wanted the explosion to distract people closer to the time of the murder. On the other hand, bombs are tricky business. A lot of them detonate at the wrong time."

"Then there could be more! I have to find Vegas and Jen and get them out of here." I whisked Mochie up onto my shoulder again to leave. "Bernie, do you want to bring the kittens and stay with me tonight?"

"Thanks. I think we'll be all right here. But I'll keep it in mind if anything else untoward happens."

Wolf kindly offered to escort me along the sidewalk so I wouldn't have to go the long way around. Carefully avoiding the areas of shattered glass, we walked fast, lest another explosion shower us with debris.

I spotted Vegas and Jen with Natasha and

Mars. Although a lot of their guests still lingered outside, their little group stood alone.

"What don't you understand about *no?*" Natasha hissed her words, but everyone within a few yards could probably hear them. "I will *not* act like a homeless person. There are plenty of hotels in this town."

"Staying with my mother for one night is hardly the equivalent of being homeless." Mars was using his diplomatic voice. The one generally reserved for reporters who criticized Mars's political clients. Natasha had crossed a line.

"I'm not staying with that woman!"

Ouch.

Vegas appeared to be unfazed by the argument, which worried me because it might mean she heard this kind of squabble too often and had grown used to them.

Jen tugged on my sleeve. "I invited Uncle Mars and Natasha to stay with us tonight."

I confess my breath caught in my throat. It was the right thing to do, of course, but my ex-husband and his lover sleeping in a bedroom across the way from mine didn't appeal to me much.

"Good heavens. You can't expect me to stay at Sophie's house. It's so . . . primitive."

Primitive? That was a new one to me. I only had one and a half bathrooms, but at least I didn't have a big hole in the wall of my kitchen. I wasn't about to pressure her, though.

"You know, this is why you don't have friends." Mars ambled off.

"What? Sophie knows her house is primitive." She threw me a nasty look, as if Mars's comment was all my fault. "I hate it when he does this. We're going to end up at his mother's house, and I won't be able to sleep a wink." Natasha chased after him.

"Come on, girls. Let's go home." We walked back to my house with Vegas worrying aloud about her "stuff" that might have been destroyed in the fire. Losing her mom and having her dad away were hard enough. I hated to think how awful it would be if she lost her material possessions, too. A person could only tolerate so many blows, and Vegas had already suffered more than her fair share.

There wasn't anything I could do about it, except try to distract her. Fortunately, as soon as the leashes and jackets had been removed, Jen seized my hand. "Come see what we made while we were babysitting Gabriel. It's so cool!"

They led the way to my den and proudly

showed me a large sign. The top line, *Bubble and Trouble,* arched in a semicircle. Underneath, in a smaller, dripping, scary Halloween font, it said, *A Coffin & Cauldron for Otherworldly Travelers.*

It was adorable and I said so.

Vegas beamed. "We made a bunch of them. Do you think Bernie could attach one over the Ye Olde Candle Shoppe sign that hangs over the sidewalk?"

"I don't see why not."

Jen sank into the sofa. "I'm beat, but I'm so relieved we finally have a great story about our haunted house. All thanks to June."

I shared her feeling and sat down next to her. "I'm afraid I have bad news."

Vegas perched on the arm of the sofa, her face ashen. "About the fire?"

"No." I didn't know how to soften the blow for them, and Vegas had already had too many horrible experiences in her young life. "The pirate we saw tonight is dead."

Jen sat up straight. "I knew it! From the vampire bite!"

"I don't know what killed him, but I seriously doubt he died from anything related to a vampire."

"But, Sophie," Vegas protested, "you saw the vampire run away."

110

"We were there, too, but we didn't kill him. Let's see what the medical examiner says first, okay? It might have been a heart attack or something."

"Yeah," said Vegas, "brought on by a vampire bite!"

"I'm afraid the really bad news is that the pirate was Patrick Starski."

"The guy dating Blake's mom," said Vegas.

"The very same. I guess Blake won't be around to help with the haunted house. We'll have to find a substitute for him. What was he supposed to do?"

Jen's eyes met mine. "He wanted to fill in for Frank as the vampire in the casket room upstairs."

Life was full of irony. "Do you want to talk about this?" I had no idea how much reassurance they needed. They didn't say anything, so I moved on, trying to open them up a bit. "So, what's with the socks around your necks? Do they keep you from getting sore throats or something?"

Jen confessed. "The socks protect our throats from vampire bites. We saw those bite marks on the pirate's neck and thought we should take precautions."

Vegas looked at me with the honest, clear eyes of youth. "Do you think Viktor Luca could be back?"

NINE

Dear Sophie,
My thirteen-year-old daughter is too old to trick-or-treat, so she's having a sleep-over. Now that she's a teen, there's a fine line between corny and cool. My husband says we should play creepy music and come up with a scary prank to spook them. I think that won't be cool enough.
    — Carol Brady in Screamer, Alabama

Dear Carol,
Buy a few bottles of bright red nail polish and begin with a bloody nail-painting session, complete with Bloody Mary Mocktails. After that, fill big bowls with kettle corn, cheesy popcorn, and buttery popcorn and host a devilish black-and-white movie horror-a-thon.
    — Sophie

"Of course not, Vegas. Whoever that man was, he was just a regular person wearing a vampire cape. That hardly makes him a vampire."

Jen and Vegas migrated into my family room and pulled out the sofa bed. I tidied up the kitchen, arranged some iced bat-shaped cookies on a platter, and made Jen's favorite cinnamon and nutmeg herbal tea. A chilling black-and-white Vincent Price movie was playing on the TV when I delivered their snack.

"Are you sure you want to sleep down here?" I asked, even though I knew the answer. It would be more fun for them to watch TV late into the night and squeal and run around. Bedrooms were boring.

I left them to their horror show, shrugged on a warm jacket, and stepped outside with Daisy. While she snuffled around the backyard, I opened the service gate that faced the street and took a few steps toward the sidewalk. Down the block, I could see lights and hear voices. I shivered and crossed my arms to stay warm. Wolf and the forensic team would have to work well into the night. Poor Maggie. She had to cope with the loss of someone so close to her and break the news to her son, Blake. I felt certain she would have a sleepless night.

113

I watched as someone dressed in black crossed the street in a stealthy manner a few houses down. The streetlights didn't do much to help illuminate him. I squinted into the dark, then chided myself for being suspicious of everyone.

But when I heard a dry leaf crunch behind me, my suspicion radar perked up again. I whirled around, but before I could raise my hands, someone cast a huge cloth that smelled of licorice over my head. A scream rose from my throat, and I flailed my arms in panic, but my short arms were no match for my assailant. While I wrestled to tear the cloth off, he pressed something against my nose and mouth with such pressure that I could hardly move. I tried to suck in air, but something was wrong. I couldn't breathe. Desperate, I kicked at him but only succeeded in losing my balance. I tried to scream again, but I couldn't get air. Wishing I'd worn daggerlike heels or at least heavy shoes of some type instead of sneakers, I slammed my foot onto his. A groan suggested I'd made contact in a painful way.

Loud barking gave me hope. Daisy! Oh no! Why had I latched the gate?

"Stop that! Help!" I recognized the voice of my best friend, Nina Reid Norwood.

The next thing I knew, my assailant

114

grunted and shoved into me. We fell as a unit, and someone lay on top of me. I floundered, fighting the cloth over my head. He'd released his grip when we fell, and I gulped air like a drowning victim. I could hear Daisy snarling and Nina yelling for help. In panic, I tried to kick my pinned legs and scramble backward. As I struggled, the cloth pulled away, and Daisy, Nina, and I found ourselves sitting on the cold brick sidewalk with a person in a vampire costume.

"Get his mask!" I shouted, trying to lunge at him from a seated position. He scrambled to his feet, and ran across the street and around the corner, a huge cape billowing from his arm as he disappeared into the night.

My heart pounded.

Nina touched my shoulder gently. "Are you okay?"

I nodded and stumbled to my feet to prove it. "Where did you come from?"

"I'm trying to catch a cat. I was about to go home to warm up for a bit when I heard Daisy barking. I opened your gate, and the two of us jumped that creep."

I hugged her. "You and Daisy just saved my life."

"Nonsense! Are you sure you're okay?"

she asked.

"I'll be fine."

"I'll walk you inside and make you some tea."

"What? You know how to heat water in the kettle?" It was a silly thing to say, but I needed to lighten up the situation. Or at least pretend that I wasn't scared out of my mind.

"Emergencies call for drastic heroics — like cooking."

"Don't worry about me. Daisy will protect me. Right, girl?"

Daisy's tail wagged, and I could have sworn that she was smiling at me. I planted a quick kiss on her head.

Nina pointed across the street. "There's the cat. Hurry up now. I need to catch that rascally fellow for his own good, but I'm not leaving you out here to be attacked again. Are you sure you don't need help?"

I waved her off.

"Well, go on then, before that kitty disappears!"

I staggered to the house, wishing I could walk more sprightly, but each step revealed a new ache where bruises were undoubtedly springing to life.

When I looked back, Nina, moving as stealthily as a jaguar, prowled toward the black cat sitting under the streetlight.

I wasn't going to hang around outside for even one minute longer. Daisy and I bolted into the sunroom, and I locked the door behind us. Just to be on the safe side, I wedged a chair underneath the handle. No one was coming in *that* way.

"Aunt Sophie?" Jen's voice came from the family room. "Is that you?"

"It's just Daisy and me." I hurried to the kitchen, called Wolf's cell phone, and told him what happened. When I hung up, I hugged Daisy like I would never let her go. I'm not much of a crier, but tears trickled down my face, wetting her fur. So much for Natasha's theory about Daisy. If it hadn't been for Nina and Daisy, who knows what might have happened?

She barked at the sound of Wolf approaching the front door. I whisked it open and flew into his arms, my breath still ragged. He shuffled inside, kicked the door closed, and held me.

Jen's voice behind me asked, "What's going on?"

I forced myself to let go of Wolf, tried to smile reassuringly at Jen and Vegas, and ushered them all into the kitchen. I collapsed into a fireside chair, and Daisy planted herself beside me. While I relayed the story, Jen put on a pot of tea, and Vegas listened with her mouth open.

"We heard barking." Vegas nervously twisted the hem of her pajama top. "It never occurred to me that you could be in danger."

Jen handed me a cup of steaming tea with milk. When I took it, I was shocked to find my hands still trembled. "It's all behind us now. Daisy and Nina are my heroines." I bent toward Daisy. "Steak is on your menu tomorrow."

She wagged her feathery tail across the floor.

People could say what they liked about dog intelligence, but I was certain Daisy understood she had helped rescue me tonight.

Wolf leaned against the kitchen island, his face troubled. "Show me where this happened."

I nodded. "Give me a minute." I asked Jen and Vegas to turn on lights in the dining and living rooms. Meanwhile, I switched on the lights in the sunroom. If the assailant was lurking around, I wanted the house to be fully lit while we were outside. I clipped a leash on Daisy, and we trekked out to the sidewalk.

"Right about here," I said.

We all stared at the sidewalk as though it might hold a secret. If it did, it wasn't giving it up.

Wolf didn't say much. He glanced toward Natasha's house and asked in which direction the person had run.

I pointed at the corner on the opposite end of the block from Natasha's.

"We have a bulletin out for people in vampire costumes, but if he's not wearing the cape, there's not much hope he'll be noticed."

"Do you think it was the same vampire we saw earlier?" asked Vegas.

"I think he was wearing the same mask," I said as we walked back to my house. But it dawned on me that I had a clue to his identity after all. I glanced at the girls. Maybe it was an overabundance of caution, but I thought it prudent not to say anything to them, lest it end up on Facebook or Twitter.

Putting on as brave and cheerful a face as I could manage, I shooed the girls back to their movie and motioned to Wolf to join me in the living room. I turned off the extra lights, and we settled on the sofa.

Before I could begin, Wolf asked, "What's your connection to Patrick?"

"None, other than the fact that his girlfriend's son, Blake, is working at the haunted house. I only met Patrick once. He threatened me, but I didn't take it seriously. It seemed like a lot of hot air — empty bullying." I eyed him. "So you think the person who attacked me was the same guy who killed Patrick?"

"Seems unlikely that there would be two guys in vampire capes running around Old Town attacking people."

He said what I'd been thinking. I scooted closer to him. "Wolf, he smelled of licorice."

"What?"

"When he threw the cape over my head, I smelled licorice. It could have been an odor on the cape, or it might even have been on his breath."

A smile crept onto Wolf's face.

"Are you making fun of me?"

"Absolutely not. I'm just imagining myself telling other cops to sniff suspects. They'll demand licorice samples so they can get it right."

I could well imagine the ribbing he would take.

Wolf's moment of levity faded fast. "If Blake is the only connection between you and Patrick, the common factor must be the haunted house, since Patrick used to rent the building. Have you found anything unusual there?"

"Nothing worth killing for. Mostly dust and cobwebs."

Wolf picked up my hand and squeezed it. "I don't want to worry you, but if this guy thinks you can identify him, he could come back to try again. You need to be on alert."

After a quick kiss, Wolf went back to work at Natasha and Mars's house.

I heard the girls scurrying back to the family room. By the time I looked in on them, they were on the sofa bed, pretending they'd been there all along. "You two okay?"

"Great!" said Jen.

I had my doubts about that, but I left them to their movie, double-checked to be sure all the doors were locked, and dragged my weary legs up the stairs with Mochie and Daisy leading the way. I opened the window a few inches to take advantage of the cool, crisp October air. Even though the vampire had attacked me in front of my own home, I felt some small degree of comfort in the police lights and murmuring voices just down the block at Natasha's.

I crawled into bed, and Mochie and Daisy nestled into my down comforter, but as exhausted as I was, I lay awake for hours, thinking about Patrick and why his killer would attack me.

■ ■ ■ ■

Screams woke us in the middle of the night. Mochie's head stretched up in alarm, like an auditory telescope, confirming that I hadn't dreamt them, and Daisy shot out the bedroom door. I could hear her heavy footsteps pounding down the old wooden stairs. I scrambled out of the warmth of my comforter and stumbled after Daisy to check on the girls. When I flicked on the lights in the family room, Vegas was sitting up on the sofa bed, holding the covers up to her chin. Jen blinked at her, seemingly confused.

Her voice trembling, Vegas said, "I saw him. I saw Viktor."

More likely Vincent Price had invaded her dreams. I sat on the edge of the bed next to her, and Mochie sprang up, purring. "Honey, there's no such thing as vampires."

Jen's eyes widened. "Yes, there is!"

She wasn't helping. I spoke gently. "I know that vampires are popular right now, but they're just based on legend. Even the original vampire, Count Dracula, was fiction."

"What about that guy in Transylvania?" asked Jen.

"Vlad the Impaler? He was a sick and very cruel man, but he wasn't really a vampire."

"But I saw him, I know I did." Vegas loosened her grip on the sheets and pointed. "He was standing right there, watching us sleep. He looked just like June described him."

Could the killer have gotten into the house? I dismissed that notion. Daisy was a friendly dog, but if someone had entered the house, she would be tracking the scent. Instead, she sat on the sofa bed kissing Jen.

"Okay, everyone into the kitchen." They followed me, and I made quick work of reviving the fire. I didn't light candles or spooky Halloween lights. Vegas didn't need her imagination inspired.

Jen retrieved milk from the refrigerator. "What about people who drink blood? Aren't they vampires?"

I popped some hot dog mummies into the oven. "There *are* people who do that. But are they immortal? They can go out into the sun, can't they? They have reflections, and they're not afraid of garlic."

"Garlic! Do you have any more?" Jen asked. "We used it all to protect Gabriel."

Fortunately, I always have plenty of garlic. They passed the next half hour stringing garlic teeth on dental floss. The kitchen smelled great, but I suspected it would take several showers for the girls to rid themselves of the pungent aroma.

I served the cute mummies — really hot dogs wrapped in bread dough with mustard drops for eyes — and I could feel the tension release.

"Vampires can go out into the sun if they have the right protection. Like a lapis stone," offered Vegas.

"Their skin glitters in the sun." Jen bit into a mummy.

I hesitated. Fiction was fun. I wasn't sure where the line was, though. Did I ruin it for them by saying it wasn't true? Or should I let them have that fantasy?

"What about ghosts? Are they real?" asked Jen.

I couldn't help looking at Faye's portrait. Until I lived in this house, I would have insisted that ghosts didn't exist. But too many unexplained things had happened, and June was thoroughly convinced that Faye's ghost resided here. I didn't know quite what to say. I dodged the question. "Have you ever met anyone who didn't have a reflection?"

Jen picked up on that right away. "Tomorrow, we'll carry our makeup compacts with us. That way, we can check the reflections of *everyone.*"

Vegas eyed me with suspicion, and I couldn't help laughing. I retrieved a shiny stainless steel pot and scooted next to the girls. I held it up, and our images reflected like they would in a fun-house mirror, completely warped. The resulting giggles and laughter finally did the trick, and I thought they might be ready for bed.

I tucked them in this time and nestled into a plush chair, my legs propped on an oversized ottoman, intending to watch them until they slept.

The next thing I knew, someone was banging the knocker on the front door and daylight was streaming into the house. The girls stirred but didn't rise. Mochie and I hurried to the front door, where Daisy already waited.

The door knocker sounded again. Someone was in a hurry. I threw open the door to find the doorkeeper vampire from Natasha's party. He held a stunning arrangement of fall flowers in an urn and a box of Teuscher Champagne Truffles.

"Oh, thank goodness." He shuffled into my foyer and set the flowers on the console. "I thought I would drop those for sure. They're very heavy." He held the truffles out to me with a smile. "For you. It's an apology."

Had he attacked me by mistake? His arrogant demeanor from the night before had vanished. He'd washed the pomade out of his dark hair, and now that he wasn't in costume, trying to act superior, his round face was actually friendly. I pretended to close the door behind him, but left it open a crack in case he turned on me.

"Thank you," I said, in spite of my confusion. "I'm not sure I understand."

"I feel just terrible about the way I treated you last night. I had no idea who you were. I thought you were just some woman off the street, and Natasha had made it very clear that I was to keep out people who weren't invited. Including Vegas!"

He'd certainly done that. I held out the truffles to him. "This really isn't necessary."

"Oh, but it is." He leaned toward me. "Don't tell Natasha, but you're really my favorite. I always read your column. You don't need an assistant, do you? I'd leave Natasha in a flash. She's a bit cranky, isn't she? I was mortified when I found out who you were. It was just so chaotic last night. Honestly, I've never been to a party like that. I guess you're used to big bashes since you're an event planner, and then to have that man die —" He stopped talking abruptly. "I woke you! You're still in your jammies. Oh, I'm so embarrassed."

The door knocker sounded again, stopping his self-conscious chatter.

The door swung open, and Natasha marched in. "Leon! What are you doing here? Shouldn't *my* assistant be at *my* house?"

He turned purple, but she didn't notice. Focusing on me, she asked, "Have you heard from Wolf?"

"Not this morning."

She clapped a hand over her forehead. "How could this happen to me? We worked so hard on this party. Everything was perfect, and then that Patrick Starski had to go and die. I hope it was natural causes. Everyone knows Maggie — just everyone! It's all over town. It's a good thing it wasn't Maggie who died. I almost killed her myself when she showed up dressed as Morticia Addams, just like me! I hand-sewed my dress while hers was off the rack, but still — what does a person have to do to be original these days? Who wears the same outfit as the hostess? That's in the worst possible taste. Patrick wore that silly pirate getup. At least Mars and I wore matching costumes. All night long everyone mistook me for Maggie, saying we look alike. Personally, I don't see it. And then the explosion in my kitchen. Could anything else have possibly gone wrong?"

She glanced at my pajamas, bright orange with flying witches and black cats. "You have to be kidding. Please tell me those aren't flannel."

They were, of course. Soft and snuggly, and I really didn't care what she thought of them.

"Did the police find you, Leon?" she asked. "They wanted to talk with you."

Leon, whose pudgy figure suggested a fondness for good food, took a step backward. "Me? What would they want with me?"

"Don't be silly. You handled the guest list and checked everyone at the door." Natasha turned to me again. "I've already heard rumors that a vampire killed Patrick."

Leon held his hands just above his tummy, twisting and turning them as though he were washing them. It wasn't lost on me that Leon had dressed as a vampire for the party.

Natasha sniffed the air. "No coffee? I desperately need coffee, and my assistant is over here instead of getting me coffee! You can imagine how little sleep we got last night at June's house. Mars is the only one who could sleep at all. He was still snoozing at his mom's when I left. Leon, are you still here? You'd better get going before the cops put out a dragnet for you."

I thought I saw a little quiver in his shoulders. He pulled his chin back rigidly like he was bracing himself. Why would he be afraid of the police? Was it possible that Leon had been the vampire we saw standing over Patrick? The man had taken off very fast. Leon didn't look like a runner, but then, when scared, even I could run at a decent clip for a short distance. He could have cut through the alley and returned to the house through the back. The vampire cape would have gone a long way in hiding his stomach. Had he accosted me last night? I leaned toward him and tried to sniff him without being obvious. He smelled faintly of lemon.

His frightened look reminded me of Maggie the day before when she was in the Hummer. What were they afraid of?

"Again, I'm very sorry, Sophie." Leon dragged out my front door as though headed to his doom.

Natasha didn't seem to notice his discomfort. "Incidentally, when people tell me how creepy my Halloween decorations are, I'm going to send them to your house. That doll is like something out of a horror movie. I never would have expected it of you. Mother thinks it's possessed."

"What doll?" I was still groggy and couldn't recall decorating with a doll. What was she talking about?

She pointed outside. Propped up on the top of one of my pumpkins stood the most hideous doll I'd ever seen. The eyes alone were enough to give me nightmares. They were completely white, with no irises or pupils, but vivid red and black ringed them against skin paler than Humphrey's. The black hair started too far back on the head, accentuating a huge forehead. "What on earth?" I picked up the doll and held it gingerly. I really didn't want to touch the horrid thing.

Still holding the doll, I stepped back inside. Natasha closed the door and leaned against it. "I don't know if Leon is going to work out. You're so lucky that you're not as busy as I am, and that you don't need an assistant. Honestly, it's hard to find good help. He came highly recommended, but sometimes I think he's like you — he likes the easy projects but isn't keen on the truly beautiful things that set me apart."

I motioned her into the kitchen, trying to hide my amusement at her insult, and dropped the doll inside a plastic bag, glad to have it out of sight. I put pumpkin spice coffee on to brew and fed Daisy one of her favorite homemade peanut butter biscuits cut in the shape of a witch's hat. I'd anticipated the possibility of haunted house volunteers dropping by in the morning and was glad I'd baked a chocolate pecan coffee ring in advance. "Did you ask your mother if she would tell fortunes at the haunted house?" I sliced the coffee ring and set it on the table.

"She's thrilled. And so am I. The police have already removed her from the roped-off area once this morning. She was using a mirror to flash the sun in some kind of protective spell.

"Sophie," she continued, her voice dropping, "do you think I'll ever live down last night's party? I'm horrified. No one in this town will ever come to a party at our house again."

"Look on the bright side — your name is probably being mentioned in every house in Old Town this morning. How bad is the damage?"

"We'll know more in a few hours when the cleanup and restoration people arrive. They're not letting us in yet. One of the firefighters said it didn't look too bad. I had to sweet-talk him into bringing me a change of clothes." She sniffed. "Everything reeks of smoke, but it beats wearing something of June's."

"At least there weren't any subsequent explosions. Do the police have any new theories, or are they still thinking the killer meant to create a distraction?"

"I was hoping you would know through your direct connection to Wolf. They haven't told me a thing." She lowered her forehead into the points of her fingers. "A murder at my party. The police better find the killer fast because if I find him first, I might be tempted to kill. A million Halloween parties in town and the killer had to pick mine?" She raised her head and fluffed her hair. "And then I had to shower in June's ancient bathroom this morning. It's like the nightmare never ends."

Daisy's ears perked. Natasha hissed, "Ixnay on the irefay."

Vegas shuffled into the kitchen. Did Natasha really think kids didn't understand pig Latin?

"Natasha!" Vegas scooted into the chair beside her. "I saw Viktor Luca last night!"

"Who?" Natasha kissed the air near Vegas's cheek. "Ugh. You stink. What is that smell? Garlic?"

Vegas grabbed a slice of the coffee ring and bit into it with gusto. "The vampire. Viktor Luca."

"You girls and your vampire obsessions." Natasha preened a bit when she said, "Wasn't my house perfect last night? I banked on vampires being the hot craze and I was so right. You know, there *is* something elegant about them — martinis and all — so much nicer than grubby mummies and zombies." She leaned toward Vegas. "Pinch off a bite of that for me."

"Do you think Viktor showed up at your party?" asked Vegas, holding out a morsel of chocolate and bread.

So much for convincing her that vampires weren't real.

Natasha raised her hands with her fingers stiffly splayed, her long nails looking very witchy. "Boo!" She plucked the chocolaty piece from Vegas's fingers and chewed it slowly, savoring every last bit. "I'm sure he wasn't there, Vegas. I don't believe I even know a Viktor."

I handed Natasha an orange mug of coffee and placed a sugar bowl in the shape of a pumpkin and a matching creamer with a green vine handle on the table.

"Do you know who bit Mr. Starski and set the fire? We saw him, you know." Vegas sniffed the coffee. "Can I have some of that?"

"Wouldn't you rather have hot chocolate?" I asked.

Vegas shook her head. "I love coffee."

I looked to Natasha for permission, but she stared at Vegas. "Bit him?"

"Jen and I saw the bite marks on his neck."

Natasha snapped her gaze to me. "Is that true? Did you see them, too?"

What I saw was my neighbor, Nina Reid Norwood, letting herself in through the kitchen door. "Why didn't you tell me about the murder at Natasha's house last night?" Daisy planted herself in front of Nina in an alert *sit* position and offered a paw. Nina withdrew a dog treat from the pocket of her quilted silk bathrobe and fed it to Daisy. "Brr, it's cold out there."

I told them to help themselves to coffee and dashed up the stairs to shower and change while Natasha brought Nina up to speed. An oversized purple T-shirt with long sleeves and a Halloween cat stitched on the front seemed perfect. I wedged into a pair of black jeans so tight that I couldn't breathe, gave up, and swapped them for blue jeans that were loaded with spandex and much more comfortable. I pulled my hair up with a big clip to keep it out of the way since we had a lot to accomplish. Glittering purple spiderweb earrings, a gift from Jen, finished off my Halloween look.

I hustled back to the kitchen to scramble eggs with ham. It wasn't the most Halloweeny breakfast, but I thought we all needed a boost of protein in our systems.

Nina rose to pour more coffee for everyone. She nudged me. "I can't believe you didn't tell me about Patrick last night! I thought the police were there because of the fire."

"You hurried off to catch that cat."

"Next time, fill me in, will you? I never would have left you alone. I never did catch the cat anyway."

I was counting on being burned-out in the evening, so I threw salty soy sauce, sweet apricot preserves, garlic, cornstarch, ginger, and orange juice into a pot and let it cook into a marinade for Chicken Scaryaki while we ate breakfast.

Slices of cantaloupe, banana monster fingers, and toast cut into the shape of pumpkins with a cookie cutter went on green plates along with the eggs and ham.

I leaned into the family room and called, "Jen, breakfast is on!"

She emerged rubbing her eyes. I noted that she still wore the sock on her neck. "Do you know anything about this?" I held open the bag that contained the horrifying doll. Jen shuddered. "It's a Living Dead Doll."

TEN

Dear Sophie,

My daughter is having a Halloween party this year, so I'm going all out. My husband found fake tombstones on sale and made a coffin for the front yard. They're all on display, but they just seem kind of uninspired.

— Not Scary in Gravestown,
Mississippi

Dear Not Scary,

You have the basics, now it's time to dress up your graveyard. How about a shovel leaning against a tree? Drop a plastic yard bag in the shape of a fresh grave and mound mulch and dirt over it. Place black flower bouquets on a couple of the gravestones. Perch a crow or two on top of one, too. Plant a plastic hand below one tombstone so it appears to be reaching out of the grave. If you have solar garden lights, prop them up behind the tombstones so there's an unearthly glow around them at night!

— Sophie

Vegas jumped up to peer in the bag. "Those dolls creep me out! Where did you get this?"

"Someone left it at the front door."

"Our door?" asked Jen, wide awake. Her eyes met Vegas's in a frightened glance.

"It was on a pumpkin by the front door," I said. "What's going on?"

"That's not good." Jen backed away from the bag. "I don't even want to touch it."

Vegas shivered. "I will. We have to know." Holding the bag with one hand, she dipped the other one inside, probed something, and screamed, dropping the doll and the bag. "It has a vampire bite on its neck!"

Jen's cheeks flared red. "It's a message from him."

I picked up the doll. "Him who?"

Jen gave me one of those impatient teen looks, like I was too dumb to live. "The vampire!"

Nina hurried over to look at it. "Gross! You mean it's a message, like — you're next?"

A spidery shiver inched down my back. I had almost been the next victim last night.

138

Had he come back and left the doll as a warning to me?

Vegas wrapped her hands around her neck protectively. "Well, duh. What else would it be?"

"A prank?" I asked hopefully. I wanted it to be something else. Anything but a threat. No matter how much the girls insisted there was a vampire, if it was a threat, it came from an ordinary, but dangerous, person.

Nina shook her head and mouthed, "Better call Wolf." She grinned at the girls. "Probably left by a boy who wants to scare you." She took the doll, closed the top of the bag, and stashed it on the console in the foyer where we wouldn't have to look at it.

I was still shaken, and I feared seeing those dead doll eyes in my dreams the way Vegas had seen Viktor. I poured a bracing mug of coffee for myself and took a few slugs in the hope it would settle my nerves. Nina resumed her place at the table, but I could see she was concerned.

"Well?" demanded Natasha, who had declined breakfast but evidently had no qualms about stealing the banana monster finger off Vegas's plate. "Did you see a vampire bite on Patrick's neck, Sophie?"

"There were two spots, but that doesn't

mean he was bitten by a vampire."

Nina stopped eating, her eyes wide. "Good heavens! I think I saw the killer without his mask last night! I was looking for that black cat in the alley when a kid in a Dracula outfit ran by. I didn't make the connection because everyone is dressed up for Halloween."

"A kid?" I said.

"You lost your cat?" asked Jen. "I would just die if I couldn't find Jasper or Alice." She frowned. "Maybe I should call the cat sitter and make sure they're okay."

"I'm sure they're fine," said Nina. "At the shelter we don't let anyone adopt black cats around Halloween — to protect them from people who might be cruel. We're rounding up black cats just to be on the safe side, and there's a big tomcat who continues to be elusive."

"Which way was he going?" I asked.

"He's been hanging around this neighborhood recently, but we've had reports of sightings down by the river, too."

Trying not to sound frustrated, I grumbled, "I meant the vampire, not the cat."

"Oh." Nina waved her fork. "He was running along the alley behind the Harts' house."

"Think you can identify him?" I bit into a crunchy piece of toast.

"There aren't any streetlights in the alley, so it was dark, but I might recognize him if I saw him again."

"You have to tell Wolf," I said. "And don't blab to other people about the fact that you saw him. You don't want to find one of those dead dolls at your door."

"Did he have long fangs for biting people?" asked Vegas.

"Vegas, we still don't know the cause of Patrick's death. Maybe the" — I chose my words very carefully for the benefit of the girls — "*man* in the vampire *costume* had nothing at all to do with Patrick Starski's death. Which brings me to another point — eat up! We have a ton of work to do before the first tours of the haunted house tonight."

After Natasha and Nina left, I rinsed the dishes and stashed them in the dishwasher while the girls changed clothes. I slid chicken tenders into a zip-top bag and poured part of the cooled Scaryaki sauce on them to marinate in the fridge until dinner.

We packed up the signs they'd made; fed Mochie, who appeared sleepy and as though he was waiting for us to leave; attached a leash to Daisy's collar; and headed for the haunted house.

Humphrey and Bernie were already there when we arrived. We divided the remaining projects, and I was amused to see that Jen had become the list keeper, following in the footsteps of her micromanaging mother. Daisy romped in the graveyard in the back while the kids helped Bernie and Humphrey spook up the mock gravestones.

I returned to the front room to tackle the chandelier. I worried about the kids, though. Was it safe for them to be exposed to members of the public who came through the haunted house? Would the killer be among the people we welcomed? Maybe I should leave them safely at home, with an adult and Daisy for protection. On the other hand, maybe the haunted house would be the safest place to be since Bernie, Humphrey, and Nina would be here with us. Wasn't there safety in numbers?

Thunk. I paused, momentarily paralyzed. It was just the normal creaking of an old building. It wasn't as though my own house didn't make sounds. I glanced around and realized I had broken my promise to myself not to be alone. *Thunk, thunk, thunk.* The noise picked up speed, and so did my heartbeat. Where was it coming from? There had to be a rational explanation.

In spite of myself, I turned with caution

toward the stairwell just in time to see a bright red ball bounce down the last three steps. I snatched it up and listened. Was someone else in the house? Had one of the kids snuck inside to play a prank?

I hurried to the kitchen and looked out the window. They were all in the backyard. Something must have dislodged the ball. It had probably been left behind by a child when the building was used for a store. I left it on the kitchen table and joined the others outside where they were attaching crows to gravestones.

"Did anyone hear from Jesse?" I asked. Given the circumstances, I didn't expect Blake to continue helping with the haunted house. I wondered if we needed to enlist extra help.

"Jesse's coming!" said Jen. "He texted me this morning."

I returned to the kitchen and hustled down the hallway before I realized something was wrong. I backed up and peered into the kitchen. The ball wasn't on the table anymore.

A chill ran through me. I tried to tell myself that there were lots of people in the house, never mind that I was fairly certain they were all out back. It could have rolled off the table, I reasoned. When I didn't spot it on the floor, I forced myself to put it out of my mind. I was overreacting to every little thing.

I climbed the ladder to work on the chandelier, and through the gauzy black curtain that hung over the window facing the street, I could just make out Maggie's huge Hummer outside. I cringed when I heard her tires spin. Reluctantly, I descended the ladder and went to open the door. I found Blake and his mother on the sidewalk in front of the haunted house.

"I'll make sure you get another school project." Maggie brushed Blake's hair with a trembling hand.

"Mom! Don't start that again." He raised his hands to cover his ears. "I'm not listening."

Maggie looked like she might burst into tears when Blake ran past me into the house and disappeared inside. Walking toward me, she pulled a pack of cigarettes from the pocket in her jacket. Tight jeans accentuated her long legs. She could have been a lanky model in her Ralph Lauren blazer, but the fancy duds couldn't erase the haunted and sleep-deprived appearance of her face.

"I'm so sorry about Patrick," I said.

She lit a cigarette. "Thanks." Her voice

quavered when she said, "Please. Don't let Blake out of your sight. I . . . I couldn't bear it if anything happened to him."

What was she so afraid of? "Is he in danger? Is there something I should know?" Had a dead doll landed on their doorstep, too?

She seized my shoulder with the grip of a falcon and whispered, "Do you know about Viktor?"

"Maggie!" A man I didn't recognize barked at her from the parked Hummer.

Her fingers flew to her mouth, covering it. "Take care of Blake," she hissed as she scurried toward her car.

Viktor? Of course! Blake went home and relayed June's exotic story to his mom. I blew off her silly fear and greeted Jesse, who ran along the sidewalk. He stopped and tossed his hair out of his eyes. "Sorry I'm late."

Daisy loped to greet him, her tail wagging in a circle. We could hear an irritated voice coming from the kitchen. We peeked in and found Jen and Vegas working feverishly to decorate the kitchen as an otherworldly dining area that we had discussed the week before.

"They're coming to the preview tonight," said Jen to Vegas.

"Bleah." Vegas stuck out her tongue. "Miss Perfect, Heather Corbin, would never miss an opportunity to chase Blake."

I could see Blake in the yard talking to Humphrey.

"You have nothing to worry about, Vegas. It's obvious that Blake doesn't care about Heather. He wouldn't be here if he wanted to spend time with her," said Jen.

"Hi," said Jesse. "What should I do?"

I ducked out and went back to my own job on the ladder.

Moments later, Blake ambled into the witch's lair and looked up at me. "Mrs. Winston? The window in Viktor's room was open when I got here. Bernie said I should ask if you opened it."

"No, honey, I didn't."

"Then who did?"

I winked at him. "Viktor?"

Blake shook his head. "No. Vampires don't exist."

Finally! A kid with some sense. "I wish you would convince Vegas and Jen of that."

"Dad made sure I knew when I was growing up. He used to sneak me Count Chocula cereal and let me watch Count von Count on Sesame Street so I would see vampires as comic and fun." He turned pensive. "I like dressing up as a vampire, but it's all

146

just in fun. Could I wrap that for you?"

"Sure!" I dismounted and handed him the black cloth that I'd been strapping around the brass. I lowered my voice a bit. "I'm so sorry about Patrick. Are you sure you feel like being here? Everyone would understand . . ."

He grasped the black cloth and scaled the ladder with athletic ease. "I'm glad Patrick is gone." His eyes met mine briefly before he focused on the light fixture. "I guess that's a terrible thing to say, but it's the truth. Did you know him?"

"Not really."

"Well, I did. I'm glad he's out of our lives. He used to spy on my mother. I *hated* him!" The fabric flew to the floor.

I picked it up and handed it to him. "You can leave some hanging shreds. They make it look creepier."

"He moved into our house." Blake's voice grew hostile. "*Our house!* And then he bossed us around and made up stupid rules. I used to lie awake at night, thinking of ways to get rid of him."

"But your mother cared for him. She must be devastated."

"Once she realizes how much control he had over us, and what a jerk he was, she'll be glad he's gone, too. All those phony-baloney people are coming by the house with food and talking about what a great guy he was." He stared down at me. "Just because he's dead doesn't mean he wasn't a bad man."

I blinked at him. Hadn't Gabriel called someone a *bad man* last night? It was a common enough phrase, but still . . .

"Does that make me an awful person?" he asked.

What could I say? "No. I think it's sad that you feel this way about him. Don't move, I'll be right back with the crystals." I walked to the kitchen entrance, only to be pushed back by three screaming banshees and Daisy, who pranced and barked like she was one of them.

"You can't come in here. This is our territory," declared Jen.

"I just wanted to retrieve my crystals for the light fixture."

"Jesse will get them for you," said Vegas.

I backed up, smiling from memories of being their age and trying to surprise my parents. Jesse raced back to me in the lair, breathless, and handed me the painted crystal prisms. I thanked him and raised them, one by one, to Blake to hang.

"Do you believe in vampires?" asked Blake.

I was beginning to get the feeling that all those phony-baloney people had kept Blake from being able to talk things out. "No, honey, I don't."

He nodded and kept working.

"Okay, you can come in now," called Jen.

I peeked first, then walked in slowly, taking in all the amazing details. Two skeletons sat at the kitchen table, now covered with an orange tablecloth. The sun flickered on warm walls, just a shade lighter than a pumpkin. A black candelabra draped with cobwebs acted as a centerpiece. The table had been set with what appeared to be hand-painted plates. "Did you make these?" I asked.

Jen beamed. "In my pottery class."

Orange with black trim on the edges, each one featured stars and moons and the image of a black Halloween cat on the orange middle. "They're fantastic, Jen!"

Black napkins had been rolled up and fastened with orange ribbons imprinted with dancing ghosts. A drink of a vile electric green shade stood before each skeleton, a piece of dainty black lace wrapped around the stem and tied in a bow.

They'd located a three-tiered cake stand somewhere, painted it orange, and glued on more of the black lace around the edges. It featured spiders on the top tier, except that a couple had escaped and made their way to the table; little white chocolate ghosts on the second tier; and tiny sugar pumpkins on the bottom tier.

Everywhere I looked in the kitchen, they had arranged delightful vignettes. Clusters of spooky pumpkins perked up the old countertops, containers bearing skull-and-crossbone labels stood behind glass cabinet doors, and bats perched on shelves.

A sign over the stove read, "Eat at Your Own Risk. They Did!" with an arrow pointing toward the graveyard in the back.

I ran from kid to kid hugging them and telling them what a fantastic job they'd done. "We'll have to take photos so your teachers and principals can see what you accomplished. It's just amazing."

Unfortunately, the kitchen clock, which moaned every fifteen minutes, reminded me that we had less than four hours before the tours began. "I think we'd better do our final walk-through to be sure everything is ready, and then grab some lunch and change into our costumes."

The kids, Daisy, Humphrey, Bernie, and I paraded through the witch's lair on our way to the foyer.

"Isn't that Mars's mother?" asked Jen.

I looked out the window. Sure enough, June stood on the sidewalk looking up at the house, her face contorted in an uncharacteristic scowl.

I continued to the foyer and opened the front door. "You're just in time to do a last round with us."

Beyond her across the street, Detective Kenner leaned against the red brick wall of a building. He lifted his head in a nod of recognition. I supposed I should be glad to know he was looking out for us, but his persistent attention to me always sent a chill along my spine.

Nina hurried along the sidewalk and joined us, distracting me from Kenner.

June smiled at her. "That hearse with the skeleton driving it is wonderful! What fun!"

She stepped inside and accompanied us up the stairs. The kids chattered nonstop, but I noticed that June remained very quiet.

When we reached the vampire's bedroom, Jesse pounced on a silver cigarette case that lay on a table under the window. "I don't remember this."

Neither did I. I looked to Humphrey and Bernie, but they seemed as perplexed as I was.

June took the thin case and turned it over. "My old eyes can't see like they used to.

This looks like it's sterling. Jen, can you see markings on it anywhere?"

Jen dutifully studied it, with Vegas looking over her shoulder. When she turned it over, they both screamed, and Jen dropped the case as though it burned her hands. "That's not funny, Blake." Her hands trembled and she refused to pick it up.

"What? I didn't do anything." Blake seemed genuinely perplexed.

I picked up the cigarette case. On an oval in the middle of the sterling silver case were the fancy engraved initials *VL*.

"Viktor Luca." June's breathy voice was barely audible.

"Oh, come on," I protested.

"What else could *VL* stand for?" asked Vegas.

"Maybe Vegas Lafferty? Or Vincent Lachen? Or Vera Luchese?" I placed the cigarette case near the martini glasses. "It's certainly elegant — wherever it came from."

I urged them to move on, but June pressed an ice-cold hand against mine. "There's something you should know."

A howl went up in the hallway, and we rushed out.

Blake held his cell phone in his hands, and the girls stood on either side of him, clearly perturbed.

"Aunt Sophie!" wailed Jen. "Heather just texted Blake and said she figured out a way to get even with you."

I was being threatened by a twelve-year-old? What next? "I'm so worried," I said sarcastically. "Come on, we don't have much time left."

I hustled everyone through the other rooms to be sure we hadn't forgotten anything major, locked up, and we trooped down to the outdoor patio of Brews and Bones. When the kids, Nina, Humphrey, and Bernie had settled down and Daisy lay at my feet, I took the opportunity to review everyone's jobs for the tours. Humphrey would be the pale grave digger in tattered clothing and a top hat who would remain motionless among the tombstones and come to life when he thought it most frightening.

Bernie had kindly offered to fill in as the vampire, but Blake insisted on that job, maintaining he had a vampire costume at home. I already knew he had the teeth.

Nina had agreed to pull the fishing lines that would animate the spiders, as well as drag a chain across the floor and flick moving eyes in a portrait upstairs.

Bernie would act as the axe murderer, and June offered to wear a witch's outfit and help hand out candied apples and treat bags. Jesse, Vegas, and Jen would lead small groups on tours through the house. I hoped we had enough adults stationed at strategic points in case pranksters visited.

I relaxed a little bit when our pulled pork lunches arrived. Most of the kids opted for the sweet tomato-based barbecue sauce, but I preferred the tangy vinegar sauce of Eastern Carolina barbecue. I had just eaten a forkful when a man with neatly trimmed hair and soft, delicate skin like a baby's stopped at our table and looked down at me with a self-satisfied smirk. He seemed vaguely familiar. It took a moment to register that I had seen him in Maggie's Hummer earlier in the day.

"Sophie Winston?" he asked.

My mouth full, I couldn't do much more than nod my head.

"The town council has cancelled the haunted house."

ELEVEN

Dear Sophie,
My daughter spotted a gorgeous witch's hat that carries a comparably gorgeous price. We can manage the rest of her witch's costume, but I'm stumped on how to make a hat, especially now that she's seen the best.
— Sabrina's Mom in Witch Lake,
Michigan

Dear Sabrina's Mom,
Buy an inexpensive hat and dress it up. Use a glue gun to adhere sequins or adhesive crystals in the shape of a moon or a cat. Add inexpensive black lace or veil fabric to the back, and you'll have a one-of-a-kind hat that can't be beat!
— Sophie

Howls of protest went up around the table, and I nearly choked on my pulled pork.

155

The man turned to the boys. "Blake, come with me. I'll take you home."

I stood up, not that I could intimidate anyone with my short stature. "Just a minute. I know everyone on the town council. Who *are* you?" He wore a navy blue crew neck sweater and, except for the patronizing smile on his face, looked like an overgrown choirboy. Since I was an event planner, I'd met a lot of people in Old Town, but I couldn't recall ever seeing him at functions before.

"Karl Corbin."

"Heather's father," hissed Blake.

The wicked smile and demand to shut down the haunted house began to make sense. So this was how the little vixen planned to cause me trouble. "Nonsense, I'm not shutting down anything. You don't represent the town council. How dare you pretend to have any authority? Blake, sit down and finish your lunch."

I couldn't help noticing Bernie trying to hide a grin. *Good!* I knew I had an ally in him. Humphrey, on the other hand, sputtered and blinked as though he'd just come out of a dead faint.

"That little witch," Vegas raised her voice, no doubt to be sure Karl heard her. "Heather's just jealous."

"Shh." Jen nudged her. "She's mad because she got in trouble last night."

Karl held out his hand. "I'd like the key to the building. You're not going to frighten any more children like you did my daughter. You might have thought it was a harmless prank, but she's traumatized, and I'm going to see to it that you're not allowed to scare any other children."

I coughed, my throat tight. "I didn't do anything to your daughter!" I swallowed a huge gulp of unsweetened iced tea. "You don't own the building, nor are you the person who gave me the key. Therefore, I will not be handing it over to you. And you are not Blake's parent. Unless I hear from his mother or father, you will not be taking him anywhere." In fact, now that I thought about it, I wondered if this was what Maggie meant when she asked me to watch out for Blake. Maybe not; Karl had been in her car, so they must be friends . . . "If you don't mind, we'd like to finish our lunch."

"You clearly don't realize who you're dealing with." Unlike Patrick, he didn't point his finger or raise his voice, but the threat was implicit. He grinned at me like I was a naive child. "I have connections in this town."

By nature, I'm not a big fighter, but I was

tired after the events of the previous night. We had worked hard on the haunted house, and if there was one thing I detested, it was people who thought they were superior to everyone else. "I really don't care who you think you are. You don't have the authority to close the haunted house or take Blake with you. Now, if you'll please excuse us."

Nina rose slowly, fixated on something. I thought she might slug Karl.

"Nina! It's okay."

She never even looked at me. She stepped sideways, moving like a panther. "Across the street. It's the black cat."

I followed her line of sight. A fat black cat sat between two pumpkins amid witches and ghosts outside a florist shop. "Are you sure he's real? He looks too perfect."

"It's him all right. Pack my lunch in a doggy bag. I'll see you back at the haunted house." She casually walked to the end of the block and crossed the street. When she was ten feet from the cat, he stretched to his full feline length and darted in the other direction. Nina sprinted after him.

The smug smile never left Karl's face. He continued to look down at me like he was endlessly amused. "Natasha told me that you're a difficult person. It's not as though you didn't know this was coming. Frank

Hart warned you to close down the haunted house."

"Frank? He ran out of there like a rabbit being chased by a dog."

"It's not safe. I'm concerned about the children."

"And what, exactly, do you think will happen to them?"

His expression never changed. "Aside from your bad influence on the children, there are malicious spirits in that house. There's no telling what they might do."

It was all *I* could do not to break into hysterical laughter. Somehow, I felt that would only exacerbate the situation. Honestly, why didn't the guy bug off already? "Thank you for the warning. We'll take care to watch out for the spirits."

Still wearing the same condescending grin, he said, "You won't be going back into that building." With that, he finally strode away.

June placed a reassuring hand over top of mine. "Beware of that man. He looks like an innocent, but a darkness lurks within him."

"Do you know him?" I asked Bernie and Humphrey.

"He comes into the bar," said Bernie. "He's never been an unpleasant customer. I don't know what he does for a living."

"He manages a local delivery service." Blake picked up a french fry.

"Who told you that? Heather?" Vegas's tone left no question about her displeasure.

Blake didn't seem to notice. "I think my dad told me. Karl's family used to own the car dealership that my folks own now. My dad says he's a self-aggrandizing malcontent."

That was a good reminder to be careful what I said around the kids. I bet Blake's father never thought *that* would be repeated in public. If Karl continued to pose a problem, we might have to call on Blake's dad. I put Karl and his nonsense out of my mind, paid the check, and sent everyone home to change into their costumes. Vegas, Jen, June, and I walked in the direction of my house.

June lagged a bit. I thought it was her age, until she whispered, "I don't know if the children should hear this, Sophie. There's something you should know about your haunted house."

We strolled on, but I watched her out of the corner of my eye.

"I didn't want to say anything until I was certain, but now there's just no doubt about it. The Bubble and Trouble really was a

160

boardinghouse once. It was the Widow Nagle's pension."

I stopped midstep. "You mean the boardinghouse where Viktor Luca lived?"

"Not only did he live there, dear, he roomed in the very bedroom on the second floor that you've set up as a vampire's lodging."

I laughed aloud. "You should definitely tell the kids. They'll lap that up."

"It doesn't worry you?"

"Why should it? It makes for a great spooky story." I grinned at her. "This is where you turn off, isn't it? You'll be at the Widow Nagle's at three o'clock?"

She promised to be there and headed east. I watched her for a few minutes. What a lovely person she was. If only all mothers-in-law could be as warm. I caught up to the girls, who gossiped endlessly about wicked Heather.

When we reached my front door, much to my surprise, Frank Hart was waiting on the stoop. I unlocked the door and told the girls to change their clothes.

I greeted Mochie and invited Frank into the kitchen. "I'd love to offer you something, but I don't have much time. I could put on some tea."

He waved a hand as though declining the

tea. "This isn't a social call. I came by because my wife and I are horrified and confused. I cannot believe you took Gabriel because I quit the haunted house."

It was official. I was *not* having a good day. "Didn't you talk with Officer Wong? I did *not* kidnap Gabriel. He showed up at my door, Frank. I was doing you a favor by not letting him run loose on the streets."

"That's not what Heather said. According to her, you banged on our doors and tried to scare her by asking questions about whether Gabriel was in bed."

"Officer Wong saw right through Heather. Next time, use a different babysitter. One who won't lose the baby."

He mashed his lips together and grasped the arms of the chair. "For your information, Heather is my wife's niece. She's very responsible. Besides, we were just across the way at Natasha and Mars's party. What I can't understand is how you got into my house."

I plopped into one of the chairs by the fireplace, exasperated with him. Mochie sprang into my lap. "What? A flaw in Heather's story? A detail she didn't work out?"

"You needn't be sarcastic. My wife is beside herself that you tried to steal Gabriel. We didn't sleep all night."

I watched him — in awe of his irrationality. He couldn't see through Heather's ridiculous lies because she was family? "Karl Corbin is your brother-in-law?"

"I can't imagine why the police don't want to pursue this. Karl says that's what happens when half the police force is in love with you."

Apparently vast exaggerations were a family trait. "Let's think this through. Let's say Heather forgot to lock the door, and I snuck into your house and stole Gabriel. Then what? You live one block down. Like you were never going to notice that Gabriel was living here?"

"You could have sold him."

"Ohhh, right. I forgot all about that stolen baby ring that I run. Do you hear how crazy you sound?"

Frank perched on the edge of his chair. "But why would Heather make that up? Why would she claim you kidnapped him?"

"Frank, she's twelve. I would guess she didn't have the courage to admit that he got away from her. How do you tell parents that you lost their child?"

Frank hadn't bothered to shave, and he ran a hand over the stubble. "I'm sorry, Sophie. What have I done? That little minx was so convincing. She said you were in the backyard making noises and trying to frighten her. Then she called the police and they found you were hiding him at your house."

"Didn't Officer Wong set you straight?"

"Heather said Wong was lying to protect you. That she was a friend of Wolf's. Can you imagine how we felt? First Patrick's death, and then we came home to find a police officer in our house and Heather claiming our child had been kidnapped."

"It's okay. Forget about it." I sat back and listened to Mochie purr.

"It's not okay, Sophie. You found Patrick's body, didn't you? You must have had a terrible night, too. I can't imagine that kind of shock."

I winced. "It's worse for the girls. They're terrified of vampires now. I hope Gabriel is too young to understand what was going on."

Frank rested his elbows on his knees and rubbed his face. "What a night. Sophie, I'm sorry. Oh, no! Heather and her dad were so upset that I'm afraid I overreacted. Heather wanted to shut down the haunted house, and I stupidly helped her by calling a member of the town council. They're going to try to prevent you from opening this afternoon."

"Frank! Then you'd better go with us and retract whatever you said. Everyone worked so hard on it — I'm not closing it. No way!"

"I can't believe I fell for Heather's lies. Someone could have snatched Gabriel, or he could have been hit by a car! I wonder if Karl knows what a devious daughter he has."

I was about to make a crack about apples that didn't fall far from the tree when Jen returned in a saucy green and black witch's costume. The bodice was green, but a long black vest hung over it and laced in the front. She wore adorable green and black horizontally striped tights and a black hat with a green and black harlequin band around it. "I thought you were going to be a cat, not a witch."

Frank applauded. "Great costume, Jen."

She took a bow. "I'm not a witch, Aunt Sophie, I'm a sorceress."

"Pardon me."

Vegas made her entrance next and swirled around to show off her costume. She wore a wedding dress that had been carefully tattered. The bottom half appeared dirty and merged into black where it trailed on the floor. A faux bloody gash had been carefully applied to her bare shoulder. She'd used white makeup to create the illusion of pallor, and her eyes were smudged with impressive black eyeliner.

Frank applauded again.

"Wow. What are you?" I asked.

"Isn't it obvious? I'm a zombie bride."

"Of course! Silly me." I didn't have half the imagination they did. I asked them to take Daisy out while I changed, and returned in minutes dressed all in black as a witch. The color helped hide my extra pounds, and I liked the sweeping cut of the skirt that came to my ankles. I'd bought an inexpensive hat and added crystals in wild swirls for fun.

With Mochie and Daisy safely in the house, Frank, the girls, and I locked the door and left. Nina caught up with us on the sidewalk. She had also dressed in black, but she looked more like a cat burglar.

Worried about a cluster of people protesting and trying to close us down, I held my breath as we rounded the corner to the haunted house. To my complete shock, a crowd had gathered and blocked the sidewalk. Heather and her father waited in front of the building, carrying signs that read, "Danger," "Do Not Enter," and "Enter at Risk of Peril."

Frank laughed aloud. "What an idiot.

166

That's like free advertising."

"Shh," I cautioned him. "Don't tell them that!"

A pungent wave of garlic overcame me when I brushed past Heather. She must have caught me sniffing because she immediately said, "I had garlic bread for lunch."

Maybe she had, but I was willing to bet she was wearing garlic, too.

I stiffened when I saw Councilman Williams. He'd been enthusiastic about the haunted house when it was proposed. Surely he hadn't changed his tune because of Karl. He glad-handed his way up the line, working the crowd. Ray stepped out of his shop and had a word with him. Frank rushed at them. I hoped he was pleading our case.

I was about to join them, ready to argue the merits of keeping the haunted house open, when Councilman Williams approached me with a huge smile. "I hear you've put together something very spooky! It's the talk of the town. Businesses up and down the street are delighted with the turnout. Carry on, Ms. Winston!" He clapped me on the back and returned to the crowd.

Karl chased after him. My stress melted

away, and I felt like collapsing on the sidewalk, but there was no time for that. I ignored Heather and Karl entirely and unlocked the front door.

"Showing your true grimy self today, Vegas?" said Heather. Her outfit of preppy green and pink plaid trousers and a matching pink sweater trimmed in the same plaid might have been considered a costume by some.

Vegas stuck out her tongue, but the banter didn't escalate because they both caught sight of Blake sweeping along the sidewalk in a vampire cape.

Nina nudged me. "Is he one of your kids?"

"He's so sexy!" Vegas breathed to Jen.

But Jen was fixated on Blake's companion, shorter and thoroughly disguised in jeans, a flannel shirt, hairy hands, and an amazing werewolf mask that covered his entire head. The front featured a long snout and bared teeth, and the back was covered in fur.

The zombie bride and the prep in pink and green rushed at Blake. Heather swooned like an obsessed fan meeting a rock star, and Vegas tried to muscle her way closer to him. Blake looked miserable.

I called to him, hoping to get him inside quickly, but Karl stopped him. "You're not going in there, son."

I was about to walk out to them and intercede, but Blake faced Karl dead-on and showed no fear. "You're not the boss of me." He'd been brave, but I noticed that he ran into the house.

Frank waved to me from the sidewalk.

"You're not coming in?" I asked.

"I'll talk to Karl, but it's going to be a long, long time before I set foot in that building again — if I ever do. Besides, I think I see that black cat Nina has been trying to catch. I believe he might be cornered now." He nodded in the direction of Ray's shop window. The cat lounged in front of stacks of books, leisurely washing his fur.

I wished Frank luck but had my doubts. Ray's shop would be like a minefield of objects for Frank to trip over, but a cat would navigate the mess and disappear in it. I wanted to ask him what he'd seen in the house, but there wasn't time. We had a show to put on, and people were waiting for us to begin.

Natasha's mother, Wanda, arrived in her fortune-telling outfit and paused on the doorstep. Her smile wavered and disappeared as she entered and looked up the stairwell. "This house is haunted."

I knew she was serious, but I suspected

that everyone else thought it was part of her act.

Nina snagged my elbow and whispered, "You have bigger problems than that. The kid in the vampire costume is the same one I saw in the alley last night after Patrick was killed."

TWELVE

Dear Natasha,
I watched your show on Halloween parties and want to recreate the fog coming out of the punch bowl. It's spooktacular! I'm a little wary of dry ice, though. Are you sure it's safe?

— Ghostly Mom in Fogg Corners,
New Hampshire

Dear Ghostly Mom,
It's so easy! You need two bowls, one that fits inside the other. Place the dry ice in the bigger bowl (be careful not to touch it because it will burn you). Pour the punch into the smaller bowl. Set the smaller bowl inside the larger one and add warm water to the big bowl. Instant fog! You don't have to be afraid of dry ice. Handle it with gloves and never touch it or eat it.

— Natasha

"Are you certain it was Blake whom you

saw?" I asked.

Nina cocked her head sympathetically. "I'm sorry, Sophie. There's no doubt about it."

Had Patrick pushed Blake too far? Had Blake taken advantage of the costume party to disguise himself and kill his mother's boyfriend? He was only a kid, but it wouldn't have been the first time a boyfriend drove a kid to murder. Had he hoped that removing Patrick would mean his parents would reconcile? I had no idea what to do. I didn't want to turn him in. On the other hand, what if he harmed someone else?

As though in a trance, Wanda walked up the stairs. The kids, silent for once, followed her, and I was right behind them. She drifted into the vampire's room and closed her eyes. "Very dark things . . . unspeakable things . . . have happened here."

Wanda held out her hands, palm sides down, and snatched them back. "The spirit in this room is very strong. He had a deep, terrible secret."

I didn't realize that June had arrived. Behind us, she chimed in, "Of course he did. Viktor was a vampire. He couldn't let anyone know."

"This is so cool," said Jesse. "Neither of

172

my grandmothers would play along like this."

Wanda fixed him with a sharp look. "This isn't pretend, young man. There's a malevolent spirit in this room."

I could hear voices downstairs. Excusing myself, I returned to the foyer and found Wolf having a look around. Blake's father, Dash, was with him, his expression grim.

"Great job, Soph! The place is scary beyond belief." Wolf bussed me on the cheek. "Sorry to interrupt, but I need to have a word with Blake. Is there somewhere we could talk in private?"

"There are a couple of chairs in the kitchen. It's far from private, but I can try to keep everyone else out of there." I showed them into the kitchen, and the clock chimed with a moan. "We're supposed to open very soon."

"Shouldn't take long," said Wolf.

I ran up the stairs, culled Blake from the little haunted house gang, and sent him to the kitchen. Whispering, I asked Bernie and Nina to keep everyone upstairs and suggested they do a few run-throughs to make sure everyone knew what to do.

I crept down the front stairs to prevent anyone from barging in. Squeals and giggles came from upstairs, but the first floor was so quiet that I couldn't help overhearing Wolf and Blake from the witch's lair.

"I didn't kill Patrick."

Wolf responded, his tone calm. "That wasn't what I asked you."

"You wouldn't have brought my dad otherwise. Look, I can save us all a lot of time. I hated Patrick."

"Blake!" Dash's voice carried a note of warning.

"The cops are going to know that soon enough, Dad. It's not like it was a secret. Even Patrick knew I hated him. But I didn't murder him."

"Where were you last night?"

"Home. Dad can verify that. He dropped me off."

"You're talking about your mother's house?"

"I know what you're getting at. Obviously, Mom and Patrick had gone to the party."

Wolf began to sound a hair testy. "Was anyone there with you?"

"No. I watched a video."

"You didn't go anywhere?"

"No! We just didn't like Patrick. Okay? He ruined everything for us."

Wolf started to speak, but Dash interrupted him. "I think that's enough. He told you he doesn't know anything. Isn't that what you needed?"

Chairs scraped along the floor, and I skedaddled to the foyer.

Wolf came through first. "What did you think?"

"About what?"

He laughed so hard it echoed in the stairwell. He kissed me, with less zeal than the night before, but it was sweet and adoring. He nuzzled my hair and whispered, "The kid's hiding something. If you find out what it is, let me know."

I already knew Blake was lying. My heart sank. I almost choked when I said, "You'd better talk to Nina. She's upstairs."

Dash and Blake joined us in the foyer, and Wolf calmly climbed the stairs, not even flinching when the automated ghost swooped down upon him.

Dash pointed at Blake, said, "Behave," and left as Ray from next door barged in.

"I believe I was promised a spot in the first tour?"

I couldn't help laughing. What was it about Halloween that got even adults excited?

I closed the door behind him. "Sure. Wait here a minute."

Blake didn't appear upset. "Do you want to take the afternoon off?" I asked.

"And miss out on the fun? No way!"

I wanted to give him a hug, but all I could think was that he might want to harm the girls if he thought they could identify him. Had he left the grisly doll on our doorstep? Had he thrown a cape over my head? He was tall enough.

"Time to start," I shouted. "Places, everyone."

We scattered to our destinations, and I played a CD of spooktacularly creepy music. Jen took the first group through. The ghost swung over their heads as she led them up the stairs, giving them their first little surprise. I could hear Jen telling the tale of Viktor Luca. A few minutes later, screams came from Viktor's bedroom, letting me know Blake had startled them. Happily, the shrieks from Viktor's room set the tone for the next group, who were having their palms read by Wanda in the foyer. Chains rattled overhead, courtesy of Nina, and something heavy dragged along the floor. I watched the expressions of the kids in the foyer. Their eyes large, they eagerly anticipated their turn.

All went well until Vegas's third tour. She motioned to her group to follow her, and they started up the stairs. But when they reached the top, a genuinely hysterical scream sent a chill through me.

"Sophie!" screamed Vegas.

I ran upstairs and found the group standing back from a snake on the floor. *I don't do snakes.* Not even a little bit. As horrified as I was, two logical thoughts made it through my hysteria. Snakes tend to slither close to walls, yet this snake was in the middle of the floor. And it wasn't trying to get away. In fact, it hadn't moved at all.

My heart pounding, I scooted closer and touched the tail with the toe of my witch boot. It didn't react. I scuffed my boot along the floor, managed to turn the snake over, and realized that it was plastic. Nevertheless, out of an abundance of caution, and a fear of snakes, I picked it up by the tail. "Go ahead with the tour. It's not real." But it had been a very scary moment, and I wondered who had tossed the snake there.

I carried it downstairs — which produced a few screams among those waiting in the foyer — through the kitchen, and out to the backyard.

Even in daylight, Humphrey cut a creepy figure in his top hat and ragged duds. The hat dipped low on his forehead. He leaned against the fence and concentrated so hard on texting that he didn't hear me coming. As I drew near, he glanced up. "You scared me! My gosh, is that thing real?" He drew back and shuddered.

"One of the kids must have thought it would be a fun prank. Probably the same one who found the cigarette case with Viktor's initials on it."

I walked to the back of the yard and propped the snake on a tree branch. Humphrey followed me with a snazzy phone in his hand. When I turned to talk to him, I thought I spied makeup on his face. I reached out and lifted the brim of the hat a little bit. Under the best circumstances, Humphrey's skin was pasty, but gray circles around his eyes made him appear cadaverous — as though he'd just risen from one of the graves in the backyard. "Yikes! Who did your makeup?"

He laughed. "One of the women over at the mortuary. I think she had entirely too much fun making me look ghoulish. I'm glad you came out here, though. I just heard from one of my contacts at the medical examiner's office."

"About Patrick?"

He nodded. "He died of asphyxiation."

"Like someone smothered him?" I inhaled deeply at the memory of not being able to breathe during my assault.

"Something like that," said Humphrey. "It

means he wasn't getting oxygen."

I feared I knew the answer, but I asked, "So he probably didn't die of natural causes?"

"I'm no physician, but I think there are a few natural causes of asphyxiation." He looked at me with those ghastly eyes. "Like medical conditions that make a person stop breathing, but that probably wasn't the case."

The fresh memory of something clamped over my nose and mouth made me think it more likely Patrick had been suffocated. "Did your contact say anything about the wounds on his neck?" I was *not* going to refer to them as a vampire bite!

"Only that it's very bizarre."

We already knew that. I glanced up at the windows. "The next group will be through any second." I touched his arm. "Keep me posted if you hear more."

I scurried into the house and ran into Wolf.

He rubbed an uneasy hand over his chin. "Nina's the third person who saw Blake in your neighborhood last night wearing his vampire costume."

"So you already knew."

"What I don't know is why he's lying about it."

I breathed a little easier. "You don't really believe he's the killer."

"I didn't say that. I have to consider him a suspect. He had motive and he was in the right place. If he had a good reason to lie, other than murder, I sure would like to know about it."

I hugged Wolf and melted into his embrace. Humphrey's revelation made me wish I could stay in Wolf's safe arms all day. My hat fell off, and I giggled like a girl when I bent to pick it up. "Have you ever heard of a Living Dead Doll?"

He made a sour face. "A woman at the medical examiner's office collects them. Pretty gruesome."

"Collects them?"

"They're not my taste, but she says they only make so many and the dolls go up in value, like other collectibles."

"Someone left one at my front door last night. The girls think it's some kind of warning because it has a vampire bite on its neck." I tried to make light of it. "I think it's just a kid playing a prank."

"I'd better have a look at it." Wolf pulled me close in a bear hug. "Don't let your guard down. Even if the doll is a joke, the killer has you on his radar."

Wolf left through the graveyard, and I hurried to the witch's lair, where June, who made an adorable witch with silver curls peeking from beneath her hat, offered a little cowboy a candied apple. I pulled aside the filmy fabric that covered the window and peeked outside. "I don't see any sign of Heather or her father." I hoped they had given up and gone home.

"Wanda put a spell on them," said June.

"What?!"

"We didn't care for their behavior, so Wanda went outside and put a spell on them." She smiled. "You should have seen the horror on their faces!"

Oh no! They would probably report us for practicing witchcraft.

"Don't be upset. It was just a silly rhyme. Wanda picked up a pumpkin" — June pretended to hold one in her hands — "and then she said, 'When this pumpkin's face you see, you will flee and leave us be.' Isn't that a hoot? And the best part is that it worked! They left right away." She chuckled with glee.

I hoped Heather and Karl shared June's amusement about it. I had a bad feeling their version of the event would be drastically different.

"Sophie, dear, the cauldron isn't fogging quite as much anymore. Do you know how to fix that?"

I withdrew an old pitcher from under the counter where I'd stashed it. "We just have to add warm water."

She took the pitcher from me. "That's easy enough."

While she fetched the water, I supervised the tour that had just ended and made sure everyone went home with a treat. I loved hearing the comments — at first.

"Man, I'm coming back at night. This is the coolest haunted house."

"The axe murderer guy was scary, but the guy in the backyard — do you think he always looks like that?"

"I bet that vampire still lives here."

"They made that up. A vampire never slept here."

"Oh no? I heard some guy died last night from a vampire bite. He probably came back here afterward and slept in that coffin."

June returned and poured water into the cauldron. Mist wafted out immediately. She cackled and wiggled her fingers at a little girl, who squealed but ran out wearing a delighted grin. "My word." June peered out the window. "There's a mob outside."

Mob? I hoped Karl hadn't brought back reinforcements.

"There you are." Officer Wong drifted into the lair gazing up at the cobwebs and purple lights. "No one expected this kind of turn-out. Must be one scary haunted house."

I didn't see any paperwork in her hands, but I waited for her to tell me the bad news that the haunted house would be closed. Jen brought another group through, and June immediately handed out goodies to children, who laughed and smiled. I was glad Wong could see the kids weren't distressed.

She examined the treats on the table. "I'm sorry to put a damper on things, but I've brought a couple of cops to make sure the crowd outside stays orderly."

"You're not shutting us down?"

"Are you kidding? Why would I do that?"

She couldn't have surprised me more. My knees went weak, and I realized how much Karl and Heather worried me.

"Hey, can I bust in line and get a tour?" she asked.

Jen nodded. "We'll say you have to make an official inspection. You can go on my next tour."

I joined June at the window. A cluster of people blocked us from seeing the end of the line. "Where did they all come from? I never anticipated this many. Especially not so many adults."

"Heather texted everybody and warned them that the house was dangerous because it was haunted by a vampire," said Jen. "And people have been texting friends when they hear the story about Viktor. I've seen them do it."

Wong laughed. "Heather the Horrid from last night? She's a piece of work. But she made your haunted house go viral. Just goes to prove that as soon as you tell people something's haunted or dangerous, they'll line up to take a peek."

"Coming through . . . coming through." I heard Natasha before I saw her. She broke through to the witch's lair and snorted in disgust. Brushing off her lavender sweater and matching trousers, she marched straight toward me. "How could you do this to me?" she hissed.

I was losing my patience with her. "What now, Natasha?"

"Don't get snippy with me. I've had to deal with fire cleanup crews all day. The kitchen was loaded with candles for ambiance and they melted all over the place. Between the hole in my kitchen wall and Patrick's death, I'm at the end of my rope. People are saying you staged Patrick's death last night to get attention for some dumb vampire story."

"I'm sure Patrick will be pleased to know he's not dead."

Wong snorted. "People can be so stupid."

Jen wasn't laughing though. "He's *not* dead. A vampire bite makes you immortal."

"Don't you dare start that rumor," I cautioned. What a nightmare.

Natasha examined the people in the lair as though she was sizing them up. "She doesn't have to start that rumor, it's common knowledge." She clapped a hand over her mouth when she realized what she'd said. "Not that I believe in that sort of foolishness."

I should have realized that anyone raised by superstitious Wanda would believe in vampires. Natasha was a no-nonsense person on so many levels, but apparently, this wasn't one of them.

I massaged my temples. "Would you be willing to make a candy run? We're going to need more of these little bags" — I held one up to show her — "and candy corn to fill them."

"Leon can do it." Natasha pulled out her phone, but before she called him, she tucked it away. "On second thought, maybe I will do it myself. Mother has suggested we buy more garlic."

"Would you get us some, too?" asked Jen. "We used ours up last night. Come on, Officer Wong. It's my turn."

Jen collected her group for the next tour, but Natasha lingered as though she wanted to say something privately.

She spoke in a hushed tone. "I think Maggie planned to kill Patrick at my party. That's why she dressed in a Morticia Addams outfit like me. People confused us all night long, and she took advantage of that. The guests aren't sure whether it was me or her they saw at certain times. It gave her a perfect alibi. She used me!"

Instinctively, I wanted to defend Maggie, just so Natasha wouldn't be correct, not to mention my desire to tweak Natasha for being so egocentric. "But I saw someone in a vampire costume running away."

"That doesn't mean he or she was the killer." With that, Natasha left to buy garlic and candy.

June's eyes narrowed as though she was scheming. "I will never understand what Mars sees in that woman. If you didn't have that nice Wolf hanging around, I'd be trying to set you up with Mars again."

I shot her a smile, but a group of kids came through and we were back to work.

When Officer Wong returned with Jen,

post tour, she pulled me aside. "That story about the vampire who stayed here? It's true."

THIRTEEN

Dear Sophie,
I'm throwing a Halloween birthday party for my daughter. As a single mom, I have to stay within a tight budget. I can handle the food and decorations, but that doesn't leave much for favors. I thought about stuffed black cats or ghosts, but I just can't afford them for so many kids.
— Creative Mom in Hallowell, Maine

Dear Creative Mom,
Put your creativity to work! Buy inexpensive small brown paper bags and adorn them with spooky stamps of ghosts. Or cut bats and moons out of construction paper, glue them on, and add a little glitter. Fill the bags with candy (homemade or bought on sale with coupons), and poke a little hole through the top to tie them shut with a

bow made of orange or black ribbon.

— Sophie

"Not you, too!" I liked Wong. I'd thought she was sensible.

"My granny was friends with the Widow Nagle. She used to tell me this story. It was exactly the same except for one thing — I never knew the vampire's name. She wouldn't utter it. She was so afraid of him that she slept clutching her rosary every night. There were mirrors all over her house, and she used to parade people in front of them, just to be sure they had reflections."

I felt terrible for Wong's grandmother. "You don't believe he was a vampire, do you?"

Wong's mouth twitched back and forth. "Granny wasn't the type to be skittish. June's story is so similar to hers that there must be some truth to it. I'll let you know what I find out."

She turned to go, but I stopped her. "Last night you said something about being warned about me? What was that about?"

Her demeanor lightened. "Everybody knows you're dating Wolf, and that Kenner is determined to win you over."

"Just the way I'd like to be known in the community," I muttered sarcastically.

She leaned toward me and spoke confidentially. "Just so you know, my money is on Wolf."

"Your money?"

"Sure. I know they say there's somebody for everyone, but I can't imagine what kind of woman would fall for Kenner. He's a sourpussed old grump. So I bet on Wolf. But now that I've seen how cute your ex is, well without that awful mustache . . ."

"It was fake. Part of the costume."

"I may have to bet on him instead."

Bet? What on earth was she talking about? My face must have revealed my confusion because she went on. "Ohhh, you didn't know about the office pool, did you?"

"The cops are betting on whether I'll wind up with Wolf or Kenner?" I could feel the hot flush of embarrassment flooding my face. The tops of my ears burned like they were aflame.

"It's all in fun, to rib the guys, you know." She winked at me and left.

I pushed through the crowd to Wanda. "Is Mercury in retrograde? Are the planets aligned to make me miserable and everyone around me nuts?"

Wanda held the palm of a young man in her hands. She turned her face toward me and said, simply, "Oh my, yes."

Swell. There wasn't a thing I could do about it, except muddle on.

Natasha returned a couple of hours later with garlic and boxes full of little treat bags. I hid them in the kitchen closet to use the next day. "That was fast."

"As soon as Leon heard they were for you, he became a little dynamo. Apparently I have to mention your name to get him to move faster."

"He seems nice." Okay, there was his unpleasant behavior of throwing us out during Natasha's party, but he was trying to do his job, and he had gone overboard in apologizing.

Natasha glanced around before whispering, "I saw him having it out with Patrick during the party."

"What do you mean?"

"They were having some sort of argument in the kitchen. I don't think they saw me, because Leon denied knowing Patrick last night. Very odd."

Leon had appeared afraid to speak with the police this morning, as well. "Did you hear what he and Patrick were discussing?"

"They made mention of money, but I couldn't hear exactly what the problem was. I'm just a bit leery of Leon now."

"I thought you suspected Maggie."

191

"I suspect both of them!"

"Have the police told you anything about the killer?"

Natasha groaned. "They interviewed Mars, Leon, and me endlessly. They even questioned my mother and June. The thing is that we don't know if the killer was one of our guests. Who would have thought so many grown men would want to play dress up as Dracula? Your Wolf made Leon and me go through the guest list and tell him who came dressed as vampires. Can you imagine? And you know how crabby Wolf and Mars are around each other, always trying to be the more clever one." She touched fingers to her forehead. "People have been calling all day long to find out if Patrick was really killed by a vampire. I'm telling you, Sophie, there's vampire mania in this town right now."

And we were adding fuel to the fire by telling the story of Viktor Luca. What lousy timing. As soon as that thought crossed my mind, I felt ashamed. Patrick had been murdered. He might have been a snob and unpleasant, but he hadn't deserved to die. Natasha and I were alive and well. We could go home and spend time with our loved ones, but everything had come to an abrupt and cruel end for Patrick — and not at the

192

hands of a vampire. He'd been killed by a mortal, someone who walked and shopped and lived among us. Someone who wanted to get rid of me.

At eight o'clock, we shut down for the night. Bernie, Humphrey, Nina, and I were beat. June and Wanda impressed me the most. They were ready to call it quits for the night, but eager to return the next day.

"That was delightful," said June. "I love being around all these adorable children. It makes me feel young again."

I hoped I would have as much energy at her age. I did notice, though, that while the rest of us walked home, June and Wanda shared a cab.

Humphrey and Bernie declined my invitation to dinner. I couldn't blame them. If I didn't have the kids to feed, I wouldn't have bothered cooking anything and would have fallen into bed.

The kids astounded me by being full of spunk. When we got home, we all changed into comfortable clothes, and Jesse and Blake lit a fire in the kitchen fireplace. The kids and Nina gathered around the kitchen table, comparing stories about the people who'd toured the house. Meanwhile, I was thrilled that Chicken Scaryaki only took fifteen minutes to cook and the Bat Cave

Risotto didn't take much longer. I made a quick salad of soft baby spinach leaves, crisp apple slices, chewy dried cranberries, crunchy pecans, and thinly sliced red onion. In spite of my determination to act normal, I found I constantly looked out the kitchen window to be sure my assailant hadn't returned. I whisked together tart apple cider vinegar, olive oil, honey, and mustard as a dressing and dinner was ready.

Nina poured sparkling apple cider for the kids and white wine for herself. I stuck with the apple cider. After the day I'd had, one glass of wine and I would be asleep at the table with my face in my plate.

As much as I loved to entertain, I was dead on my feet, and didn't mind one bit when the door knocker sounded and Blake's father, Dash, whisked the boys away. Daisy and I walked Nina home.

Nina stopped in the middle of the street. As though she had read my mind she asked, "Do you think he could be stalking us right now?"

We stared up and down the quiet block.

"I'm sleeping over. Don't bother arguing with me about it. My husband is away, and I'm not even fostering a dog at the moment."

At her house, she stuffed nightclothes,

face creams, a toothbrush, and the CD player on which she listened to books and which she couldn't sleep without into a bag made of recycled fibers by impoverished women in Africa.

Nina locked her front door and nearly propelled me across the street to my house. "I don't see anyone, do you?"

"Not a soul."

We checked on the girls in the family room and told them Nina would be staying over. They were underwhelmed. Vegas bowed her head texting, and Jen painted her toenails. Dramatic music from an old Christopher Lee vampire movie played in the background.

They barely acknowledged us when we said good night. Fine by me. I couldn't keep my eyes open one minute longer. Thank goodness the beds upstairs were made and ready for company. Nina opted to sleep in June's favorite room with a huge canopy bed, across the hall from my bedroom. I bid her good night, slid under the comforter, felt Mochie and Daisy settle on the bed with me, and was asleep in seconds.

I woke to the sound of Daisy howling. Rolling over, I squinted at the clock. Four in the morning. What was she thinking? Groggy, I stumbled down the stairs. "Daisy!" I hissed. "Shh." She wagged her tail when she saw me but didn't budge from her position by the door in the sunroom. I turned on a light.

"Come on, Daisy. It's the middle of the night."

Mochie sat nearby, feigning disinterest by washing his face.

Daisy released another woeful howl. "Shh. You'll wake Nina and the girls." Who was I kidding? Daisy was only feet away from the family room. Jen and Vegas were probably awake by now.

"Too late. What's going on?" Nina rubbed her eyes.

"I have no idea."

Nina's eyes widened and suddenly she didn't look sleepy. "The killer!" She turned off the light.

We peered through the windows into the dark backyard. No sign of a murderer or evidence of devilish rabbits or other nocturnal creatures.

"I don't see anything. Come to bed, Daisy. I'm pooped."

She refused to move. "Sit there all night if you like, but quit howling." She flapped her feathery tail against the floor.

I peeked into the family room. Neither of the girls stirred. Amazing. Kids could sleep through anything. Mochie flashed by me, and before I could stop him, he flew onto the bed, landing squarely on one of the girls — and sank into the depths of the comforter. I switched on a lamp and pulled back the covers, only to find carefully placed pillows and no girls.

"Oh no!" Nina's deep grumble reflected what I felt.

"Let's not leap to conclusions. I'll check the kitchen."

When they weren't there, Nina and I sped through the house, looking in bedrooms, the den, the living room. In the end, we could come to only one conclusion. They had sneaked out, and Daisy had tried to tell us.

FOURTEEN

Dear Natasha,
I'm planning an elegant Halloween cel-
ebration. I loathe the ticky-tacky decora-
tions most people use. No spiderwebs or
mummies for me. I rather like the natural
shape of pumpkins, but the color — oh,
please! It doesn't go with anything!
                    — No Halloween Kitsch in
                    Pumpkin Bend, Arkansas

Dear No Halloween Kitsch,
Make the most out of pumpkins by paint-
ing them gold. Gilding them adds a touch
of class that will impress even your most
discerning friends.
                    — Natasha

"Maybe they're at Mars's house?" I couldn't
fathom why Vegas might want to go home
in the middle of the night, but stranger
things had happened.

198

I attached Daisy's leash, grabbed a coat, and stuffed my cell phone in the pocket.

"Hold it there, Lone Ranger. You're not going by yourself." Nina reached for her coat.

"What if the kids come back?"

Her lips mashed into an annoyed straight line. "Hurry! I'll give you three minutes to cross the street. If I don't hear from you, I'm calling the Marines."

Daisy and I ventured into the cold night. On high alert for any sign of movement, I ran across the street, climbed the stairs to the front door, and called Nina to let her know we were safe.

I rang the doorbell and heard the familiar two-note foghorn of the Addams Family doorbell. No doubt still from the party.

Mars answered the door, his hair mussed and one eye closed. He wore a navy blue bathrobe. "Soph?" He reached out to rub Daisy's head.

"Jen and Vegas are gone. I thought they might have come here."

Mars's closed eye opened, and the drowsiness left his face. "They're missing?"

"They arranged their pillows so it would look like they were asleep under the covers."

"That's not like Jen." He rubbed his

forehead in a gesture I knew very well. "They haven't turned up here. C'mon, we need to talk."

Talk? That didn't sound good. I followed him into Natasha's kitchen expecting a disaster area. For a room in which an explosion had taken place recently, it sparkled. The stainless appliances shone as if just cleaned. The countertops and sleek European cabinets gleamed silver, too. She'd painted the walls a pale gray-blue; even the tile floor was a matte bluish gray. If I hadn't been so worried about the girls, I might have been tempted to run through the kitchen leaving fingerprints on all that shiny steel. The hole in the wall had already been framed and drywalled. The only reminder of the explosion was a plastic tarp billowing in the gap where a new window would fit.

"This is amazing." I sniffed the air. "It barely smells of smoke. How did you do that so fast?"

"Minimal damage. It looked much worse than it was. Bad enough that it blew out the window, but on the whole we were very lucky. That, and the restoration crew worked fast to get away from Natasha."

I made a mental note to put Natasha in charge the next time I needed something done fast. I focused on Mars. He still looked like the good old boy he was. His face retained a fresh, youthful quality, even though the years had aged it a bit. He picked up the phone. "Have you tried calling Jen?"

I buried my face in my hands. How stupid of me. I'd been so upset and sleepy that I hadn't thought about the fact that they had cell phones. Taking the phone from Mars, I dialed Jen's number. "It's defaulting to voice mail. Try Vegas."

Mars hung up the telephone. "We can't call Vegas." He leaned against a counter, careful not to touch it with his hands. "We took her phone away to punish her."

"Punish? What for?"

He exhaled with his eyes closed. They snapped open when he said, "For sneaking out in the middle of the night."

"She's done this before? You might have told me! I wouldn't have left them alone for even a second."

"Natasha didn't want to share."

"What?! She'd rather Vegas drag Jen off somewhere with her?"

"I'm sorry, Soph. I'm so, so sorry. I never should have listened to Nat. You know how she is about appearances. She didn't want anyone to know we were having trouble controlling Vegas."

I stood beside him, facing the counter, and placed my hands on it, pressing hard to control my anger.

"Uh, Soph. No fingerprints, please. Natasha has a fit when she sees fingerprints."

He had to be kidding. It was childish, but I promptly mashed my palms against the counter in several places. "I really don't understand you, Mars. Why on earth do you stay with her?"

I thought he was about to answer, when a voice behind me demanded, "What's going on in here?"

Natasha. I didn't bother looking at her. "Thanks to your decision not to tell me that Vegas has a tendency to run away in the middle of the night" — I whirled around — "now Jen and Vegas are missing."

Natasha lifted a manicured hand to her forehead. "Vegas isn't that kind of girl."

"Cut the act. Mars already confessed."

She lowered her hand and must have forgotten about being dramatic when she clomped over to us. "I thought we were going to keep that private."

"It's just Sophie. Besides, Vegas is the one who blew it by taking off again. Where do you think she went?"

"What is Daisy doing in my kitchen?"

When neither Mars nor I removed Daisy,

Natasha sagged. "Why do these things have to happen to me? I planned such a perfect party, but one of the guests managed to get himself murdered by a vampire of all things, which means no one will *ever* come to one of my parties again; someone blew up part of my kitchen; now this with Vegas; and a *dog* in my kitchen. What else can possibly go wrong?"

"Not that I mean to detract from your tale of woe, but where did Vegas go last time?" I asked. "Maybe she went there again."

A look passed between Mars and Natasha. She pressed her fingers over her mouth. "This is bad. It was bad enough last time, but now it's even worse."

"We have to call," said Mars. "We can't just let them run around by themselves."

"Suppose we let Sophie in on what we're talking about," I suggested.

"Maybe we should wait an hour or so. See if they come home on their own," Natasha said.

"Maybe we should call the police and let them help us find the girls," I said, lifting the phone.

"No police!" They said it in unison, and Natasha swiped the phone from my hand.

I stared at them. "Where are they?"

Natasha pulled the belt tighter on her robin's egg blue silk bathrobe. "Last time, Vegas snuck out to meet Blake. Patrick was a complete jerk about it. You can't imagine how awful he was."

Actually, I could.

"If we call the police, they'll think there's a connection between Patrick's murder and the fight we had over the kids," said Natasha. "Of all the people to die at our party. We couldn't have handpicked a worse candidate."

"Why did you invite him, then?"

Natasha scowled. "Guest lists are impossible. I didn't want to include Patrick, but I couldn't invite Maggie without inviting him. You know, Maggie is quite influential because she owns fifty percent of that car dealership."

"Seemed okay to me. Making amends, you know," said Mars.

Wonderful. They'd had an ugly argument with Patrick, invited him to their party, and someone had murdered him. *That wouldn't reflect badly on them.* "Just for the record, I think you should know that finding Jen is more important to me than hiding your argument with Patrick from the cops."

Mars nodded as though he understood, but Natasha gasped, "You wouldn't!"

"You bet I would."

Mars rested his hand on my arm. "There's another reason we don't want the police involved. It might throw Vegas into the juvenile social services system. Nat and I aren't perfect parents, but we're getting along. I really don't want to open that door with her mother missing and her dad overseas."

Unfortunately, I understood that. Vegas wasn't a bad kid. If she were living with me, I would feel the same way. "How about if I call Maggie to see if the kids are there?"

Mars nodded again and picked up the phone, but Natasha pressed her hands to the sides of her head like she thought her world would end.

"We have to do it. We can't just let Vegas run wild," he said, dialing the number.

I took the phone from him. It rang and rang, and finally kicked over to voice mail. I left a message. "Do you have Blake's number?" I asked.

Natasha left the kitchen for a moment and returned with a yellow sticky note on which a number had been scribbled. I dialed the number, but it, too, rolled over to voice mail. I was beginning to hate the person who invented voice mail.

I stashed the sticky note in my pocket.

"I'm going over there. Do you know the address?"

"I know where they live. Give me a second to change, and I'll come with you." Mars left the kitchen at a jog.

"Is there anywhere else she might have gone?" I asked Natasha.

"There's always the possibility that your perfect Jen wanted to sneak out to meet some boy."

She said it in a snarky tone that I didn't appreciate, but I had to concede that it was a possibility. "Are you sure Vegas doesn't have her phone? She was texting when I said good night to the girls."

"Not unless she bought a new phone that we don't know about."

Mars bounded into the kitchen. "Let's go."

Daisy pranced ahead of us in the dark, delighted about her nighttime stroll.

Mars yanked at the zipper of his jacket uncomfortably. "I'm sorry about this, Soph. I never should have listened to Nat. We should have told you. Nat has her good sides, but keeping up appearances at all costs is getting painfully old." He took Daisy's leash from me. "Our relationship might not have been perfect, but I never gave a single thought to leaving fingerprints

206

on anything." He smiled at me. "We had some good times, didn't we?"

We walked six blocks, mostly in silence. I debated telling him about the attack on me, unsure why I was reluctant to tell him. Due to the late hour, no lights glimmered in windows. A bone-chilling wind blew along the old brick sidewalk, scuttling dead leaves past our ankles and whipping them up around our heads. Rushing air howled by us, and as we hurried past historic houses, I was overcome by an awareness of the people who had walked the same streets two hundred years before. Except for the pumpkins and Halloween decorations, the historic houses and brick sidewalks probably hadn't changed very much. It wasn't hard to imagine the ghosts of decades gone by brushing past us.

Or a contemporary murderer lurking around a corner. For our mutual safety, I finally told him what had happened to me. He stopped and even in the dim light of the moon and the streetlamps, I could see his shock.

He hugged me. "Why didn't you call? I could have helped."

"I'm fine. Once he was gone, there wasn't anything anyone could do."

We continued walking. "Why would Patrick's murderer want to kill you?"

"I wish I knew. Wolf thinks he feared I could identify him."

Mars cut a sharp glance at me. "I had a chat with Wolf. He's not such a bad guy."

"I wouldn't date him if he was."

Mars smiled. "You always did have good taste in men."

"Very funny."

"The current assumption is that the killer planned ahead. This wasn't a random murder. Someone had it in for Patrick and took advantage of the party to wear a costume and hide his identity. But his attack on you puts all that in a different light. He's a chilling character, Sophie — think how much moxie it took to kill someone right out on the sidewalk in the open where anyone could see."

"He did a good job of concealing his identity. I saw him up close twice, but I can't tell you anything that would help identify him. He was covered head to toe."

"What about his shoes?"

"I don't even know what kind of shoes you're wearing right now. Who looks at shoes?"

"He obviously knew Patrick and was able to lure him outside, but he must have been waiting for you. Did he go after your neck like he was planning to bite you?"

"Not at all. He held his hand over my nose and mouth, and I couldn't breathe."

"Then why bother leaving bite marks on Patrick when it would have been so much easier to bash him over the head or stab him?"

Mars turned and walked up a short flight of stairs to a red brick town house with dark shutters. Beautiful ironwork mini-balconies accented long windows that looked out to the street.

"Nice house," I said.

"Maggie got it in the divorce. There's a lot of money in car dealerships." Mars rang the bell.

"She's not into Halloween." Not even one pumpkin sat by the door.

Moments later a light illuminated an elegant fan-shaped window over the door, and I heard movement inside. A drowsy Maggie opened the door crying, "Marsie! You came back." She reached for him and held on.

I took Daisy's leash from him, and we stepped inside. An elaborate mirror hung over a console, reflecting us and making the foyer appear larger.

Mars unwound Maggie's arms from his neck, apologized for waking her, and explained that we had called first. "Jen and Vegas are missing, and we wondered if they might be here."

She leaned against him as though she could barely stand. "I don't know a Jen, and Patrick told Blake he wasn't allowed to see Vegas anymore."

As sweetly as I could, I asked, "Would you mind checking Blake's room to see if he's there? Maybe he knows where they are."

As though she was drunk, she flung one arm in the direction of the stairs. "Be my guest."

I handed Daisy's leash to Mars and seized the opportunity to dash up the stairs, even though I didn't have a clue where Blake's bedroom might be.

I could hear Maggie cooing, as if to a baby, "You have a doggie. I like doggies." She gasped. "I should get a dog!"

I turned right and peered into what was clearly the master bedroom. She'd left the light on, and it reflected in an entire wall of floor-to-ceiling mirrors. I thought I heard someone scuttle away. "Blake?" I called. "Blake?"

When no one answered, I flicked on the light in the next room. The nautical decor suggested I'd found Blake's bedroom. Either Maggie had a knack for decorating, or she'd hired a good designer. A blue palette offered a backdrop for red accents and seashore memories. The bed, however, looked amazingly like the girls' bed had. Pillows were lumped in the middle, and Blake was not tucked in like he should have been.

I swallowed hard and gazed around, looking for a clue that would let me know he wasn't the killer. It was stupid of me, but I couldn't help thinking that the girls had probably met the prime suspect in Patrick's murder by themselves in the dark of night. This couldn't be happening.

I turned off the light and called Blake's name again. He had no reason to hide from me. "Blake? The girls won't be in trouble. I just need to find them. Can't you help me?"

If he was there, he didn't come forward. I pulled out my cell phone, pressed in Blake's number, and listened. Either he had turned it off or it wasn't nearby.

I rushed down the stairs and found Mars seated in the living room. Maggie roamed, flipping open one decorative box after another, complaining about not finding any cigarettes.

Mars shrugged at me and made a little circle near his head with his forefinger, like he thought she was nuts.

"Maggie," I said. "Blake's not in his room."

She looked at me and held onto an accent table to keep from swaying. "He's probably with that girl, Vegas. They're working together on the haunted house. Patrick tried to put a stop to that, but Blake threw a fit." She sank into a chair covered in a gorgeous floral print on a black background, and grunted in a most unladylike manner. "Blake hated Patrick. Did you know that? Patrick took such good care of us. He was our protector, and my little Blakey hated him. There's no one to watch over us now."

She sounded drunk. I shot a glance at Mars, who lifted his eyebrows like he hadn't a clue.

He leaned toward Maggie. "Where would he have gone?"

"I don't know," she whispered. "Do you think they really sleep in coffins?"

That was too weird for me. "Maggie!" I raised my voice to get her attention. "Where is Blake?"

Maggie dug in the pockets of her dressing gown. She pulled out a plastic medicine bottle and stared at it.

Mars launched to his feet and gently removed it from her hand. He read the label. "Sleeping pills. That explains a lot."

He handed them back to Maggie, who promptly opened the container and shook half a dozen into her hand. "Maybe we should leave these where she won't find them."

"Good idea." I took the pills, located the kitchen, and stashed them under a bag of peas in the freezer. I shouldn't have been snooping, but was it really snooping if something was right out in the open? Two aperitif glasses stood on a drying mat next to the sink, along with an ornate, serrated spoon. I sniffed the air, but it didn't smell of licorice. I bent closer to the empty glasses. They must have been washed. I couldn't pick up a scent. Aside from the fact that she shouldn't have been mixing sleeping pills with alcohol, Maggie had every right to a drink, and given what she'd been through with Patrick's death, who could blame her for having a nightcap with a friend? It gave me pause, though, and bolstered my suspicion that someone was hiding from us upstairs.

When I returned, Maggie had stretched out on the sofa and was holding Mars's hand. He tried to withdraw it, but that prompted her to moan, "Don't leave me. Please!" Her voice shrank to a tiny whisper. "I'm next."

"You're next for what?" I asked, but she had drifted off to sleep.

"Think she'll be okay?" asked Mars.

I nodded and opened the door. Outside on the stoop, I said, "There's someone else in the house."

"Who?"

"Don't know. There were two wineglasses in the sink, and I thought I heard someone hiding from me upstairs. It could have been Blake. He doesn't have a reason to avoid me, but I guess it could have been him."

We walked down the steps to the brick sidewalk. A couple strolled by us, their arms around each other. Across the way, a man walked by in the other direction. A frigid wind blew along the street. The lights in pumpkins had been doused hours ago, and none of the cute electric lights glowed, leaving shadowy images of witches and skeletons. Definitely creepy — the kids would have loved it.

"What about Jesse? Do you know where he lives?" I asked. "Oh, wait! Do you think they would have gone to Blake's dad's house? What's his name? Dash?"

We strolled to the next block as we spoke.

"Soph, I don't want to worry you, but kids don't sneak out at night to go where there are adults who will make them go home."

Mars was right. As I tried to imagine where they would have gone, a familiar license plate on a parked car struck a chord with me. I whipped around and looked back at Maggie's house, half a block away. Nudging Mars, I said, "I guess when you don't want people to know you're sleeping over, you should park farther away."

FIFTEEN

Dear Sophie,
For years, my husband has hung cute little ghosts from a tree by our front steps. When our children were small, they were perfect. Now that the kids are older, I'm wondering how to make those friendly ghosties a little scarier. Bwaha-haha!
> —Wicked Mom in Dead Mans Crossing, Indiana

Dear Wicked Mom,
Search for an old suit and a gauzy or lacy white dress in secondhand and thrift shops. Stuff them with newspapers or biodegradable packing peanuts. Attach stuffed gloves for hands. Notice what's missing? Now you have a headless couple to greet your kids and their friends. Want to make them a little bit more gory? Dribble red paint around the

collars and down the front.

— Sophie

"Aw, that's a real shame," said Mars. "I never expected it of him."

The streetlight shone brightly on a vanity license plate that left no doubt about the identity of the owner — HRTWIN. Everyone who lived on our block and jostled for parking spots knew Frank Hart's license plate based on his name and store — Hart Wine. No wonder the person in Maggie's house hid from me.

"Frank's wife is lovely. What would possess him to leave her for Maggie, who appears to be a mess, and only lost her boyfriend yesterday?" I gasped as the obvious dawned on me. "You don't think he murdered Patrick to get him out of the way?"

"Wouldn't be the first time that had happened."

"Would they be foolish enough to spend the night together so soon after Patrick's death?"

"People do a lot of stupid things for love."

I squinted at him, getting the feeling he wasn't just talking about Frank and Maggie. Whatever he meant, it would have to wait. Finding Jen came first. "Mars, I'm worried. Three people saw Blake in our

217

neighborhood the night Patrick was murdered. I think we have to call the cops."

He turned and grasped my shoulders. "Not yet. Please, Soph. Once we start that ball rolling, we won't be able to stop it, and it could have lifelong repercussions for Vegas."

Repercussions worse than death?

"Let's give it one more try," he said. "Where would you go if you were a kid out on the town in the middle of the night?"

"The waterfront? The park? Market Square?"

If his expression was any indication, Mars was as concerned as I was. "We'll start with the park."

I dialed my home number while we walked, in the hope that Jen had returned. Nina reported that she hadn't returned or called. At the park, the moon shimmered on the Potomac River, but we were the only people present. Under other circumstances, I'd have thought it romantic, but the pressure of finding Jen weighed on me. I faced Mars. "So much for the park."

In one swift move, he wrapped his arms around me and kissed me with a fervor that made me melt. I should have pushed him away, should have protested, should have jumped aside. Instead, I lingered in the

218

warmth of his embrace, excited by the unexpected, yet comfortable with the familiarity of his scent and body.

He released me, his fingers sliding down to caress mine. I had no idea what to do or say. This was the last thing in the world that I'd expected. *Correction. My reaction was the last thing I'd expected.* I thought I was content in my relationship with Wolf. I thought I was officially over Mars, and that we had settled into an easy friendship. Yet, now, under enormous pressure, when I should have been thinking about Jen, I yearned for more. How could this be happening? Maybe this was how people reacted in times of extreme stress — they sought comfort wherever they could find it.

Despite my consternation, Mars looked down at me, smiling like the happiest man in Virginia. "I could have lost you forever." He ruffled the fur on Daisy's neck. "I thank my lucky stars that Daisy protected you."

Wordlessly, we turned and walked toward King Street. Mars still held one of my hands. Should I gently untwine my fingers? Should I yank my hand away? No, I would have done that instinctively; instead, I'd held on. What was wrong with me?

"We're in luck," whispered Mars. "There are kids hanging out near the fountains. Act casual. Maybe we can get close and see if Jen and Vegas are there."

Act casual? When my heart was pounding so hard I thought everyone could hear it, and I was worried about becoming the other woman for my ex-husband? *Focus on Jen.* That was the solution. Nothing else was important right now. I would have to sort out my feelings later.

Mars wrapped his arm around my waist, and there was little I could do except loop my arm around him. We paraded by the kids, who ignored us. Neither Jen nor Vegas was among them. Their conversation slowed me considerably, though, because I wanted to listen in when I realized they were talking about the haunted house.

"That vampire bedroom is so cool. You think my mother would let me sleep in a coffin?" The boy laughed under the streetlights, and I could see vampire fangs in his mouth. "She'd freak!"

"Eww." A girl shifted away from him. "That would creep me out."

A second boy snickered. "If you're so scared of vampires, what are you doing out at night when they roam around looking for necks to bite?"

She clutched her throat with both hands. "I'm wearing a bulky turtleneck and garlic, and I borrowed my sister's cross necklace. It's sterling silver. I figure that ought to cover it."

"You have to come with us tomorrow night."

A girl responded. "As long as I don't have to sleep there. I'm not as brave, or as stupid, as those girls. Why would you spend the night in a vampire's bedroom when everyone knows two vampires are on the loose?"

Two vampires?

I felt the tension in Mars's arm. "The haunted house," he whispered.

We turned as a unit and his arm fell away when we raced in the direction of Bubble and Trouble. I'd had no idea it would prove to be such a fitting name.

Mars ran with Daisy on a regular basis, but it didn't take long for me to get winded. He slowed to a walk, clearly for my benefit, but it annoyed me. Ex-husbands weren't supposed to be so considerate.

A gaggle of kids clustered on the sidewalk outside Bubble and Trouble. Some sat cross-legged, and a couple of them smoked cigarettes. The house looked dark and quiet when we approached it. No lights shone in the windows.

"What are you doing here?" I asked the

kids, hoping I would see Jen or Vegas among them.

"We're waiting for the vampires," said a gangly boy.

"They have to come home before dawn," offered a girl with pumpkin orange streaks in her hair.

"Go home." I said it in what I hoped was a firm, I'm-in-charge voice. "No vampires are coming."

"How do you know?" asked the boy.

"Because there are no such things as vampires. Now scoot!"

They took their sweet time leaving and certainly grumbled about it. I could hardly wait to find out if Jen and Vegas were inside. Had the older kids outside frightened them? Mars was about to pound on the door. I grabbed his wrist to stop him. "Wait a second. If we knock on the door, they can run out through the gate in the backyard. For that matter, they could just hang out and pretend they're not inside. They'll fear it's these kids trying to get in."

"Good thinking. I'll jog around and head them off the back way. Give me a couple minutes to get back there." He handed me the leash and scanned the street. "If anyone appears, just shout, and I'll come running back. I don't like leaving you alone."

Mars sped along the deserted sidewalk and disappeared around the corner.

I couldn't say if it was the dead leaves rustling or the bare branches silhouetted against the night sky, but a chilling shiver rattled through me. I hoped Jen was inside, safe and sound. What could have possessed her to run around in the middle of the night?

I figured Mars had made it to the backyard, and, saying a little prayer, I pounded on the front door. No one answered. For absolutely no good reason, I tried the door handle. It was locked. Why hadn't I brought the key? I thought I heard scuffling. "Jen?" I called.

The door handle shifted. I clutched my phone in my hand, ready to dial for help yet mindful that calling the police could result in dire consequences for Vegas.

Mars swung the door open from inside. "How did you get in?"

He reached into his pocket and pulled a credit card out of his wallet. "I resorted to old tricks. Ray needs to put a better lock on that back door." He switched on the foyer light. "Vegas?"

His call shook through the house. I reminded myself that it wasn't haunted, nor was there any such thing as a vampire. So why was I nervous?

Gathering courage, I tried to laugh at myself and started up the stairs. Something swept over my head — a blast of air — and I screamed.

"What was that?" asked Mars.

"You felt it, too?" At least I hadn't lost my mind. To make matters worse, the automated ghost swung in our direction.

Daisy didn't care, though, and bounded past me. Her nose to the floor, she shot to the door leading to the vampire's bedroom.

Mars tried the doorknob, but it was locked. Screams rose inside.

I pounded on the door. "Jen? Vegas? Are you in there?"

Mars sounded as afraid as me when he barked, "Open this door right now!"

A timid voice came from inside. "Aunt Sophie?"

She was alive! "Open the door, Jen!"

Mars and I could hear muddled whispering on the other side of the door. Half of me wanted to knock the door down and hug her, while the other half wanted to give Jen the worst scolding she'd ever had.

"Prove it's you," said Jen.

Prove? I looked to Mars. "Daisy is here with us. Open up!"

"Ask Sophie something to which only she

would know the answer, Jen," said Mars.

More whispering ensued. Jen's tender voice finally asked, "What are the names of my cats?"

"Your dad is George, your mom is Laci, your nana is Inga, and your Ragdoll cats are Jasper and Alice."

The lock clanked, the door opened, and Jen hurled herself at me with the velocity of a tornado, thus dispelling any lingering intention to chew her out. Vegas launched at Mars in much the same way, leaving Jesse and Blake looking very uncomfortable.

Each of them wore a chain of garlic. "Is everyone okay?" I asked. Jen clung to me like she would never let go. I held her away just enough to see her cute little face. "Are you hurt?"

"No. But, Aunt Sophie, this house really is haunted."

Mars winced and looked up at the ceiling.

"Oh, Jen." My voice clearly reflected my disbelief, because the other three all started talking at once.

Mars whistled to get their attention. "Do you boys have your cell phones with you?"

Jesse looked a little bit sheepish when he said, "We turned them off so the vampires wouldn't hear them if they rang."

"Call your parents and tell them to pick

you up at Sophie's house in about ten minutes. Now — down the stairs!" He jerked a thumb over his shoulder.

The kids obeyed, and I could hear Jesse trying to explain to his mom why he was calling her in the middle of the night. I wasn't sure Blake's mom would understand. She had enough trouble driving when she *wasn't* drugged. I caught up to Blake in the foyer. "I think you should call your dad, not Maggie." Blake cringed a little when I said that, and I had a feeling I knew which of his parents he couldn't manipulate.

I started for the kitchen to lock up when something crashed upstairs. I rushed back to the foyer. A quick head count verified that everyone was accounted for. Daisy galloped up the stairs, and Mars took them two at a time with the boys on his heels. Before they reached the landing on the second floor, footsteps slammed down the back stairs.

It didn't help that the girls screamed like banshees and grabbed hold of me. I lunged from their grasp and shot to the kitchen, just in time to see a dark figure fleeing through the mock graveyard and out the gate.

Sixteen

Dear Sophie,
I'm having a few friends over for a Halloween dinner, but I'm stumped about a centerpiece. I don't want anything too gross, like a tombstone or a coffin, and pumpkins just seem so juvenile. What can I do that's creepy but elegant?
— Saucy Sorceress in Little Hell,
Virginia

Dear Saucy Sorceress,
Haunt secondhand shops in search of one or two old candelabra. Even ugly or chipped ones will do. Spray paint them black and add candles. For an extra touch of bling, wrap them with crystal ice garlands or glue crystals on them. They'll be an unexpected touch of gloomy glamour on a table or a sideboard.

— Sophie

Mars, Daisy, and the boys charged down the back stairs and met us in the kitchen.

Vegas screamed, "It was him. It was Viktor. He was here the whole time!"

Jesse looked at me earnestly. "Sunrise is at seven twenty-six. He'll be back by then to get into the coffin. We should bring a wooden stake and a sledgehammer."

I didn't know whether to be horrified or to laugh. "Everyone listen to me." I tried my best to sound rational, even though I'd been through some extremely troubling hours, and I still quivered from the knowledge that someone had been in the house with us. "Vampires do not exist. That was an ordinary person, just like you and me. There will be no stakes or sledgehammers." On second thought, I added, "Or silver bullets. Mars, if you'll lock the back door, I think we should make our way home." I held a hand out to Jen. "I presume you have the key?"

I admit I was pleased to see remorse in her eyes when she handed it to me.

Mars returned and we doused the lights. When I secured the front door, I overheard Vegas mutter to Blake, "Stay close, okay? I can't believe she's going to make us walk home in the dark when she knows there's a vampire on the loose."

How was I ever going to convince them?

We marched silently to my house, Mars, Daisy, and me bringing up the rear so we would see if one of our charges strayed away. Mars glanced at me. "What a night."

Dash Bennett waited by his car when we arrived. He leaned against the red SUV, his arms folded over his chest. Even bed head and a grumpy expression didn't diminish his good looks. "I'm so sorry about this."

Nina opened the front door for us, and I invited Dash into the house. Behind his back, Nina raised her eyebrows and mouthed "Wow," which I interpreted as admiration for Dash.

Mars struck a fire in the kitchen fireplace as though he still lived there, and I put on hot chocolate, in the hope that the warm milk would help us all relax and get a little sleep. We needed to have a showdown with the kids first, though, which I dreaded.

The door knocker sounded, giving us all a few more minutes before the confrontation. When I opened the door, I found a petite woman with high cheekbones and a chic haircut that framed her delicate face. Her resemblance to Jesse left no question that she was his mom. She introduced herself as Dana Unterberger and apologized for Jesse's behavior. I led her into the kitchen, where she glared at her child and took a seat at the table.

Mars leaned against the kitchen counter, and in a no-nonsense tone, he said, "Explain yourselves."

To her credit, Jen looked miserable when she said, "Aunt Sophie, they're saying you put the vampire bite mark on Patrick's neck to make people think Viktor was back and get publicity for the haunted house."

How could anyone think anything so absurd? "Where did you hear that?"

Jesse chimed in, "It's all over the Net. On Facebook and Twitter."

I took a deep breath. This wasn't about me or any stupid rumors. I ladled hot chocolate into mugs with assorted Halloween images on them, and topped them off with miniature marshmallows. "That should teach you that you cannot believe every silly thing someone puts on the Internet. There's no filter for accuracy, you know." I passed out the mugs.

Mars frowned at them. "Even if that's true, it doesn't explain your middle-of-the-night foray."

I handed Dash a mug. He thanked me, but I noticed he didn't seem terribly upset with Blake, who appeared more relaxed than the rest of the kids.

It was Jen who finally broke. "We did it for you, Aunt Sophie. We thought if we spied on the vampire, we would know who he was, and then Wolf could capture him so you wouldn't be in danger anymore."

"He goes there every night. That's why the window is open. He flies in and out as a bat," said Vegas.

Every adult in the room raised eyebrows at Vegas's bat explanation.

I didn't know what to say. I was honored that they would go to such lengths for me, but that wasn't the right attitude — it would only encourage more irresponsible behavior. While I was thinking, Jen continued.

"And Heather changed her relationship status on Facebook."

Blake's face blazed crimson. "It was a lie."

Jen focused on me. "Heather said she was in a relationship with Blake. That" — she glanced at Vegas — "a revolting zombie bride had tried to move into her territory, and she'd better back off."

I tried to keep a stern face. Relief swept over me, though, because I now had a hunch that the frightening dead doll had come from Heather the Horrid. Apparently, that girl was determined to torment Vegas. "What does that have to do with anything?"

Vegas finally spoke. "She said she was

meeting Blake at the haunted house."

Jesse's mother, Dana, tapped her finger-nail on the table. "That doesn't explain why you were involved in this caper, young man!"

"Mom," said Jesse, "the house is really haunted. For real. You wouldn't believe what was going on in there last night. There's this cigarette case with Viktor Luca's initials on it and it disappeared. Blake had it in his hand one minute, then he set it down next to the wine bottles, and we walked over to the spider room, and when we came back, the case was gone."

"And Viktor's room smelled like cigarette smoke, but none of us were smoking," added Jen.

"And this red ball bounced down the stairs," said Blake. "It was in the lair down-stairs the last time we saw it, so how did it get up to the second floor?"

The hairs on the back of my neck stood up even though I was certain there were reasonable explanations for everything. I had to believe them because I'd seen the ball bounce down the stairs myself.

Vegas shuddered. "There were these things, like little vortexes of air, that flashed over our heads when we turned out the lights. We think they were ghosts."

Mars sounded surprisingly patient when he said, "Need I remind you that a fifth person fled the house when Sophie and I arrived? Someone had fun playing a major prank on you guys."

There was something about the way he said it that gave me pause. He was too calm and dismissive.

"Thanks for coming, everyone." Mars stood and shook hands with Dash. "Let's get these vagabonds to bed. That's the end of the haunted house for these four!"

"Oh no!" Jesse's mother jumped up. "Could I please speak with the parents privately?"

Leaving the kids with Nina, I ushered the other adults into the living room. No one bothered to sit down. We clustered in a little huddle.

Dana placed her hands together under her chin as though she were praying. "Jesse is a bright boy. Unfortunately, you wouldn't know that from his grades. We're working hard on applying ourselves. The thing is that he's getting extra credit for this project and he *cannot* mess it up. Seriously. It will be a nightmare. It could even mean repeating the year."

Mars said, "Then he can continue by himself."

Dana's eyebrows rose in alarm. "That won't work. If the others don't get credit, there will be all sorts of questions about why they didn't finish the project and put in their hours. It will all come out, and Jesse is the one who'll suffer." She looked at the ceiling and drew a deep breath. "Please don't think that I'm not upset about my child running around on the streets in the middle of the night — but they didn't do anything horrible. No one got hurt. They didn't break windows or vandalize anything or do drugs. C'mon, it could have been a lot worse."

Dash tilted his head. "I have to agree. If this becomes a disciplinary matter at the school, it could jeopardize Blake's participation on the tennis team. As far as I'm concerned, it was a childish prank that the parents should handle. I see no need to involve the school."

I knew Mars was going to agree to protect Vegas. "I'm not Jen's parent, but all things considered, it's probably best if the parents handle this."

Their relief was palpable. For a second, I thought they might high-five.

"However" — they froze and I could feel their apprehension — "I am not going to babysit them. We have dozens of kids going through the haunted house, and I can't possibly keep my eyes on all of them, plus our four rascals. You have to accompany them. You can wear costumes, and we'll give you roles to play. That way each of you will be responsible for your own child."

Dana eagerly seized on my suggestion. "That's fair."

Dash didn't seem too pleased. His hands on his hips, he stared at the floor. "If there's no alternative, I guess I'll have to agree."

Dash and Dana collected their sons and left after promising to show up an hour before the haunted house opened for business.

Mars crooked a finger at Vegas. She shuffled toward him, her head down. "Get your things. You're going home."

"But I'm staying here!"

"Not tonight, you're not."

It was sort of silly to say that since dawn would break in about an hour. However, I desperately needed sleep, and it would be easier if the girls weren't together, plotting.

I held out my hand to Jen. "Cell phone, please."

Horrified, she clutched it to her chest. "What if I need it?"

"You won't need it when you're sleeping. Hand it over and hightail it for the third-floor bedroom."

Her mouth pursed, and she banged the cell phone into my hand as she marched by me and clomped up the stairs.

Mars followed Vegas out. He turned to me, and I wanted to ask him what he thought had happened at the haunted house, but I decided it might be something best said out of earshot of the girls. Instead of saying good night, he said, "I'll be back as soon as I make sure Vegas is safely home."

"What for?" It wasn't the nicest way to ask, but exhaustion had kicked social politeness right out of me.

"I'm not leaving you alone. Someone has to protect you."

"Nina and Daisy are here with us. We'll be fine. Maybe you'd better make sure Vegas doesn't pull another stunt."

He protested, but I stuck to my guns, locked the door behind him, and followed Nina upstairs to bed.

Not surprisingly, I slept late the next morning. Neither Mochie nor Daisy was in my bedroom when I woke. The rich aroma of coffee wafted to me as I trotted downstairs. Nina never made coffee. Aha. Jen must be trying to make amends. That was sweet.

But there was no one in the kitchen. Not

even Mochie. I poured myself a mug of pumpkin spice coffee with a hint of nutmeg and strolled through the family room to the sunroom. Not a soul to be seen. It was nearly noon, and the sun had heated the brick floor. I longed to plop onto the sofa and lounge, but I knew I'd better find my little delinquent.

I ventured up the stairs and heard voices one flight up. Had Vegas returned? I'd better make sure Natasha, Mars, and I called each other to confirm where the girls were supposed to be so they couldn't pull any more stunts. I padded up the stairs. June and Nina sat on chairs near an open storage-area door, looking through mementos. Jen clambered over boxes and odd pieces of old furniture, while Mochie and Daisy sniffed every corner.

"I found another one, Gramma June!" Her tone became decidedly more somber when she added as properly as a British schoolgirl, "Good morning, Aunt Sophie."

Gramma June? Some serious bonding had been going on while I slept.

Jen handed June a gold box tied with a ribbon. June opened it and cried, "Here he is!"

Nina and I peered over her shoulder at a box full of photos. "Good morning. I assume you put on the coffee, June?"

"That was Jen's idea," said June. "Look what she found. She's such a big help."

Ohhh, someone had already told her tale of woe to Gramma June to acquire a sympathetic ally.

June held up a picture. I recognized June and her sister, Faye, raising cut crystal martini glasses in a toast. June tapped the photo with her fingernail. "See the man in the corner?"

He probably didn't know the photo had been taken. It captured him in profile, with a straight nose and lustrous wavy hair. I could imagine him playing the role of a sensitive 1960s poet and strumming a guitar.

"That's Viktor." June handed the photo to Nina and continued perusing the contents of the box.

Nina studied the photo. "I'm not surprised that women flocked to him. He looks like he should pose for the cover of a romance novel."

"Add that seductive accent, and he was nearly irresistible."

I stretched, ready for a second cuppa.

June turned to me. "Nina says the kids had quite a scare last night. It's a shame some ghosts are malicious."

Under my breath, so Jen wouldn't hear, I said, "Please, June, we don't want to encourage them."

She waved her forefinger at me. "Don't underestimate the powers of spirits. They're not all as sweet as Faye."

I was surrounded by believers. What happened to just enjoying Halloween as fun? Citing my need for a second cup of coffee, I hustled down to my bedroom and pulled on my favorite hang-around-the-house chamois soft trousers and a cinnamon fleece sweatshirt that did nothing for me but felt soft and cozy. I should have showered and fixed my hair properly, but I really wanted that second cup of coffee after the long night. I wound my ponytail around a hair stick to pin it up and hurried to the kitchen. Lunch would soon be in order. I was just pouring my second cup when I looked out the kitchen window and saw Humphrey step out of a parked car. He'd barely taken two steps when Mars and Vegas jaywalked across the street in the direction of my house and joined him as he walked toward my front door.

SEVENTEEN

Dear Natasha,
I thought the competition to have the best Christmas decorations was bad, but now the drive is on to impress the neighbors with Halloween decor. There are so many wonderful things we could do, but my boys and their friends aren't easy to spook anymore. All my hard work with pumpkins and branches and lights goes unappreciated. Any fresh ideas?
— Den Leader Dad in Wolf's Head,
Georgia

Dear Den Leader Dad,
Play a prank on your sons. Use PVC pipe to construct a human-sized cage. Enlist the assistance of a friend and dress him in a werewolf or Frankenstein costume. Put a strobe light on him inside the cage and let him surprise the neighborhood kids by

being "alive" when they least expect it.
— Natasha

I met them at the front door and glanced around for another dreaded dead doll. Fortunately, I didn't see one. "Has something happened, or is this some kind of intervention?"

Humphrey murmured, "We need to talk."

Nina raced down the stairs. "I hate being out of the loop! What's going on?"

Vegas didn't bother saying hello. "Where's Jen?"

I pointed upstairs. She took off like she hadn't seen Jen in months. Mars slung an arm around my shoulders. "I hope it's okay. Vegas pestered me to death about coming over here. She *had* to see Jen. Brrr, it's cold in here. No wonder you look like a polar bear."

He strode straight to the kitchen fireplace and tossed logs in with kindling.

Nina scowled at me. "Why do I feel like I've missed something?"

If she only knew. Nina was my best friend, and had I been Jen's age, I probably would have pulled her aside and spewed the details of Mars's kiss the night before. But in the light of day, that romantic moment seemed like something I had only dreamed and in

241

any event was perhaps best left unmentioned.

A fire blazed by the time I poured coffee for everyone. I did a quick head count and decided paella was in order for the cold day. While Mars brought Humphrey up to speed about our late-night excursion and the attack on me, I watched chicken legs brown in a deep cast-iron pan. I added sausage slices, along with paprika for flavor, and set them aside when they were done. I poured the rice into the pan with golden yellow saffron and a sprinkling of oregano, and turned the mixture to coat the rice. Finally, I poured in clam juice and diced tomatoes and mixed in the sausage and chicken. I ladled the entire mixture into a baking dish, covered it, and slid it into the oven.

I joined Nina, Humphrey, and Mars at the kitchen table. In the company of my close friends, I dared to ask, "Mars, last night I got the feeling you knew something that you didn't tell us."

He leaned back in his chair. "Four kids saw things — things that appeared, things that went missing. One of those four seemed less spooked than the others. Plus, we caught a fifth person tearing out of the house, and we know that Heather was instrumental in the shenanigans. When I do the math, I'm hoping it doesn't mean that Heather is really our boy Blake's honey, and that the two of them are pulling some kind of cruel joke on Vegas."

I was stunned. Heather had already proven her propensity for maliciousness, but it hadn't occurred to me that Blake might be in on it, and that poor Vegas could be their target. What a sad and frightening notion. "If that's the case, it would explain the appearance of the dead doll on our doorstep. I bet she left it there to scare Vegas."

Nina poured herself another cup of coffee. "Gee, Blake seems like such a nice kid. However, if Mars's theory is right, it would explain what he was doing in the alley the night of Patrick's death. He probably knew Heather was babysitting, and paid her a visit to neck."

"It doesn't explain why he was wearing his vampire costume. It reflects on him poorly either way. Either he's being mean to Vegas, or he killed Patrick." I toyed with my coffee mug. "I'm thinking about sending Jen down to stay with my parents. It's gotten too dangerous. I thought I could keep an eye on her, but last night she proved that was only my naive stupidity."

Humphrey frowned and tapped his foot on the floor.

"Bad timing," muttered Nina.

I didn't understand what she meant until seconds later when Jen barreled up from behind me. She planted her fists on her hips. "You don't mean that!"

I could barely bring myself to look at her face out of fear that I would cave in. "I do mean it. What if something had happened to you last night? Your parents trusted me to take care of you, and now there's a killer on the loose who probably thinks we can identify him. You would be much safer with your grandparents."

Vegas walked up to Jen and stood beside her like a warrior reinforcement. "We were fine! None of us was hurt or bitten by a vampire last night!"

I thought Jen might cry. She wrapped her arms around my shoulders from behind and rested her head against mine. "If I leave, there won't be anyone to watch over *you*."

Uh-uh. I wasn't falling for that. It also meant no birthday party with her friends.

Nina crossed her arms over her chest. "Did you know that several people, including me, saw Blake in the alley the night of Patrick's death?"

"Blake!" Jen released me.

June settled at the table. "Oh my! He has such nice manners. I would never have

244

thought it of him."

Mars's eyes widened in surprise. "Mom! I didn't know you were here."

"The girls and I have had the best time looking through Faye's old things."

Vegas glared at Nina. "You're wrong. It must have been someone who looked like Blake."

"I'm sorry, honey," said Nina. "He was even wearing his vampire cape."

Jen crossed one arm over her chest like Nina, but she held her elbow with her hand and used the other hand to tap her lips. "Verrrry interesting."

I wanted to giggle at her dramatic sleuthing pose, but bit my lip.

"What do you know, Jen?" asked Humphrey.

"Blake wouldn't do anything like that," she said. "He's . . . he's cerebral, like you, Humphrey. Yet . . . there's more going on than meets the eye, or he would have told Vegas and me about it."

"I agree with Jen," said Humphrey. "That's why I'm here. I overheard a couple of cops talking about Blake this morning. He's young, but he could have easily coaxed Patrick outside. Their theory was that he jumped on top of one of the hay bales, which would have given him a height advantage, and clamped something over Patrick's nose to asphyxiate him."

"The person who accosted me wasn't standing on anything."

Except for Humphrey, my friends didn't do a very good job hiding their amusement.

"Sophie, I feel quite confident that Blake is endowed with sufficient height to attack you." Humphrey's deadpan seriousness brought the rest of them to laughter.

"No!" shouted Vegas, stomping her foot. "You know it couldn't have been Blake."

Humphrey drew back at her outburst. "I'm inclined to be of the same mind. I spent hours working with Blake on the haunted house. He's not a killer." He leaned toward me. "We have to help him."

"Maybe that's a good idea." Nina stirred her coffee. "His mother certainly won't be of any assistance to him. She's been an oddball as long as I've known her. Afraid of her own shadow."

"I can't imagine it was the boy," said Humphrey. "Most adults can't figure out how to asphyxiate someone without leaving any marks on the body. It's unlikely a child could be so clever."

"But there *were* marks on the body — the vampire bite," said Jen.

"He didn't die from loss of blood,

though," explained Humphrey. "He died because he couldn't get air."

Jen's little forehead wrinkled, and a tidal wave of guilt swept over me. She was entirely too young for this. Humphrey's explanation had been simple and clinical, which was good, but I wondered if she and Vegas should be exposed to any of it.

Jen's lips pulled tight, and she threw a doubtful glance at Vegas. "I'm sorry, Aunt Sophie. I'm really, really sorry, and I promise I'll never sneak out or do anything like that again. Ever. Pinky-swear." She held out her pinky and twined it with mine. "Now can I stay? Pleeeease? I don't want to miss out on the haunted house fun." Her head bowed, she added, "Or my party."

Mars rested his hand on top of mine. I thought Nina's eyes might bug right out of her head. While I was debating how to extract my hand without hurting Mars's feelings or drawing everyone else's attention to the situation, Mars said, "Sophie, if we send the girls to stay with someone else, the killer will be convinced that they know something. They might even be in more danger from him. There's safety in numbers. You'll all be safer if you stay together. I can sleep over to protect you."

Whoa! I suspected I was the only person

in the room who was shocked by his suggestion. "No, no, no. That's not necessary. I think Jen was wrong about the killer leaving the dead doll. That must have been the work of Heather the Horrid."

June interrupted me with a sly smile. "Don't be so quick to turn Mars down. Remember, Viktor was able to take advantage of Peggy Zane when they were alone together."

I slid my hand out from under Mars's and leaped to my feet. "I have to make cornbread!" I preheated the other oven and slid a square cast-iron pan into it to warm so the cornbread would sizzle and form a crust when I poured in the batter. Glad that I could busy myself and hide my face, which burned from embarrassment and must have been the color of red wine, I stirred together cornmeal, tangy buttermilk, and a can of creamed corn.

Humphrey puffed up his chest. "I can take turns with Mars."

Good heavens! Surely Humphrey wasn't serious? I finally looked at my friends.

Nina grinned at me, and it wasn't a sweet I'm-your-concerned-friend grin, it was a sneaky this-is-going-to-be-hilarious smirk. "That's settled then. One big sleepover. I'm in."

I had to resist the urge to stick my tongue out at her. I poured the cornbread mixture into the hot pan and slid it back into the oven to bake. Looking for a reason not to return to my seat next to Mars, I checked the paella and added peas and shrimp while savoring the tempting aroma that wafted from the pot. But the food didn't distract me for long. Jen sat on the window seat, stroking Mochie's fur, and I couldn't help worrying about her. Part of me yearned to ship her to safety. Was Mars right? Would the killer be misled into thinking Jen could identify him and had gone into hiding? She deserved a second chance, I reasoned, and I could always change my mind and cart her down to my parents' home in the country. For now, I would keep a close eye on her.

I opened the cupboard and took down green majolica-style plates from Portugal. When I ladled the paella onto them, the saffron color of the rice contrasted nicely with the green of the plates. Mars ticked me off by rising to assist me. When had he become so helpful? He graciously handed out the plates, along with forks, knives, and orange and green napkins imprinted with huge golden mums.

I slid the platter of cornbread squares onto the middle of the table, where everyone could help themselves. "I guess it would send the wrong message to shut down the haunted house."

The cry that rose could probably be heard all the way down to the river.

"We're sticking together." Jen raised a piece of cornbread like it was a saber. "All for one and one for all." She looked at me, her brow furrowed. "Right, Aunt Sophie?"

I picked up a piece of cornbread and mimicked her battle stance. "You bet!" I was in it up to my ears now.

June buttered a piece of cornbread. "I don't know these people as well as you do, but I'm usually a good judge of character. Young Blake is a proper gentleman. He's not a calculating killer. I'm all for tracking down the real killer to assist that young man."

I had other reasons to uncover the killer — namely so I wouldn't have to look over my shoulder every minute or worry about Jen's safety. Plus it drove me nuts that everyone felt obligated to protect me. "Blake never made a secret of his hatred for Patrick. Don't you think a twelve-year-old would be smart enough to keep those feelings private if he planned to murder someone?" I asked.

"Thirteen," corrected Jen.

I continued with my train of thought. "I like Dash, but maybe he couldn't deal with the divorce, and he killed Patrick out of jealousy. That's a lot more likely."

Vegas stared at her plate, her arms hanging limply by her sides.

"Don't you like paella?" I asked.

She nodded and pushed it with her fork, but didn't take a bite.

"We love paella!" said Mars. "Natasha won't cook anything that comes out of one pan. Vegas and I sneak out for fun food. Don't we, Vegas?"

"I just feel so terrible about Blake." Vegas toyed with her spoon. "I don't understand why he would have come here wearing his vampire costume. Why didn't he mention it? He couldn't have killed Patrick. I mean, he hated him and all, but he wouldn't have killed him. I wish we could do something to help him."

"Can we help Blake, Aunt Sophie? You've been involved in murder investigations before. Couldn't we please help him by finding the real killer?" asked Jen. "We'll do whatever you tell us."

Humphrey reached for cornbread. "I, for one, like young Blake. Jen's quite right. He's an insightful young man. Besides, there's a question to be answered here. When we

251

know the answer, we will know the identity of the killer."

Everyone stopped eating and paid attention.

"The murderer went to lengths to make it appear that a vampire killed Patrick. Why?"

It was a good question.

"Publicity?" Humphrey looked at me.

I sagged. "Humphrey! You know me better than that. Staging a vampire bite is one thing, but killing someone? Oh please! This is the same thing the kids were talking about last night. I had nothing to do with it." I raised my empty hand in protest. "In spite of whatever idiotic rumors might be on the Internet."

"A person would have to be insane to murder someone for publicity for a haunted house." Nina smacked Humphrey playfully.

"Suppose the killer wanted to cast suspicion on someone else?" Humphrey directed his reply to Nina.

"Wait a minute," I cried. "Are you implying that someone killed Patrick to make me look guilty? That's crazy. Besides, I only met him one time."

"Exactly." Nina smiled smugly. "You see, Humphrey, you may think you've got this figured out, but what you're saying makes no sense."

Humphrey didn't seem convinced. "Really? You tell me why the killer would go to those extremes."

Nina answered testily. "Why would someone carve a mark in a victim's skin or take a memento? Killers are nuts."

"By definition, really," said Humphrey. "However, I seriously doubt that we have a deranged vampire killer running through the streets of Old Town."

June leaned toward me. "Even if it's not a demented wild man, it's someone very dangerous, and someone in our midst. I warned Mars to be careful because the killer is most likely on his guest list. I don't know what possessed the murderer to go after Patrick, but he's clearly a troubled person and not above doing it again. I certainly hope the police have better leads than a little boy." She pushed back her platinum gray hair, checking her chignon with her fingers. "Sophie, dear, I had such fun going through Faye's things this morning. She certainly knew how to have fun, especially on Halloween."

I let out a sigh of relief and mentally thanked June for changing the subject.

"Those old pictures were cool," said Jen.

Mars sputtered. "Aunt Faye scared me half to death when I was a little boy. She dressed some girl in a filmy white dress and made her walk across the stair landing. From the foyer, it looked like she was floating. For years I was convinced that the little girl ghost was in this house somewhere."

June laughed so hard her shoulders shook. "We couldn't convince you that it was pretend. I miss her parties."

In a completely stilted voice, like she'd rehearsed what she was going to say, Jen piped up, "We should have a Faye-style party here on Halloween for my birthday."

"What a good idea, Jen!" exclaimed June. "Sophie, do you have anyone to hand out candy at your door while you're at the haunted house on Halloween? I could do that for you and get things ready for the party."

Their little conversation happened so fast that it was like watching a ping-pong game. We had planned to have a party. What were they up to? "If I didn't know better, I would think you two were related. June, I would love for you to pass out candy to kids while we're at the haunted house."

June smiled like it was all settled. "Wonderful! Faye always set up a midnight buffet on Halloween. According to Wanda, that's when the barrier between us and the spirit world is the weakest and they can communicate with us the best."

It was a conspiracy. I looked around the table at the pleased expressions and wondered if I was the only one who hadn't been in on this little plan. A midnight buffet wasn't a big deal — well, maybe to Jen. It might seem exotically adult.

"Everyone can bring a dish, that way it won't be so much work, and we'll have a marvelous time!" June winked at Jen, as though she was thrilled they'd accomplished their little party scheme.

I had to admit that a midnight dinner sounded like fun. They could have just asked me. There had been no need for a grand conspiracy. I didn't want to ruin their fun, though. They clearly thought they'd accomplished something special.

We finished off the Halloween cupcakes I'd baked, and everyone scattered to don their haunted house attire. Mars took Daisy for a walk while the girls changed clothes. I was cleaning up the kitchen when the phone rang.

I didn't recognize the voice. The man blathered incoherently. Thinking he must have reached a wrong number, I almost hung up, but he managed to say, "It's Dash. Maggie collapsed and we're at the hospital."

EIGHTEEN

Dear Natasha,
I'm supposed to make costumes for my daughter and son, but I can't sew. I don't even have a sewing machine and if I did, I wouldn't know where to start. All the other mommies seem to have a sewing gene that I was born without. I've asked around, but it's too expensive to hire a seamstress to make a costume that they'll outgrow by next year.
— All Thumbs in Casper, Wyoming

Dear All Thumbs,
There's no longer any excuse for those who don't sew. Iron-on tape will accomplish almost anything you need to create a great costume. Begin with a hoodie and sweatpants or tights. You can create fabulous costumes by simply attaching felt. Add red felt wings with black felt dots to a black hoodie and tights and you have

a ladybug. Cut a felt tunic to attach to a green hoodie and tights, add a faux sword, and your son will be a Knight of the Round Table. Or go with pink, and add a huge swirl of tulle and a few sparkles to dress your princess.

— Natasha

I finally managed to deduce that Dash needed a favor. He didn't want Blake to see his mother in her current state. Would I pick him up at the hospital and take him to the haunted house? Of course I would. I rushed to change into my witch costume, and the second Mars returned with Daisy, I arranged for him to walk the girls to the haunted house.

When I arrived at the hospital, the first familiar face I saw belonged to Wolf. The sterile surroundings took on an ominous note. As fond as I was of Wolf, his presence signified death. I hoped Maggie hadn't been killed. A quick check around the emergency waiting room sent shivers along my arms. No sign of Blake.

I drew closer to Wolf and Dash and realized that Wolf held a Living Dead Doll and that Frank Hart was with them.

Wolf didn't bother greeting me. He held up the doll. "Maggie received one of these, too. Is this what yours looks like?"

"Similar. This one has red eyes with pupils. Ours has white eyeballs."

"Maggie opened the front door and found it on the stoop," said Frank. "She became so agitated that she couldn't inhale. I went to get a paper bag for her to breathe into and when I returned, she had passed out."

I was a little bit surprised that he admitted to being at Maggie's house, not to mention the fact that he had come to the hospital, since he had a wife of his own. Was their affair public knowledge?

Wolf turned the doll. "Does yours have these little bite marks drawn on the neck?"

I nodded. "I guess that eliminates any possibility of coincidence. How is she?" I asked, holding my breath and hoping the answer would be positive.

Dash rubbed his jaw with his palm. "She'll be fine. Maggie is . . . high-strung on her best days. Patrick's murder sent her into a tailspin. I'd like to know what idiot left this doll for her. That was the last thing in the world she needed."

"Where's Blake?" I asked.

"I sent him to the car to get his duffel bag with the costume in it. He should be back any minute."

"Would it be okay if I peeked in on Maggie and said hello?" Thank goodness she would be all right.

"Sure." Dash pointed me in the direction of her ER room.

I followed the direction of his finger.

"Sophie! Wait." I was reaching for the door handle when Dash jogged over to me.

He bent his head to whisper in my ear. "Maggie doesn't know that Blake is dressing as a vampire this Halloween. She has an irrational fear of vampires. Stupid, I know, but it would be better if you didn't mention it."

I pulled back to face him but kept my voice low. "How could his mother not know about his Halloween costume?"

Dash tilted his head from side to side and exhaled. "It's complicated. That's why I've been picking him up. He leaves it at my place or in my car so she won't know about it."

"Do you realize that Patrick found vampire teeth in Blake's bedroom?"

He whisked a hand through the air but spoke softly in spite of his aggravation. "Is there anyone who didn't hear about that? Didn't you have wax lips as a kid? Sheesh. The way Patrick carried on you would have thought they found heroin in Blake's room."

"I'll try to steer clear of vampires," I assured him.

He nodded and pushed the door open for me.

Maggie was sitting up, looking none the worse for the wear. "Do you have a cigarette?"

"I'm sorry, I don't smoke."

She twisted in the bed restlessly. "They took mine away from me. You'd think they would understand that I need them to calm my nerves." Her eyes narrowed. "You're Mars's friend."

Close enough. "Yes. We spoke the other day about Blake when you dropped him off at the haunted house."

"Could you hand me my purse?"

I hoped there weren't cigarettes hidden in it but handed it to her anyway.

Maggie dug deep in the bag. "Here it is." She withdrew a mirror, and with all the drama of an old vampire-slaying movie, she turned it toward me and leaned forward to look at my reflection.

I could see it, and I guessed she could, too.

She held it up and tried to examine her neck. Her voice broke when she said, "I can't see. Do I have a bite?"

Fear welled up in me. What would I say if

she had two bloody dots on her neck? Fortunately, she didn't, and I realized that she had briefly sucked me into her hysteria.

She cupped her forehead in her palm. "I was so worried that I only had three days to live. Patrick didn't even get *that*."

What could I possibly say to ease her mind? "I received one of those dolls, too."

She sat up in alarm. "When?"

"We found it yesterday morning."

She reached for my hand with both of hers. "You have less than thirty-six hours left. You mustn't be alone. Do you understand? I'll call Mars and explain it to him. He has to protect you. I'm sure you have silver jewelry. Wear it all, especially necklaces and crucifixes."

Very nice, Sophie. Not only did you fall right into the vampire trap, but you've managed to exacerbate the situation. I had no idea what to say. Would she become agitated if I told her I didn't believe in vampires? I couldn't take that chance. It was probably best if I humored her.

"Do you need anything?" I asked.

"Garlic. I don't have any garlic."

Were the grocers in Old Town experiencing an unprecedented run on garlic? I smiled and promised I would tell Dash.

She reached out and clutched my arm.

"I'm sorry, Sophie. I'm so, so sorry. We could have been friends. I have to warn you, though — don't come after me when you're immortal and you need to drink blood. I'll fight you with everything I have."

With that unsettling notion, I backed out of the room and bumped into Dash, who must have been waiting outside the door.

"It's called sanguivoriphobia," he said. "Fear of vampires. She can't help it. She's seen countless shrinks, but she can't let it go."

"That's why she has so many mirrors in her house?"

"She usually wears one on a chain, too." He massaged the back of his neck. "Most of the time it doesn't interfere with her life, not too much anyway. She coped very well until Patrick's death. I suspect it was important to Blake to dress as a vampire to overcome the fears she tried to instill in him. He needed to prove to himself that nothing adverse would happen. That he could take the costume off, and it would never mean anything more than playing a character. That it was only pretend."

"No wonder Patrick's death threw her. Not only was she dealing with losing someone she loved, but . . ." I stopped talking as I put it all together. ". . . The marks on his neck. She's afraid that Patrick is immortal and will return to her to bite her! Poor Maggie!"

"She'll get over it once the vampire hullabaloo dies down again. Until then, she needs to be sheltered from inane rumors. I don't know how this will all play out. Before Patrick's death, Blake asked if he could live with me." He tried to smile, but I could see sadness in his expression. "You must think we're nuts. Most of the time, Maggie is functional, and we're lucky to have such a great kid. Look, I've told Wolf about Maggie's sanguivoriphobia, but other than that, only family and some close friends know about it. I'd appreciate it if you could keep it quiet. I can't afford to be known as the vampire-fearing car dealer."

Blake ran up to us carrying a large duffel bag. "Thanks for picking me up, Ms. Winston."

"I'm glad to help. Are you ready to go?"

Dash flashed me a look that I interpreted to mean *please get him out of here.*

I waved at Wolf and hustled Blake to my car. We were pulling out of the parking garage when Blake leaned forward and twisted to get a better look at a car that had stopped for a parking voucher.

"Is that Heather and her dad?" I asked.

Blake's mouth worked into a half smile. "Yeah."

I wished I could see into his head and know if he and Heather had cooked up something. I didn't want to overstep my boundaries by questioning Blake, but the news that someone had left a dead doll on Maggie's doorstep changed everything. I had hoped Heather had left that chilling doll on our doorstep, but why would she leave one for Maggie? If she was chasing Blake, as the girls believed, and as she'd demonstrated through her attention to him, why would she want to scare his mother — or him, for that matter?

The appearance of that doll had shifted my theories. It connected us in some way to Maggie and Blake. The person who left it must have meant to scare or warn us. If it was intended as a warning, it didn't make sense that the doll would land on Patrick and Maggie's doorstep *after* Patrick's death. If the killer left the dolls, wouldn't he have sent his ominous message before Patrick's death?

Unless I missed my guess, Dash, and maybe Dash's lawyer, had told Blake not to talk about the night Patrick was murdered. I went with a broader question that didn't point a finger at Blake. "Who do you think

264

killed Patrick?"

He didn't pause for a second. "Ray Barnett. The guy who runs that old junk shop."

The car swerved a bit. I hadn't expected to hear that. "Why would you think Ray killed him?"

"Patrick complained about him all the time. Not just regular griping. He accused Ray of stuff."

"What kind of stuff?"

"Patrick blamed Ray for putting his candle shop out of business. My dad says that Patrick has a lousy head for financial matters, but Patrick claimed Ray charged too much rent and refused to repair the building. They were always fighting about it. Patrick got behind on the rent, so my mom paid it for a few months. I thought my dad would bust his guts over that. Man, was he mad. So then Mom quit paying Patrick's rent, and Ray used to call the house all the time bugging Patrick for the money. Patrick said Ray cheated him and he wouldn't pay Ray if his life depended on it."

Maybe it had. Ray told me he had put out the word that no one should do business with Patrick. Had Patrick threatened Ray? Had their argument escalated to the point where Ray had done Patrick in?

I glanced over at Blake, who must have

gotten a gene for calmness in the face of crisis from Dash. He certainly hadn't received it from Maggie.

"Everybody hated Patrick. I don't know why my mom kept him around. My dad didn't like Patrick, either. He said Patrick was a moocher, a leach who would latch onto somebody and suck them dry."

I guessed Dash's ears must be ringing by now. Blake apparently had no filter regarding what he repeated.

He studied his hands. "Did you know that I'm a suspect?"

Yikes! I chose my words carefully. "You didn't make your hatred of Patrick a secret."

"You can hate a person without killing him. I hate a kid on the tennis team who thinks he's better than the rest of us, but I wouldn't kill him." He snorted. "I might put itching powder in his shorts, but he wouldn't be worth going to jail for."

I hadn't spent much time getting to know Blake. Maybe Jen and the others were right about him. For a young teen, he seemed fairly levelheaded.

I slowed as we cruised into Old Town and the number of pedestrians increased. We drove by Hart Wine, and I hit the brakes in shock.

266

NINETEEN

Dear Sophie,
After many years of fun Halloween parties, my twin daughters have declared this year's party a no-costume zone. They're at the age where nothing is cool enough. I'm afraid this party will be a complete disaster. What can I do about this no-costume edict?
— Party Mom in Seven Devils,
North Carolina

Dear Party Mom,
Don't worry, they'll outgrow the I'm-too-cool-for-a-costume stage. In the meantime, buy an assortment of hats at secondhand and thrift shops — enough for each guest to have one, plus a few extra. Provide a few pots of Halloween makeup in the powder room, and even your girls will get into the fun when their

guests wear funky hats and makeup!

— Sophie

A life-sized vampire with a skull for a face stood in the show window of Hart Wine. Above him hung a banner that read *"A Taste of Immortality."* Bottles of wine surrounded him, stacked on boxes. I had a hunch they were Vampire wines.

"Pretty cool, huh?" said Blake. "Everybody is talking about it."

Blake might have been impressed, but to me it meant Frank had access to a vampire costume. "When did he put it up?"

"I don't know. Around the beginning of the month, I think."

The person in the car behind me honked. I had stopped traffic. Reluctantly, I pressed the gas pedal and my SUV rolled on, but Frank still dominated my thoughts. So many people had suggested that the killer left a vampire bite on Patrick's neck for publicity. I'd thought it ridiculous. What kind of person would kill for publicity? Frank's chilling Taste of Immortality promotion forced me to reconsider. Frank had attended the party, clearly placing him at the scene of the crime. Natasha or Leon would know if he'd dressed as a vampire.

I dropped Blake off in front of the haunted

house. To my amazement, a line of eager people had already formed even though the scheduled opening time wasn't for another forty-five minutes. When Blake was safely inside, I drove toward my own house, looking for a parking place on the street. Fortunately, I was able to find a spot close to home.

Mindful of the time, I hurried along the brick sidewalk, feeling very witchy in my costume. Pumpkins and elegant fall wreaths decorated the old homes I passed, and dry leaves crunched under my boots.

I seemed to be making a lot of noise in my rush. I paused for a second and heard footsteps behind me. The horror of my attack overwhelmed me, and I ran like the devil pursued me.

My breath came heavy and a burning sensation hit my chest. I stopped, bent over to catch my breath, and looked back. I didn't see anyone who appeared to be following me. Straightening up, I noted that a nearby service gate swung as though someone had just gone through it. Was someone hiding behind it?

Across the street, people walked along, enjoying the weather and historical ambiance of Old Town. Their relaxed demeanor made me chide myself for overreacting.

Those old gates swung in breezes all the time. And the cracking leaves I'd heard were probably just rustling in the wind.

I turned and continued on my way, but I did jaywalk across the street to be closer to the calm tourists. In spite of myself, I looked over my shoulder every few minutes. When I saw a figure on the other side of the street dodge behind a delivery van, I no longer thought my panic ridiculous. I sprinted ahead, winding my way between people who strolled and paused to examine store windows.

Unfortunately, to reach the haunted house, I had to cross the street again, which would put me closer to my stalker. In case he had followed me to the other side, I jogged between cars in slow-moving traffic. When I reached the corner, I fled for the haunted house, flung open the door, and slammed it shut behind me.

Wanda, seated at her fortune-telling table, frowned at me.

Mars emerged from the lair dressed in his Gomez Addams outfit. "There you are! Everything okay? You're out of breath."

"He's following me," I croaked.

"Where? Did you see him? I'll nab him." He reached for the doorknob.

"I didn't get a good look."

270

"Soph! Should I man the front door, so I can watch who comes and goes?" He winked at me and pretended to kiss my arm from fingers to shoulder, but it didn't feel like he was pretending.

Ordinarily, I wouldn't have thought a thing about it, but after our moment last night, I forced myself to pull away and straighten my witch costume. Putting on a smile, I pretended to be fine, took a deep breath, and entered the lair.

June had already replenished the caramel apples and treat bags. An ominous cloud wafted from the cauldron.

"Thanks for taking care of all this, June."

"My pleasure. I hear Blake's mother will recover?"

I drew the gauzy window covering aside to see if my stalker was watching. "She'll be . . ."

Two vampires tapped the window and flashed their fangs.

I screeched.

June ran to my aid. "A little Halloween scare. Are you all right, dear?"

What could I say? No matter how much I wanted to deny it, my nerves were frayed.

The vampires high-fived and waved at us.

June smiled and waved back at them. "Isn't it marvelous that men in their early

271

twenties would dress in heavily ruffled white shirts and black leather jackets cut in a style that would have pleased George Washington? And in his old stomping grounds at that."

Fighting my fear, I looked out the window again. Detective Kenner walked by. Where had he been when I was being followed?

People waited patiently for us to open the doors. Adorable three-foot-tall princesses and a short frog, several superheroes, ghouls, and rock stars waited among the vampires. Many had removed masks and some only wore makeup, but the ones with masks that pulled over their heads, completely concealing their identities, worried me.

"Lovely," I choked. I dashed to the kitchen and searched the closet for a leftover piece of cardboard and a marker. There wasn't time to fashion anything cute, so I simply wrote in block letters, "PLEASE REMOVE ALL MASKS BEFORE ENTERING." That should do the trick. At least we would be able to see who toured the house.

I breathed a sigh of relief. Surrounded by friends, I would be safe. It was time to open the haunted house and let the fun begin.

When I opened the door to post the sign, Jesse rushed in with his mom, Dana. Humphrey followed behind them.

"So sorry we're late." Dana grimaced. "This was Jesse's idea. I hope it's okay." She wore a pink 1950s poodle skirt with a demure black top and apron. She'd used white makeup all over her face and drawn black circles around her eyes, a black triangle on her nose, and garish grinning teeth over her lips, giving her pretty face the look of a skull.

"Isn't it cool?" asked Jesse. "She can pretend to be cooking in the kitchen and then when she turns around — whammo — she's a skeleton!"

Dana giggled. "This is fun, even for adults. You've got quite a crowd out there."

Upstairs, someone screamed. A shiver-down-to-your-toes scream.

"Wow," said Dana. "Is that a recording? It's very effective."

We'd listened to all our spooky CDs repeatedly the day before. "That was real." I cautioned myself not to overreact since it was probably one of the kids scaring another one.

A door slammed and we heard the scream again. I rushed to the foot of the stairs. Natasha stood at the top, clutching her heart as though she was about to collapse.

"You okay?" I asked.

"You could have told me there's a body in the coffin!" She gripped the stair rail for support.

I had a strong hunch that someone was playing a trick on her, but I hastened up the stairs with Mars right behind me. I opened the door carefully, but nothing appeared to be amiss.

Mars lifted the lid on the casket. "Trying to get us in the spirit, Nat?"

One hand still on her chest, she inched over to look inside. "There was somebody in there. Really. He had fangs! And . . . and a vampire cape folded over him. His hands were crossed over his chest."

"It wasn't me," said Blake. "I was with Vegas. Right?"

Vegas blushed. Her black lipstick had smeared. A hundred and one adults in the house, and we still couldn't stop them from smooching.

"Sophie, the window in Viktor's room was open again when I got here this morning." Blake spoke earnestly. I didn't think he meant to pull my leg.

"Did anyone open it?" I asked.

We all looked around at each other, but if the prankster was present, he didn't speak up.

"Who cares about a window? There was a

vampire in that casket!"

I didn't want to embarrass Natasha in front of the kids. "Great prank, Natasha! You had us all going. Everybody back to your stations."

They filed out, a lucky thing because Natasha grew stormy. "He was there! I am not making this up. You're acting like I'm pretending."

Mars placed a reassuring hand on Natasha's arm. "It's Halloween. I'm sure someone was playing a prank."

She yanked her arm away from him. "Perhaps you didn't notice that the door slammed behind me. How did that prankster get out of the room?"

"He probably slipped out right behind you. What are you doing here anyway?"

Her eyes narrowed. "Why shouldn't I be here? You, Vegas, my mom — our entire household is here."

"Why don't you join the first group going through the house?" I suggested. "I bet you'd enjoy it."

"To hear that ridiculous story about a vampire that June told my mother? Honestly, June shouldn't be walking around on the streets anymore. She's delusional."

Just yesterday Natasha had talked as though she believed in vampires. We'd been through this before with her. I couldn't grasp why she thought it normal for her own mother to believe in the supernatural, but she couldn't deal with that sort of behavior from June. I turned slowly, hoping no one, and especially not June, had heard Natasha.

June stood in the doorway, her face flushed, her lips drawn into bitter lines. She huffed and retreated down the stairs.

Mars massaged his forehead. "Don't start that again, Natasha. Now, go home. All you've done is cause a ruckus."

She drew herself erect and glided past me on her way out. "There was a vampire in that casket — I'm telling you."

I didn't envy Mars. He had two women on his hands who were undoubtedly angry with one another and would put him in the middle.

"Are we ready?" Jen's voice echoed up the stairs.

Blake hustled in to take his place as the vampire. I was relieved I didn't have to deal with Natasha and her issues at the moment. I ducked down the back stairs and the show was under way.

Dash arrived two hours later wrapped like a mummy. Blake had begged him not to hang out in the vampire's bedroom, so he'd agreed to float from room to room to graveyard. If I hadn't recognized his voice, I wouldn't have known who was wrapped in those shreds.

"How's Maggie?" I asked.

"Worried about you!"

We could hear a group coming through the kitchen. They shrieked, no doubt at Dana. Dash raised his arms and held them out like a sleepwalker. He marched to the kitchen like a stiff mummy and the gleeful screams rang out again.

I smiled for the first time in hours. Patrick's killer had placed a curse on Maggie and me. I hoped I wasn't quite as nervous as Maggie yet, but I was certain I'd been followed to the haunted house.

A soft touch on my shoulder made me swing around, fists clenched. Bernie raised his hands as though I held a gun. "Mars just told me about the killer attacking you and the plan to sleep over. I'm going to trade off with Mars and Humphrey. Dash says that Maggie has friends lined up to stay with her. We can do the same for you."

It was a lovely thought, but I hated feeling so needy. "I am not san-guin-vor-iphobic or whatever it's called."

"Of course you're not. But under the costume there was a live, breathing killer, and for some reason, he wants to exact his vengeance on you. We're not going to give him the opportunity."

I had mixed feelings. What wonderful friends I had. They were willing to give up the comforts of their own homes just to watch over me. On the other hand, I *hated* imposing on them. Reaching out, I hugged Bernie. "Thank you."

He returned to his house-haunting duties, and June waltzed over to me. "Such a lovely boy. I don't understand why he's not married. Your generation is a mystery to me."

I hadn't given Bernie's marital status much thought. "I guess he's busy running the restaurant. He probably doesn't have much time to date."

She leaned toward me and whispered, "Dana's completely in love with his British accent."

"June! You little matchmaker."

She grinned. "What's life without a little love?"

I handed bags of candy to children, but my mind wasn't on my job. In between tours, I hurried up the back stairs to find Nina.

"What are you doing here?" she hissed.

"Will you come with me when we're done here tonight? I need to do a little nosing around."

She perked up. "You bet! Count me in."

I scuttled across the hall to Mars. "Could you watch the girls for a few hours tonight? Maybe take them out for pizza?"

"Sure."

I could hear the tour coming through and dashed down to the kitchen and through to the lair. Minutes later, when I was handing out treats, Mars showed up.

"Do you have a date with Wolf?"

"Wolf? No, I have plans with Nina."

"Oh. Okay." He disappeared into the kitchen, and I could hear his footsteps on the stairs.

Officer Wong burst through the gaggle of kids exiting. "I thought all of Old Town came through here yesterday, but the line outside seems even longer tonight. And the merchants on this street are making the most of it. Did you know that Ray has set out an ancient soft drink machine? He's making a bundle."

June lifted an eyebrow. "He jumps on every opportunity, doesn't he?"

Wong motioned for her to come closer to us. "I called my granny to ask her what she remembered about your Viktor Luca. She almost got the vapors just hearing his name."

That piqued June's interest. "Your granny

knew him?"

"She used to help out the Widow Nagle. Did a lot of the baking for her."

"Is your granny Opal Jones?" asked June.

Wong smiled. "Do you know her?"

"Know her? Opal was famous for her sweet potato pie. She made it for the Widow Nagle to serve to her boarders."

"She's living in Florida, but she still bakes those sweet potato pies for a local restaurant down there."

June focused on me. "You see? I'm not a loon like Natasha thinks. Other people remember Viktor."

"Granny couldn't believe it when I brought up his name. She said she has nightmares about him. That she'd be here, in the kitchen, stirring something on the stove, and without any warning, he would be behind her, watching. No footsteps, no sound at all, like he appeared out of thin air. She said dove necklaces were really popular with the peace movement and all, and a lot of people wore them, but Viktor wore a necklace with a bat on it that grossed her out."

June clasped her hands in excitement. "We found pictures of him wearing that bat. It was silver with glowing ruby eyes."

"Granny said it looked silver, but he

refused to touch silver. Not even when Mrs. Nagle brought out her good silver flatware. He wouldn't eat with it. He insisted on using stainless. Granny thinks the bat was white gold."

June beamed. "You kids thought I was making all this up. Viktor was a vampire."

Was I the only person in the world who didn't believe that vampires exist? I didn't know Wong well enough to read her yet.

"Did you know about the cat?" Wong asked June.

TWENTY

Dear Natasha,
I love Halloween, but my apartment complex restricts what I'm allowed to do outside on my doorstep. I refuse to allow them to squelch my Halloween spirit, though! What can I do in my windows for maximum impact?
  — Sneaky One in Trickum, Georgia

Dear Sneaky One,
Surely they can't complain if your lights are turned on. Dangle black cutouts of spiders, scary cats, and ghostly images in your windows and be sure the lights are on to highlight them! The scarier, the better!

  — Natasha

"The black cat! I'd forgotten all about it," said June.

Wong eagerly filled me in. "There was a

282

huge black cat, solid black, no white what-soever. It hated Viktor. It would hang out in the backyard and screech like a Halloween cat when it saw him."

"It was a stray," added June. "He loathed that cat. It would show up in the oddest places, like it was following him." She gasped. "Like that cat Nina is looking for!"

Wong looked at me. "Is that true? There's a black cat on the loose?"

No amount of coaxing or bribes could possibly have persuaded me to reveal the fact that the murderer nearly tripped over a black cat when he ran from the scene of the crime. I wasn't going to feed the vampire hysteria.

I tilted my head. "Don't you think there's usually a stray black cat around?"

June made a little sputtering noise as though she was pooh-poohing me. "Officer Wong, we're having a midnight meal at Sophie's house tomorrow night." She lowered her head a bit in a coy manner. "You know, that's when the dead are best able to communicate. Won't you come? It's a buffet. Maybe you could bring Opal's sweet potato pie?"

"I would if she'd share the recipe! I made her promise to write it down and put it in a safe so I can inherit it. Maybe I can coax it out of her with information about the black cat and Viktor. She's afraid Viktor is back and warned me not to end up like Peggy!"

Fortunately, I could hear another group coming through. I tried to wind up the conversation on a realistic note. "I'm sure Peggy died of natural causes."

Wong snapped her fingers. "Of course. They must have performed an autopsy." She waved good-bye to June and me and fled before the oncoming troop of ghosts and goblins.

At eight o'clock, I was thrilled to close for the night. Only one more night to go. The next day would be Halloween and the insane vampire craze would finally fade away.

I sought out Jen. "Sweetie, you're having dinner with Mars and Vegas tonight, okay?"

Her face wrinkled in dismay. "Who will protect you?"

"Nina. We're . . . going to visit a sick friend." I hated lying, but if I wasn't careful, Jen would insist on coming with us. Besides, it wasn't a total lie. I did hope to stop by Maggie's house.

She cast a suspicious glance my way. "All right. But you better be careful. Do you have your cell phone?"

I pulled it out of my pocket. Even better, I

retrieved my bag and returned Jen's cell phone to her.

She wrapped her arms around me. "Thanks for having faith in me."

Excited chatter filled the house as the participants filed out. I locked the front door behind them and we scattered in all directions.

Nina grinned at me. "You're wearing that?"

I smoothed the skirt of my witch outfit. "I don't want to waste time going home to change. Come on."

"Where are we going?"

"Hart Wine."

"Ohhh, you picked the right gal for that. I love to haunt wine and liquor stores."

"Do you know anything about it?" I asked.

"I know I never shop there. Frank's prices are way too high. You can buy the same thing a couple of blocks away for significantly less. What are we shopping for?"

"Nothing. We're sleuthing."

"Interesting. I assume this has something to do with Patrick's murder?"

I talked as we walked. We didn't have much time before the store closed. "Frank was at Mars and Natasha's party the night of the murder, placing him at the scene. The next night, when Mars and I went to Maggie's house, someone hid from me and there were two empty glasses in the sink. His car was parked half a block away from Maggie's house."

"The night after Patrick died? That's fast! Unless they'd been seeing each other all along."

"That's what Mars said. Then Humphrey asked why anyone would go to the trouble of making it appear that a vampire killed Patrick. I couldn't imagine a good reason, but it turns out that" — we stopped in front of Hart Wine — "well, you can see for yourself. Frank Hart is using the vampire excitement to sell wine."

We walked into the store, which was silent except for the sound of a ticking clock. A bored clerk leaned against the wall behind the cash register, texting on a phone.

"Pretty quiet in here," I said.

"Yeah."

Evidently, he wasn't the talkative sort. "Is the vampire in the window bringing in business?"

He slid his phone under the counter. "You'd think so. A lot of people stop and look at it, but they don't usually come in. You interested in a bottle of wine? The Vampire wine is actually pretty good."

Nina had migrated toward the cash register. "Do I smell licorice?"

"Everybody asks that. You're probably smelling the licorice sticks we sell." He pointed to a jar full of black licorice. Some people think eating licorice when they drink red wine brings out the nuances." He straightened the Vampire wine bottles. "Frank is into gimmicks."

"Is it always this dead?" I asked.

He shrugged. "It is when I'm here. But hey, Frank's usually on time with my paycheck and that's all I care about."

I felt obligated to buy something. I picked out a bottle of ChocoVine, a French Cabernet combined with chocolate, and paid four dollars more for it than I would have at the grocery store.

We thanked him and left. "I think we have our man. The place reeked of licorice!" I hated what it would do to Gabriel. The darling little boy with everything going for him would soon see his world collapse. "I guess I should call Wolf and tell him." I pulled out my cell phone.

In front of the gruesome skeleton vampire in the window, Nina grabbed my elbow. "Tell him to come right away. We have company."

"Where?"

"He's standing in a dark, recessed doorway across the street, watching us."

I tried not to be obvious, but there was no way to see across the street without turning around. I lifted my arm and pretended to look at a watch even though I wasn't wearing one. My heart pounded in my ears, but I reasoned that the search for the killer might soon be over. Nina and I needed to keep him engaged until Wolf arrived. My head bent, I raised my eyes to look for him. If Nina hadn't pointed him out, I never would have noticed him lurking there. I could make out the outline of a person, but little more.

"Let's move away from the show window so it won't be so obvious that I'm calling someone." I inserted an earbud in my ear and pressed in Wolf's number while we strolled.

When Wolf answered, I told him where we were and that the killer was behind us.

"Stay on the line with me and head toward King Street where there are lots of people."

"No problem. We're already doing that."

"I'm just a few blocks away in my car. Don't turn to look for me. I'm hoping I can spot him from behind."

More to Nina than to Wolf, I said, "He must have been watching Bubble and Trouble. He probably tailed us from there when we closed up. Wolf, we're turning south onto King Street." I welcomed the brighter lights and bustle of pedestrians.

"Slow down," Wolf replied. "We're not going to be able to identify this guy once he makes it onto King Street and mixes with the crowds."

A restaurant door to our right burst open and teenagers in costumes poured out onto the sidewalk. Whooping and hollering, they danced and ran with youthful exuberance across the street where Wolf was driving. There were so many of them, I thought they would never stop streaming past us.

I heard Wolf grunt. "Where did the circus come from?"

Circus was the perfect description. The kids wore colorful costumes, some danced, some walked backward, a couple swung around the lampposts. It was the worst imaginable timing.

"You lost him, didn't you?" I asked. "Where are you?" I tugged at Nina and we retraced our footsteps.

Wolf walked toward us on the side street. "What a lousy break."

"No worries. We figured out who the killer is. It's Frank Hart. He's having an affair with Maggie."

Wolf rarely showed much emotion, but

this time his face registered surprise. "Frank?"

I explained about the licorice connection.

Wolf rubbed his forehead before slinging an arm around me.

Nina flashed me a grin. "You're so adorable together."

"I appreciate the help. Really, I do. But I can't base a case on licorice. Do you know how many people eat licorice? A lot of them probably buy it at Frank's store."

"But what about his affair with Maggie?" protested Nina.

"Don't worry, we'll be looking into that." He gently squeezed my shoulder. "You didn't actually see him at Maggie's house, right? It could have been someone else."

I wrenched away from him. "Excuse me. He was with Maggie when she found the dead doll, and he's the one who accompanied her to the hospital."

"Maybe they're just friends. Maybe Frank was a buddy of Patrick's and he's helping her get through a rough time," said Wolf.

"That's not how it looks to me." Nina frowned at him.

"I'm not saying that Frank isn't our guy." Wolf maintained his cool. "But I have to be able to make a case against a suspect. I can't just arrest someone on suspicion of a love affair and a fondness for licorice."

He could not have said it in a nicer way. No sarcasm, frustration, or anger tinged his voice.

I felt a fool. Of course he needed more information. "I'm sorry. I was just so eager to pin this on him and get him off the streets. It was totally selfish of me. I'm looking over my shoulder with every step I take and overreacting to the smallest things. I guess I wanted to have it over with."

"Who could blame you?" Nina shot me a sympathetic look. "I was a basket case when I thought someone was after me last year." She scowled at Wolf. "Don't you have any leads yet?"

He suppressed a smile and leaned over to kiss my cheek. "None that I can share with the likes of you. Be careful, Soph."

He strode away into the night, and Nina tugged at me. "Visiting a wine store without sampling anything is just a cruel tease. C'mon, I need a drink."

It was the least I could do for her since she'd been kind enough to come along and protect me. "Think we should walk up to Bernie's? The killer might still be hanging around here."

"We might learn more by sticking around Frank's neighborhood. Maybe we'll bore our stalker and he'll leave." She pulled open the door to a trendy restaurant and motioned me inside.

We settled at the bar and Nina ordered an Immortal Kiss.

The bartender, a young fellow with a bohemian goatee, said, "Mrs. Norwood, I have no idea what that is." Nina rose, and he held up his outstretched palm. "Hold it! I got into a lot of trouble the last time you came behind the bar to mix your own drink."

"Then you'll have to make it for me." Nina rattled off the ingredients as the bartender raced to keep up. "Parrot Bay Passion Fruit Rum and Absolut Raspberri. Oh! And a splash of ginger ale. Don't you want one, Sophie? Soph?"

The din in the room faded, and I was only marginally aware of Nina's question. She might have moved on to fun drinks, but my mind still focused on the person who attacked me and killed Patrick. Right in front of me, at the other end of the bar, one of the suspects lifted his glass to me in a toast.

TWENTY-ONE

Dear Sophie,
My wife spent a small fortune on Halloween decorations. In spite of our efforts, our front porch, lawn, and foyer don't look spooky. What can we do to jazz up our decor?
— Perfectly Boring in Boos, Illinois

Dear Perfectly Boring,
Adding a few imperfections will put the spook into your decor. Don't line up decorations perfectly, and don't make them symmetrical. Think off-kilter! Leaning tombstones, rusty lanterns, drooping spiderwebs, and the unexpected will provide the spooky punch you seek.

— Sophie

I shivered even though he was just being sociable. Red flags jumped up in my head, warning me that someone had been tailing Nina and me, and that it might just be the guy at the end of the bar. Leon collected his drink and napkin and made his way through the crowd toward us.

"Sophie, what's wrong with you? Give her an Immortal Kiss, too." Nina nudged me. "What is it?"

By that time, Leon had reached us. I did my best to hide my angst. "Have you met Leon? He's Natasha's new assistant. This is Nina Reid Norwood. She lives on our block."

"Natasha's assistant? You poor thing!" Nina clapped a couple of fingers over her mouth. "Or are you one of her adoring minions?"

"Is Nina friend or foe?" he asked me.

"Friend." I chuckled at his question and some of my fears abated. He seemed like a nice guy.

"Let's get a table so we can talk." Nina moved us all to a tiny table in the corner. I sat with my back to the wall, just in case another suspect showed up.

The bartender followed with our drinks.

"So give us the dirt on Natasha." Nina sipped her drink.

"She's frantic about Patrick's murder and the impact it will have on her reputation.

Honestly, I hope the boys in blue catch the killer before she does because I think I'd rather face the law than Natasha's wrath."

"She's looking for the killer?" Nina asked.

"Mostly lip service. It's all she talks about."

I sipped my Immortal Kiss, surprised by the fruity flavor. "Who does Natasha suspect?"

"She's obsessed with Maggie. One of these days I'll walk in and find she has fashioned a chart of Maggie's movements that night. Frankly, though, I think it's because she's still irritated that Maggie wore a Morticia Addams outfit and stole Natasha's thunder."

Nina giggled. "I'm sorry I missed that! Ohhh, I wonder if I could find a Morticia Addams dress by tomorrow night. I bet Natasha will wear hers, and it would aggravate her to no end if I turned up in one, too." She leaned toward Leon. "We're having a midnight buffet at Sophie's house tomorrow night. You have to come. It's potluck, so bring something."

Leon sat up straighter. "Really? I'd love to come. But I can promise you one thing — I'm not dressing as a vampire this time. I was mortified to see so many other vampires at Natasha's party."

A perfect opportunity to find out about Frank. "What was Frank Hart wearing that night?"

Leon lifted his eyebrows. In a dusky tone, he said, "Frank, eh? You know, I remember him talking with Patrick."

"What was he wearing?"

"De rigueur for men in attendance, vampire deluxe."

Nina signaled the bartender for another round of drinks. I clamped my hand over the top of my glass. I needed my wits about me.

"Did you know Patrick?" I asked.

Leon shifted in his chair uncomfortably.

"You can tell *us!*" A stranger listening in would have thought Nina was an old confidant of Leon's.

"Promise you won't inform Natasha? She'd fire me if she found out."

Nina pretended to zip her lips with her fingers.

"I worked for Patrick. One painfully long month, I worked in his candle shop. Now, I'm not saying I'm a clever businessman, but, honey, I understand retail, and I know how to set up a display. Patrick had no imagination whatsoever. He thought candles should be stacked like cat food cans in a grocery store."

Nina took a long swig of her drink. "Why shouldn't Natasha know that?"

"Because he fired me. If she finds out, she'll do the same." Leon's chest heaved. "He was supposed to pay me every two weeks. He didn't pay me after the first two weeks, but I let it go because I knew we didn't sell much. I figured he would pay me as soon as he could. When two more weeks passed, I had to tell him I couldn't continue to work without a paycheck. That louse accused me of stealing cash from the register. Nothing could be more untrue. It just isn't in my nature to do anything like that. All he had to do was compare inventory to receipts to prove it. I might poke fun at people and enjoy having a good time, but I'm not a thief. Heaven knows I'm not perfect, but my momma did not raise any sticky-fingered children."

"Did he ever pay you?" asked Nina.

"The crook blackmailed me. I went back to the store to insist he pay me, and he threatened to tell everyone I'd stolen from him. What could I do? How do you prove you didn't do something? I couldn't force him to do an inventory or show me his books. It was cowardly of me, but I backed away. I didn't know how to fight him. He had a lot of clout in this community, and I couldn't afford to be known as a thief — even if it wasn't true." Leon emptied his drink in one long gulp. "Oh dear, I'm sure I'm cursed now that I've spoken ill of the dead."

If that was the case, Leon wouldn't be the only cursed resident of Old Town. "Did you ever see Patrick argue with anyone else?"

"He must be turning in his grave like a rotisserie chicken with all this nasty gossip about him." He paused and leaned over the table as though he was speaking confidentially. "Ray from next door came in all the time. At first I thought he was snooping, but it turned out that Patrick hadn't paid his rent, and the old coot wanted to see if we were selling anything. It's quite ironic, really. Have you seen Ray's shop? *Ugh.* If he sells one item, I bet it's a great day. If Ray didn't own the building, he would be behind on the rent, too. That old man is such a character. He acts like he just rode in from the Wild West. The way he ranted, it wouldn't surprise me one bit to find out he did Patrick in."

"Was he invited to Natasha's party?" Somehow I couldn't imagine Natasha putting Ray on her guest list of Old Town's elite.

"Are you kidding? He most certainly was

not on the guest list. I can assure you of that! I do wonder, though, if he has an alibi. How could we find out?" Leon addressed his question to Nina.

"Sophie and I will pay him a visit tomorrow morning." She finished her second drink.

"Be careful," warned Leon. "You can't come right out and ask or he'll be onto the fact that we suspect him."

Nina giggled. "Oh, darlin', Sophie and I know how to handle an interrogation. He won't know what hit him."

I wondered if Leon realized that he'd just been the victim of one of our interrogations. I whipped out my wallet and paid our check before Nina could order more drinks. "I think we'd better be on our way. I'm so glad we had this opportunity to chat with you, Leon."

"We'll see you at the Halloween party!" Nina waved and followed me out the door. "What a great guy! I feel like we have a spy in the enemy camp!"

We giggled like silly schoolgirls as we walked up King Street. "You do know that he's a suspect?" I turned the corner so we were headed east.

"No!" Nina's giggles subsided. "Do you

think he was telling the truth about being fired?"

"We're about to find out. I thought we might drop in on Maggie to see how she's doing. She would know the scoop about Leon and Patrick."

"Unless Patrick lied to her. He might not have wanted her to know his business was such a shambles."

"True," I said. "But Blake told me his mother paid the rent at Patrick's shop. She must have realized something was wrong."

"But we women can be blind to the faults of the men we love."

Nina was certainly right about that.

She slid her arm under mine so they linked at the elbow, and drew me close. "He's following us again."

I slowed and was turning my head when Nina whispered, "Don't look!"

"Would you rather he caught us off guard? We have to know where he is and cross the street or something." We'd already arrived on Maggie's block and left the hubbub and crowds of King Street behind. The only soul outside was someone parallel parking a car.

In spite of Nina's warning, I glanced back. A shadowy figure darted behind a tree. "Our best bet is to jaywalk across the street and head straight to Maggie's house." Shivers shuttled along my arms as we changed our direction and jogged across the street and up the stairs to Maggie's front door. I rang the bell somewhat impatiently and whipped around to see where he had gone.

"I've lost him. Where is he?" A note of panic had crept into Nina's voice. "Oh my gosh! The cat!"

I squinted. "Where?"

"On the other side of the street. He just ducked under someone's gate."

"Who is it?" Maggie called.

I pounded on the door. "Maggie! Let us in. Hurry! It's Sophie and a friend."

In the quiet night, we could hear a little discussion inside the house.

Nina clamped onto my arm with strength I hadn't known she possessed. "He's coming up the sidewalk!"

A man strode toward us with an assured gait.

This time Nina banged on the door.

It swung open, but Maggie's eyes didn't focus on us. "No!" she howled.

I was certain the killer must be right behind us. My feet seemed locked in position. I turned my head and saw a vampire, his cape flying out behind him, running along the other side of the street.

Nina screamed like she'd seen her mother-in-law, and the man who'd been striding toward us walked up the steps.

"What's all the fuss about?" With a fluid movement, Dash used one hand to push back his hair. A stalker he wasn't.

Nina slammed her hand over her chest. "You nearly gave me a heart attack."

"What are *you* doing here again?" Dash didn't bother to hide his annoyance.

For a split second, I thought he was talking to Nina and me, but then I realized that Karl Corbin clutched Maggie in his arms and was murmuring something soothing in her ear.

"Didn't you see the vampire?" Karl asked Dash.

Dash pushed past Karl into the house, and Nina and I quickly followed.

"So what? It's the night before Halloween and some kid ran down the street in a vampire cape. Maggie, you will be the death of me yet." Dash sucked in a huge breath of air and distorted his stunning features by vigorously rubbing his face with his hand. He disappeared into the kitchen, leaving us with Karl and Maggie, who held her hands over her nose and mouth.

She stretched her arms out to me. "I'm so glad you're still alive! I thought I would never see you again, well, unless you came to bite me." She lifted my hair off my neck and examined it with a gorgeous smile.

"Karl, honey, would you be a lamb and open a bottle of wine?" Maggie stroked his upper arm. He smiled at her and headed toward the kitchen.

She showed us to the living room and invited us to have a seat.

Dash stalked in, looking angry. In a low tone, he said, "Maggie, how many times have I warned you about Karl?"

She actually batted her eyelashes and preened. "We're divorced now, baby. You don't get to tell me who I can see."

"Karl is going to be the same kind of disastrous nightmare that Patrick was. Why do you insist on surrounding yourself with pathetic losers?"

Unfortunately, Karl had stepped in, carrying a bottle of red wine, and overheard Dash's comment. His expression remained the same, calm and irritatingly placid, just as it had the day he tried to shut down the haunted house and take Blake home. "Who is having wine? How many glasses do we need?"

When he'd returned to the kitchen, Maggie whispered, "Do you think he heard? I'd hate for Karl to be offended. He's been such a help to me."

I thought Dash might go through the roof. "Of course he heard! I want you to get rid of him, and Frank, too."

Maggie lifted her shoulders in a coyly pleased motion and grinned at us. "Don't you just love a jealous man?"

I watched Dash and Maggie carefully. There were stranger things going on between them than between Mars and me. I rushed to change the subject before Karl returned. "Maggie, did Patrick ever say anything about a guy named Leon?"

"The one who worked for him? The man was a nightmare. I know it's hard to find good help, but Patrick had nothing but problems with him. Patrick couldn't even get away for lunch when Leon was working because he couldn't trust Leon to be there alone. And when he let him go! Oh!" She threw her hands into the air. "Leon actually came back to the shop one day and threatened Patrick." Her eyes opened wide. "You think he's the vampire! Of course! The police asked me about Leon."

Dash had settled into a cushy chair and crossed his ankle over his knee. "Were you there when Leon threatened Patrick?"

"You never trusted Patrick." Maggie blinked uncomfortably. "Yes, as it happened, I was in the store at the time."

Karl finally returned carrying a tray of wineglasses and the wine bottle. He poured the wine, handed a glass to each of us, and said, *"Salud!"*

Dash eyed him. "Aren't you having any?"

Karl's unchanging expression with the pleasant smile unnerved me. "Not with the vampire on the loose."

Was he joking or serious? I couldn't tell, but he didn't pour a glass of wine for himself, and I noted that Dash refused to drink his. Moving fast to stop Nina, I accidentally knocked her glass sideways and it spilled all over her.

"Sophie!"

"I'm so sorry. What a mess."

Dash brought Nina a towel.

She dabbed at her trousers. "Ugh. I think we'd better go. I'm sopping wet." She glared at me and lifted her lip in a playful growl.

"It's getting late. Maybe we should all head home. Can I give you a lift, Karl?" Dash looked him in the eyes.

"Thanks, but I'll help Maggie clean up."

If Dash had been a cartoon character, the top of his head would have opened and steam would have poured out. He accompanied Nina and me out the door. It shut behind us, and he looked back at it, his mouth tight with anger. "Just so you know, Maggie was lying about being there when Leon threatened Patrick."

"How do you know that?" asked Nina.

"She won't go into that building."

"You're right!" I should have realized. "She refused to come into the haunted house. But why would she lie about it?"

Dash laughed, albeit somewhat bitterly. "So I wouldn't be right about Patrick. He lied to her all the time, and she's beginning to figure that out, but she won't admit it yet. You've seen her at her worst, but she can be a strong-willed and stubborn woman."

"And what was with not drinking the wine?" I put Dash on the spot, but I didn't care.

One corner of his mouth turned up and the other one turned down. "I make it a rule never to drink if the host isn't having any from the same bottle."

TWENTY-TWO

Dear Natasha,
I've been trying to think of something dif-
ferent for a Halloween party with mostly
preteen boys. Over the years, other moms
have served spaghetti brains and grape
eyeballs. What can I do that would be
fresh?
— Wicked Hostess in Bloody Corners,
Ohio

Dear Wicked Hostess,
Throw a mad scientist party. Drape a table
with black fabric. Buy beakers and test
tubes to use for drinks. Add some curling
tubing to mix cranberry juice with blueberry
juice. Decorate with microscopes. Set up
a cauldron of dry ice to waft over the table
and set the mood. Hire a magician or
friend to dress as a mad scientist and
perform tricks as entertainment. And don't
forget to hand out safety goggles to each

Nina gasped and gazed at her wet trousers. "You think he poisoned the wine?"

"Nah. He couldn't explain away that many dead bodies. I don't trust him, though. He, ah . . . well, you don't need to know the whole sordid history."

He started to walk, but I grabbed his sleeve. "Yes, I think we do need to know. Could he have killed Patrick?"

"My history with Karl has nothing to do with Patrick."

If I had learned one thing about murder, it was that everything, every tiny detail, was important. How could I get Dash to talk? "I understand his family owned your car dealership at one time?"

Dash bent his head forward and stared at the ground, which I was beginning to recognize as his pensive mode. "It was in his family for generations. His grandfather and great-uncle started it. Karl practically grew up there because his father took over from them. I guess it all seemed preordained to him. He thought the business would go on, and the money would keep flowing in, and all he had to do was cash a paycheck. But when the economy slowed, Karl's dad realized that he hadn't raised a business-man." Dash inhaled deeply. "Maggie and I got very lucky. We had started a used car lot a long time ago. That was how I met Karl's dad. He liked me, I guess because I came from the school of hardscrabble, and when he saw that the family business needed more than he could give it at his age, he made me an offer" — he held his palms up in a helpless gesture — "that I couldn't refuse. As part of the deal, I took Karl on as a salesman. As you might expect, he was childish and drove customers away, so I had to let him go. He always was sweet on Maggie, though. I've warned her about him."

Dash grunted. "Maggie doesn't get it. She thinks I'm being possessive when I caution her about the men who flock around her. They're after her money, but she can't see that. She's vulnerable and an easy target. The only silver lining in Patrick's murder is that Maggie won't be marrying him."

"I had no idea they were engaged," I said.

"Oh, yeah. Blake was incredibly upset about it. We knew Maggie was nothing but a meal ticket to Patrick. Now I have to figure out how to protect her from Karl."

"What happened to Karl's wife?" Nina buttoned her jacket and turned the collar up.

"She took off with her share of the money from the sale. It's a real shame she left Heather with her dad."

"Her mother left her?" I could hardly believe my ears. Heather had been so cruel to Vegas about her missing mom. Who would have thought it? Heather knew what would hurt Vegas because she was experiencing the same feelings of loss.

"Excuse me." Dash's eyes narrowed as a vampire rushed us from behind, veered, and ran into the street.

Dash leaped after him and gave chase for half a block.

"That guy has some moxie!" Nina beckoned to me and started to jog after him.

I had little choice but to follow. Of course, three of us would be better able to restrain the killer than just Dash alone. I pulled out my cell phone to call Wolf but only got voice mail.

Ahead of me, Dash tackled the vampire at the edge of the sidewalk. A third man emerged from the shadows and leaped on top of them. A fourth shadowy person ran across the street and joined the melee. They fell in what appeared to be a painful manner. By the time I reached them, Dash had stood up. He pulled the vampire away from the other two and shoved him behind his back.

Bernie and Humphrey lunged toward Dash until the vampire, who was an entire head shorter than Dash, peeked around at them. The person in the vampire cape was none other than Blake. He bit his upper lip and waited behind his dad, as though he expected his father to yell at him.

Panting, Bernie and Humphrey stared at Blake.

Dash asked him calmly, "What do you think you're doing?"

Blake shifted from foot to foot, almost in a rocking motion. "I thought if Mom saw a vampire when you came to the door, that she would fall into your arms. I didn't know stupid Karl would be there."

Dash pulled his son to him in a bear hug and leaned his head against Blake's. When he released Blake, Dash ran a fatherly hand over his son's mussed hair. "The next time you pull a stunt like that, tell me first so we can work out the details." Although Dash smiled, his eyes conveyed sorrow. He waved at us. "Sorry if this scamp scared you. I'd better get him home."

"Hold it!" Bernie tried to catch his breath. "I've been following Sophie for days. The killer has been tailing her, too. How do we know Blake isn't following her?"

"You?" Humphrey frowned at Bernie. "*I've* been tailing Sophie."

"Looks like you two have been chasing each other." Dash wrapped a protective arm around his son's shoulders and started toward their car. I heard him ask, "Feel like tacos tonight?"

Nina wiped her nose with a tissue and sniffled. "How sad was that? And Dash was so sweet! If I weren't married, I'd be chasing him!"

"Which one of you followed us to Hart Wine tonight?"

Both Humphrey and Bernie raised their hands.

"And which one of you followed me to the haunted house this afternoon?"

Humphrey cleared his throat. "That would have been me."

I couldn't help laughing. "You've had me so scared! Why didn't you tell me and walk with me?"

Bernie cocked his head. "You're sort of independent."

"You would have objected," said Humphrey.

They were right. They were so right! "From now on, no sneaky following me, okay?"

Nina was laughing so hard she couldn't breathe. She waved both of her hands in front of her face. "I'd like to change clothes and get some dinner. Who's up for a drink?"

The four of us started for my house.

"Soph," said Nina, "you don't think Dash killed Patrick, do you?"

"I'd have to say he's on my list of suspects. Did you see how jealous he was of Karl tonight?"

"I was afraid you would say that. So there's Ray, who is clearly sharper than he looks. He could have pulled it off. And then there's adorable, chubby Leon, who fought with Patrick about something. Whether he stole from Patrick or Patrick blackmailed him doesn't really matter, I guess. They had an altercation and there was clearly residual anger."

"Don't forget Frank and the licorice and his affair with Maggie," I added.

Humphrey cleared his throat. "I'm not sure we can eliminate Maggie herself. I don't wish to appear prudish, but does it seem to anyone else that she is involved with a lot of men? Patrick, then Frank, who is married by the way, and now apparently Karl, too?"

I couldn't help coming to Maggie's defense. "Just because we've seen her with them doesn't mean she's, um, *involved* with all of them." I wanted to honor Dash's request that I not blab about her sanguivoriphobia. "I think she's afraid to be alone. Your point is well taken, though, Humphrey. It does appear that she might have been seeing Frank prior to Patrick's death."

Bernie chimed in. "I hate to say it, but I guess we have to include little Blake. That performance tonight was touching. He really wants his mom and dad to reunite. That's a pretty powerful motive."

I nodded. "And we know he was in the area when the murder was committed."

"I guess that wraps it up. Did I leave anyone out?" asked Nina.

"Only all the men at the party who were dressed as vampires. Rats! I meant to ask Maggie about Ray tonight."

Humphrey took a detour to his car, and the rest of us walked up to my front door and let ourselves in.

The wintery scent of burning wood filled the air, and Daisy bounded to me, her tail circling like an airplane propeller. I wrapped my arms around her neck for a doggie hug and continued patting her as we walked into the kitchen.

Jen sat at the kitchen table, and Mars was poking the fire, but Vegas prowled like a

314

caged tiger.

"Hi." It was a feeble thing to say, but I wasn't sure what we were walking into. Something was afoot.

"Maggie is a vampire." Vegas handed me a photograph. In it, Maggie wore an off-the-shoulder dress with a wide red belt and a voluminous skirt. She posed in front of my dining room fireplace with Viktor Luca, who wore the bat necklace Officer Wong had told us about.

Nina peered at it and exchanged glances with Mars and me. "Where did you get this?" she asked.

Jen squirmed. "It was upstairs in one of Faye's old boxes."

"I hope it was okay to let them snoop around up there." Mars placed the brass wood poker in its stand.

I nodded. "Of course. I just don't understand this photograph. It's clearly old." I flipped it. "No writing on the back. This is the guy June said was Viktor Luca, right, girls?" I passed it to Bernie.

"We called Gramma June. She's on her way over." Jen picked up Mochie and head-butted with him.

Mars elbowed me. "Gramma June. Isn't that great?"

Nina sniffed the air. "I'm starved. I don't

smell food. Did you eat?"

"I could eat again," said Jen. "Natasha invited me to *dine* with them."

Uh-oh. No wonder she was hungry. "What was on the menu?"

"Sea urchins on weird toast, and black ink squid pasta. I think you should invite Vegas over here more often for real food." Jen wrinkled her nose. "I really don't like seeing a creature's legs and stuff when I'm eating it."

I couldn't blame her because I felt the same way. "How about mac and cheese?"

"Yes! With a little bacon?" When we laughed at him, Mars forced himself to sound more mature. "I mean real mac and cheese, not one made with sea urchins or cilantro or wine."

"Real mac and cheese," I assured him, filling a pot with water for the elbow macaroni.

Vegas licked her lip. "Can we eat it in our pajamas?"

What was with these two? "Of course."

Jen and Vegas flew out of the kitchen and up the stairs, sounding like a herd of elephants. Daisy galloped along behind them.

Mars tried to be subtle, edging toward the foyer and the stairs.

"You brought pajamas?"

"That was the deal, remember? I'm staying here to watch out for you." He shot out of the kitchen and up the stairs, no doubt to avoid my response. Ready to ditch my witch costume, I followed them and changed into Halloween pajamas.

When I returned, a soft tapping sound came from the kitchen door. Humphrey peered in at us, and Nina waltzed over to let him in.

"It's freezing out there tonight!" He placed a bundle on the fireside chair and held his hands toward the fire to warm them.

"Let me guess. Are those pajamas?"

"Why, yes. Where will I be sleeping?"

"You have a choice between the third-floor bedroom and the sofa bed in the family room."

"I'm feeling rather left out." Bernie laughed.

"It seems most logical that I would sleep on the first floor to intercept intruders," said Humphrey.

I walked into the foyer and shouted up the stairs. Jen appeared on the third-floor landing, looking down at me. I asked her to bring fresh linens for the sofa bed and returned to the kitchen, where I laid strips of bacon in a frying pan. The heavenly scent wafted up to me immediately, reminding me that I hadn't had dinner.

Nina handed Humphrey the picture of Viktor and Maggie. "Here, genius. Figure out how Maggie can be in this photograph."

"I'm not sure he knows Maggie." I popped cheeses into the food processor to shred them so they would melt quickly.

Humphrey took the photo and studied it. "I don't know her well, but we *have* met. My mortuary is handling the arrangements for Patrick." He flipped the photo over. "Is this some sort of trick? I'm told one can do almost anything on a computer. Although I don't believe they make this kind of photo stock anymore. It was popular when I was a child."

I transferred the cheeses to a pot, along with milk, butter, and chopped onion, and stirred while it all melted together.

The knocker at the door sounded. "Keep cooking. I'm starved." Bernie hurried to the foyer. He returned in seconds with June.

Stripping off gloves, June asked, "Where's Jen? Is she all right? I came as soon as I got her message."

"I'm sorry if she scared you, June." I had no sooner spoken than Jen, Vegas, and Daisy charged into the kitchen, followed by a slower and tired Mars.

"Mom!" He kissed his mother on the

cheek. "Wow, you're cold."

Bernie took her coat and hung it up in the foyer closet while June settled in a fireside chair.

"What's the problem, Jen, dear?" She gazed around at us. "Or would you rather we spoke privately?"

"It's okay if everyone hears, Gramma June." Jen spied the picture in Humphrey's hands. "May I?" She handed it to June.

"These old photos bring back so many wonderful memories. *Ugh.* There's that crazy bat Viktor always wore."

"What we want to know is — how can Maggie be in that picture?" Jen leaned over June's shoulder.

"Sweetie, that's not Maggie. It's Peggy Zane, the woman Viktor killed." A tiny shudder rippled through June's shoulders. "He must have been planning her demise even then."

Everyone except me clustered close to June for another look at the picture.

I poured the cheese mixture over the elbow noodles, spooned it into individual ramekins, and slid them all into the oven on a tray.

"They're the spitting image of each other!" Nina frowned at me. "Stick Maggie in that dress and do her hair in a 1960s flip and you couldn't possibly tell them apart."

Vegas droned somberly, "We think Maggie is a vampire. She returned to Old Town, and now Viktor is back, too, looking for her."

It took every ounce of willpower I could muster not to scream. I inhaled deeply to calm myself and spoke as quietly as possible. I had to be the voice of reason.

"Vegas, Jen, I know we've been having a lot of fun with the haunted house. It's fabulous to imagine giant spiders and zombies and werewolves, and yes, vampires. But those things don't really exist." I flashed a look of warning at June and hoped she understood that I needed her to back me up. "Vampires are creatures of our imaginations. They're fun in movies and books, but just like talking rabbits and flying pigs, they're only make-believe. Maggie is *not* a vampire."

"What about Viktor Luca?" Vegas looked to June for an answer.

I jumped in before June had a chance. There was no telling what she might say. "Viktor was an odd man who apparently killed someone and then took off. He wasn't a vampire."

June's lips drew into a tight line. "I suppose you're going to say Faye's ghost doesn't exist?"

Good grief. Couldn't she cut me a break? Ghosts weren't the problem. All eyes were on me. What could I say? I suspected that Faye's presence was in my house. More specifically right above June's head. Faye's portrait often swung to a cant for no reason. Living in this old house had opened my mind to the possibility of ghosts. If I agreed to the possibility of ghosts, though, it would undercut my argument against vampires. Not to mention that if I declared that ghosts didn't exist, I would insult June, who was convinced that she could speak with her deceased sister, Faye, in my kitchen.

"Nonsense." To my surprise, it was Humphrey who spoke up in his textbook matter-of-fact way. "One cannot compare ghosts with vampires. Ghosts are ethereal, most likely existing on another plane. While their existence is a subject of debate, there are logical theories explaining the phenomenon. Vampires, to the contrary, are completely fabricated. To start with, there's the issue of immortality, which is physically impossible. While people may choose to drink blood, there is no scientific basis for believing that it has any impact on their longevity and may frequently be the cause of death since they would be subject to the various diseases of their victims."

Were Vegas and Jen buying his explanation? They both looked pensive.

"How do you explain the fact that June saw a mausoleum with Viktor's name on it and that he had died a hundred years before?" Vegas locked her eyes on Humphrey.

"That's a very old trick. People often assume names of the dead when they wish to conceal their identities. Viktor probably saw the name and liked it. He undoubtedly thought himself clever for giving the cemetery as his address in Paris."

I shot a very grateful smile at Humphrey. He puffed up his chest, proud of himself.

While the others talked about Viktor, I checked on the macaroni and cheese. The aroma that wafted into the kitchen brought groans from my friends. Jen jumped up to set the table, and Daisy promptly sat at the island counter and offered me a paw.

"Too hot, Daisy. You have to wait." As though she understood, she wagged her tail across the floor but didn't budge.

I'd never seen everyone move so fast. I didn't have to ask anyone to help. Nina took drink orders, and Humphrey delivered them to the table. Mars donned oven mitts to deliver a piping hot ramekin to each place setting, and everyone took their seats.

"You act like you haven't eaten all day." I placed a napkin in my lap.

Their mouths were too full to respond.

Amid appreciative murmurs and occasional chatter about vampires, the mac and cheese disappeared. Vegas, Jen, Daisy, and Mars even licked their bowls.

Vegas smacked her lips. "Mars, do you think Natasha would notice if we came over here for real food once in a while?"

"I think we should try. We could tell her we've joined a fish lure tying league so she wouldn't come with us." Mars stretched and rubbed Daisy's head.

"Maybe you should suggest that Natasha vary her menu to include the things you like to eat."

Bernie, Vegas, and Mars burst into uncontrolled laughter at my suggestion. It didn't really come as a shock. Natasha might have told Karl that I was difficult, but she was the one who was unbending. I'd hoped that Vegas's living with Mars and Natasha might force Natasha to consider someone else's needs. Apparently not.

Humphrey helped me wash the dishes while Bernie, Mars, and Daisy walked June home. We all chuckled about Mars donning a coat over his pajamas for the little excursion. The girls weren't happy when I asked for their cell phones, but I wasn't taking any chances on middle-of-the-night texting. On Bernie and Mars's return, we hit the sack with a full house.

I woke from a deep sleep when Daisy jumped off my bed. Her heavy paws pounded down the wooden stairs, and I became conscious of scuffling noises under my window. I dragged myself from bed, opened the window, and looked out. Two people appeared to be fighting in front of my house. Unless I was mistaken, one grabbed the other from behind, much as the killer had attacked me.

Twenty-Three

Dear Sophie,
I'm supposed to bring a cake to my son's school for a Halloween celebration. It's a money-raising function and while all the other mommies are domestic divas, I don't bake. I've been warned not to bring a store-bought cake. What's a mom to do?
— Desperate in Ding Dong, Texas

Dear Desperate,
Get out the Ding Dongs and make a haunted house. No baking required. Use graham crackers, gummy worms, candy corn, licorice — go wild in the candy aisle. Mini chocolate bars make great roofing tiles, and don't forget to include a few marshmallow ghosts. Use royal icing as glue. I'm willing to bet your "cake" will be the most popular!
— Sophie

I shot down the stairs and opened the front door. Daisy galloped out and barked but didn't jump on the killer as she had before. Hoping he would be afraid and run, I flicked on the outdoor lights and shouted, "I'm calling the police!"

"I'm on it!" Nina ran down the stairs and headed toward the kitchen telephone.

Maybe I didn't have the strength to wrestle the killer to the ground and keep him here until the police arrived, but this time I was determined to be able to identify him. I dashed for a flashlight and flew back. Training it on the head of the attacker, I realized with a shock that Humphrey rode someone piggyback. Someone who staggered around flailing his arms as though barely able to take slender Humphrey's weight. Humphrey clung tenaciously to the person, who was dressed in black all the way up to the stocking cap he wore, concealing his hair.

Just as I was contemplating whether I should join the brawl to stop it, the groans and utterances began to sound familiar.

"Help! Sophie, don't just stand there. Help me!" A woman's voice.

Moving cautiously, I scooted to the other side of them and aimed my flashlight at the face of the person in black. "Natasha?"

"Get him off me!"

When Humphrey loosened his grip, Natasha grabbed his arm and flipped him onto the ground on his back. She applied her running-shoe-clad foot to his neck.

"Natasha!" I flicked the light on Humphrey's face so she could see him. "It's only Humphrey."

She was breathing so heavily, I wasn't sure she heard me. It must have taken a moment to register with her. "He jumped me from behind."

I reached out to Humphrey and helped him stand up.

He whacked the back of his pajama pants with his hands. "You were unlocking the door! What were you doing snooping and trying to sneak into the house? Sophie, she was going from window to window, peering in. I thought she was Patrick's killer looking for you."

Natasha straightened her oversized black sweatshirt.

"You *are* dressed like a cat burglar. I don't think I've ever seen you all in black." I'd never seen her hair stuffed under anything, either. It was always perfectly coiffed.

Nina stood in the doorway holding Mochie. "I've cancelled the cops."

"Where's Mars?" demanded Natasha.

"Upstairs, asleep." Couldn't she just have

called him instead of coming over in the dead of night?

"You couldn't come up with a better lie than that? He's clearly not here."

"See for yourself." I gestured toward the house. If she insisted on waking him, that was her business.

Natasha pushed past Nina and floated up the stairs with the grace of a beauty queen.

Humphrey and I retreated to the kitchen with Nina. I preheated the oven and scrounged in the freezer for a midnight snack.

Nina set Mochie on the window seat. "What's your preferred poison, Humphrey?"

"Poison? I didn't do anything wrong. I was trying to protect Sophie."

Nina shook her head in mock dismay. "A drink, Humphrey. I'll fix you a drink."

"Oh! Hot tea would be nice."

Nina spluttered and disappeared into the foyer.

I imagined she was on her way to fetch liquor, so I filled the kettle with water and set it on the stove to heat. "Are you okay? Need a bandage or anything?" I popped sliced frozen Quadruple Chocolate Chip Cookie dough into the oven.

Humphrey pulled back his pajama sleeves

and examined his arms. "Just bruised, I think."

"What happened?"

Nina returned with her recent favorite — butterscotch schnapps — as well as bottles of rum and Godiva chocolate liqueur. She helped herself to cordial glasses and set them on the table.

Humphrey massaged his neck. "I think Natasha has lost her mind. I woke to the sound of eerie scratching on the sliding glass door to the family room. I thought it was branches or leaves and didn't pay much attention at first. Then I remembered about the killer and looked over just in time to see her hunched over and sneaking toward the backyard. Naturally, in the dark I couldn't tell who it was. I thought the murderer had arrived to do you in. So I crept to the sunroom and watched her. I thought she was a man. She turned, ran back through the service alley, and peered into the bay window in the kitchen. I let myself out the kitchen door, tiptoed toward her, and jumped her when she tried to unlock your front door."

"Thank you so much, muttonhead. I'm going to be sore for a week." Natasha strode into the kitchen, pulled off her cap, and sat down at the kitchen table.

"Godiva?" Nina twisted the top off the bottle.

"Please." Natasha glared at Humphrey.

"Did you find Mars?" I poured herbal cinnamon apple spice tea into the black Halloween mugs for all of us.

"Yes." She didn't sound happy about it.

"Sound asleep, I guess?" I arranged the cookies on a platter and placed it in the middle of the table, along with napkins.

"That man could sleep through an erupting volcano. We'd find him the next day like the people in Pompeii, covered in lava."

Why did I suspect that she was trying to avoid the subject of her midnight raid?

"Well?" Nina swallowed a bite of cookie and leaned toward her. "Are you going to tell us why you're dressed like a ninja warrior?"

Natasha sat back in her chair and tented her fingers over her nose and mouth. She huffed a heavy sigh. "Mars is having an affair with Maggie Bennett."

I almost spewed my tea. "Why on earth would you think that?"

"A woman knows, Sophie. He took her home after Patrick was killed. He didn't have to do that. He should have stayed with me, to comfort *me*. And I have come to the sad conclusion that her appearance at my

330

party as Morticia Addams was no co-incidence. She knew he would be dressed as Morticia's husband, Gomez."

"I hardly think —"

She interrupted me. "He's entirely too happy. He keeps making excuses to be out of the house, like that nonsense about having to work on the haunted house."

"Actually," I said, "that's true. It was part of the deal."

Her eyes tightened and her mouth worked into an angry slash. "I know he's with her. I just can't catch them together."

"In that case, shouldn't you be over at Maggie's house, sneaking around her yard?" Nina plucked another cookie off the plate.

"I went there first. That house is impossible to see into. She bricked off the service alley on the side of the house, and there's no alley in back whatsoever. I had to go one street back, guess where her house might be on the block, and sneak through some stranger's yard only to find there's a huge brick fence separating the backyards of the properties. Maggie's house is like a fortress."

Natasha broke off a thumbnail-sized piece of cookie and popped it into her mouth. "Then I thought Mars would be sleeping in your family room, and that if I could see in and the sofa sleeper was empty, I would know he wasn't here."

"Maybe you're just wrong about Mars having an affair." I swallowed a large gulp of butterscotch schnapps and hoped it would calm me enough to sleep. Natasha's pronouncement, not to mention my own feelings of guilt, had set every hair on my head on edge.

"How long have you known me?" Natasha's eyes flashed a stormy warning. "*I am never wrong.*"

Halloween morning blew in with a vicious wind that howled at the windows. Gray skies accented bare tree limbs that reached up like the gnarled fingers of witches. I slid into a fuzzy purple bathrobe, snuggly and warm, yet shapeless and unattractive, which would be best if Mars was up and about. No one was stirring yet. Glad for the time alone, I fed Daisy and Mochie and put on toasted praline coffee and turkey sausages that made my mouth water the second they hit the pan and sizzled.

I poured a mug of coffee and did a head count for Jen's birthday party. Seventeen people at least. Taking advantage of the quiet, I mixed a double batch of Jen's favorite chocolate cake — eggs, flour, butter, melted bittersweet chocolate — poured it into two sheet-cake pans and one small round pan, and slid them into the oven to bake.

I had just closed the oven door when Mars came in, rubbing his hands as though he was cold.

I poured a mug of coffee for him and, instead of adding milk and sugar the way he liked it, set sugar and milk on the table along with spoons. Maybe it was silly of me, but I didn't want to encourage him in even the tiniest manner. It felt like a betrayal, even if Natasha had lured him away from me once. Besides, there was Wolf to think about. In the chaos of the moment, with a killer on the loose, I wasn't in a place where I wanted to choose between Mars and Wolf. Maintaining the status quo seemed wisest.

Mars struck a fire in the fireplace, and happily, Humphrey woke and staggered into the kitchen, stretching and making unpleasant faces. "Your Natasha can inflict some serious damage when she flips a man onto the ground."

"Natasha?" Mars continued poking at tiny flames to encourage them.

Humphrey took the mug of coffee I offered and rubbed his shoulder. "I believe I need to see a chiropractor. She was here last night. You slept through the whole thing. Seems she thinks you're having an affair with Maggie."

Trust Humphrey to launch into exactly the subject I wanted to avoid. To my utter surprise, Mars didn't react at all, except to smile.

"You're not worried?" asked Humphrey.

"She's just insecure. Last week I had an affair with a woman who works in the back of the bakery. She's probably a very nice woman, but she's fifteen years older than me, and I've never seen her without a hairnet. The week before it was the mayor's wife."

"Why don't you marry Natasha already?" Humphrey spooned more sugar into his coffee.

My eyes met Mars's with dread.

"I guess I'm not ready to take that plunge, old man." Mars smacked Humphrey on the back in a very masculine motion and joined him at the table.

I avoided Mars's gaze and busied myself slicing apples for a maple syrup and apple french bread casserole for Jen's birthday breakfast. Her mother had left a list of instructions that would keep Jen happy all day, and it began with her favorite breakfast.

Mars didn't let me get away with avoiding him. He paraded up to the kitchen island

and plucked a piece of sausage from the pan, making sure he caught my attention.

When the door knocker sounded, I dropped my paring knife, glad for the opportunity to escape to the foyer. Expecting to see Natasha, I whipped the door open, only to find Officer Wong on my doorstep.

"Wong! Come on in. How about a cup of coffee?"

She followed me to the kitchen. "I'd love a cup of java. It's been a long morning already. I'm here on official business, though." Wong gazed from Humphrey to Mars to me. "Guess I should have worn my PJs. What is this? Some kind of adult slumber party?"

"We're sleeping over to protect Sophie from the killer." Humphrey poured a cup of coffee for Wong and handed it to her. "Sausage?" He pointed at the skillet.

"Don't mind if I do. You have good friends, Sophie."

"What's the official business? Have I been accused of stealing a baby again?" I sipped my coffee.

"Nope. This time you've been accused of stealing a husband."

I choked. Literally choked. Mars patted me on the back as my eyes watered, and I gasped for air. Had Natasha figured out that

Mars was interested in me? "I haven't stolen anyone . . ." I wiped my eyes and glared at Mars.

TWENTY-FOUR

Dear Natasha,
We're having a Halloween party and we've been poring over magazines for outdoor decorating ideas, but nothing seems original enough. What could we do that's different?

— Going Batty in Transylvania, Louisiana

Dear Going Batty,
Cut bat shapes out of sturdy cardboard and cover with black plastic garbage bags, leaving extra for a flutter effect at the wings. Use glue to secure the plastic. Place two holes in each bat body and string fishing line through the bats, knotting them in place. If you want them to flash at night, outline or paint them with glow-in-the-dark paint. Attach the top of the fishing line to your gutter and the bottom to a heavy brick or block. When the

"Yeaaah." Wong sounded bored and didn't seem to equate my choking episode with guilt. "That's what I figured, but they sent me over here to have a look around."

Mars was standing in front of her. Since when did the police get involved in affairs anyway? "They?" I coughed and swallowed coffee in tiny sips to settle my throat.

"His wife called when he didn't come home last night. Normally we wouldn't react this way to a missing husband, but with the killer on the loose and attacking people, we're checking it out. He's probably shacked up with some honey." Wong smiled at me. "I told them it wasn't you, but they wanted me to come over and have a look around."

Mars held up his hands. "No searching anything without a warrant."

Wong's mouth swung to the left in annoyance. "That's probably good advice most of the time, but his wife is pressing us to get a search warrant for your house."

It felt like my world had spun out of control. "Who? For heaven's sake, who are you talking about?"

Wong blinked at me. "Frank Hart."

"Ohhh." I fell backward into one of the fireside chairs. "What a relief." I waved a hand at her. "That I know about." I pointed at Mars. "Mars was with me and can back me up. Frank is having an affair with Maggie."

Wong's brow furrowed. "Patrick's Maggie?"

"The very same."

"Jumpin' jiminey! Does Wolf know about this? If their affair started before Patrick was killed, then there's a good chance Frank is the killer."

Mars squinted at her. "Jumping jiminey?"

"Have you got a problem with that?" Wong eyed him with cop intensity.

"No. Nooooo."

"Wolf knows." I was breathing normally again. And I knew something about myself. I was *not* cut out for having an affair. Not that I would have anyway for the basic moral reasons, but I could barely live with the guilt of a kiss from a man who used to be my husband and technically wasn't married. Nope, nope, nope. Not even a chance of that.

"Mind if I have a look around, just to quell everyone's fears?" Wong gestured toward the family room.

"Go ahead. Nina is asleep on the second

floor, and Bernie and the girls are sleeping in bedrooms on the third floor."

"Sophie! That's extremely unwise."

"Mars, I have nothing to hide. Frankly, I'd rather have Wong or Wolf take a stroll through the house than have some overly eager team come in here and turn my house upside down. Besides, if Frank is really missing, I don't want them wasting their time thinking I'm hiding him here."

I flicked my fingers at Wong, motioning at her to go ahead. The oven timer trilled, and I pulled the cakes from the oven and set them on racks to cool. With any luck, I would have a chance to whip up the frosting and ice them before the birthday girl bounded down the stairs.

"I thought they needed some kind of evidence to get a search warrant. You know, a good reason to believe that they'll find what they're looking for," mused Humphrey. "Wonder what they have on you?"

"Nothing!" How could he even think that?

"It's probably a bluff." Mars poured more coffee for me, and added sugar and cream, just the way I liked it. "Wonder what happens when it turns out he was at Maggie's? Do the cops tell Frank's wife and the jig is up?"

"I suspect the jig was up when he didn't

come home last night — with or without cops involved." I took my mug from him. "Thanks for fixing my coffee."

Wong ambled into the kitchen from the foyer. "This is a really cool house. Nina says to tell you she'll be down shortly."

"I gather you didn't find Frank Hart hiding in a closet?" I sipped my coffee, a little bit aggravated that, after all these years, Mars remembered how I took it and had gotten it right.

"Not even one rattling skeleton." She sniffed the air. "It smells great in here. My mouth is watering." She cast a wistful look at the cakes cooling on the counter. "Gotta go. Duty calls."

Mars saw her to the door, and I turned out the cakes and cut them.

Humphrey looked over my shoulder. "I don't understand what you're doing."

I offered him a piece of cake that I had trimmed. "I hope you'll see in a minute." I cut the sheet cakes into mirror images of each other, placed them on a long rectangular cake board, and wedged the small round cake between them, but a little bit low.

While Humphrey and Mars studied my creation and guessed what it might be, I covered the cake with a thin layer of raspberry buttercream, flavored with Chambord raspberry liqueur. It wasn't until I began to pipe a rich dark chocolate frosting onto the cake that they exclaimed, "It's a bat!"

Jen and Vegas bounded into the kitchen full of energy, just as I slid the cake into the refrigerator. Jen twirled around. "I'm thirteen! Do I look more mature?"

Her purple pajamas featured black Halloween cats and laughing bats, which made Jen look more like a seven-year-old, but we all assured her that she had miraculously turned into a sophisticated teenager overnight.

I checked the time. Jen's mother, the micromanager who'd had trouble leaving her daughter on her birthday, had provided instructions for the entire day. In fifteen minutes Jen's parents would be calling. I hustled to the closet where I'd hidden her birthday gifts and brought them into the kitchen singing "Happy Birthday."

Jen had just ripped open a fancy box when the phone rang. "It's the watch I wanted!"

I handed her the telephone so she could talk to her parents.

After breakfast, the girls changed clothes, and Mrs. Ferguson, the mother of Jen's other best friend, Lilly, arrived to take the girls on a day of shopping, mani-pedis, and lunch at Tysons Corner — all prearranged by Jen's mom and dad.

Humphrey and Bernie left, and Nina, with a sly grin that I didn't like one bit, went home to shower and change, leaving me with Mars.

We tidied the kitchen, and although there wasn't a reason in the world for me to be uncomfortable, I was. Not to mention that I had a little snooping in mind and wanted to get away from Mars for a while to sleuth. When a tap came at the kitchen door and Bernie returned, I flew to open the door and kissed him on the cheek.

"Mars, would you be a sweetheart and take Daisy out for a walk?" I handed him her leash.

For one horrible second, I thought he might kiss me when he took the leash from my hand. I ducked and kissed the top of Daisy's head to avoid him.

As soon as he left, I grabbed Bernie by the forearms. "I'm begging you, please tell Mars that you'll walk me to town. You don't have to stay with me."

"But what about the killer?"

"It's broad daylight! What's he going to do? Jump me in front of a gazillion people on King Street?"

Bernie pulled me into a hug. "Promise

you'll stay out of danger."

I high-fived him. "Thank you!" I hurried upstairs to shower and change into black jeans and a long-sleeved black T-shirt with three delicate sequin pumpkins on the front. I wanted to be ready to fly out the door.

Mars accepted Bernie's proposal, not surprising since I suspected Mars was itching to go home and change out of his jammies. For safety's sake, and for fun, I took Daisy with me on my little excursion. True to his word, Bernie turned off at his restaurant, The Laughing Hound, leaving me blissfully alone for the first time in days. Daisy pranced among costumed people on the sidewalk, apparently undisturbed by their odd attire and masks.

We headed in the direction of the haunted house because I wanted to have a word with Ray. If Leon could be believed, Ray knew quite a bit about Patrick. I didn't imagine that the looney old guy could be the killer, though. Somehow, he just didn't seem the type to bite someone's neck.

The bell at the door of Le Parisien Antiques clanked softly when we entered. I hoped Ray wouldn't mind a dog in his shop. After all, Daisy couldn't exactly make a bigger mess of the place. We wound our way to the middle of the store where the cash register sat on a counter. "Ray?" I looked around but didn't see anyone.

In the dim light, it appeared that the door leading upstairs to his living quarters stood ajar. Maybe he'd gone up for a minute. I wandered through strange collections of old yard statues, weather-beaten fence gates, and the occasional piece of vintage furniture — to the door. I knocked on it. "Ray?"

A second later I heard giggling. "Oh, Ray!" A woman's voice. It seemed vaguely familiar. Feeling enormously guilty, I waited for her to say something else so I could identify her.

When no more words burbled forth in the next few seconds, shame overcame me. What did I think I was doing? I came to talk to Ray, not to uncover the identity of his lady friend. That was none of my business!

I steered Daisy away from the door, wondering what kind of woman would find crusty old Ray attractive. All I wanted to do was leave, get out of there before Ray and his friend discovered us. I could feel my face flushing at the thought of it.

Daisy had other ideas. She plunged through a graveyard of old sinks and stuck her nose under a drop cloth that looked like it might have been a tent once. Just what I needed. I tugged at her, but she had hold of something. "Drop! Drop, Daisy!" She knew the command but didn't comply. Imagining how filthy it might be, I lifted the cloth. Daisy had discovered a set of deer antlers.

"For heaven's sake, Daisy — let go already," I hissed.

If dogs could sigh, I think she did. I turned in a rush to leave the store, but in a flicker of ominous recognition, I shifted back around. Ray had mounted another set of antlers on the wall, and there, neatly draped on a clothes hanger, a vampire cape, complete with stand-up collar, dangled in the air.

Blake thought Ray killed Patrick, but I hadn't taken him seriously. The expansive space loomed around me, dark and sinister. A corpse could disappear in there far too easily. "C'mon, Daisy!" We jumped over sinks and boxes of old paperbacks in our eagerness to reach the door. I flung it open and we raced outside into the cool, crisp air of fall, where everything seemed heavenly mundane. Daisy looked up at me, wagging her tail as if she wanted to run that obstacle course again.

I rubbed under her chin. "How about a nice, boring ride to the grocery store?"

After I unloaded groceries, I made myself a turkey sandwich with mayo and a touch of raspberry jam, wistfully looking forward to Thanksgiving and cranberry sauce. Daisy and Mochie shared my turkey lunch. While we ate, I boiled potatoes for Ghost Potatoes to serve at the Halloween potluck that night, glad I could mash them in advance.

With the potatoes stashed in the refrigerator, I collected the bags of candy I'd bought to replenish our diminished stash at the haunted house. The unexpected response to the haunted house had resulted in a depletion of our caramel apples. Visitors would have to make do with little totes of candy.

Daisy and I walked back to the haunted house to meet Bernie and Humphrey, with Detective Kenner following us at a distance. I waited for him at the front door of the haunted house. He crossed the street and pretended he didn't see me. "Hey, Kenner! Want to come in?"

He couldn't have looked more surprised if I'd confessed undying love. He gave me a little wave and disappeared into a shop. I hoped I'd embarrassed him enough to make him stop tailing me.

Humphrey set up orange and black bags on the table in the lair like little soldiers, while Bernie and I ripped open sacks of candy and chocolate bars and started filling the bags.

"Do you hear that?" Humphrey gazed upward.

"It's a haunted house, silly." I dropped miniature chocolate bars into the bags. "There are supposed to be eerie noises."

"Everyone stop speaking. I hear it, too. So does Daisy." Bernie held up his palm to quiet us.

A faint scrabbling came from the second floor. Wordlessly, we followed Bernie up the stairs.

"Did we leave this door closed?" He pointed to Viktor Luca's room.

"One of the kids might have." I mentally kicked myself for not touring the entire house every night before we left.

Bernie's eyes met mine. He wasted no time opening the door.

Cool air and a breeze hit us immediately. "The window is open again. How does that happen every night?" I walked over and pushed the curtains aside to examine it. "Just an old double-hung window."

The scrabbling noise came again, and a squirrel jumped from the roof to a tree in the backyard.

"One mystery solved," Humphrey quipped.

"We're lucky it didn't come in through the open window." Bernie's eyes met mine, and I suspected we were thinking the same thing.

Bernie laughed. "I bet that little scamp has been getting inside the house. He's probably the one making the noises that scared Frank and the kids. I hope he doesn't have a nest or a family inside the house." Bernie opened the closet door.

Fortunately, it was empty — no sign of a squirrel home. He started to close it when I thought I saw a tiny glimmer. "Wait a sec." I walked into the closet, just wide and deep enough for one person. Bending down, I peered at the old wood floor and almost missed the little glint. I couldn't get a good hold on it. It seemed to be stuck under the wall. "I need something very thin to pry with."

Bernie immediately produced a Swiss Army knife. He leaned over me. "I don't see anything."

"It's probably an old gum wrapper wedged in a crevice." I worked the knife next to the object and wiggled it gently. A tiny bit slid forward. "It looks like a chain. Like jewelry."

Bernie tried so hard to see it that he nearly tumbled on top of me. And suddenly, soundlessly, the back wall of the closet opened like a door.

TWENTY-FIVE

Dear Sophie,
It's my year to throw a party for the kids on the block. They range in age, and I can't imagine how we're going to entertain them.
— Black Widow in Spiderweb,
South Carolina

Dear Black Widow,
Get them out of your house and let them run through the neighborhood! Arrange with the other moms and dads to provide spooky items for a scavenger hunt. Divide them into two or three age groups so the little ones have a chance, too.
— Sophie

"What's going on?" Humphrey asked.
Bernie and I shushed him.
I stood up, and for one long minute, Bernie and I stared into a chaotic storeroom. A

rolltop desk and leather office chair in a corner appeared to serve as a home office. We crept out, and I tiptoed to the window. A perfect view of the graveyard in the back of the haunted house!

Humphrey whispered, "Where are we? I feel like I went through a time-warp portal."

"This has to be the apartment over top of Le Parisien Antiques." I crossed the room and peeked out the door into a hallway.

"Has to be," said Bernie. "Plus it reeks of smoke."

I motioned to them. "Get a load of this!" I tiptoed into the hallway. At the top of the stairs was a built-in bookcase with an arched top. Nearly identical to the one in the haunted house.

We clustered before it and Bernie stifled a laugh. "That explains the bouncing red ball! I've heard about these things. Most of them have been closed up by now, but they hark back to Prohibition. When the authorities came, they would pass the liquor over to their neighbor to hide. I bet this has a hidden door that opens. In some towns, you could walk an entire block through hidden doors of houses with shared walls."

"We're going to get caught!" I detected a tinge of panic in Humphrey's tone.

We skittered back to the closet. "So Ray is

behind all this," I said. "He must have been the masked man Natasha saw in the casket. What a rascal! He's had a grand time scaring everyone. Instead of confronting him, we should use the door to play a trick on him!"

Bernie chuckled. "The old guy has been opening the window every night to rid the room of the smell of smoke after he comes through."

We were safely back in Viktor Luca's room in the haunted house, but we still kept our laughter and voices down. Before closing the door on Ray's side, I kneeled to see if I could pull out the jewelry. It stuck under the wall just where the door hinged. Prying a little harder with the knife finally worked and a necklace flew across the tiny closet.

We closed the door in a hurry, and I picked up the necklace — a silver-colored bat hung on the chain. Ruby eyes gleamed at us.

"What a peculiar piece." Bernie flipped it over and held it up to the light. "Isn't this —"

"It's the necklace Viktor Luca was wearing in the picture June found. The one where he was posing next to my fireplace with his victim, Peggy Zane."

Humphrey frowned at me. "You mean

that necklace has been stuck there for decades?"

"Either that or Ray dropped it and couldn't see where it went. Maybe someone came into the house and interrupted him and he didn't have time to retrieve it."

Humphrey took the necklace from Bernie. "I'm inclined to believe the latter. It's not tarnished."

"Someone, maybe Wong, said it was white gold. A vampire couldn't wear silver," I teased. "Is it marked?"

Bernie chuckled at my joke, but Humphrey snorted with disdain. "Oh, yes. Viktor the vampire." He pulled out reading glasses and peered at it. "The number 750 is stamped on the back."

"Eighteen karat. Someone must be very sorry he lost it." According to June, Viktor left in a hurry. It wasn't inconceivable that he might have dropped it in his haste to pack.

"Someone? I think we can safely assume it was Ray." Humphrey handed the white gold bat to me.

Bernie studied the hidden door between the two buildings. "Is there any possibility that Viktor and Ray could be the same person?"

Humphrey and I burst into laughter.

354

"So he's not the same dashing bloke that June remembers. He's about the right age, isn't he?" Bernie remained serious.

"I have some trouble imagining that the rough-and-tumble Texan was a refined European gigolo adored by Old Town hostesses." I slid the bat necklace into my pocket. It would have been safer around my neck, but the mere thought of wearing it creeped me out.

"Bernie does have a point," said Humphrey. "Some people are quite adept at reinventing themselves." He paused for a moment. "What was that?"

"Shh. Probably Ray." I listened, hoping he would come through the hidden door, proving he knew about it.

Even in the stillness, the slight rustling was barely audible. The low moan that followed came from behind us. We turned around slowly.

There was only one option. The sounds had to be coming from the casket.

My breath caught in my throat. Bernie recoiled and stared like he was momentarily paralyzed. Daisy barked and backed up.

"It's a trick," said Humphrey. "It has to be."

Bernie looked from the casket to the hidden door and back. "Do you think Ray installed some kind of moaning gadget to scare the kids? A tape that he can set off with a remote control?"

When the next moan arose, an ear-splitting scream followed it. Natasha stood in the doorway. "Viktor! I told you I saw someone in there. It's Viktor!"

Footsteps slammed against the old stairs, and Natasha shrieked again.

"Aunt Sophie? Are you here?"

"Jen?"

Jen arrived on the landing first. "We wanted to show Mrs. Ferguson . . ."

She stopped talking when the moaning inside the casket began again. Vegas screamed and Jen ran to me.

Bernie leaned over to open the lid.

"No!" Vegas ran into the bedroom and seized his hands. "Viktor is in there. Don't unleash him!"

"Hello? Is someone there? Let me out!"

We all took a step back at the sound of the muffled voice. Daisy barked and pranced but didn't go closer.

"Who's in there?" Mrs. Ferguson and Lilly peered into the room.

"I'm so sorry. I don't know." The woman must have thought us all nuts.

"It's a vampire! You cannot let him out." Vegas yanked on Bernie's arm, trying to

356

draw him away from the casket.

How would we ever convince her? I was about to tell her that a real person, not a vampire, must be in there when Bernie reasoned with her.

"It's daylight, Vegas. Humphrey, open the drapes all the way, please."

The heavy velvet curtains billowed a bit. Humphrey pulled them aside. I wished sun would flood the room, but gloomy gray daylight filtered in.

"If Viktor or any other vampire happens to be in there, he'll shrivel and die in the light of day." Bernie's lovely accent always made him sound knowledgeable. He bent forward and tried to lift the top. It didn't open. He tried again. "It's jammed or something."

Humphrey tapped Bernie's shoulder. "You don't know how to do it. Step aside, neophyte."

Fear rippled through us when something thunked against the inside of the lid. I held Jen close.

Humphrey lifted the lid.

We crowded around for a better look at — Frank Hart.

He groaned and opened one eye.

"Can you sit up?" Bernie reached for him.

Frank inhaled deeply and sputtered. He

held up one hand as though it took enormous strength. Bernie moved around behind Frank's head and reached inside the casket to help him up. Humphrey tugged on the hand Frank had extended.

Frank wobbled, but between the two of them, Bernie and Humphrey managed to hoist him up and out.

"Thank you. Thank you." Frank rubbed his face wearily, then gripped his forehead. "What a headache. Oh no. This is the haunted room. I couldn't figure out where I was." He breathed erratically and staggered when he walked, but he was clearly determined to leave the vampire's bedroom.

Bernie walked down the stairs in front of him to prevent him from tumbling. Frank scrambled for the door, ripped it open, and lurched past Bernie in his eagerness to depart.

We scrabbled after him. He hadn't bothered to close the door, so we piled out of the house single file and joined him on the sidewalk, where he appeared to have collapsed. He sat on the brick sidewalk, holding his head in his hands.

"How did you get in there?" I asked.

Frank's nostrils flared. "That room is cursed. I knew it was trouble when I worked on the haunted house."

358

"See, Aunt Sophie? It's not just us dumb kids who think mysterious things happen in there." Jen placed her hands on her hips, reminding me of my mother.

Bernie's mouth twitched to the side. "How did you come to be in the casket, Frank?"

He massaged his head. As if he was trying to remember, his brow furrowed, and he studied us. "I . . . don't know."

Bernie all but picked him up. He helped Frank over to a bench.

"Sorry, I feel a little woozy. Since the big vampire scare, every night around eleven I've taken a stroll to the wine store to make sure kids haven't broken in. The vampire in the window has attracted a lot of attention, and you can imagine how much damage kids could do to wine bottles. I was passing the entrance to the alley that runs behind the haunted house when someone grabbed me from behind and pulled me into . . ." — he paused — "a graveyard?"

He must have meant the faux graveyard in the back of the haunted house.

"I remember . . ." He winced and scratched at his neck. "Oh no! What's that? Do I have a bite on my neck?" He pulled down his turtleneck.

Screeching, Vegas jumped away, tumbling

to the sidewalk. She scrambled backward. "What is that?"

"It's there, isn't it?" He touched his neck and flinched. "He grabbed me from behind. I woke up in the casket and couldn't breathe. I thought I was dying, and I remember pressing all the way around, on the top and the sides, until I found that hole. I reached through it and what a relief not to touch dirt. For a while there . . ." Frank sniffled, unable to control his emotions. ". . . I was afraid I'd been buried alive. I don't know. I guess I used up the oxygen inside the casket, because when I found the hole and stuck my nose and mouth up against it, my head cleared some."

I took a closer look at his neck. A red dot, like the ones on Patrick's neck, bled slightly. In the spot where the second dot would have been, something clung to him. Something . . . slimy. "I think you'd better go to the emergency room." I walked away a few steps and dialed 911.

Officer Wong arrived on the scene first. "What kind of mischief are you up to now?" I didn't want Frank to become hysterical, so I whispered to her about the thing on his neck. Her demeanor changed immediately. Wong leaned toward his neck and moved his turtleneck gently to have a look. Horror registered on her face. She released the fabric and turned a bright smile on Frank. She had the sense to keep Frank talking. He told her what had happened. "How come your pants are wet?"

I hadn't noticed, but the bottom foot or so of Frank's trousers looked like he had waded through a shallow stream.

He reached down and lifted his pant leg, revealing a screaming red ankle. "Ow. It feels burned."

Wong took a closer look. "That's what I'd say."

The sirens of the ambulance drew near. A good thing because that ankle appeared extremely painful to me. "Someone burned you and doused the flame?" I didn't even want to imagine that anyone would do something so cruel.

Frank held his forehead with one hand. "I don't know. I remember the pain, but I couldn't reach my ankle in that horrible coffin."

The ambulance arrived and EMTs piled out as Wolf strode along the sidewalk toward us. He arrived just in time to watch one of the EMTs gingerly touch the thing on Frank's neck.

"What the devil is that?" Wolf leaned back when the EMT tweaked it off Frank's neck.

He held it up for Wolf to see. "A leach."

Frank keeled over into a dead faint.

The EMT dropped the leach into a plastic bag. "They're mostly harmless. Ugly little suckers." He peered at Frank's neck as they loaded him onto a gurney. "They do make a nice round wound."

The girls clustered together, muttering, "Eww."

Mrs. Ferguson watched, her eyes huge. "This was the most interesting thing I've seen in years. Lilly, honey, I think we should go now, before anything else happens."

Lilly must have had other ideas, because she drew her mother into a hushed argument.

When the ambulance drove away, Wolf looked up at the haunted house. "Sorry, Sophie. I know it's Halloween and that it's your big day, but this is now a crime scene." He slid a gentle arm around my shoulders. "I'm sorry to be the bad guy who shuts you down, but we have one murder and two attempted murders. You understand, don't you?"

For the sake of the girls, I pulled myself together. "We understand completely. We're having a midnight dinner for Jen's birthday tonight. If you're not busy, maybe you could come?"

He squeezed my shoulder. "I'll try to swing by. I miss seeing you."

A little argument broke out among the girls. "Hey! What's going on?" I asked.

Mrs. Ferguson's mouth puckered like she'd bitten into a lemon. "Lilly would like to stay for Jen's party. Under the circumstances, though, I don't think it's wise. In fact, I wonder if the girls shouldn't come to our house tonight."

"Thank you, Mrs. Ferguson, but my Uncle Mars and Gramma June will be coming. Bernie and Humphrey and Nina, too. I wouldn't want to disappoint them." Jen spoke with confidence and extreme politeness, but then her tone elevated a notch, like she thought she was pleading a losing case. "We're having a midnight dinner!"

Lilly didn't bother being gracious. "Mom! Jen is my BFF! I can't miss her birthday party."

Mrs. Ferguson calmly removed car keys from her purse. "Now, Lilly, let's not make a scene out here on the sidewalk."

Lilly turned her back on her mother. "I'm staying with Jen like we planned and that's final."

Bernie stepped toward Mrs. Ferguson. "She'll be fine. We'll have a great time, won't we, Lilly?"

Ray gamboled out of his shop. "What the blazes is going on?" He eyed the cops stringing yellow police tape along the front of the haunted house.

I chose my words carefully, so he wouldn't know I thought he could be the killer. "Someone attacked Frank Hart. The police have shut us down. I'm afraid that's the end of the haunted house."

"Is he dead?" Ray's brusqueness sounded callous.

"No." I almost added that he'd been taken to the hospital, but reconsidered at the last second. If Ray had tried to murder Frank, I didn't want him to know where he could find him to finish the job.

Ray scowled. "Wolf, this is overkill. You can't close down the haunted house just because Frank went on a bender or concocted a story for the benefit of his wife."

Wolf didn't bother to look at him. "That's why it's police business, Ray. It's our job to figure out what happened."

Ray muttered, "They have no business closing you on Halloween. I'll bet that horse trader, Karl, is behind this." He took a few steps toward Wolf.

"Wait." I hurried up to him. "Why would you think Karl is responsible?"

"He's all hat and no cattle. He has that

innocent baby face, but I never saw a slicker smile. He and Patrick were two of a kind — thought the world owed them everything. Their kind doesn't understand a hard day's work and the respect that comes from it. Don't know what crawled up Karl's pants, but he was bound and determined to shut you down before you even opened the doors."

I didn't care for Karl or his condescending smirk, but Patrick had been murdered before the incident with Gabriel and Heather. Karl hadn't made a fuss about closing the haunted house until the day after Patrick's death. Of course, he could have mugged Frank and stuck him in the casket. Would he do that to his own brother-in-law?

No one knew about the leaches yet. If the faux vampire bites turned out to be the same on Patrick and Frank, then it meant the same person had attacked them. I couldn't help rubbing my own neck. Had I come close to having leaches applied to me? *Ugh.*

The girls squealed in horror, jolting me out of my selfish thoughts.

Jen aimed a quivering finger in the direction of Ray's feet.

TWENTY-SIX

Dear Natasha,
My husband and I were roped into the lo-
cal high school Halloween party. I'm glad
we'll be keeping the kids off the streets
and that they'll have adult supervision, but
they're bored with little kid party ideas.
— Mr. and Mrs. Munster in Kill Devil Hills,
North Carolina

Dear Mr. and Mrs. Munster,
Involve the kids by having a group cos-
tume contest. They can dress as charac-
ters in their favorite movie, band, or TV
show. Decorate with a creature feature
theme and the kids will have a ball.
— Natasha

Mrs. Ferguson pushed Lilly behind her.

I didn't see anything. Ray wore navy and
maroon slippers, the kind with fabric encas-
ing the toes and open backs that slapped

the ground when he walked.

Wolf sprang toward him. "Take off the slipper."

"What in tarnation . . . what is that thing?" Ray slid his bare foot out of the shoe and bent to peer at it.

I edged closer. On top of the slipper, a slimy worm, just like the one that had been attached to Frank's neck, writhed slowly.

"You . . ." I clamped a hand over my mouth to keep from finishing the sentence I almost blurted. Blake had been right all along. The leach gave Ray away. He must have nabbed Frank and left him in the casket. Only Ray didn't realize that one of the leaches had landed on his shoe. It was a dead giveaway.

I had never considered myself particularly squeamish, yet the leaches and the realization that Ray killed Patrick sent chills rippling through me.

Wolf tore his gaze from the leach and shifted it to me. "Was Ray in the haunted house with you?"

"Not today." Wolf's meaning became immediately clear. Most people didn't happen to have leaches hanging around their residences. Ray had to be the killer.

Ray held up his hands and backed away from Wolf. "Now hold everything there. I got me a feeling that you're jumping to some kind of conclusion. What's going on here? And what is that thing?"

I was proud of the girls for not blurting anything that might clue him in and make Wolf's job harder.

"Oh my word! It's a leach. He's the killer!" Mrs. Ferguson apparently did not grasp the importance of keeping details quiet so the police could question the suspect.

"A leach?" Ray's mouth pulled back in disgust. He limped toward it, raised his slipper-clad foot, and appeared to be ready to stomp on the leach, but Wolf stopped him.

Ray directed a grumpy look at me. "What you doin' with leaches in my building?"

So he knew that was where he'd picked it up! Confirmation that he'd been in the haunted house when we weren't there.

He glanced around at the people gawking at him and the leach. "Look, I haven't been in any swamps or wherever those things come from. Is that why you're shutting down the building? Because there are leaches loose in there? How the blazes did something like that happen? Some kid let them loose as a Halloween gag?"

Either Ray was a talented actor, or he

didn't know anything about the leaches. Risking Wolf's ire, I challenged him. "So you admit that you entered the house last night or early this morning?"

Wolf shot me a look of daggers. "I think we'd better talk about this at the station, Ray."

Ray's eyes took on the appearance of a trapped animal's and his mouth worked itself around in a full circle when he realized he'd been caught. His turkey neck wobbled. "Hold it, I'm not going anywhere. I haven't done anything more than play an entertaining Halloween prank on the kids. It was all just in good fun. Though I have to say that I scared Frank Hart more than any of the children." His eyes opened wide, as though he'd just realized he'd incriminated himself. "I mean days ago. I scared Frank so good he wouldn't even go back in there." His face wrinkled, and his bushy eyebrows nearly met over his nose. "Hold everything! If Frank was afraid to go back inside — what was he doing in there today?"

He gave such an innocent impression that I almost believed him. Questioning people was hard. How did Wolf know if they were lying?

Jen marched up and stood beside me, her hands planted on her hips in bossy mode.

369

"You're the one who opened the window every night!" Her eyes narrowed with suspicion and she shook a finger at him. "Did you plant the cigarette case with Viktor's initials?"

Ray guffawed. "You're one smart filly. I have an old engraving machine in the back and carved *VL* on it. Thought that added a spooky touch!" He beamed, clearly proud of himself.

Vegas joined us. "How did you make those little whooshes of air that flew over our heads?"

Ray ran his thumb and forefinger along the edges of his mouth and focused on me. "I thought those were one of your tricks."

Crafty old coot. Was he denying responsibility so the kids would still be spooked about something? I just shook my head at him.

Wolf held out his arm as though he meant to steer Ray. "Come on. I have some questions for you."

They walked away, and Lilly chirped, "Now I can stay for the party! The cops have the killer, Mom!"

Mrs. Ferguson sighed. "Lilly Michelle Ferguson, you are to call me every fifteen minutes."

Lilly grabbed her mom in a bear hug.

370

"Thanks, Mom! I promise I'll call to let you know I'm okay."

Mrs. Ferguson kissed her daughter and walked by me. She paused, ever so briefly, and hissed, "Jen's mother is going to hear about this!"

I forced a smile that probably didn't appear sincere. What else could I do? Jen's mother would hear about it all right — from me! It wasn't as though I'd *planned* a murder for Jen's visit.

With the cops swarming our beloved haunted house, there wasn't anything to do except head home. Humphrey and Bernie promised Jen they would be at her party before they turned down King Street. We walked in the other direction, encountering goblins and ghosts, both small and tall.

On my block, twinkling orange lights illuminated houses and bushes as dusk filtered in. Evil pumpkins grimaced at us, and eerie music could be heard all the way to the sidewalk.

When we reached my house, Jen and her girlfriends tore up the stairs to change clothes, chattering nonstop. The door knocker sounded ten minutes later. I grabbed a bag of miniature Reese's peanut butter cups to rip open. I hadn't anticipated trick-or-treaters quite so soon.

But it was June who waited on the stoop wearing her Mochie cat costume. She sailed past me into the house. "Jen called me. She, Lilly, and Vegas need a little bit of help getting ready for the party."

Why did I feel left out? Even though I was delighted by the budding relationship between Jen and her Gramma June, I had a funny feeling they were up to something.

I located the orange bowl with a gnarled green witch hand that automatically cackled and grabbed hands when they reached for candy. In a gravelly voice it asked, "Want some candyyyy?" I filled it until a variety of sweets threatened to spill out of it, and I set it on the console in the foyer, so it would be ready when kids came by.

Since it would be a very late night, I made a pot of strong coffee and went upstairs to change clothes. As much as I loved my witch costume, I'd grown tired of it and donned a Wilma Flintstone dress I'd worn once to an event. I fastened chunky rock beads around my neck and fixed a faux bone in my hair. Best of all, I slid my feet into comfortable, barely there sandals.

The girls dodged me so I wouldn't see them when I went downstairs. I poured myself a mug of coffee and retreated to my tiny den all alone to make phone calls about the haunted house being closed. From the den, I could hear footsteps dashing up and down stairs. Even my loyal buddies, Mochie and Daisy, had forsaken me for the excitement upstairs. At least they were having fun.

I chose my words carefully when I made my calls because I didn't want to start unfounded rumors. Trying hard to keep Frank's and Ray's names out of it, I simply told most of the people that we'd found something there that caused the police to rope it off for further examination. I assured all the volunteers and their parents that our party was still on.

By the time I emerged, the world outside had grown dark. The door knocker sounded, and I could hear faint voices whispering on the other side of the door. I opened it to Harry Potter and his friends. No older than seven, they shrieked with delight when the witch hand in the candy bowl moved and the scary voice spoke to them. Over and over, they stuck their hands in to set it off, staring in awe. I waved at their moms and dads and closed the door.

When I turned around, June stood at the bottom of the stairs.

"Introducing the Be Witched Sisters!" June hit a button on a small gadget in her hand and lively 1920s music played. Jen,

Vegas, and Lilly appeared at the top of the stairs in flapper outfits and, one by one, strutted down to the music.

"Aren't they wonderful dresses?" exclaimed Jen. "We found them today for seventy-five percent off."

A light knock at the door reminded me all too much of the night Patrick died.

Jen checked the peephole. "I don't see anybody. Do you think it could be Gabriel?"

She opened the door, and little Gabriel, wearing his cute devil costume, solemnly held out a bag.

"I'm surprised his mother let him come here," I whispered. "Hi, Gabriel!"

"It's not his mother." Vegas stared past him at the sidewalk. "Heather the Horrid brought him."

June, Lilly, and I crowded closer for a better look.

"I bet she came to spy." It hadn't taken Lilly long to join the we-hate-Heather team.

"She must be freezing!" June said.

"She couldn't have found a more revealing costume unless she wore a bikini as Malibu Barbie," said Vegas.

The girls might not be old enough to recognize Heather's costume, but the long blond ponytail gathered in a little tube at the top of her head, bare midriff, and see-through pants that blew in the breeze screamed *I Dream of Jeannie.*

Heather made a forty-five degree turn, snaked her arms out to the sides, and writhed more like an inept pole dancer than a graceful belly dancer.

"What does she think she's doing?" June snorted. "I could shake my booty better than that. Oh, my word! What is that?"

In the distance, a headless skeleton walked toward Heather, its bones gleaming through the dark night. A moment later, the silhouettes of other people with the skeleton took shape. "Is that the boys coming down the street?" I asked.

Tittering and primping commenced around us. June shook her head. "Were we like that at their age?"

"Worse!" No sooner had I spoken than the girls shot out to the sidewalk. Gabriel had beat them there, but Heather was so entranced by dancing for the approaching skeleton that she didn't notice Gabriel stepping off the curb into the street.

I ran out the door, but by the time I reached them, Jen had already grabbed Gabriel and held him in her arms. Between Jen yammering at Heather about Gabriel and Vegas yelling at Heather about Blake, not to mention Heather shouting at both of them, it was utter teen chaos. Why wasn't I one of those people who could stick two fingers in my mouth and whistle?

I reached for Gabriel, who gawked at the skeleton. Fortunately, I knew the boy behind the bones. Blake must have had enough of being a vampire. "Jen, would you take your friends into the house, please?"

Three other kids whom I'd seen visiting the haunted house followed them. With my agreement, Jen's mom had invited a total of seven kids to help her celebrate. Vegas remained behind, her hip cocked and her arms folded over her chest.

Holding Gabriel out to Heather, I hoped she would be responsible enough to care for him. His mother must have entrusted Gabriel to her niece again. I took a deep breath. I had enough going on. If Gabriel's mother had confidence in Heather, it was none of my business. Was it? I hated to hand the little guy over to her. "Maybe you should wind up the trick-or-treating. It's getting dark for someone Gabriel's age."

She grabbed Gabriel. "I hear you're having a party."

I couldn't believe it, but the wistfulness in her voice made me feel sorry for her. For fleeting seconds, I wanted to invite her to join us. The poor girl had virtually been abandoned by her mother. Every bad call she made seemed to be a cry for attention. Was that why she had fixated on Blake? Was she seeking the attention she couldn't get from her parents?

"That's right. And you're not invited." Glee rang in Vegas's words.

Ouch! I had a feeling that might be retribution for Heather's crack about Vegas's mom.

Heather leveled a glare at Vegas that could only come from a reality show contestant or an overly confident teenage girl. "Stay away from Blake."

"And if I don't?"

"Consider yourself warned."

"Enough of that! In the house. Now!" I gave Vegas a gentle shove to get her moving. No wonder they called it *in loco parentis*. Teens would drive anyone loco.

Relieved when Vegas was inside, I shut the door behind us and reminded myself that in less than twenty-four hours, Vegas, Blake, and Heather would no longer be my responsibility.

Vegas joined the other kids, and I hustled to the kitchen to make punch. Mars slouched comfortably in one of the fireside chairs with Mochie rubbing his head against Mars's chin. Halloween candles glowed; the fire crackled, throwing shadows on the wall; and tiny orange lights illuminated the work areas. In spite of the spooky decor, my kitchen oozed warmth and comfort.

"Where did you come from?"

"I avoided the teen angst scene out front and came through the service alley." Daisy sidled up to his chair for petting.

June bustled in with Jesse, Blake, and Humphrey right behind her. She stopped dead when she saw Mars. "I didn't know you were here. You look so . . . content."

"I am. Even in this Gomez Addams getup."

"I thought you were handing out candy at your house. Where's the dry ice, Sophie?"

I pointed June toward the cooler where I'd stashed it.

Mars sighed. "They fired me because I wasn't doling out the candy right."

If he'd said that about anyone other than Natasha, I wouldn't have believed it. I noticed I wasn't the only one stifling a laugh. How could anyone not pass out candy correctly? I poured equal amounts of apple cider and orange juice into the punch bowl and added ginger ale for a touch of sparkle and sweetness.

June handed me a black kettle in which she had placed dry ice. "I love this stuff. We never used it creatively when I was young. Honestly, I was always a little bit afraid of it."

"For good reason. Just be sure you don't burn yourself. Terrific costume, Blake." Up close, I could see that the skeleton bones covered a black T-shirt, trousers, gloves, and shoe covers. "Tired of being a vampire?"

"No. But my mom will be here later. She, uh, doesn't like vampires."

"How's she doing?"

Blake followed me to the sink and whispered, "She's talking about Dad a lot." His eyes twinkled and he wiggled his eyebrows.

The door opened and a gust of wind blew into the kitchen. Bernie, dressed as Cyrano de Bergerac with a frighteningly long nose, swept in with panache. "Gomez Addams!" Bernie withdrew a play sword from a sheath on his hip. "I challenge you to a duel for the hand of our fair lady."

Mars leaped to his feet, dodged behind the island, located my two-foot-long knife-sharpening honing steel, and wielded it like a sword. He and Bernie danced in a mock sword fight, alarming Daisy, who barked at them both.

Fortunately, Wong arrived, looking so elegant that the guys ceased their battle to bow to her. She wore a low-cut bright yellow dress adorned with pearls and sequins. She'd styled her hair in a pouffy pageboy and wore a tiara atop her head.

Humphrey could hardly take his eyes off Wong's ample cleavage. "Who are you supposed to be?"

Wong sashayed over to him. "Oprah, silly! Tonight, I am the queen of the world."

I knew the dreamy look that clouded Humphrey's eyes.

Apparently Wong recognized it, too. "Down, fella. I already married the Wong man once."

Bernie and I burst into laughter.

Humphrey, never one to pick up on humor very fast, said, "Is that how you got your name?"

"You betcha! I got the name, the cat, a vintage convertible that lives in the repair shop, and half of his pension."

Humphrey's cell phone jingled a spooky tune. He excused himself to answer it but soon returned, his pale face flushed. "The medical examiner confirmed that the marks on Patrick's neck were made by leaches. They secrete a blood thinner that was present in both Patrick's and Frank's wounds."

Wong glowered at Humphrey. "That's privileged information. You're not supposed to know that."

Humphrey smiled at her like a bad boy, pleased to have gained her attention. "I have connections."

"Gross! I think I'd rather be bitten by a vampire," said Blake.

"Leaches." Bernie scratched his head. "Where would Ray get leaches?"

"They're still in use. Leach saliva contains a compound that prohibits blood clotting. It's called leach therapy." Trust Humphrey to know about a disgusting practice.

Wong gave him an evil eye. "Who told you that?"

Humphrey regarded her oddly. "Isn't it general knowledge?"

My mouth puckered at the thought. I'd come very close to some of that therapy. "You're saying the leaches didn't kill Patrick."

"Not in that small amount," said Humphrey. "Besides, they already determined that Patrick died from asphyxiation."

"It can't be hard to confirm Ray as the killer then," I said. "It's not like he could walk into Leaches R Us and buy half a dozen. That should narrow things down for the police considerably."

Wong sighed. "Probably not. Aside from collecting them yourself in shallow waters where they live, it seems one can buy them online. They're not even expensive."

"Hey, Blake!" Jesse snapped the hair out of his eyes. It fell back immediately but looked adorable above the doggie snout he wore. "It's dry ice like that guy had on the video we watched. I dare you to touch it."

Blake regarded him with the boredom of an old man who had seen it all. "Don't mess with that."

Bernie and Mars ceased their mock fight and looked over Jesse's shoulder.

"Fraidy cat," sneered Jesse. "This stuff is harmless. They just put all those warnings on there for little kids. Watch. I'll eat a piece and nothing will happen." He reached for the dry ice.

TWENTY-SEVEN

Dear Sophie,
My children want to carve a pumpkin, but they're too little, and I'm afraid they'll be hurt with the sharp tools. Is there a way to soften pumpkins?
— Mona Blunt in Tenkiller Lake,
Oklahoma

Dear Mona,
Skip the carving altogether and let your little ones paint scary faces on pumpkins with glow-in-the-dark paint!
— Sophie

"No!" I lunged at Jesse and inserted my hand between his hand and the ice. "That will burn you."

He laughed. "How can ice burn you? It's just frozen water."

Frank's ankle! Why hadn't I thought of that before? "Dry ice burns bare skin. It's not hot, but it can burn you like frostbite."

Bernie nodded. "It's not water, Jesse, it's carbon dioxide. We use it sometimes in the restaurant. Can't keep it in a sealed container, though" — he grabbed my arm — "because it displaces the oxygen."

"The killer didn't know about the hole in the casket!" Bernie and I said it in unison.

I dashed to the phone to call Wolf. As I dialed, I asked, "Is it possible that the murderer suffocated Patrick with dry ice? When he attacked me, he held something over my nose, and I couldn't breathe."

"Was he wearing gloves when he murdered Patrick?" Bernie looked to me for an answer.

I tried to remember details. The cape and the mask seemed so vivid to me. "He might have. I'm not sure. He seemed like a mannequin. Gloves would have fit that image. I might have noticed he was real if he hadn't worn gloves."

"A bit sick if you ask me," said Bernie, "but technically I suppose it could work. If he placed the dry ice in a loosely woven cloth, cotton perhaps, and held it over the victim's nose and mouth —"

Humphrey interrupted Bernie with all the excitement of a schoolboy. "It would be a double whammy. The victim would exhale carbon dioxide, then inhale the additional

384

carbon dioxide wafting from the dry ice and suffocate."

I shuddered, realizing that I had been only breaths away from that fate.

Wolf answered his phone and I jumped right into our theory.

"We were talking about Frank in the coffin, and it dawned on us that the killer might be using dry ice to kill people. He could have placed it in the coffin around Frank's feet. If the hole hadn't been there, the carbon dioxide would have suffocated Frank. Plus, if he set the dry ice around Frank's ankles, it would have burned his bare skin."

"Why were the ends of his pants wet?" asked Wolf. "I thought dry ice went straight from a frozen form to a gas form."

"I don't know — unless the killer poured some water over the dry ice to speed up the process. We're also thinking that he might have suffocated Patrick by holding dry ice over his nose and mouth. Same principle."

After a stunned silence, he said, "I think you might be onto something. That's the first theory to make any sense at all."

I hung up, thrilled that we had helped with the investigation. "There's only one problem. If we're right about the dry ice, then Ray wasn't the killer. He knew about the hole in his wife's casket."

Bernie shook his head. "Don't count the old fellow out so quickly. He probably thought the concentration of carbon dioxide in that small bedroom would be sufficient to kill Frank anyway. Dry ice labels always warn against letting it dissipate in a small room, or a tent even, because the oxygen will be depleted and people can suffocate."

"It's that window that's always open. The killer didn't anticipate that," said Humphrey.

I glanced at Blake. He knew about the window. How much had he known about dry ice?

Gazing around at the somber faces in my kitchen, I said, "Hey, this is a party! Come on, let's shove the furniture out of the way in the sunroom for some dancing!"

"Dancing?" Humphrey spat the word with disapproval.

Mars, Bernie, and I whipped the sunroom into shape quickly. Tiny lights twinkled overhead and gleamed on the glittery wings of bats I'd hung from the glass roof with suction cups. The overall effect was positively romantic. In short order, "Love Potion No. 9" began to play. Bernie and I were the first to make fools of ourselves dancing, but Wong promptly lured Humphrey out to wiggle to the music. Before long, June and the kids joined us, and my house rocked!

I had to bow out to prepare Dead Man's Bones for dinner, but the music and fun went on in the sunroom. Catching my breath, I rushed through the family room on my way to the kitchen, where I immediately preheated both ovens and pulled racks of baby back pork ribs from the refrigerator. I swayed to the music as I minced fresh garlic and mixed it with apricot jam and soy sauce. Such an unlikely combination of ingredients, yet one of my favorites, even when it wasn't Halloween.

I hauled my mashed potatoes out, spooned them into a pastry bag, and squeezed little ghosties onto an oblong baking dish. In minutes, an army of three-inch-tall ghosts stood at attention. I was cutting raisins to use as tiny ghost eyes when Nina showed up at the kitchen door.

She let herself in and set a large box on the counter. "Great music!" As threatened, she wore a Morticia Addams gown. "Is Natasha here yet?"

"No. What's in the box?"

"We were supposed to bring something."

"But you don't cook."

"I brought chocolate-iced Krispy Kreme doughnuts with an orange drizzle on them for Halloween."

I nearly dropped the knife in my eagerness to dive into that box.

"Feel like dancing, Morticia? I'm sure Gomez would be thrilled if you twirled about with him."

She disappeared in the direction of the sunroom, and I finished poking tiny raisin bits into the ghosts' heads as eyes. Checking the time, I lined baking sheets with aluminum foil for easy rib cleanup, placed the ribs on them, and shoved them into the two ovens. I set the timer for twenty minutes so I wouldn't forget to baste them with the sauce.

The music almost drowned out Mochie's growl, but I caught him prancing on the window seat like a scared Halloween cat, his back arched high. "What's with you?"

I started toward him, but someone knocked on the front door, and I hurried off in the opposite direction.

Maggie walked in dressed as Morticia Addams. Natasha would hate having two other women present wearing the same costume. A pretty good Halloween prank, actually. "Do you find it hard to walk?"

Maggie groaned. "I hope fashion never goes this way!" She looked out the door and called, "Come on, honey."

The one person I would never have invited strode into my house.

Maggie had brought Patrick to Natasha and Mars's party, and now she'd invited Karl Corbin to Jen's celebration. I could only hope it wasn't a bad omen. I didn't like the fact that "Lil' Red Riding Hood" began to play in the sunroom.

Karl couldn't have appeared more sinister if he'd tried. He wore a black leather jacket over a black T-shirt and jeans, a tight silver necklace of dagger charms, and a black hat that swooped into a long point over his eyes. "Hello, Sophie. It was so nice of you to include me."

I bit back all the retorts that came to mind. "That's quite a necklace. I'm afraid I don't recognize the outfit. Who are you supposed to be?"

"A vampire hunter."

"You came to the wrong place," I joked. "I haven't seen a single vampire tonight."

Maggie giggled like a schoolgirl. "I think it's positively swashbuckling!"

"If that's what you like, wait until you see Bernie." I showed them along the hallway to the sunroom.

Maggie hung back and whispered, "Is Dash here yet?"

"Not that I know of."

389

She leaned down to my ear. "I hope you don't mind that I brought Karl. He always makes Dash so jealous." Maggie disappeared among the dancers, leaving me to wonder if she wanted to make Dash jealous because she still loved him and wanted him back, or to annoy him, or to make herself feel special with two men fighting over her.

The door behind me burst open. Natasha waddled in like a duck in the Morticia Addams costume. "Where is Mars?" she demanded. "This stuff is heavy, and it's impossible to walk in this dress."

I strode toward her, biting my upper lip to conceal my amusement about three women in the same costume. It might just kill Natasha.

She shoved a casserole at me. "Can you please take this? Mom insisted on making it. Mom, for heaven's sake, stop that! You're going to embarrass me!"

Wanda quite literally Texas two-stepped into my house — in the arms of Ray! A Stetson sat atop his head and snakeskin adorned his boots.

Choking back my shock at seeing him, I stepped aside to let them dance through the hallway to the sunroom. Morticia number three was about to shuffle off, but I managed to snag her arm in spite of the heavy casserole I held. "What's he doing out of jail?"

Natasha answered as matter-of-factly as if she were telling me the weather. "He wasn't arrested."

"You brought the murderer to the party? Are you out of your mind?"

"You're joking, right? Surely you don't think that lumbering old troglodyte is a killer."

"I saw Ray with a gun when Patrick paid him a visit."

Natasha flipped a hand through the air. "The man likes to pretend he's a big bad Western hero. That didn't mean a thing. Patrick wasn't shot!"

Something wasn't quite right. Natasha usually detested men like Ray. She hadn't invited him to her party. "Who do you think killed Patrick?"

"It's between Frank Hart, who has been acting very strange, and —"

I interrupted her. "Frank? I think he's out of the running. You saw him stuck in a casket this morning with a leach on him."

"He did that on purpose to throw suspicion onto someone else." She tsked. "And you fell for it."

"Who's the other contender?"

She twirled slowly, constrained by her

tight dress. "Leon. He —" She stopped talking abruptly and raised her voice when she continued. "Leon! What a fab costume!"

Leon joined us wearing a wig reminiscent of Viktor Luca's wavy hair. "I hope you don't mind, some lady let me in the side door. I left my famous worms and eyeballs, really short spaghetti and meatballs in blooooooood sauce, on the kitchen counter." He tugged self-consciously on the boxy white shirt he wore over trousers cut in tatters below his knees. Instead of shoes, he wore giant faux bare feet with hairy toes.

"Frodo?" I guessed.

He clapped his hands together. "I'm so glad you figured it out." To Natasha he said, "I told you other people would appreciate Frodo."

Natasha peeked into the dining room. "You're using dry ice. It's my absolute favorite Halloween effect. I love the way it drifts across everything, like a spooky night fog." She sniffled. "I saved some to use tonight, but the explosion in my kitchen blasted it to smithereens."

Red flags went off in my head. "You saved it? How?"

"I put it into a huge glass jug and screwed on the top good and tight."

Leon and Natasha looked at me innocently. "I hate to be the bearer of bad news, but you blew up your own kitchen with a homemade bomb."

"What? Nonsense. I would never do that."

"You can't put dry ice in an airtight container. It will explode like a bomb."

Natasha's expression changed to one of horror. "I had no idea," she whispered. Her shock didn't last long. "It catches fire?"

"I don't think so. Maybe the resulting shrapnel knocked over a candle."

"Leon! Why didn't you tell me that? What am I paying you for?" scolded Natasha.

To his credit, Leon didn't lash out at her like I would have. "Is that 'I Put A Spell On You' playing? Bette is one of my favorites. Come on, Natasha!" They scuttled off to the sunroom, Natasha barely able to walk in her narrow skirt and Leon taking giant steps with his huge feet. I was sorry I wouldn't be there to see him dance in those things.

I returned to the kitchen to baste the ribs with the thick sauce. The bacon-like smell of the cooking pork reminded me that dinner was being served very late, and I was hungry. Only fifteen minutes to serving time.

The door knocker sounded again. I didn't think anyone was missing, and it was too late for trick-or-treaters. I opened the door to find a round woman dressed in a flowing black caftan. "Yes?"

She focused on the plaque on my house. "I adore these historic homes. Spirits simply thrive in them."

How peculiar. I was getting ready to say that she must have the wrong address when Wanda swooped up beside me.

"Madame Poisson! I'm so glad you could join us." Wanda swept her arm to the side and bowed slightly, inviting the stranger in as though she were royalty.

Natasha greeted Madame Poisson in the foyer and air-kissed her on both cheeks. "What a delight that you could come."

What were they up to? Why hadn't anyone told me this woman had been invited?

"The buffet will be ready shortly, but first, you simply must see the kitchen." Wanda took a large tote bag from Madame Poisson, deposited it on the console, and escorted her to my kitchen, which surprised me since Natasha loathed my kitchen.

"Do you feel it?" asked Wanda.

Madame Poisson closed her eyes and held her hands out before her. "Oh my, yes. The spirit is very strong in here."

The painting of Mars's Aunt Faye hanging on the stone wall slid to a tilt. That often happened when Natasha came to visit, but I had a feeling that this time, Faye was telling us what she thought of Madame Poisson.

Madame opened her eyes and sniffed the air. "Ribs? It's so rare that anyone serves food at a séance. I'm famished. Lead the way, Wanda!"

Séance? I grabbed Natasha's arm as she turned to follow them. "Who *is* this woman?"

TWENTY-EIGHT

Dear Natasha,
You carve such gorgeous images on pumpkins. My pumpkins look like my tod-dler hacked them out with a dull fork. How do you make those intricate images?
— The Butcher in Pumpkintown,
South Carolina

Dear The Butcher,
I suspect you're not using the right tools. Pumpkins have a tough outer shell. Ditch the plastic toy tools. To create shadows and depth, one has to have control over how much of the rind one removes. I recommend wood-carving tools, rotary tools, and sturdy saws to make a pumpkin a piece of art. One of my favorite tricks is using a paddle bit on an electric drill to make holes all over the pumpkin.
— Natasha

Natasha frowned at me. "Madame Poisson

is one of the best mediums on the East Coast. We're so fortunate that we were able to get her on short notice and on Halloween of all nights."

"That should suggest something to you. Wait a minute. Hold everything. *You* invited her?"

"My mother, actually. Don't look at me like that. It was your darling June who suggested it, and little Jen begged for entertainment for her birthday party."

"Yet no one thought to consult me?" I had a vague memory of a mischievous moment between June and Jen. *Those rascals!*

"Really, Sophie. You can be a bit staid. You're so predictable. When is the last time you did anything unexpected? And you needn't be snarky about it. Of all people, I'd think you would want to hear what she has to say."

"About ghosts in my house?"

"Honestly, Sophie, sometimes you're so dense. No wonder Mars left you. Madame Poisson will be contacting Patrick, and he can tell us who killed him."

"The séance ought to be held in your house then. That's where he was killed."

Natasha inhaled sharply as though I had offended her. Her teeth clenched, she said, "It was on the sidewalk."

I might not be the smartest cookie around, but I did see an interesting flaw in her plan. "So then, you don't think vampires exist?"

"I didn't say *that!* We were talking about ghosts."

"You can't have it both ways, Natasha. Either he's a ghost or he's immortal."

Shock registered on her face. Who was dense now? I'm ashamed to admit that I turned away quickly to hide a smile of immense satisfaction, and poked my head into the dining room to watch our Ghost Whisperer.

Madame Poisson's fortuitous availability on Halloween seemed a little bit suspicious to me. I began to deliver the dinner dishes to the buffet and watched her eye them, dinner plate in hand.

Unlike Natasha, whose fingernails looked so perfect that I wondered if she had just had them done, Madame Poisson's short, unpolished nails and chapped skin indicated she worked with her hands. The spray of gray emerging at the roots of the hair on the sides of her face led me to think she might be in her late fifties. She wore it up in a twist, very elegant and a good choice for her round face. Oversized rings adorned her fingers, and multiple necklaces jangled about her neck.

When I brought in the ribs, she filled a plate and peeked into my living room, as though assessing her seating options. Wanda quickly offered her a chair at the dining room table, treating her like a queen, or at least a princess.

I really didn't mind the séance. I had never been to one and thought it might be fun. But I wasn't crazy about the fact that it had been arranged behind my back.

I snagged Jen as she walked by. "What do you know about a séance?"

Jen brightened. "Is she here?"

"Hold it. How did this happen?"

She shifted her feet and couldn't look me in the eye. "June asked you if we could have a party like Faye used to have — and Faye always had a séance."

June hurried over. "Don't be upset with Jen, dear. I'm afraid I'm the instigator this time."

"June! Do you really think the medium can contact Patrick?"

"You never know which spirits might be hanging around. It was always so much fun when Faye had a séance. It's just so appropriate for Halloween, and I thought it would be delightful entertainment for little Jennie's party."

Jennie? If I had called her that, Jen would

have pitched a fit. The truth is that I wouldn't have chewed out June under any circumstances. If I'd thought Natasha was the instigator, I wouldn't have been as kind.

Dash snagged my arm. "How about a dance?" He led the way to the sunroom.

"When did you arrive?"

"Mars let Dana and me in."

"Dana? Did you . . . come together?" Maggie would be very unhappy if that were the case.

"No. Just got here at the same time."

I took advantage of his friendliness to pry a little bit. "Did you go to Natasha's party?"

"Gosh, no. I hate that kind of overblown pretentious gathering where everyone is trying to impress everyone else." He swung me around. "This is what I call a party!"

When the music ended, I excused myself to get the food on the buffet.

While the others helped themselves to dinner, I made a quick check of the candles in the sunroom. I didn't need any accidents like Natasha's explosion. Voices floated to me from my den. Hushed, but definitely angry.

"Stay away from me. And from my mother!"

Blake? They hadn't fully closed the door. I edged sideways to see through the crack.

The lights were off, but glowing bones left little mistake that Blake was one of the speakers.

A sinister chuckle. "You have to accept that I'm going to be part of your mother's life. She loves me, and we'll probably marry."

"You stay away from her!" Blake lowered his tone. "If you don't, you'll end up like Patrick."

Blake barreled out of the den and down the hall. I stepped behind a huge ficus plant. Karl followed at a leisurely pace. The glimmer of the sparkling lights overhead caught his face. For once, the mocking smirk had vanished.

"Sooophie!"

Thank goodness Natasha hadn't charged into the sunroom a moment earlier. "What are you doing back there?"

"Blowing out candles. What's up?"

She inhaled deeply and ran her hands down her hips as though dredging up courage. "I need your help. I'm afraid Mars is having an affair."

I couldn't breathe. I tried to speak but my voice squeaked and the next thing I knew, I was having a coughing fit. When I'd regained my composure, I said, "I'm certain that you're mistaken."

"No, a woman knows these things."

Really? The way I should have known when I was married to Mars and you started making eyes at him?

She shook her head and gazed into the darkness of my backyard. "He's seeing Maggie. I'm sure of it. That's why she turned up in that Morticia outfit again. He's over there all the time — ever since Patrick died."

What could I say? *It's not Maggie, and I know that for a fact because it's me he's interested in.* I reminded myself that nothing had happened. Nothing except a toe-tingling kiss that made me feel like the other woman. For all I knew, he *was* having an affair with Maggie. What was I thinking? That wasn't Mars's style at all. I knew him better than that. "I'm sure you have nothing to worry about, Natasha."

"That's easy for you to say. Haven't you noticed that Maggie is trying to look like me? He's obviously attracted to tall, willowy women with lustrous dark hair." She kept her eyes on the hallway as though she expected Mars to come looking for her. "At least I don't have to worry about him being attracted to you. Help me spy on him, will you?" Without waiting for an answer, she waddled up the hallway like a tall penguin.

I followed at a discreet distance, and

wound up next to Karl at the buffet.

"I understand your ex-husband's family once owned this house." He helped himself to the Ghost Potatoes.

"His aunt." I didn't feel the need to explain that I'd bought Mars out in our divorce.

He responded with an *uum* sound. Could an *uum* carry a note of disapproval, or was I imagining things because I didn't like the guy or his daughter?

"The dining and living rooms are huge by Old Town standards."

Although I was sorely tempted to respond with an *uum*, I helped myself to ribs and said, "Mars's Aunt Faye was well known for her parties. She built the addition expanding the downstairs."

It may have been rude of me, but the last thing in the world I wanted was to eat my dinner next to Karl. My food would stick in my throat for sure. I swung around, desperate to find a spot between two people. Fortunately, Bernie motioned to me and scooched over to make room on the sofa. I plopped down next to him and took a second to gaze around.

Fires blazed in the living and dining rooms, which joined through a large opening in the wall between the rooms. Faye had thought about party traffic patterns when she added on. All the electric lights had been doused, leaving us with flickering flames in jack-o-lanterns and masses of candles. The dim lights danced on the faces of our guests, adding to the spooky mood. If Faye was floating about checking out the partygoers in their outlandish garb, I thought she must be quite pleased.

With June, Jen, and Vegas helping out, the midnight buffet had been a snap. After finishing my dinner, I delivered the large bat cake to the sideboard, and Vegas carried in the other desserts people had brought. Jen made the rounds with mugs, coffee, hot cider, and tea. I placed an assortment of liqueurs on the buffet so those inclined to doctor their drinks or have an after-dinner drink could help themselves. Either I didn't have what Karl preferred, or he couldn't wait, because he poured something from a flask into his drink and Maggie's.

While June assisted me in wrapping the dinner leftovers and wedging them into the bulging fridge, I conceded that Jen's party had been a success so far, in spite of the presence of Karl and Ray.

I returned to the dining room, where Mars stoked the fireplace, much as he had during our marriage, which made me a hair uncomfortable. Normally, I would have simply been appreciative, but given his recent behavior, every simple gesture, no matter how kind and well intended, unnerved me a bit.

Bernie sidled up to me. "Our fearless soothsayer has made it a point to speak in depth with Blake and Maggie. Dash avoided her for the most part, but I'd say she did a fairly good job of milking details about Patrick."

After Madame Poisson had sampled each dessert and pronounced the double fudge cake her favorite, she retrieved her bag from the foyer and asked us to bring chairs from the dining room to the living room. At her direction, we placed them between the sofa and arm chairs so they formed a circle of sorts, and everyone took a seat.

"Please join hands, but do not allow your knees to touch."

I sat again and took the hands of Jen on my left and Bernie on my right. Across the way, Nina's eyes seemed to twinkle with excited anticipation in the candlelight.

"Close your eyes and concentrate on Patrick."

The fire crackled in the background. I peeked and saw that most of my friends had followed her instructions.

"I feel the disruption of a nonbeliever. You must believe and feel love for the departed or his spirit will not visit us."

I tried. Really I did. After all, I believed that Faye's spirit moved her portrait in the kitchen. Why shouldn't I believe that Madame Poisson had the ability to contact the dead?

I peeked again, amused by the fact that Vegas and Jen had closed their eyes and were participating. If they brought up a vampire again, I would have to point out to them, as I had to Natasha, that Patrick couldn't be both a vampire and a ghost.

"Concentrate," Madame Poisson intoned. "Welcome spirits. The hour of midnight on All Hallows' Eve is nigh. The barriers to Earth are at their lowest. Come forth and make your presence known."

Twenty-Nine

Dear Sophie,
I love the idea of a witch-themed decor for Halloween. I have the candlesticks and the cauldron, the ravens, and the black cat. What else should I include?
— Endora in Witch Hazel, Oregon

Dear Endora,
Don't forget to make a broom! Find a thick, misshapen stick and tie straw or twigs around the bottom. You'll also need a spell book. Check your local used bookstore for a very thick book. Age it a little with droplets of water or by singeing it. Lay it, opened, next to a crooked candle and insert a handwritten note or two about spells!
— Sophie

I heard a click and my eyes popped wide open. Madame Poisson had brought a CD player. The "Funeral March" sonata by Chopin began to play. I wasn't the only one surprised by her choice of music. Bernie squeezed my hand so tight that I knew if I looked at him I wouldn't be able to stop from breaking out in laughter.

Madame Poisson turned the music down. The ominous death march played in the background, setting a somber mood. "Yes," she murmured. "Thank you." She nodded her head, as though she could hear someone speaking. "Thank you, dear. Is your name Patrick?" She paused. "Thank you. Patrick is here with us. He says he misses his family."

Maggie sniffled.

"He wants you to know that his vision has returned. He can see perfectly now."

Either Patrick had an eye problem I didn't know about, or someone told Madame Poisson about the eye patch he wore as part of his pirate costume, and she misunderstood. Dash was biting his upper lip so hard that his lower lip trembled, so I had a feeling it might be the latter.

"What . . . what about his neck?" murmured Maggie.

"It's completely healed now."

She dodged that one.

"So he's n-not a vampire?" Maggie's eyes

were closed and the muscles in her neck stretched taut with tension.

Madame Poisson's eyes grew large, and she stared at Maggie in horror. "Thank you, thank you. Patrick assures me he has passed over and is not a vampire. Wait . . . is someone else with us? Please come forward and speak to me."

I fully expected her to say Faye had arrived.

"She's wearing a gorgeous dress, a green . . . silk, I think, with a tight bodice and a long full skirt like a ball gown." Madame raised her head and shifted from side to side. "She says she's pleased to have company in her home. She remembers her parents throwing her coming out party in this very room in 1860."

Apparently no one had mentioned to Madame Poisson that the living room was an addition built by Faye in the 1960s.

"No! Wait! Patrick? Patrick, are you still with us?" Panic resonated in Maggie's voice.

"Paaatrick," intoned Madame Poisson. "Paaatrick, are you here? Yes. Yes, thank you. I'm seeing several people now. They're all waiting their turn."

"Ask Patrick who murdered him." Maggie's entire body curved forward. I hoped she wouldn't fall off her chair.

"He's saying the killer was male. Someone who resented him. Someone single, or whose wife has left him." A gust of wind blew out the candles in front of her, splashing hot melted wax onto her hands and arms. Madame screamed, shrill and prolonged, setting off a chain of screams from Vegas, Jen, and Lilly.

A ghastly cat screech rattled through the house, provoking more screams.

I jumped up and ran to Madame Poisson. "I'm so sorry!"

"You have a spirit in this house!" Her nostrils flared.

Wanda helped her stand and rushed her in the direction of my powder room, while I shot toward the kitchen to check on Mochie. Jen and her friends followed me.

Mochie stood on the window seat, his back arched like a Halloween cat. Daisy had wedged under the table and managed to get her two front paws on the window seat. She growled at the window.

Outside, something slammed against the glass and disappeared in an instant.

"What was that?" Dana stood behind Jesse with a protective hand on his shoulder as though ready to whisk him out of harm's way should it happen again.

I wasn't quite sure. Daisy barked at it, and

Mochie hissed.

"It's a vampire trying to get into the house," cried Vegas.

"Nonsense." I spoke firmly. I didn't know *what* it was, but it most certainly was not a vampire.

The bang on the window startled us when it happened again. But this time, an unearthly yowl accompanied it, and claws scrabbled at the window for a foothold.

I inched onto the window seat with Mochie and Daisy.

"No, Sophie," screamed Jen. "Don't get so close!"

I peered into the darkness and flinched backward at the third strike against the window. My closeness paid off, though. The black cat Nina had chased through Old Town must have seen Mochie through the window. It was an old-fashioned cat fight, but, thankfully, the glass separated them. I heaved a huge sigh of relief. "Somebody get Nina and tell her the black cat is outside." The way it had been running from her, if it saw Nina, it would probably take off and forget about Mochie.

I'd momentarily forgotten about Nina's tight dress. I met her waddling into the foyer.

"I can't catch a cat in this get-up! I can

barely bend to sit down, much less be agile enough to grab that elusive fellow. Are you sure it's him?" She opened the front door. "What are you two doing out here?"

Vegas and Lilly raised their forefingers to their mouths and shushed her.

I stepped outside with them and closed the door behind me so Daisy and Mochie wouldn't escape and chase the black cat.

"Jen's after the cat," whispered Vegas.

Jen's flapper dress wasn't exactly cat-catching garb, either. I needn't have worried. She ran to us, breathless.

"He jumped the gate to the backyard. Aunt Sophie, I smelled licorice."

Nina snorted. "Cats don't eat licorice. Oh!" Her eyes grew wide and she threw her arms in the air. "Hurry, hurry!"

"Nina, you keep the girls inside, please," I said. "I don't want them out there. Jen, go get Mars or Bernie and tell them what's going on so they won't be noisy when they come outside."

I breezed past Natasha, Wanda, and Maggie, who were begging Madame Poisson to give the spirits another chance.

"Perhaps if I could have a bit of brandy for my nerves . . ."

As quietly as I could, I let myself out the kitchen door. For a long moment, I simply listened and allowed my eyes to adjust to the darkness in my service alley. Faint laughter, low and male, came from the backyard. I crept in that direction.

The light of the moon illuminated two figures. Keeping close to the fence, I ducked behind the potting shed. Their voices became clear.

"Why don't you come in? They've got some kind of phony pretending she can speak to Patrick in the hereafter."

"I'd like to, but after my absence last night, my wife is about to blow a gasket. She thinks I'm in the basement. Won't take her long to catch on. If you hadn't been so close, I wouldn't have been able to bring you a refill."

"You really don't remember anything about last night?"

"A total blackout. Even in college I never did anything like that."

A gentle breeze brushed my neck. I swiped at it and realized Bernie had snuck up on me and blown at my neck to get my attention.

"I hear you came to the party with Maggie. You've been seeing a lot of her."

"That's pretty funny coming from you. Does my sister know how much time *you've* been spending with Maggie?"

"Maggie is a close family friend."

"Is that what they're calling it these days?"

Bernie spoke to me so close that his breath warmed my ear. "Who is it?"

"I think one of them is Frank."

"Peculiar. The other one must be a guest?"

Mars darted up behind Bernie and crouched with us. "I see them. What do we do?"

Good question. Their little meeting at my back gate surely qualified as odd behavior, but they hadn't done or said anything suspicious. So far their only possible connection to the killer was the aroma of licorice, but Frank's presence explained that. Wolf's words rang in my ears. He couldn't make an arrest based on the smell of licorice.

I shrugged and held up my open palms. Maybe there wasn't anything to do. Maybe we were being totally foolish to huddle behind my potting shed and eavesdrop.

The light of the moon caught a glimmer around one man's neck, revealing a chain of daggers and giving away Karl's identity. His flask caught a moonbeam as Frank poured something into it. Good heavens! With all the wines and liqueurs available to him at my house, he still needed something special that Frank had to bring to him?

Bernie nudged me. "Absinthe. Smells like

414

licorice."

For pity's sake. Was Karl so addicted to the stuff that he had called his brother-in-law for a refill? Better yet, why would Frank dare to go out in the dark and amble through an alley after being so brutally attacked the night before? I motioned to Bernie and Mars to scoot back to the house, but before any of us had moved, my back gate creaked open.

THIRTY

Dear Natasha,
I saw the first part of your show where you said bowls were a lazy way to hand out candy. I had to go to work and missed your solution.
— Domestic Diva in Chocolate Bayou,
Texas

Dear Domestic Diva,
Make a candy topiary! Hot glue a Styrofoam ball to the top of an urn. Glue a dowel rod into the top center. Add a slightly smaller ball on top of the dowel rod. Cover the rod with Halloween ribbon. Hot glue candy to the balls and you'll have a creative and beautiful candy topiary!
— Natasha

Heather stomped into my backyard and pumped her fists on her hips. "There you are! I knew it. This is just like the night

416

Patrick died when I got into so much trouble. You two are out running around and having a great time, while I have to babysit the monster child."

"What are you doing here? I thought you promised to go straight home after your babysitting job. And keep your voice down. You don't want *Blake* to hear you making a fuss, do you?" The inflection Karl placed on Blake's name suggested to me that it wasn't the first time he'd used the threat of Blake to obtain Heather's cooperation.

"You never come home anymore." Heather's voice broke like she was crying. "I hate waking up in the middle of the night and knowing you're not there. Everybody thinks I'm so cool because I can do anything I want. You know the night everybody went to the haunted house? I was there, too. I instigated it! But I didn't get into trouble because I was smart enough to run down the back stairs and out of the house before they caught me. You weren't home and didn't know that I wasn't home, either. Ever since Mom left, nobody cares about me."

I wanted to jump up and hug her in spite of all the mean things she'd done. Poor kid.

"What's that?" she asked. "Ugh, I hate this stuff. Both of you smell like it all the time. I'll never eat another piece of licorice as long as I live."

"Heather," Karl's tone carried a warning, "let's not make a fuss in front of Uncle Frank. You go on home now, and we'll talk about this tomorrow."

"Are you coming home tonight?" The plaintive note in her voice made me sad for her.

"I'll buy you new ugly dolls tomorrow, okay?"

"I — don't — want — a — doll." She spaced her words for emphasis, and her tone had turned as ugly and frightening as the dolls.

"Why don't you go home with Uncle Frank? You can spend the night there, and I'll pick you up in the morning."

"Oh no you don't. She's your problem, not ours."

"Aunt Anna already locked the doors and told me to go home." She sounded like a lost little girl.

I couldn't believe they would speak so cruelly in front of Heather. No wonder she'd become a mean girl. She'd learned to be unkind. I couldn't even imagine the hurt she felt at being unwanted. Maybe it wasn't surprising that she lashed out at other people, like Vegas. It also explained her indifference to her cousin, Gabriel.

"Fine. I'll just walk the streets then, and one day you'll both be sorry! One of you might be sorry sooner than you expect . . ." Heather sniffled and left through the gate.

"What did she mean by that? You don't think she'd turn me in, do you?" asked Frank.

Her father snickered. "Who would believe her?"

An awkward pause followed, as though each waited for the other to make the first move.

"Mars!" Natasha's voice shot through the night like an angry bullet.

Bernie and Mars moaned, and for a moment, I thought they'd given us away. Unfortunately, things only got worse when Natasha shuffled across the lawn in tiny Morticia steps, shouting at Karl. "Mars, is that you? You better not be with another woman!"

I clamped a hand over my mouth. Bernie poked me gently, and I knew he was cracking up, too.

"It's not funny," Mars hissed.

Frank fled out the gate.

Karl stashed his flask inside his jacket and ambled toward Natasha. "Lost your man, have you?" He wrapped an arm around her waist. "Don't want you tripping in that sexy gown."

"You're such a gentleman. Tell me about Maggie. Is your relationship serious?"

"Not if I can have you instead."

"Oh you! Seriously. I need to know. Are you . . . with her every night?"

"We're not living together — yet — if that's what you're asking."

"Well, I'm all for encouraging your relationship. Maybe we'll have you and Maggie over for dinner. Do you like Lamb Wellington?"

Their voices faded, and we heard the sunroom door close.

"Looks like you're having dinner guests soon." I stood up and stretched, stiff from crouching.

"What's up with Maggie and Karl? For a moment, I thought Karl and Frank would come to blows over Maggie. And why is Natasha being so snoopy about it? What have I missed?" asked Bernie.

"Natasha think Mars is having an affair with Maggie."

"Which is nonsense," Mars muttered.

"I think Maggie is using Karl to make Dash jealous," I added. "So what's the deal with absinthe?" I asked Bernie. "I thought it was illegal."

420

"Not anymore. We have it at the bar. Mates of mine who consider themselves connoisseurs of the stuff claim most of the legal U. S. versions are watered down and not the real thing. It has quite a history of murder, suicide, and death because it was made with wormwood, which contains a toxin called thujone. The U. S. limits the amount of thujone, thus leading to the complaints. People thought drinking absinthe led to madness. It's a hundred and six proof — more likely it led to being completely snockered."

"Lovely," I said.

"They call it The Green Fairy. Addicts say they get high on it. They pour it over a spoonful of sugar to take off the bitter edge. I don't see the attraction myself, but it looks like Frank has been cultivating a bootleg business."

We walked toward the house and when we entered, I avoided Mars's eyes. The guilt of that kiss still haunted me. I should probably face him and have a little talk to straighten everything out — but not during a party that had already disintegrated into chaos.

I shooed everyone out of the kitchen. Maggie lingered behind, and I caught her rinsing her wineglass.

421

"You don't need to clean up!"

She glanced at the doorway and whispered, "I'm not. Karl and Frank have a thing for this awful drink called absinthe. It knocks me for a loop, so I keep pouring it out." She chuckled. "I have a large fern in my living room that's nearly dead because I keep dumping this stuff in it."

"Why don't you just tell them you don't care for it?"

She tilted her head. "When did I become such a wuss?" She scratched her cheek and studied the floor. "When Patrick was murdered. And the doll showed up. I've been scared to death with that vampire on the loose. That's why I'm always begging Frank or Karl to stick around. I'm . . . I'm afraid to be alone. I wish Dash would come home." She gasped and looked at my neck. "I don't have to tell you. The vampire tried to bite you!"

No one else was in the kitchen. I motioned to her to sit in one of the fireside chairs, and I eased into the other one. "Please don't be upset with Dash, but he told me about your condition. The thing is, I don't think a vampire attacked me or killed Patrick. It was a real, mortal person. As far as I know, you and I are the only people to have received the dolls. The only connection I can think of is the kids. Don't you suppose someone like Heather left them?"

"You mean it wasn't meant for me? Why would Heather leave Blake a doll? No, Sophie, I fear you're wrong about that. Someone sent those dolls as messages for us."

"Why would they want to scare us?" I asked. "If I wanted to attack or hurt someone, I don't think I would send a warning so he would be on the lookout."

"Sophie!" Jen peeked in at us. "Madame Poisson is about to begin again."

"We'll be right there."

Jen ran back to the other guests.

"You don't believe in vampires, do you?" asked Maggie.

It seemed unkind to tell someone with a fear of vampires that I didn't think they existed, but it seemed important to be honest about it. "I'm sorry, Maggie — no, I don't."

"That's okay. Most people don't understand because no one in their family was killed by a vampire. They are, indeed, very real and extremely devious and dangerous."

For once I was speechless. Dash had said Maggie had been to countless shrinks about her problem. If they hadn't been able to convince her that vampires couldn't exist, then I surely couldn't!

Wong wandered into the kitchen. "Ooo. Girl talk?" She drew up a chair. "Who are we talking about? Karl or Dash?"

Maggie flapped her hand through the air. "I'm not interested in Karl."

Wong frowned. "What about Frank?"

"Oh, my word!" Maggie sat up straight. "Please tell me people don't think I'm *seeing* them both. What must they think of me?"

Wong and I exchanged a look.

Maggie shrank back against her chair. "It's not like that! I'm not sleeping with them! I'm just afraid to be alone. I know he's coming for me." Her voice trailed off, and I got the impression Maggie needed to talk.

"It's okay. You can trust Wong." At least I thought she could.

Maggie started with a tremor in her voice. "A couple of years before I was born, a vampire by the name of Viktor Luca lived in Old Town."

Wong jumped back in her seat, and I could feel my eyes widen.

"You've heard of him?" asked Maggie. "I thought I was the only one left who knew about Viktor. You see, he bit my Aunt Peggy on the neck, and she died three days later."

That explained Maggie's resemblance to

424

Peggy. Where had we put the picture? I rose to look for it.

Wong pounded the arm of her chair with her fist. "Peggy Zane was your aunt? Wait until my granny hears about this! She used to help out at the Widow Nagle's boardinghouse . . ."

". . . where Viktor lived." Maggie finished Wong's sentence. "That's why I was sick with worry about Blake working there."

I couldn't quite follow her logic. "You thought he would be harmed? But Viktor has been gone for decades."

Maggie laughed like I was naive. "Decades mean nothing to vampires. They're like days or weeks to them. All my life I've know that Viktor would come back, looking for me."

I found the photo. "Here it is." I handed it to her, and Wong leaned over to have a look.

"Now that's scary," said Wong. "Girl, you are the spitting image of Peggy."

"I'm named after her, too — Margaret. They tried to call me Peggy, but when I turned seven, I overheard my mom and her mother talking about Viktor. From that day on, I insisted on being called Maggie."

"He's not bad looking for a vampire. Very artsy. Nothing personal, Maggie, but they both had weird taste in jewelry."

The bat necklace! How could I have forgotten it? It must be in my pants pocket upstairs. I didn't dare show it to Maggie, though. If she'd been scared before, she would flip out at seeing the necklace. I bent over the two of them to see the picture again. There was no question in my mind that the bat hanging from a chain on Viktor's neck was the very same one we'd found earlier today in the haunted house. A shiver ran down my back. Surely that confirmed the stories about Viktor living there.

"That bat is weird enough, but what does Peggy have on?" Wong pointed at the photo.

"That's her astrological sign. She was a Scorpio. They were big on that sort of thing back then. You know, Age of Aquarius and all that. Would you mind if I kept this photograph, Sophie?"

"I'd be delighted. And I bet Faye would be, too." I glanced up at her portrait on the wall over Maggie's head. It didn't swing to the side.

"Everybody's waiting!" Jen poked her head in from the foyer again.

"We're coming right now." I motioned to Maggie and Wong.

Minutes later, we were back in our seats holding hands. Madame Poisson called to the spirits, beseeching them to speak to her.

426

Only this time, the occasional slurred word caused me to wonder if she had overfortified herself with wine.

"Shpeak to me. Are you with ush, Patrick? Oh! Oh! Who are you?"

I knew I should have had my eyes shut, but Madame's performance was simply too good not to peek. Besides, watching everyone else yielded some interesting information, too. Dash couldn't take his eyes off Maggie and Karl. Maggie bowed her head, but Karl, eyes wide open, focused on Madame. Blake's gaze darted from his dad to his mom and back. Ray scanned us as if he hoped to identify Patrick's killer.

"I can't make out what you're saying. There's a man and a woman. The woman keeps pointing at a picture. She seems oddly familiar." Madame gasped. "It's the woman on your wall in the kitchen — she just bared her shoulder like in the portrait. She seems very happy. But the man . . . Who are you? Are you Patrick? If you're Patrick, send us a sign."

"Bwahahahahaha!" Cackling came from my kitchen. "Want some candyyyy?"

THIRTY-ONE

Dear Natasha,
I'm hoping to do a voodoo Halloween decor. Any ideas besides the obvious ones?
 — Witchy Mama in Spook Hill, Maryland

Dear Witchy Mama,
How about shrinking some heads? Peel apples and carve faces in them. Allow them to shrivel. Display in groups, or as a grisly decorative treat on a dessert platter.
 — Natasha

In spite of the screams, I jumped up and ran to the kitchen, Bernie on my heels. We came to an abrupt halt in the doorway. All was quiet, and except for Mochie, the kitchen was empty. Mochie walked innocently toward us. I opened a pouch of salmon cat food and emptied it into his bowl.

The cackling candy dish sat on the counter, undisturbed.

Karl sidled into the kitchen. "Did you hire someone to hang out and make noises?"

"Hardly. I never heard of Madame Poisson before she showed up tonight, and I'm not the one who invited her. I had no idea she would be here."

Karl frowned. "Then how did Madame Poisson arrange for that cackling?"

"That's what we're all wondering," said Bernie.

We returned to the living room, where Maggie pleaded with Madame Poisson. "Please, just one more try. You clearly reached Patrick. Everyone heard it. He has to tell us who killed him."

How could he manage that by cackling? Would Madame pretend to translate?

"I need a little bracer. Excuse me." She made a beeline for my kitchen, poking Karl on the way.

The second Karl left the living room, Dash said to Maggie, "I'd like a quick word with you, please."

What was up with these people? I watched Jen and her friends, who remained seated, discussing the mysterious cackle.

Bernie whispered, "What's with Karl and the medium? Do you think they're a team?"

There was only one way to find out. "Would anyone care for another cup of coffee or tea?" When no one replied, I said, "I guess it's just the two of us, Bernie."

Acting casual, we sauntered into the kitchen in time to see Karl pouring liquid from his flask into Madame Poisson's teacup.

She seemed a little bit pale to me. I suspected she'd already had too much to drink. I edged up beside her. Her teacup trembled in her hand.

"Do you feel all right?" I asked.

"Honey, I hate to be the one to tell you this, but you got ghosts in your house!"

I shouldn't have teased her, but the temptation to tweak her a little bit seized me. "The young woman in the ball gown?"

"Okay, not her so much, but those others" — she stopped for a gulp of liquor — "I don't know where they came from!"

"Didn't they come because you called them?"

She stared at me, blinking. "I suppose they did! Except that one woman, the one right there in the picture." She pointed at Faye's portrait. "She acts like she lives here, flitting around from one to the other like she thinks she's the hostess."

Suddenly I didn't feel quite so smug. That

430

sounded like Faye. I chuckled. "You almost had me. Someone told you that Faye threw a lot of parties."

"Okay, yes. Wanda disclosed that, but she's really here. I'm seeing her. When she's not playing hostess, she hovers around June."

Karl snorted. "What nonsense. It's a pity that you prey on vulnerable people and take their money."

Madame Poisson didn't flinch. "Is it nonsense? How can you be so sure?" She must have been used to convincing nonbelievers because she regained her composure quickly, and I got the feeling she was on familiar territory. "Were you good friends with Patrick?"

"I knew him socially." Karl resumed his supercilious smile.

"That explains why he came in here with you."

"That's not funny!" Karl stormed off toward the living room, but I noticed that he kept looking over his shoulder. "Maggie, it's time to go."

I struggled not to laugh out loud. "I believe you've scared him."

"Serves him right, though he does have the most wonderful liquor. A lot of nonbelievers are easily shaken. They have their doubts. You know, mediums help many people. We put their hearts and minds at rest about their loved ones in the great beyond. We even bring them closure when they have unfinished business with the dearly departed."

Maggie rushed at Madame Poisson. "I don't wish to pressure you, but I fear Karl has become impatient. Could we try to contact Patrick one last time? Please?"

"Yes, dear, of course." Madame Poisson followed Maggie back to the circle in the living room and took her place.

When I sat down and joined hands with Bernie and Jen again, Madame began to hum.

She stopped and muttered, "Good heavens! What are you doing? I don't know what that means. Charades? We have to play ghost charades? Okay, look, I watched *Ghost* about fifty times, but this isn't anything like that. You're going to have to give me some help."

Maggie appeared to be the only one with her eyes closed. "Please, Patrick. Tell us the name of the vampire!"

"Aha. Good," said Madame Poisson. "First name. No? First word? You look like you're doing the *YMCA* dance. How about this? I'll ask questions and you answer by knocking. Once for yes, twice for no."

432

She cleared her throat. "Was it a man?"

Mars and Jen broke into smiles. We waited for a response, everyone except Maggie looking around as though we expected to see spirits.

To my complete amazement, we heard a tiny ping in the sunroom.

Mars leaped to his feet.

Madame Poisson motioned him to sit. "Do not disturb the spirits. Is he here with us tonight?"

I found myself holding my breath. When we heard another ping in the sunroom, Bernie leaned over and whispered, "How is she doing that?"

I shrugged. I had no idea. Even worse, only nine of the people sitting in my living room were men, and I could eliminate everyone except Leon, Dash, Ray, Karl, and, I supposed, Blake. Of course, we all knew that the pings didn't mean anything. Still, they were very odd . . .

Madame Poisson breathed heavily. She swayed ever so gently, her eyes closed. Beads of perspiration broke out on her brow, she lifted a hand, her head tilted back, and she slid from her chair onto the floor with a *thump*.

"Madame Poisson!" Wanda flew to her side.

I rushed to them. "Is this part of the act?" I realized that was a stupid question right away. No one could perspire on command.

"I'm calling an ambulance," said Nina, borrowing Humphrey's cell phone.

She'd probably had too much to drink, but to be on the safe side, an ambulance might be a good idea. "What's in your flask, Karl?"

He folded his arms over his jacket as though protecting it. The smug grin returned. "Flask?"

He had to be kidding. "Yes, you poured something into Madame's drink."

In spite of her glitzy outfit, Wong's police persona took over. "There's not a person here who didn't see you pouring a liquid from your flask."

"Just a little booze, honey. Nothing that would make her swoon. Unless, of course, she's delirious about me."

He might have intended it as a joke, but his timing couldn't have been worse. Madame Poisson struggled for breath.

"Hand over the flask. Didn't Frank pour something in it outside?" Bernie held out his hand. "The doctors will need to analyze it."

The smug smile left Karl's face, and he appeared frightened. He turned the flask over to Bernie. "It's supposed to be absinthe. But maybe that scumbag did pour something else in there. Maybe he wanted to harm me!" He gripped the back of a chair and eased into it, as though he no longer had the strength to stand.

"I thought you were friends," said Maggie.

Karl's head turned slowly as he looked up at her. "I can't believe this. But maybe he's jealous of our relationship and wanted me out of the way — maybe he got rid of Patrick, too."

Maggie stumbled backward, but Dash was quick to catch her before she fell. "No! That can't be right."

The door knocker sounded, and I rushed to the foyer. EMTs flooded into my living room. Bernie promptly turned the poisonous flask over to them. I shooed the guests out to give Madame Poisson a bit of privacy. In moments, they had loaded her onto a gurney. A hush fell over us as they rolled her out to the ambulance.

A crash blasted through the dead air. I shot along the hallway to the back of the house. In the sunroom, Vegas and Blake clutched each other but stared in shocked silence at shattered glass littering the floor. Cold air blew through a gaping hole in a panel of glass in the sunroom.

Vegas screamed like she'd seen Viktor.

On the opposite side of the gaping hole, a vampire bared his teeth at us. I recoiled. There wasn't a doubt in my mind that the vicious mask looking in at us was the very same one I had seen on the vampire who fled the scene of Patrick's murder.

The vampire turned and ran into the dark recesses of my backyard. Daisy barked at the door to be let out. I considered chasing the vampire, but the recollection of my previous encounter came flooding back. The last thing I wanted was to be attacked again. "Nina!"

"Right behind you, darlin'."

"Would you please corral Daisy and Mochie in a bedroom until we get this cleaned up?"

She coaxed Daisy away. My heart pounded as I raced through the house, looking for the suspects. Ray was offering to drive Wanda and June to the hospital so they could be with Madame Poisson. Outside, Wolf had arrived and appeared to be questioning Karl. Dash comforted Maggie in the kitchen, and Leon asked me for a dustpan. So much for the list of suspects. Karl had to be right. The only person not accounted for was Frank.

I returned to the sunroom, where Bernie, Mars, Leon, and Humphrey were busy cleaning up glass shards.

Bernie handed me a plant. "We're supposing this was thrown at the window. The shards of its pot are scattered about the floor."

The plant bore one flower of three delicately striped leaves and a podlike stamen in the center. "Is this an orchid?"

Maggie's voice came from behind me. *"Dracula vampira."* She refused to touch it. "It's a vampire orchid."

"It had to be Frank. I'll be right back to help clean up this mess." I carried the flower to the front door. The ambulance pulled away, leaving Wong and Wolf on the sidewalk in a discussion. I joined them and turned the flower over to Wolf, explaining what happened. "I guess Frank is the killer after all. Everyone else was here. I'm positive that the person who hurled this through the window was wearing the same mask as Patrick's vampire. There are probably lots of those masks, but what are the odds that someone would wear an identical mask to commit a random act of vandalism and pick my house?"

Wolf studied the flower, but I could see that he was deep in thought. "If Frank poisoned the absinthe, why would he come back here and throw a vampire orchid at your house? I hear you're one of the witnesses who saw Frank pouring a liquid into Karl's flask?"

I nodded. "Mars, Bernie, and me."

Wolf sighed. "Mars is always in the picture, isn't he? I should have come to this party. I've never been to a séance." He leaned over to kiss my cheek. "I'm heading up to Frank's house. This should be interesting."

I spent the next fifteen minutes saying good night to everyone. Maggie seemed disappointed that Karl was driving her home. Dana and Dash split the job of delivering Jen's young friends to their homes. Natasha put her foot down and insisted Mars accompany her to their house. By the time I shut the front door and locked it, only Jen, Vegas, and Lilly remained. They dragged off to bed, exhausted.

I puttered around the kitchen, cleaning up and thinking about what Wolf had said. If Frank poisoned Karl, why would he come back and throw a flowerpot at my house? Wouldn't he have the good sense to stay away and wait for the phone call that Karl was in the hospital or dead? I peered out the window in the hope Wolf might come

438

back to tell me what had happened. At three in the morning, though, I just didn't have enough steam left in me to stay up and wait. I checked to be sure all the doors were locked and went up to bed with Daisy and Mochie.

THIRTY-TWO

Dear Sophie,
For Halloween, I was planning to simply hand out candy to trick-or-treaters. My new stepchildren insist their mother always bakes a cake in the shape of a pumpkin. Where do I buy the cake pan for that?

— Wicked Stepmother in
Satan's Kingdom, Massachusetts

Dear Wicked Stepmother,
You probably already have the pan. Bake two Bundt cakes. Turn one upside down and glue it to the other one with icing. Frost with pumpkin-colored icing. Use a flat-bottom ice cream cone for the stem and cover with green icing. Voila! Pumpkin cake!

— Sophie

We all slept late on November first. I

440

lounged in bed for a few minutes, until I heard faint cackling. I didn't know how Madame Poisson had accomplished that the night before, but I couldn't take chances. There might be someone in the kitchen.

I walked down the stairs, trying to avoid the creakier parts. Peeking in the kitchen, I didn't see anyone except Daisy and Mochie. I made a quick tour of the downstairs. Nothing was out of place.

I made a pot of strong tea, and when I was pulling eggs out of the fridge to make a hollandaise sauce for eggs Benedict, the cackling began again behind me. I whipped around. Mochie sat beside the cackling bowl. When it stopped, he gingerly inserted a paw into the bowl, just far enough to make the hand move and set off the cackling again. I swung him up in the air, laughing, then nuzzled his face.

Looking up at Faye's portrait over my fireplace, I said, "Well, that was some party last night. If you were there, I hope you had fun."

Carrying a steaming mug of tea, I accompanied Daisy to the backyard. She snuffled where Mars, Bernie, and I had hidden behind the potting shed, as well as by the gate, where Frank had poured poison into Karl's flask. I returned to the kitchen and added shallots and white wine to a pot to reduce, but no matter what, my thoughts returned to Frank. Had he really been so obsessed with Maggie that he felt compelled to kill his rivals? He'd attended Natasha's party dressed as a vampire. He must have stashed the mask somewhere that night, or dashed home to get it. The girls and I had the bad luck to come upon him right after he murdered Patrick. He took off and returned later to attack me. He must have feared I could identify him.

But why had he claimed that *he'd* been attacked? Why had he jumped into the casket at the haunted house and adhered a leach to himself? That seemed peculiar. Had he thought it would throw suspicion on someone else? Wouldn't he have been afraid of suffocating in the casket? It didn't make sense that he returned to throw the vampire orchid through my window, either. And what about his conversation in my yard with Karl? Did he see Bernie, Mars, and me watching? If that was the case, why did he pour the poison liquid into Karl's flask? Why wouldn't he have said he didn't have any or made some other excuse?

I separated three eggs into bowls and whisked the yolks. There were too many things that didn't make sense. The more I thought about it, though, the more I concluded that someone wanted to scare Maggie. Even Blake had thought he could use a vampire costume to frighten his mother back into his father's arms. Whoever killed Patrick and left the bite on his neck must have known about Maggie's fear of vampires. "He certainly didn't love her, though. It was cruel to manipulate Maggie through her fear," I muttered.

Jen yawned as she entered the kitchen. Daisy ran to her, wagging her tail. Jen petted Daisy but made a point of wrapping her arms around me. "Thanks for the party, and for not sending me away. This was the most exciting birthday I've ever had! Some of the kids who were here last night have been texting about the séance and the poison. Everybody thinks I'm really cool."

"Tea? Are Vegas and Lilly still asleep?" I poured tea into a mug for her.

"Yes, and it's a good thing. Vegas is going to be plenty mad when she gets up."

"Did something happen?"

"Heather texted everyone about Blake kissing a flapper bimbo in the sunroom last night. I don't know why she's so mean. She's pretty and smart and has everything. Vegas says she's the kid that sets the trends all the others copy at school — you know, designer clothes and all that stuff. She could have any boy she wants, except for Blake."

I grinned since Jen and I were both wearing comfy, anti-designer flannel pajamas. "Sometimes appearances are misleading. The truth is that Heather's father didn't inherit the business he thought he would receive. It was sold, and Heather's mother took half the money, divorced Karl, and moved away. Karl pretends to be a doting dad, but Heather is alone a lot, sometimes all night long. We really ought to feel sorry for her. I suspect that she's often mean to get attention."

Jen frowned at me. "That's so sad. You'd think she'd be nicer to Vegas, instead of calling her names."

I let out a little gasp and removed the pot from the stove. "Wait a minute. If Heather saw Blake kissing Vegas in the sunroom, then maybe it was Heather who threw the vampire orchid at the window last night."

"Yeah! She would have been plenty angry. Except where did she get a vampire orchid — or the mask?"

Pieces of the puzzle fell into place so fast that my head spun. "From the killer — her father. Karl didn't dispose of the mask! And he's been using props, like Heather's Dead dolls, to scare Maggie and me. I bet that vampire orchid was going to land at Maggie's front door to frighten her. But last night, Heather was angry and hurt. She went home and got her father's precious orchid and the mask, and came back here intending to smash the plant in front of him to get his attention. But when she saw Vegas and Blake kissing, she became angry and threw the orchid at the window."

"So you think Heather's father killed Patrick? I feel horrible for her. Her mother ditched her and now her dad's going to jail?"

Footsteps thundered on the creaky old stairs on my foyer. "The other girls must be up. I need to call Wolf and tell him it's Karl, not Frank!"

Jen twitched her mouth around, making faces. "When I came in, didn't I hear you say that someone who loved Maggie wouldn't be so cruel?"

I dialed Wolf's number and placed my finger on my nose like we were playing charades. "Exactly. But you see, Karl never loved Maggie. He didn't care if he hurt her. He wanted to scare her into needing him. Dash had Karl pegged right all along. What Karl really wanted was control of Maggie's share of the car dealership — the one his family used to own."

Jen picked up Mochie and paced toward me. "So he might have murdered Maggie eventually, too."

I stared at my young niece, surprised by her intuitiveness. "Perish the thought, but I bet you're right."

My call rang through to Wolf's voice mail. I left an urgent message, saying that I thought Karl had murdered Patrick.

When Lilly and Vegas joined us for breakfast, I made a point of changing the subject, but it was impossible. The girls bubbled over about the events of the night before.

Lilly sat on the banquette cross-legged. "That was the most exciting night of my life! Wait until the kids at school hear about your birthday party, Jen. That séance was awesome."

"I wish I went to your school." Vegas poured herself a cup of tea. "Then I wouldn't have to deal with Heather. She's so mean! I'll get her back, though."

I set a plate of eggs Benedict in front of Lilly. "Vegas, wouldn't it be better to turn the other cheek? The more you respond to Heather, the more you egg her on. She's trying to upset you, so when you retaliate, you're pleasing her. That means she hit home and hurt your feelings."

Vegas sat down but drew herself as erect

as Natasha would have. "I can't stand by and let her abuse me. I'm tired of her calling me ugly names. This time I'm getting her good."

"Uh-oh." Jen cut into the soft egg on her plate. "What are you going to do?"

Vegas smiled. "You'll see."

At one o'clock exactly, Lilly's mother arrived to pick up Jen and Lilly. There was a flurry of good-byes, and Jen whispered, "Call me tonight and tell me what happens with Karl."

"I'll be calling all right. Your poor parents won't believe what happened, and now that they're back I don't want them hearing it from Lilly's mom."

When the car pulled away, Daisy and I walked Vegas home. Mars answered the door and said in a voice so loud that I knew he wanted someone to hear him, "Sure! I'd be happy to walk Daisy!"

Vegas barged past him into the house, and Mars whispered to me, "Wanda brought Madame Poo Poo home. I can't take one more minute of all that psychic stuff."

"I'm sure Daisy would be most pleased to rescue you. She could use a good long walk."

Unfortunately, he grabbed a jacket and left, walking down the street with Daisy and me, just like old times.

"Was Madame Poisson really poisoned?" I asked.

"Apparently so. She's lucky she didn't drink more of that stuff. Now that she'll be okay, I think they're conjuring up some sort of spell to make me marry Natasha."

I laughed. "It wouldn't be the first time."

"Probably not."

Wolf rounded the corner from the side street and walked toward us. Once again, he kissed me with a fervor that surprised me. I hated that I thought it was for Mars's benefit and not because Wolf had missed me. "You two going someplace?"

"I just took Vegas home, and Mars wanted to walk Daisy. Have time for a cup of coffee while I fill you in?"

Mars perked up. "There's been a development? Daisy wouldn't mind if I had a cup of coffee first."

Wolf didn't seem all too happy that Mars accompanied us back to my house.

I whipped up mocha lattes in no time and shared my new theories about Karl and Heather.

Wolf leaned back in his chair. "That would explain why we didn't find the mask in Frank's house. His wife claims they've never had any orchids. I tend to believe her because I didn't see a single plant anywhere in the house. They're not the houseplant type, I guess."

Stroking Daisy's head, Mars said, "Wow. So Karl was the killer, and last night when Madame Poisson fainted, he switched it around fast. Frank didn't try to kill Karl out of jealousy over Maggie; it must have been the other way around. Karl wanted Frank out of the way, so he tried to kill Frank using the dry ice in the casket."

"I'll bet anything that Frank lied to us when we found him in the casket. He *claimed* he didn't remember anything, but I bet he knew perfectly well that Karl tried to kill him. That's why he meant to poison him last night." I shook my head. "That was a close one."

Mars scratched behind Daisy's ears. "Frank probably thought he had to kill Karl, before Karl could make another attempt on Frank's life."

Wolf scowled. "He should have come to the police."

"He couldn't," I said. "Karl would have turned in Frank's bootlegging absinthe business. That's how he was making a living. Not with his legal but overpriced wines."

Wolf rose. "Sorry to run, but I have a lot

to do. No time for lounging at the moment." He squeezed my shoulder affectionately. "I promise I'll make time for us when this is over." Wolf stepped out the kitchen door. Through the window, I could see him making a phone call and walking with great haste.

"Sherlock, I believe you've cracked the case," quipped Mars. He latched Daisy's leash onto her collar. "Ready for our run?" She wagged her tail and led him to the door.

The phone rang as the door closed behind them. "Aunt Sophie? It's Jen. Remember how Vegas said she would get even with Heather? Well, Vegas sent out a text this morning" — her voice rose in pitch — "from *my* phone saying that *her* dad is a hero, not a murderer disguised as a vampire. She must have heard us talking about Karl this morning because I didn't tell her."

I dropped the phone and ran to the door. "Mars!" I motioned to him to come back, and returned to the phone. "Sorry about that, sweetie. I'm glad you called to let me know. Did your parents make it home okay?"

She assured me they had. Hanging up, I said to Mars, who had just entered, "Vegas might be in trouble. She sent out a text ac-

cusing Heather's dad of being the murderer."

Mars blanched. He turned around and ran
across the street with Daisy before I could
grab my jacket. By the time I climbed the
stairs to his front door, he was already in
the foyer yelling for Vegas.

Natasha emerged from the dining room.
"Mars! We don't shout like heathens in this
house."

"Where's Vegas?"

"Probably in her room. I sent her up there
and told her to do any homework due tomorrow."

Mars handed me the leash and raced upstairs.

Natasha cast a displeased glance at Daisy.
"Would you mind waiting outside?"

Mars's wild dash up the stairs reminded
me of the night the kids went missing. I
wasn't about to budge. I looked Natasha
squarely in the eye and said, "Yes, I would
mind waiting outside."

She drew back as though I'd said she
resembled a wart-covered toad. "Really,
Sophie! There's no reason . . ."

I tuned her out when Mars reappeared at
the top of the stairs. He shook his head.

I turned right and, over Natasha's objections, scouted out the living room, dining

room, kitchen, and powder room with Daisy. By the time we'd finished, Natasha had raised her voice like a heathen, and Mars had checked out the lower level.

"She's not here." Worry rang in Mars's tone. "Think, Natasha, did she say anything?"

"Please don't tell me she sneaked out to meet Blake again."

I hoped her absence meant something so innocent. "Did you return her phone to her?"

Natasha sighed. "No!"

"Her computer!" Mars ran upstairs again and returned in seconds. "Heather posted on Facebook that she's meeting Blake where the vampire sleeps."

"The haunted house."

Mars nodded. "Nat, stay here and call us immediately if she comes back."

"I hate it when you two do this. What's going on?"

On my way out the door, I said, "Karl is the killer. Apparently Vegas broadcast that fact to her whole class."

Natasha clutched her throat. "I'll ask Madame Poisson to find out where Vegas went."

I called Wolf and filled him in during our fast walk to the haunted house. He promised

452

to meet us there.

"We should cut down the alley in back and scope out the situation first, just in case we're right, and Karl took her there," said Mars.

"I have a better idea." We passed the entrance to the alley and rounded the corner exactly as Wolf parked across the street.

We stopped in front of Le Parisien Antiques, and Wolf jogged over to us.

Afraid Ray might be closed on Sundays, I held my breath when I tried the door, but it pushed open easily, setting off the almost imperceptible *bing-bong* announcing us.

Mars whispered, "What are you doing? We don't have time for this."

"Have a little faith and follow me." I cut through the maze of old junk to the door leading up the stairs. Daisy sniffed as we walked, happy to be back in the land of the exotic and weird. I knocked softly, not daring to make noise that might be heard next door in the haunted house. We didn't have time to wait, though, so I tiptoed up the stairs with Daisy next to me and Mars and Wolf right behind.

We found Ray in the kitchen, chowing down on takeout ribs. Placing a finger over my lips, I bent over to him and explained in a whisper what was happening.

"Well, don't that beat all!" He rose from his chair, wiped his barbecue-sauce-covered fingers on a kitchen towel, and lumbered into his office. The closet door must have had well-oiled hinges, because it swung open without so much as a tiny creak.

Wolf and Mars looked on in amazement as Ray opened the panel between the two rooms. Daisy whimpered.

I glanced out the window and saw an unmarked car idling in the alley. "Did you call for backup?" I asked Wolf.

"Of course." He entered the closet and leaned an ear against the door on the other side. He retreated for a moment. "She's in there. I can hear her making a racket."

He returned to the closet and opened the door to the vampire room in the haunted house, just a crack. He pushed it open a little wider.

"Daisy, stay!" I said.

I could hear sobbing.

Although we shouldn't have, when Wolf finally stepped into the vampire's bedroom, the three of us did, too. Wolf opened the casket, and Vegas screamed as though she were being skinned alive.

He reached for her, and she wrapped her arms around his neck, still crying. He swung her up out of the casket and carried her into the safety of Ray's apartment.

I heard footsteps on the stairs of the haunted house and pushed Mars through the opening so I could follow. I closed the closet door in the nick of time.

We scooted through, and Ray closed the panel in between the rooms. A scant minute later, we heard Karl look into the closet on the other side.

Vegas bawled. She sat in the desk chair and in between sobs, swore to Mars that she would never, ever go anywhere by herself again, *ever!* He hugged her, and she clung to him like a baby monkey clinging to its parent.

I left Mars comforting her and dashed down the stairs with Daisy. I was dying to know what Karl would do when he realized Vegas had disappeared.

Daisy and I stepped out of Le Parisien Antiques, onto the sidewalk. Kenner watched the entrance from his position across the street. Wong waited on the sidewalk, like I did, only on the other side of the haunted house.

The door flew open, and Karl stumbled out in a hurry, just as Frank had the day Ray spooked him. Karl didn't notice any of us. He turned and looked up at the windows as though he thought he might see Vegas — or Viktor.

Wong made quick work of handcuffing him.

The constant smirk had finally left Karl's face — for good, I hoped. "You! I should have gotten rid of you and the girls right away. I was afraid you'd recognized me."

"That's where you were wrong. Your own daughter gave you away by wearing your vampire mask last night."

The look of astonishment on his face was priceless.

Detective Kenner strolled across the street and asked, "Is the kid okay?"

Daisy growled at him.

"Traumatized, but I suspect she'll be fine." He studied me. "You had a close call this time."

I met his gaze dead on. "Thank goodness no one, and by that I mean *you,* will be following me anymore."

"Just watching out for you." He grasped Karl's upper arm and steered him to a waiting squad car.

Wolf strode out of the house. "Karl wasn't taking any chances this time. He patched the hole in the casket with plastic and slid it against the wall."

A chill ran down my back. "He wanted

her to suffocate?"

"That's how it looks. Seems Heather sent out a text about meeting Blake at the haunted house. That's why Vegas came down here. I suspect we'll find it was Karl who sent the text from Heather's phone."

Mars and Vegas emerged from Ray's store. I thought Mars was trying to prevent her from seeing Karl or the squad car. I waved my fingers at him, and the two of them walked away.

Wolf kissed my cheek. "I'll be in touch in a couple of days."

Before I knew it, Daisy and I were blissfully alone. We strolled home, and no one followed us or cared.

The next morning, I finally attacked my growing pile of laundry. Linens, towels, and clothes, I carried them all down the stairs. As I sorted them into piles, I felt something hard in a pants pocket. I reached inside and pulled out the white gold bat on a chain that had been Viktor's.

I looked up at Faye's portrait. "So what do I do with this thing?" *Good heavens!* I was beginning to talk with Faye, like June did. The necklace brought back memories, many of them painful for a lot of people. It didn't seem right to sell it, and if Viktor had relatives or heirs, we didn't know about them.

Late in the afternoon, I took Daisy for a walk down to the haunted house. There wasn't any police tape, so I assumed we could enter.

I walked up the stairs to Viktor's room, pulled open the curtains, and opened the window for some fresh air. I placed Viktor's bat necklace on a table under the window, wondering what I should do with it.

The door slammed downstairs. I didn't have to worry about the killer anymore, but my heart raced anyway. I walked into the hallway, ready to bolt down the back stairs if necessary. Fortunately, it was only Wong. She waved and jogged up the steps.

"I thought I might find you here." Her chest heaved as she caught her breath. "You'll be happy to know that Karl is officially under arrest for Patrick's murder. They'll be bringing attempted murder charges for his attacks on you and Frank."

Me? I shivered at the thought. "So he did try to kill Frank with dry ice in the casket?"

"Sure did. Frank told all." She winked at me. "Just so you know, it will be in the paper soon. I'm not divulging privileged information. Frank was afraid Karl would try to kill him again and decided it was best to take the offensive and murder Karl first, so he's being charged with attempted murder, too. He might get hit with some moonshining charges for his illegal absinthe operation."

"Why was he interested in Maggie? Did he really love her? She said they never had an affair."

"Money. Frank's wine shop hasn't been in the black in over a year. He's broke and was looking for someone to funnel money at him. Speaking of Maggie" — Wong waved a sheaf of papers at me — "it took some doing, but I have it. Peggy Zane didn't die from a vampire bite. Her official cause of death, according to the coroner's report, is acute myocardial infarction."

"A heart attack? Wouldn't you think they would have made that public?"

"Apparently they did, but it doesn't make for a great story. People probably remembered the vampire part, not the mundane everyday part."

"What about the neck? Any bites?"

Wong sighed. "Sort of sad, actually." She read from a paper in her hand. "Two puncture wounds to the neck consistent with piercing by the pincers on a scorpion necklace she wore, probably due to a fall." Wong looked over my shoulder. "Is that . . . it can't be!"

The ruby eyes of the bat shimmered even though dusk had set in and the sun was long gone. "We found it jammed under the wall in the closet. I . . . I don't know what to do with it. It must have been there for decades. I wonder if I shouldn't put it back. Maybe it belongs here. Sort of like a time capsule for someone else to find someday."

A rustling overhead caused us to look up as a little vortex of air descended. A bat settled on the table next to the necklace to look at us.

I wasn't fond of bats, but it did explain the mysterious little things that flew over our heads. "Eww. I bet bats have nested in the attic."

It grabbed the necklace and flew out the open window.

We rushed to the window in time to see the bat swoop toward the ground. The big black cat Nina had been chasing leaped at the bat but missed him and yowled in frustration.

My eyes met Wong's and a clamminess crept down my back.

Wong threw a hand over her heart. Horror in her eyes, she held out her little finger and said, "Pinky swear. We never mention this to Maggie."

RECIPES & COOKING TIPS

DEAD MAN'S BONES

(Sophie says these are great in the summer on the grill, too. They only take about half an hour on the grill.)

1 slab baby back pork ribs
4 garlic cloves, chopped
3/4 cup apricot preserves
1/4 cup soy sauce

Preheat the oven to 425 degrees. Line a shallow roasting pan with aluminum foil (makes for much easier cleanup!). Lay the slab of baby back ribs on it, meat side up, and roast in oven for 20 minutes. Meanwhile, mix the garlic, apricot preserves, and soy sauce in a small bowl. Remove ribs, flip bone side up, and slather with half the sauce. Roast 15 minutes. Remove ribs, flip to meat side up, and baste with the remaining sauce. Roast another 15 minutes and they should be done. When done, they will tear apart easily between the bones. Slice into two-bone portions and serve!

GHOST POTATOES

3 pounds white potatoes
Salt
3/4 cup milk (Sophie uses skim)
1/4 cup (1/2 stick) butter
2 egg yolks
Raisins

1. Peel potatoes and cut into large cubes. Place in large pot with enough water to cover them. Add 1 teaspoon salt. Bring to a boil. When they boil, turn down the heat a bit and cook them until easily pierced by a fork, about 15–20 minutes.
2. Drain the potatoes and return to the pot.
3. Pour the milk into a 2-cup Pyrex measuring cup, add the butter, and microwave until nicely warm but not hot.
4. Whisk the egg yolks a bit with a fork, then add just a bit of the warm milk to them and whisk again. (Tempering the eggs this way will prevent them from seizing when added to the hot potatoes.) Add the yolks to the milk in the measuring cup.
5. Using an electric mixer, mash the potatoes, slowly adding the milk mixture. Mix

until mashed, but don't over-mix, or they'll get gummy. Salt to taste. (Mashed potatoes are best when the potatoes are put through a ricer. However, to save time and energy, Sophie usually puts them in her KitchenAid mixer to mash them.)

6. Preheat the oven to 375 degrees.
7. Butter a shallow baking dish.
8. Spread about 1/3 of the potatoes on the bottom of the pan. Spoon the remaining potatoes into a pastry bag with a large tip. Don't have one? Use a plastic freezer bag and snip a hole in the corner. Squeeze out ghosts!
9. Cut the raisins lengthwise and slice into little bits. Place two raisin pieces on each ghost as eyes.
10. Bake about 20 minutes. The tops should have a tiny golden tip.

NOTE:

Sophie had some leftover potatoes that had not been baked, so she scooped them into a container and stuck them in the fridge for two days. When she took them out, she found they were very malleable. Sophie pressed the potatoes into a funky goblin shape (or try another shape — your imagination is your only limitation!), decorated him with almonds, and popped him into a 400-degree preheated oven. He tasted just as good as the ghosts had days before!

DRACULA DEFENSE SHIELD
1 or more garlic heads
Olive oil
Salt
Rustic loaf of bread, sliced

Preheat the oven to 375 degrees. Remove the loose, papery skin around the heads of garlic, leaving the cluster of garlic cloves intact. Slice off the top 1/4 to 1/3 of the head, exposing the interior of the garlic cloves. Brush with olive oil and sprinkle with salt. Roast for 50 minutes or until soft. Squeeze out the soft garlic and spread on a slice of bread. Vampires are guaranteed to flee!

CHICKEN SCARYAKI
(Monster Fingers)
3 tablespoons cornstarch
1 cup orange juice
1/2 cup soy sauce
2 teaspoons minced garlic
6 tablespoons apricot preserves
1/4 teaspoon ginger
1 package chicken tenders (about 9 chicken

tenders)
Almonds, sliced or halved

Whisk the cornstarch into the orange juice until dissolved. Pour into a small pot, along with the soy sauce, garlic, apricot preserves, and ginger. Stir or whisk. Bring to a gentle boil, stirring constantly. Cook at a gentle boil for approximately 1 minute, stirring. Set aside to cool. When cool, pour 1 cup of the teriyaki sauce into a zip-top bag and add the chicken tenders. Squeeze out the air and be sure the meat is covered with the sauce. Marinate in the refrigerator for at least 1 hour. Refrigerate the remainder of the marinade.

Preheat the oven to 375 degrees. Cover a baking sheet with aluminum foil. Place the chicken tenders on the foil and squeeze any excess marinade in the bag onto them. Place one almond slice or half on the pointy end of each chicken tender (as a fingernail). Bake 15 minutes. Warm the reserved marinade and serve in little bowls as a dipping sauce.

MUMMIES
1 package refrigerator crescent rolls
1 package hot dogs (beef, chicken, or soy,

doesn't matter)
Yellow mustard

Preheat the oven to 375 degrees. Unroll the crescent dough and slice into long strips. Wrap one strip around each hot dog, leaving a small part uncovered where the eyes will be. Use mustard to create two dot eyes. Bake 12–15 minutes or until light golden brown.

BAT CAVE RISOTTO

2 tablespoons butter
2 tablespoons olive oil
1 cup arborio (risotto) rice
1 onion, chopped
1/2 cup diced ham
2 15-ounce cans black beans
2 cups chicken stock
2 cloves garlic, minced
1 tablespoon dark brown sugar
3/4 teaspoon cumin

Place butter and olive oil in a wide, shallow microwaveable dish. Microwave on high for 2 minutes.

Add remaining ingredients. Stir. Microwave for 9 minutes on high.

Stir again and microwave for another 9 minutes on high. Stir again and microwave for 9 more minutes.

Remove and let stand for a couple of minutes. Salt to taste.

IMMORTAL KISS
1 ounce Parrot Bay Passion Fruit Rum
1 ounce Absolut Raspberri Vodka
2 ounces each pomegranate juice, grape juice, and ginger ale
Splash of grenadine syrup

In a tall glass, mix together the rum, vodka, juices, and ginger ale. Add a splash of grenadine, and serve.

BREAKFAST MONSTER FINGERS
1 banana
Almonds, halved or sliced lengthwise
Any red jam (strawberry, raspberry, whatever you like)

Slice the banana in half, then slice each half lengthwise. Press an almond slice on the narrow end of each "finger" as a fingernail. Broken edges only add to the scary look. Smear a little bit of jam where the finger was "cut off," and using a toothpick dipped in the jam, dab a little bit of "blood" along the finger.

AUTUMN PUNCH

1 part apple cider
1 part orange juice
2 parts ginger ale

Mix together all ingredients and serve.

MAG'S FAMOUS SWEET POTATO PIE

4–5 medium sweet potatoes
3 eggs, lightly beaten
1 1/2 cups sugar
1/2 cup butter
2 cups milk
2 unbaked 9 to 10-inch pie shells

Preheat the oven to 325 degrees. Cut potatoes into large chunks and boil until done. Peel and mash with a potato masher until pulp forms. Mix in beaten eggs, sugar, and butter. Using an electric mixer, beat thoroughly, then add milk. Beat again until well mixed. Pour half of the mixture into each of the two pie shells. Bake about 55 minutes or until the crust is brown and the mixture is set.

Makes two 9 to 10-inch pies.

ABOUT THE AUTHOR

Krista Davis is the national bestselling author of the Domestic Diva Mysteries. Her first book, *The Diva Runs Out of Thyme,* was nominated for an Agatha Award. Krista lives in the Blue Ridge Mountains of Virginia with an Ocicat named Mochie and a brood of dogs. Her friends and family complain about being guinea pigs for her recipes, but she notices that they keep coming back for more. Visit Krista at her website, www.krista davis.com, and the blow www.mysterylovers kitchen.com.

The employees of Thorndike Press hope you have enjoyed this Large Print book. All our Thorndike, Wheeler, and Kennebec Large Print titles are designed for easy reading, and all our books are made to last. Other Thorndike Press Large Print books are available at your library, through selected bookstores, or directly from us.

For information about titles, please call:

(800) 223-1244

or visit our Web site at:

http://gale.cengage.com/thorndike

To share your comments, please write:

Publisher
Thorndike Press
10 Water St., Suite 310
Waterville, ME 04901

471